Totally Bound Publishing books by Aurelia T. Evans

Single Books
Red Queen

Arcanium
Fortune
Carousel
Aerial
Ringmaster
Contortion
Spider
Funhouse
Haunted
Skeletons

I0662178

Anthologies
Wild After Dark: Intervention

Collections
Frost Bite: Gravedigger

Arcanium

SKELETONS

AURELIA T. EVANS

SKELETONS

Chapter One

Vivian had expected more from Arcanium.

When she'd arrived at the Renaissance faire that the freak-show circus had paired with, Arcanium was little more than a collection of small tents and booths attached to the far edge like barnacles. The way her friends had described it the previous year, it was supposed to be the kinky steampunk party everyone needed in their life. But she'd been in the hospital again back then and hadn't been released until after the circus had already moved on.

There were harnesses everywhere the eye could see, leather and lace, bustiers and kickass boots. The Spider Woman creature...thing...person was tied up in white rope, and to Vivian's untrained eye, it looked authentic. But kink was more than outfits, and steampunk was more than cogs and gears, although there was a good bit of that, too.

And to Vivian's disappointment, the big top that her friends had all talked about was nowhere to be found. Any tents set up along the perimeter were small, and any open-air performances were seemingly spontaneous and limited in scope. There was no sign of the hot, homoerotic trapeze artists Lupe had mentioned.

As Vivian slipped through the crowd in her flowy gypsy skirt and peasant blouse — the closest she had to appropriate for the venue, although if the circus had been actually kinky, she would have had a few other things to contribute, she noted the performance times were unpredictable and the offerings slim, but the freak show was fucking beautiful. The kink and steampunk nods in the circus were more perfunctory than devoted homages, but the parasitic circus' enthusiasm for natural and unnatural weirdness seemed unmatched by anything she'd ever been to or seen before. Sure, she'd seen circus movies and shit, but those cheated enough that these freaks — the ones that were definitely real, at least — were worth a look.

But a look only lasted about fifteen minutes, and what else was she supposed to do with her time?

She abandoned the circus to return to the faire, where at least they had turkey legs she could pick at while watching falconers, wondering whether anyone would catch the irony. No one did, but the birds of prey kept her attention and the falconers weren't too bad either. She supposed they'd seen plenty of pressed cleavage in their day, but she leaned forward with her elbows on her knees and she wasn't wearing a bra. After the act, that distracted the sandy blond with an overgrown but somehow sparse beard. She smiled, finished what she was going to finish with the turkey leg, which was a little dry and how the hell did a single person eat the whole thing without looking pregnant when they were done? Vivian had only chosen it for the irony, anyway, and if even the falconer couldn't spot it, she needed to move on.

She was that close to throwing in the towel and leaving to drink heavily elsewhere — someplace where the pissy beers didn't cost an arm and a turkey leg to buy — when she heard music. And not the usual Celtic crap that sounded like it belonged on one of those soundtracks found at souvenir gift shops.

Vivian abandoned the falconer without a thought to follow the siren song of rock and roll where it didn't belong.

There was no stage, no curtains, nothing but a bare-bones set-up of amps, speakers and instruments next to the circus' food court. On the bass drum, someone had painted 'Skellies' in spiky script. And on an easel, a sign with the same script read *Karaoke — Auditions for Lead Singer.*

"Seriously?" Vivian muttered.

"Seriously," a man said behind her.

She could have sworn no one had been there, and as he stepped around her, the continued impression that he didn't displace the air was the weirdest, most unsettling feeling. Even though he was pretty as sin, she leaned away.

Pretty, indeed. Gently toned muscles wrapped around his bones. He was shorter than her, but when he looked up, he didn't seem to take it personally. He walked with absolute confidence as far away from arrogance as Vivian had ever seen on an attractive man who looked like he hadn't met a weight machine he hadn't tried.

Actually, there was fluidity to his strength that suggested something other than the gym. He wasn't a bodybuilder, wasn't absolutely ripped like the strongman. He was lean but not slender, like someone who could do all the weird fitness moves—a trapeze artist or a dancer, maybe. Since he wasn't with anyone, she wasn't sure whether he was supposed to be one of the trapeze artists she'd been looking for, although she was pretty sure one was supposed to be blond and the other black, while this man's close, curly hair was on the brown side of auburn.

He wore nothing but a gold bracelet around his arm—which had to be fake, because this kind of circus couldn't support that amount of real gold—and a pair of cotton pants that practically invited her to look. She couldn't see detail, but with the light beige color of the pants, he certainly wasn't wearing anything under them.

She didn't hide that she was studying his body, and he appeared unfazed by the inspection. He didn't preen or flex, didn't glare, didn't inspect her back—just sat down on one of the picnic tables that had been set up in front of the band. In spite of decent guitar riffs and beats coming from the practicing instrumentalists, people hadn't congregated yet.

"I didn't know circuses were in the habit of gleaning talent from their audiences," Vivian said. "Seems kind of desperate, don't you think?"

His hazel eyes looked a little sad—something in the set of his eyebrows—but he curved his lips in a grin. "Oh, it *is* desperate, in its own way. I'm afraid a good number of my performers had to leave en masse due to an illness that swept through my circus, with many lingering side effects. Now I'm working with a skeleton crew. I'd ask you to pardon the pun, but it just seems all too appropriate."

Vivian raised her eyebrow. "*Your* performers?"

When he didn't seem to mind her sidling closer, she climbed onto the picnic table and sat on the edge next to him — close enough to telegraph a certain amount of interest, although she wasn't in heat or anything.

"My circus. My monkeys." He raised his chin in acknowledgment to the guitarist, a pale man in a see-through shirt screened to look like the bones of a torso. He'd pulled back his long black hair, and when he glimpsed her talking to the shirtless man, he gave a too-wide smile. Despite his white teeth, he reeked of cigarettes from all the way where she sat. Yet she still couldn't get anything but a visual off the man next to her, who crossed his legs like some kind of bohemian model.

"So you're the one who's desperate, then," she said.

"I'm always on the lookout for talent, love. There's no shame in soliciting, and our audience has some fun in the process."

"You ever found anyone this way?"

The man nodded toward the acrylic drum sheet. "Shane, our drummer. Bringing her on allowed Lennon to take a permanent place as guitarist, which he much prefers."

Shane transitioned into a new beat, shaking her bald head and clenching her teeth — at least the ones in her mouth. The place on the left side of her scalp, which Vivian had initially thought was a tattoo, was dimensional in the right profile. Vivian blinked, squinted to find where poreless latex smoothed into pored skin — because if Vivian didn't know any better, a fang-filled mouth formed a crevice along Shane's scalp, like some kind of science fiction brain surgery gone horribly wrong.

As Shane moved, twisting on her chair and closing her eyes to the music, she revealed other places where the eerily realistic mouths opened in wet, red gashes wherever the skintight, bloody, white latex dress cut away from her body—along her shoulder, slashed diagonally over her belly, in place of a navel. Her entire body seemed to have been prepared for a glimpse of horror from every angle. She was skinny, her jutting collarbone, hipbones, knees, elbows and shoulder blades accentuated by the light layer of makeup that made a suggestion of a skull on her face and bones over her exposed ribs and spine.

Vivian dwelled on the beautiful angles of her thin fingers around the drumsticks with more than a little envy.

"Like oddities, talent is everywhere if you're willing to do what it takes to find it," the man said. "Or create it for yourself. Arcanium is undergoing a much-needed transformation, and if we are to survive, it needs to be fast. Bell Madoc, fortune teller and illusionist, at your humble service, my lady. I don't believe I caught your name." He held out a hand for her to shake.

At least when she took his hand, his flesh was solid and warm, almost hot.

"Vivian. I've never heard Bell as a first name before."

"It's short for a number of names I have taken. I am the Bell, book and candle behind the magic of Arcanium, and it does as well as anything."

Vivian turned back to the practicing band. A woman had stepped behind the keyboard and was fiddling with the volume. She wore a long black lace skirt and bralette that appeared to cover only what was absolutely necessary for legal reasons, all the better to show off the incredibly detailed body paint that created the illusion that the woman was only a skeleton.

Vivian was beginning to sense a theme.

Unlike Lennon, the guitarist, who only briefly nodded to the band's name, and Shane, whose skeleton makeup was soft, like a faint overlay of a skeleton illustration, the keyboardist had gone all out, filling in her body with black where the bones hadn't been painted on in minute anatomical detail. The woman wasn't as slender as Shane, didn't have the same skeletal structure already exposed. Instead, she seemed downright soft — which seemed to be coming back into fashion, but Vivian preferred angles to curves and bones to flesh. When she turned an envious eye, it was to women like Shane every time.

The keyboardist clearly had a background in belly-dancing, because she swayed sinuously to Shane's beat as she joined the warm-up, her hips seeming independent of her spine.

A pair of similarly skeletonized women gradually took their places behind Lennon, one of them picking up a steampunked electric violin. They were even thinner than Shane — emaciated, with their skin tight on their bones. In comparison to them, Vivian felt bloated, the flesh over her stomach like gelatin, her hips too broad, her breasts heavy, her thighs pressed too tightly against each other.

She could starve herself for months and die less skinny than they were. With her arm pressed to her belly, which felt like rolls of fat to her, she fought against the grumbling in her abdomen telling her how hungry she still was. Her eyes burned, as though the hatred she felt for their skeletal bodies could literally shoot out through her sockets. No such luck. The two girls muttered to each other — the instrumentalist smiling, the backup singer not — and none of them spontaneously combusted.

"More stray talent?" Vivian asked.

"The violinist, Lily, answered a classified. It wasn't what she'd thought she'd be using her classical training for, I'm sure, but she seems to enjoy the circus' particular challenges. The other two were mined from auditions like this. Oh, they aren't strictly auditions, Vivian. If you simply want to sing with my Skeletons, you're more than welcome to take the mic."

Vivian tore her gaze from the women of the band. "Okay, mind telling me why you're buttering me up?"

If he'd been giving out any kind of signal for sex, she'd get it—maybe even be down for something somewhere private, since he was a lot more attractive to her than the falconer—and not just in the looks department. But he wasn't signaling. In fact, despite the bare chest, suggestive pants and the way he sat too close for an acquaintance, he seemed to deliberately not send fuckboy vibes in her direction. But the performer-owner of a circus just deciding to cozy up to a random stranger in the middle of his barebones circus? It seemed like more than coincidence, even suspicious.

"Because you didn't seem happy," Bell said. "Happiness is certainly not guaranteed here, but boredom simply won't do."

"I followed the music, didn't I? It sounds better than your average midlife-crisis garage band. What were the odds I'd find a good, hard sound at a freak show?"

"I thought I'd try something new." Bell rested his chin on his fist and narrowed his eyes in the classic Thinker pose that somehow looked deliberate and unpretentious at the same time. "It's definitely new. But test audiences like you seem to like it and so does my cast. The whole circus stops whenever they do their set."

"No offense, but this isn't a circus," Vivian said.

"Oh?" Vivian expected him to get defensive, but his expression remained neutral, and she couldn't tell whether he was hiding anything behind it.

She was used to understanding men. Men, like dogs, were easy. They wanted money, power, sex and a maternal figure. Period. All a person needed to do was figure out which one they needed to be at any given time. But Bell wasn't giving away his position. Vivian twisted her skirt between her fingers and tried not to clench her teeth.

"This is a freak show with circus elements. If it can't stand on its own, it's not a circus. It's circus kitsch."

"Before my cast got sick, it was a circus."

"Talk to me again when it doesn't need a geeky craft fair pretending to be Renaissance to prop it up." Vivian shrugged. "Don't get me wrong. I'm here at the geeky craft fair, aren't I? I didn't come here to mock it. But just because I like pewter dragons on necklaces doesn't mean everything's okay. I *came* here for the Two Thousand Twenty-Second Cumming of Mick Jagger, but this is kind of just...Steven Tyler in his grandma's wardrobe. It's not that he can't pull it off, but it's not what I came here for."

"I understand." He rested a hand on her shoulder, his thumb brushing the edge of her collarbone. Warmth deepened his eyes, his hold the first stirring of something sexual. Not blatant, like a hand to the thigh or the ass, but his skin was on her bare skin, a caress light but deliberate. "While Arcanium is in transition, why not help make it the circus you wanted it to be?"

Vivian scoffed. "I still can't figure out what *this* is."

"This?"

"*This*." She gestured to the length of him then finished off at the hand at her shoulder. "Talking honey. Humoring me when I'm clearly not humoring you. Trying to get me to go up there."

He withdrew but not abruptly. He trailed his fingertips down her shoulder, suggesting again that he wasn't ashamed of what he was doing—whatever he was doing.

"I just want you to enjoy yourself. I'm allowed to narrow my focus to a single guest, Vivian. It's difficult to thrill a crowd of people every day the circus opens. I find it much easier to please one person at a time."

"Is that why you play fortune teller instead of Ringmaster?" She inclined her head toward the tall, dark drink of water who glowered a head taller than the tallest normal man. That, along with the breadth of his shoulders and the downright evil glare, kept everyone an arm's length away. Vivian didn't know him, but she already liked him, and not just because his bare chest was more ruggedly masculine than Bell's.

"I'm an entertainer. I like to see the sparkle in a guest's eyes when they experience the magic we offer. Faces blend together, but a single face in front of me? I'll remember that with an elephant's memory. For instance, I'm accustomed to boredom by those who come to an interactive buffet like this but still can't remove themselves from the constant stimulation of their phones. They're bored in lines, bored at exhibits, glowingly bored in my big top tent. But you haven't picked up your phone once. A pretty young woman such as yourself, yet you came here alone, not a single person to accompany you. Yours is a different kind of boredom."

Vivian stopped watching the dancing, playing and singing Skeletons in front of her and straightened. "Looks like they're not the only ones picking up their phones. What have you been reading up on?"

"Where exactly would I put a phone in this outfit?" Bell replied mildly.

"Same place they put 'em in prison."

16

"I'm afraid it's never become that dire. I own a computer, but I've never been able to abide phones. They've only become more annoying as time goes on. And they all have this buzzing sound most people can't hear, like electrical wires." He gestured to his ears. "It's distracting."

"And your floodlights, Christmas lights and sound equipment don't use electricity?" Vivian said.

"It's not electricity. It's whatever whispers across space when people speak idle words into the universe."

"You're so melodramatic." She shook her head and looked away from him again.

"Thank you. Will you consider gracing us with a song? My cast likes to bet, and so do I."

"Bet on what?" Vivian asked.

"Talent."

"You haven't known me five minutes, man." She ran her hands through her hair and shook her head. "No. I think I'll just watch. This isn't really my scene. And to stand up in front of everyone looking like this when those women out there are... Talent doesn't mean shit. I wish I looked like them instead."

Bell sighed. "I don't suppose it makes much difference if I say you already look like them."

"It doesn't matter what you *think* I look like. It only matters what I see in the mirror, because I'm the one who has to live with it, not you." She slid off of the table and slung her purse over her head to hang crossways down her body. "Besides, didn't you say you were a fortune teller? Don't you already know whether I can sing or not?"

"I like to be surprised." Bell climbed down, too, but though he faced her, he didn't pursue. He gestured toward the band with an ironic little flourish. "Surprise me, Vivian, if you can."

"Is that a challenge?"

"Let's just say you remind me of the worst traits of people I have lost."

The insult came so fast from so far left field that she didn't expect it to hurt as it did. She wound the purse strap around her hand to keep from hitting him in front of witnesses.

"To be fair," he said, "it makes me homesick for what Arcanium was. But I'd like to think you have more to offer than that. I'll tell you what I do know, love. I know you're competitive as hell. Don't disappoint me. I have a substantial sum riding on you."

"Why should I go up there and help you win, asshole? Why shouldn't I just leave and make you pay out?"

Bell shrugged. The smile of a gracious host returned. "I only pay out if you try but can't. Do think about it. And if you want a real taste of the truth afterward, come to my fortune teller's tent. I think we'd both be much more satisfied discussing such things in private, don't you think?"

The smug son of a bitch bowed then wove through the thickening crowd to speak with the Bearded Lady. Vivian didn't know whether to sneak up behind him and kick him in the balls or whether she should just stalk away and not spare the circus any more of her time, money or energy.

She did neither, though she had the sneaking suspicion that Bell had switched tactics on purpose after buttering her up hadn't worked, that it had all been part of some grander manipulation.

But he was right about at least one thing. She *was* competitive as hell.

And it didn't help that people were starting to sing.

Apparently, the band's repertoire included not just rock, metal and punk but a number of pop and dance standards as well—with an edgier spin, of course, although the keyboard could bring it down to something gentler. Vivian almost laughed when they did, because it was really something to see a seven-foot-tall mountain of a man. She thought he was literally called the Mountain, because he was shaped like a barrel, almost as wide as he was tall but more solid than fat—with a tiny, disproportionate head in the crowd, bobbing to a nineties Celine Dion power ballad.

A nineties Celine Dion power ballad that was being slaughtered by someone who should never have been given a device that amplified sound. The woman appeared unwinded by the laughter, singing *It's All Coming Back to Me Now* on what had to have been her third or fourth tankard of ale.

Vivian didn't understand how people could drink like that without saying things they really shouldn't and doing things that made people give them more than a side-eye. Maybe they did say and do things they shouldn't, but most people didn't do or say the kinds of things she did when tipsy. She wasn't a nice drunk, and she'd learned early on not to drink when she was in danger of being in other people's company. When she was alone and didn't have to wake up in the morning, she could drink as much as she damn well wanted.

Control. She'd learned that after her first round at the hospital. If losing control had put her there, maintaining it kept her out, even though nothing had changed. There had been a few lapses since, but she had enough control that nobody had to know why. Nobody ever had to know *her*. And as long as no one knew her, she could do as she pleased—anything within her complete control.

For instance, leaving before the ear-splitting caterwauling could strip the paint off her toes. She didn't have to stay for this. There was nothing keeping her here—no gates, no fences, no walls, no chains.

Vivian stood from the table and pushed her way through the crowd. In a matter of seconds, someone else took her prime seat—just one more reason to move on. The press of flesh around her, the scent of sweat, of meat, of sugar and cream and beer knotted her hollow stomach, twisted it into a clenching cramp. And the noise didn't help. If someone would just hit that woman over the head with a two-by-four, nothing would ever come back to her again, no matter how someone touched her.

That particular agony finally ended just as Vivian reached the far edge of the not-insignificant crowd. Really, she hadn't realized how big it had grown, with circus folk, circus fans—she could tell by the costumes, which had more glitter than the ones there for the Ren faire—Ren faire fans and regular Joes and Joannas with their kids and friends and family. On the outside of that, a girl could breathe again.

By the time she caught her breath, a deep voice yelled to the crowd, "Good afternoon, everyone! *Now* who's ready to rock?"

She considered turning around just to make sure it wasn't the guitarist, because she hadn't expected that rich voice to come out of his white, reedy, nicotine-stained body. Vivian supposed some people went for that, but pale British rock wannabes had never been her thing. The accent was sometimes lovely, but grease was for fish and chips, not complexion, and she didn't actually want to fuck Mick Jagger. Billy Idol, maybe.

And Bell kind of looked like him, if he ever decided to go platinum…

Shit, there her mind went again, to that infuriating rodent playing some kind of game with her. And with the return of Bell to her mind, she couldn't help but turn back, furious at the helplessness of her own reactions — as though someone had read up that free will was an illusion and decided to have a little fun with her.

Instead of the guitarist, though, a tall, thick, three-breasted, busty drag queen belted out a surprisingly good rendition of *I Would Do Anything For Love* in a rich baritone that shouldn't have worked — like something out of a campy Jim Steinman horror musical, which was somehow the charm of it. The drag queen strutted across the uneven ground in six-inch heels — not stilettos, but nothing a person wanted to be walking on grass in — bellowing into the microphone with every indication that she'd been classically trained and could probably dominate a concert hall even without a mic.

Vivian crossed her arms over her chest and stayed through the whole song. She even clapped at the end with the rest. The drag queen gave the Human Spider a high five as she left the makeshift stage, all three boobs jiggling like they were real in the blue-sequined black leather and lace dress.

But when another drunken crooner who thought he could sing ambled up to the mic, Vivian turned on her heel once more, pressing her hands to her ears as she headed back into the Ren faire for the exit.

Before leaving, she stopped at the fairground bathrooms, which were an exercise in degradation all on their own — just one step up from portable toilets, gross from the cinderblocks to the seat covers. But she didn't want to use a gas station or fast food restaurant bathroom either, and she had to pee.

Inside the stall, she could still hear the muffled butchering of *Radioactive*.

'Why not help make it the circus you wanted it to be?'

All she wanted to do was leave. That goddamn effete little elf. She'd talked to him for only a few minutes and he'd infiltrated her mind as though he'd been there for years. She was supposed to be the puppeteer, not the puppet. *Never* any man's puppet.

Vivian slammed her hand against the stall door, uncaring that there were other people in the bathroom. Then she stuffed her sleeve in her mouth, covered herself with her light cardigan and screamed, digging her nails into her cheek.

"Are you okay?" someone asked from a few stalls down.

Vivian spat out her sleeve then forced a smile onto her face to change the quality of her voice. "I'm fine. Thank you."

She closed her eyes and took deep, long breaths until the urge to throw herself against the wall had passed. Then she adjusted her cardigan to hide the wet spot on her sleeve where she'd stifled her scream, straightened her shirt and stepped out of the stall. In front of the mirror, she pulled lipstick out from her purse to touch up with dark red and checked her hair, ignoring the curious stares from other people going in and coming out of stalls.

Vivian stepped out of the bathrooms. But she stopped in her tracks right before the ticket booths, wincing, when another guest started butchering *Living on a Prayer*.

"Oh, for fuck's sake."

She turned on her heel and strode back toward the circus, where the band had transitioned into a much-needed instrumental break. Thank God she didn't need to hear someone ruin *Don't Stop Believin'*. The electric guitar and electric violin played the melody as a duet, and the audience sang along together. In concert, the tone-deaf singers were overwhelmed by the swell of the sound. Audience singing was always a little flat to the ears and slightly creepy, like praying or saying the Pledge. But *Don't Stop Believin'* was *Don't Stop Believin'*. People didn't just listen to a song like that.

Vivian edged the crowd toward the front, where most of the circus folk congregated away from the good angles but close enough to support their own. Here, she got a better look at freaks that hadn't been wandering in her direction during her earlier time in Arcanium. The drag queen was taller than Vivian had been able to tell from a distance. In her heels, she was half a head taller than the Ringmaster, who looked thoroughly unhappy to be there.

Up close, Vivian was almost certain the drag queen's boobs weren't some kind of stuffed latex prosthetic but actual implants, and those implants were quality. Girl showed some serious devotion to her craft. Her hair was a wig but a good one, and she was talking with another woman next to her—at least Vivian thought they were a woman until they turned their head to reveal a nicely trimmed sandy mustache and goatee, a shade redder than their feathery, ambiguous hair. They were dressed in a slim, natty suit and held a black and silver cane—more Marlene Dietrich than Cary Grant, especially with the second button of their shirt undone to expose the lacy edge of a bra that provided decent and undeniable cleavage. But their hips were slim, buttocks more masculine, and with facial hair, their face appeared male. If Vivian wasn't mistaken, there was quite a bulge in the front of the tailored, pressed trousers, enhanced by the cut, but they could have been packing.

Vivian thought Arcanium might get a lot of angry letters from both sides of the aisle because of those two, but it was no significant concern for her. She mostly just wished she could pull off a suit like that, plus the drag queen's heels.

Next to the suited individual, a man had coiled — yes, coiled — his long, glimmering tan body into a seat to watch the show, his scaled head nodding with the beat and a smile on his heavily made-up face. How long did it take these people to do themselves up every day? Vivian allotted thirty minutes to her routine, but she hated every minute of it, especially when it was still dark outside in the morning. Some of these transformations had to take hours.

The Mountain was indeed mountainous, and the Bearded Lady was a different creature entirely from the suited individual, furred all over like a dark ginger cat, with a pirate queen's cleavage and a long beard any lumberjack would envy.

Next to her, Bell hooked his arm through hers. If Vivian weren't looking closely, Bell would seem like the gay best friend — intense, intimate, ultimately nonthreatening. But when he kissed the Bearded Lady's neck, there was nothing playful about it.

This damn circus. No, like she'd said, not yet a circus. *This damn freak show.* She couldn't pin a piece of it down. If they'd just had men on stilts, a couple of tumbling, rainbow-colored clowns and an elephant, she'd know what she was getting into. But a skinless woman had nails, pins and letter openers all over her like a pincushion, an armless black man moved like a backup dancer to the music and the Patchwork Pirate was almost scarier to Vivian than the creepy-ass clowns Arcanium *did* have, because she literally looked like someone had taken apart a sweet-faced hooker and put her back together again. On top of that, Vivian had no idea what the little girl's body with the big-ass man's head on it was supposed to be.

Twisted or missing limbs, face paint, gymnastic skills—these were all things she would have understood. But in the harsh light of day, the freaks looked real, more real than anything computer- or makeup-generated, and they were different from any other freaks she'd ever set eyes on.

If Bell had asked her what she thought of the circus now, she might have been more generous. The freaks were all the stranger close together and against a backdrop of so many normal people. When walking behind the oddities, she was the one who felt freakish. She often felt that way in a crowd, but this was different—as though she'd stepped into the *Twilight Zone* world where pig-faced normals pointed and laughed at her deformities, where she was the trespasser to lock away and they the holders of the keys. It was an unpleasant, upside-down emotion.

But when the Bearded Lady turned around at the sound of grass crunching behind her, there was a brief flash of fear in the formidable woman's expression. Perhaps the Bearded Lady saw a brief reflection of her own fear, because she calmed and gestured Vivian forward, indicating the stage in an unspoken query.

A forty-year-old bar singer got there first, calling for *Piano Man*. The keyboardist and guitarist rolled their eyes, but they dutifully played the intro as unironically as possible.

Enough was enough.

"Would you be so good as to hold my purse and jacket for a moment?" Vivian's mother had raised a girl who knew how to say polite things in passive-aggressive ways.

The first line of the song made Vivian want to rip the man's throat out. Instead, she strode forward, stepped right in front of him, angled herself toward the band members rather than the audience and pulled the neckline of her shirt to the side to expose one breast.

The man's mouth stayed open, but nothing came out of it anymore.

"Great, now that we've stopped this train wreck..." Vivian covered her breast again and made a cutting motion over her throat to convince the instrumentalists to stop, which they did with a certain amount of gratitude. "Don't let the door hit you on the way out, bitch."

"Whore," the man muttered, but after being briefly stunned by the flash of bare boob, he staggered off.

That was more like it—more how men were supposed to act whenever she did anything.

Vivian assumed the place at center mic. She glanced over her shoulder at the band. "Do you do *Paint It Black*?"

"Thank the devil and all his minions," the guitarist said, changing the setting on his amp and checking back with the keyboardist. "But if you can't sing, I may have to kill you."

"Stuff it, ciggie. Just play the damn song."

The man smiled as he gave her the British two-finger salute. Then the keyboardist started on her first notes, a higher-register minor-key harpsichord setting that tickled the hairs on the back of Vivian's neck. She turned back to the microphone and waited for her musical cue.

With the abrupt shift from harpsichord to the electric guitar's power chord and the drummer joining in with a crash, Vivian closed her eyes. There wasn't a lot in the world she liked. Pizza was at the top of her list. Music that shuddered through her sternum was another.

After the keyboardist did a lead-in string of notes and the drums withdrew, Vivian grasped the microphone. With butterflies in her stomach but hornets in her head, she took on the first verse, favoring it with her warmer lower register, just a hint of a rasp within the sweetness. It wasn't perfect. They hadn't rehearsed, and it took a minute for Vivian's vocal chords to finds their muscle memory. But Vivian knew how to improvise, and once the guitar whined a third above her voice, something clicked.

The instrumentalists started following her, with dramatic pauses when they weren't sure what she was going to do. They were professionals, and she'd sung in bands before back in high school and college. She had no formal training, unlike the keyboardist, the violinist or the drag queen, and she didn't always play well with others, but she'd learned what her voice could do in the silences. And when she brought the melody up an octave, relishing in the demon rock goddess growl she could conjure on command, she soaked in the sound of cheers from the crowd and circus freaks alike.

In spite of the lyrics, she couldn't hold back a smile. It had been years since she'd performed, since she'd even sung along with the radio.

She'd missed this—the power chords, the electric violin soaring up to ugly-beautiful heights, the toothsome woman going Animal on the drums, words growling out of her chest like a demon. And at the end, she pulled the demon back, with clearer, sweeter notes floating up into her head, the entire crowd quiet to hear.

God, how I've missed this.

The applause didn't suck either, especially when the drummer did her own version through a descending drum solo.

"You got a standing O, rude woman." The guitarist grinned as he changed his amp setting again.

"I guess a standing O is better than no O at all."

"You're weird, and I like you."

Vivian bit back the impulse to ask if he wanted sex later. She couldn't stand even the slightest bit of cigarette smoke, but he did have a good smile.

"I think they want one more." The keyboardist had a pleasantly gentle alto, the kind that would do much better in the singer-songwriter genre. "What are you up for?"

"I was on my way out. I just wanted to stop the bad." Vivian put the microphone back on its stand and raised her hands as she backed away. "What you do now is up to you."

The keyboardist grinned then started on the first few notes of *My Immortal*.

Vivian tilted her head, saying '*Seriously?*' again without even opening her mouth.

"People love it even when they hate it," the keyboardist said. "Come on."

Vivian shook her head, but the crowd clapped to encourage her and the violinist added her plaintive strings to the repeating intro.

Vivian backed away again. "I don't remember the lyrics."

"Don't worry about that."

Vivian jumped then whipped around. Someone needed to put a fucking bell on Bell, because he just didn't *feel* like a person, the way all the little cells on skin could sense anyone else close by. She hated that he'd made her jump in front of hundreds of people.

"An audition is all about showing range," Bell said, "and never saying no."

"This isn't an audition," Vivian replied. "It's a rescue mission, and I've done my part. I'm out of here."

Bell nodded to the sign — *Karaoke — Auditions for Lead Singer*.

"Yeah, well, I did the karaoke part of it."

Bell caught her hand before she could walk past him. "You don't get to choose whether this is an audition, Vivian. You've been in dead-end office jobs for years because that's all you can manage while keeping your secrets. Don't you want something a little more exciting? Something a little stranger?"

Vivian hesitated, swallowing back another nauseating wave of fear, a different quality this time than when she'd been behind the freaks. She wasn't sure if Bell's hand would squeeze, grinding her bones within his grip.

"This isn't my audition." And when she pulled her hand away, he did release her. "I'll do one more song if it'll get you out of my face, but then I'm going home."

"I know how this day will end, Vivian, and it's not how you expect." He touched her chin, lifting her face, then brushed her cheek. She swore he was going to kiss her, and to her utter humiliation, she was weighing whether she'd let him or not. But Bell sank back into his freakshow crowd, clapping with the rest of them to encourage her to take center stage.

The crowd cheered harder and higher as she returned to the microphone. She waited for the keyboardist and violinist to cycle through the introduction again and cue her in.

She kept her voice soft, clear, reining in the vibrato and only bringing in the barest harshness during the bridge. And in spite of being in a fairground, with all sorts of ambient sounds and people doing other things—even though it seemed like the whole world had congregated in front of the band—everything else seemed to go silent. She'd rarely sung for people who weren't friends or friends of friends before, and never for a crowd this big.

The keyboardist was right. Even when someone said they hated this song, they secretly loved it, because a good minor key got through all the cracks and crevices, and for a few minutes, it made her feel something other than angry. Maybe that showed, because everyone—young and old, boomer and hipster, normal and freak—applauded again. And her smile might have been shy, without a trace of coyness.

"Thank you," she muttered into the mic. Then she determinedly walked back the direction she came, rounding the crowd away from Bell. The Bearded Lady handed her the jacket and purse with a smile. Vivian didn't bother checking her wallet. She was even agreeable when the drag queen raised a hand for her to fist bump.

She was almost out of the sparse Arcanium midway when Bell grabbed her by the back of the neck and covered her mouth to keep anyone from hearing her scream.

"You're not going to sneak away from me that easily, love. We have some unfinished business."

Chapter Two

"Let go of me! Let go of me, fucking piss bowl!" Or at least that's what she tried to say, but he'd firmly planted his hand over her mouth.

Bell pulled her to the other side of the midway booths, farther away from the crowd, toward the sad-looking funhouse that Vivian hadn't even bothered trying because it looked like a collection of construction offices mashed together.

That was also where Bell had set up his fortune teller's tent. She didn't need to be a psychic to know that. It said *Fortunes* on the awning above the open tent flap.

In surprisingly little time, considering she was kicking and wrenching against him without hesitation, spitting and trying to bite his hand as hard as she could, he'd dragged her like a clever caveman into the tent, somehow drawing the flap down again in the process.

Between the scarves, incense, candles and shitload of crystals, his tent practically dripped mysticism. Vivian could already tell she was going to hate the incense with a blinding passion. She had far too sensitive of a nose to stand most burning things that weren't food. Cigarette smoke, incense and strong perfumes made her want to stab things — as though she needed another reason to kill Bell.

Her teeth finally found purchase on his palm, and she sank them in as hard as she could.

Bell hurled her onto the Persian rug and shook his hand, flicking thick blood drops onto the weave. "Son of a *bitch*!"

Vivian spat out the piece of bloody skin still between her teeth. She scrambled toward the door, but just as she reached the closed tent flap, he grabbed her by the neck again and swept his leg against the backs of hers, pulling her, weak, back into the main room. He shoved her away from him and pointed down at her.

"Just stay there. I'm not going to hurt you."

"That's what people say right before they hurt you."

"I didn't say you shouldn't be afraid when I pulled you from your path, did I? Your reaction was perfectly reasonable, as was mine when you bit off a piece of my hand." He held it up, blood dripping down his arm like raspberry sauce. "But I'm not going to hurt you."

She tried to get around him. He shoved her back by her sternum with his good hand. She would have tried again — there was no statute of limitations on escape — but with his bleeding hand not a few feet away, she got an eyeful of the edges of the wound wriggling inward.

It startled her so much that she stopped. As the wound completely closed, the blood that had covered the front of his hand and forearm absorbed into his skin until there wasn't so much as a stain or a scab.

"Now that I have your attention," he said quietly, "would you rather continue this stand-off or would you like to sit down?"

"I'll fucking stand, thank you. What the fuck is going on? Is this latex? Was that even blood?" Vivian grabbed his hand, poked and prodded at it, scratched at the light calluses and his forearm, looking for somewhere that the blood and seemingly exposed flesh could have gone, some hidden sleeve he could have slipped things into. But a shirtless man didn't have many places to conceal sleight-of-hand tricks, as he'd already pointed out. This time he didn't stop her or push her away, not even when she scraped her nails over his skin so hard that it drew blood again.

"It's better if you don't break yourself trying to figure out what the trick is, Vivian. It's just gone. We have more important things to discuss."

"Something like that doesn't just happen and we pretend it doesn't happen."

"I think we need to talk about your future."

Vivian let go of his hand, unable to find so much as a seam in his skin that she hadn't made by scratching him to find one. "I don't think that's any of your business. Now let me go."

"You can leave this tent, but you'll never be allowed beyond the edge of the fairgrounds. Not unless I let you out, and that would only be under special circumstances."

"Wait, so this is supposed to be an actual abduction?" Vivian laughed, looking around at the filmy ceiling. She was in a tent, and the door was a tent flap. Fort Knox it wasn't.

"For the sake of simplicity, yes."

She laughed again, but though Bell smiled, all trace of pain gone from his forehead and the creases in the corners of his eyes, he didn't laugh back.

"Okay, joke's over, man. I'm leaving."

"Your fate was sealed before you ever stepped foot on that stage, but when you did, you gave my power the direction it needed. Your audition went very well, love. You're perfect for what I always wanted the Skellies to be."

"What, a symphonic metal cover band?" Vivian crossed her arms. "Wait, I know what this is. Did Fernanda put you up to this? Did she tell you to freak me out so they can put up some lame video on YouTube or something? If I see a video of me singing go viral, man, I'm going to make sure something much bloodier goes viral."

"I never received a phone call, e-mail, text message or smoke signal from anyone named Fernanda," Bell said. "I'm in league with no one. I just know what I want."

"And you want me, is that it? You want this?" Vivian slipped a hand between her legs and another over her breast and squeezed. "I don't know if you've noticed, you crazy motherfucker, but I fight back, and I don't mind drawing blood. You won't have anything to fuck me with when I'm through with you."

She shoved past him again, but this time he grabbed her by the hair and yanked her back against his body. And he was a lot harder and hotter than Vivian could have expected just from looking at him.

"You have all of Lizzie's crudeness but none of her grace. It's a shame I don't like you nearly as much as I do her. I have no absolutely no interest in fucking you, handing you over to someone else to fuck you or having people pay me to fuck you."

Ordinary girls probably wouldn't be more offended by the fact he didn't want her than the fact he fully intended to kidnap her. But her brain kept sticking on the first point, and he seemed to realize it, because he brought his mouth to her ear, close enough that her body reacted the way a body did.

"All I want you to do is exactly what you did in front of that crowd for as long as I decide to keep you. Depending on how you adapt to my world, it might not be for very long. Then you can go about your dull, bad telenovela life as though it's something worth hurrying off to. Do you know why I don't like you, Vivian?"

When he wanted to, he sounded like sex. Even though she hated him right now, she imagined what hating him between the covers would feel like.

"Because you forgot to take your blue pills this morning?" she replied through clenched teeth.

"Oh, believe me, that's never been my problem." He was so close that his lips brushed the shell of her ear, and Vivian kind of hated her body just as much as she hated him right now.

"Could have fooled me. Let me go."

"I don't like you, Vivian, because I know you." He leaned in even closer, practically kissing her ear as he whispered, "I know what you are."

She stopped fighting to escape his grip, panting from the effort. There was that spike of fear again, unwanted and more powerful than expected. "What are you talking about?"

He stroked her disheveled hair. "I know what you are, and I know what you've done."

"You don't know jack, you shriveled garden slug."

"I know what you did to Fernanda. I know why you're here alone, not a single one of your friends available to come with you. I know why you can't advance in any job you get and why you've been discreetly let go from three of them. I know why all of the bands that took you for your voice still kicked you out. And I know why you went into that hospital the first time and why they made you stay. I know why you went to the hospital again last year, and I know what you hid from them. For all the secrets you've kept in your life, you have none from me."

"Because you're a goddamn psychic?" She'd known how to make herself cry since she was ten, but for tears to spring to her eyes without her forcing them was like lemon juice on a wound.

"Exactly."

"Balls. You really have talked to Fernanda. Or Simón. Or somebody. Once you knew my name, you looked me up, asked the wrong people some questions and got just enough to make that viral video really fucking juicy."

"I haven't talked to anyone, and we've already established there's nowhere on me to hide a phone."

Up close and personal, she could confirm that he didn't have any underwear under his trousers, and he really didn't have space to put anything but his dick.

"You're staying here in Arcanium. You'll complete the band, tide over the guests while I continue to get Arcanium back on its feet. And you'll get to do one of the few things that makes your block of ice carved into the shape of a heart happy."

"Over my block-of-ice dead body," she snarled.

"Oh, I'll do worse. If you try to leave Arcanium, you'll experience the most unpleasant sensations you've ever felt in your life, and I know you've felt plenty."

"Fuck you and the stupid circus you rode in on. Go fuck yourself." The harder she wrenched away from him, the more she strained her own arms in the attempts.

Finally, she shed her last bit of pride and screamed. And she could scream long and loud. But Bell didn't make any attempt to cover her mouth this time.

Somehow, that was scarier than anything he'd done so far.

When she needed breath, he loosened his hold on her hair and whispered, "They can't hear you."

Then he stepped away.

Vivian darted forward, scrabbling at the edges of the tent flap, pulling at strings, digging at seams. But the strings wouldn't move, the seams wouldn't break and the canvas tent flap seemed fused to the rest of the tent. She knelt on the grass to crawl underneath the edge of the tent, but the canvas was thick, the stakes on the outside pulling it taut, and it wouldn't lift more than a few inches from the ground. She screamed through the crack. Bell still didn't try to stop her.

Finally, she climbed to her feet and whirled around, taking in the sight of all the crystals around her and trying to figure out which one would be best to launch at his head. They'd probably be heavy as hell, but there were a few wands that she could swing at him like a lead pipe.

"I dare you to do it. I dare you to crack open my skull with one of these beautiful geological prisons." Bell picked up a rose quartz the size and length of a good cucumber. "I think you'll find yourself as successful as your attempt to bite me."

"I did bite you. I broke the skin. And it hurt you. You were bleeding." Vivian rocked back and forth on her heels, torn between grabbing one of the stones and the fact he didn't seem all that concerned.

"But I'm not bleeding anymore, am I? Don't bother trying to understand, my dear. It defies all laws but mine."

She grabbed one of the agate balls from the sideboard and threw it at the shelves at the other end of the tent, knocking over candles and breaking both the agate ball and another one of the crystals. Bell barely blinked. "Stop talking crazy and tell me what the hell is going on here."

"I thought I was perfectly clear. You're trapped, Vivian. I'm taking you. You're part of Arcanium now. It's time for you to help make this the circus you wanted to see."

"You goddamn motherfucker." She lifted an amethyst geode that was a lot heavier than it looked and flung it as hard as she could at him.

He lifted a finger. The geode stopped in midair.

"These aren't tricks. No pulleys. No latex. No gimmicks. Oh, I use a few of them here and there to sell the mystique in a package that people can understand, but this is magic, love. As fierce as you are, as unflinching and unhesitating as you are, you are no match for me. You're only human."

"And if I'm *only* human, what does that make you, oh great and powerful one?"

"If you're not inclined to listen to me when I'm being calm, reasonable and rational, I don't see how my answering that question is going to do either of us any good. All that matters is that you're mine and you can't leave. As soon as this day is over, you'll be sharing a tent with the rest of the Skellies, despite my not wanting to inflict you on anyone else."

Okay, now he was just being insulting.

"If you loathe me as much as I loathe you, why drag me along and *inflict* me on everyone else in your circus? I'm fully willing to share the misery, and if you're so 'psychic', you'd know that." She relaxed her shoulders and spine and turned on the sweet, but his demeanor didn't change. "Come on, man. Let me out of here. You'll never have to see me again, won't have to wake up every day to someone devoted to making your life a living hell."

"We'll get into the consequences for everything you're thinking about doing later. You have no power to make my life a living hell, and enough of my people have gone through hell that they'll scarcely tolerate a skinny little girl like you trying to put them through it again. I wouldn't test them or me, my dear. I'm fiercely protective of my people, especially from any dangers within — more than I ever was before. I owe them that much."

He stepped closer, one bare, delicate foot in front of the other. When he reached for her face to touch her cheek again, she flinched as though he would hit her. But though the threat had been implicit, he did nothing more than brush her hair back behind her ear.

"As for why I won't let you go, well, now we get into the crux of *your* problem rather than mine. You made a wish, which allowed me to bring you into Arcanium, and your talent allows me to shape how. But you didn't wish for a good voice, did you? You already had that. No, you wished to look like my Skeletons. I'm bound to fulfill the wish, one way or another, but if I did and let you loose, your health would take a severe turn for the worse. You already know how bad that can be, don't you, Vivian?"

He grabbed her wrists when she tried to claw his eyes out.

"You son of a bitch," she hissed. "What the fuck do you know about it? You know shit, you hear me? You know *shit* about me."

"I. Know. *Everything*." He forced her hands back to her sides, close enough now to kiss. "Everything. I know what I'm bringing into Arcanium. I think you're worth it for what you can add to the circus, but the transition isn't going to be easy for either of us, because you always look for the loopholes, don't you? But I don't have any for you to exploit. If you step out of line, you'll be punished in far more terrible ways than anything on the outside. If I need to, I'll make this place *your* hell. But I don't want to. You've had enough of that, and deep down, I'm simply not a demon—no matter what you believe of me right now."

Until then, he'd been close only in proximity, nothing beyond the barest suggestiveness in his posture, his touch, his words, despite how her body reacted to them. But facing her directly, his body brushing hers with every slight movement, his bright, almost amber eyes burning into hers then glancing down to her mouth, the slight cant of his hips... Every signal he had withheld before slipped through, to her utter confusion. He'd said he hadn't wanted her, and maybe he hadn't five minutes ago, but something had changed. Maybe he got off on caging her in, or maybe he got off on her trying to kill him. It wouldn't be her first time with a man into either of those things. That was something she knew how to deal with.

Vivian stopped fighting and brought her hips deliberately against his erection. She swallowed when she realized just how little he needed those little blue pills. But she angled her head and parted her lips, inviting him to kiss her. Inviting him to try. She might even let him, for a few seconds.

He brought a finger between their mouths and pressed it against her lips. "No. That's not what I want from you."

"Could have fooled me," she murmured against his finger then licked up to the tip.

"You and I both know there's a difference between biology and desire." He let go of her other wrist and withdrew. "You're not ready for someone like me, not even close."

"You think an awful lot of yourself, don't you, asshole?"

"I know myself, as I know you. Do you know yourself, Vivian? Do you look in the mirror and see who you are?"

He gestured to the side of the room. A full-length mirror in an ornate antique frame was propped against the shelves of crystals, candles and sculptures. It hadn't been there a minute ago, otherwise it would have shattered when she'd thrown the agate ball, and it looked too heavy to have been stealthily placed there by unseen assistants.

"Fucking *stop* that." She tried to turn away from herself, but Bell grabbed her arm hard enough to bruise and forced her back around.

"No. We have all kinds of mirrors here in Arcanium. There's the makeup vanity in Kitty's tent. There are several full-length mirrors like this one in the Skeleton residential tent. There's an entire Hall of Mirrors in my haunted funhouse. You'll eventually have to confront them all. Might as well begin now. I'll give you the choice I gave to my other Skeletons, a choice my original Skeleton never had because she was born that way."

"What the fuck you talking about, fucking crazy white dude?" She was at the end of her patience. All she wanted to do was leave this goddamn circus and go home to down a whole bottle of wine in her goddamn bathtub.

"Sandra was born with a wasting disease she couldn't control. She came to Arcanium voluntarily, although she didn't know what we were. She was looking for a steady job until she died, something that would help her pay down her medical bills and the debt she'd accumulated trying to figure out what was wrong. I kept her skeletal for my circus, but I took away her pain, her aches, her weak heart and the fog in her mind. She eventually wished herself free, and I gave her the health she'd never had. All my new Skeletons, however, came into the circus wishing to lose weight they didn't need to lose, with distortions in their perception, distortions in their expectations, delusions almost as strong as your own and compulsions stronger. But they started out normal, like you. Look at yourself, Vivian. Look at yourself and don't look away from that mirror until we're through."

His tone brooked no refusal. Usually, that didn't mean shit to Vivian, but she found herself obeying, confronted by the inescapable image of her body as she had always seen herself. The image she knew was wrong.

"I know what you see," he said. "It's a shame your perception has been so distorted for so long that you're unable to see what you look like, although you seem comfortable exploiting what other people see."

Bell came up behind her. She could see him just fine. But herself… Every place that wasn't bone looked like blubber. Every curve that wasn't an angle looked like cellulite. She could use a mirror to put makeup on and do her hair, and she could glance in a reflection to check her clothes. But to see herself, her whole body, was to see something that disgusted, repulsed, repelled her. She knew she wasn't an ogre, because as Bell had pointed out, she wouldn't be able to use men as adeptly as she did if she was as repulsive as she seemed to herself. But knowing and seeing were two different parts of her brain, and knowing that it wasn't real didn't help her see any better.

"How can you know what I see?" Anger had seeped from her voice. With her softer words that in no way meant she'd melted for him, he rewarded her with another almost tender touch along her throat. He obviously liked to touch. Some people were like that, and Vivian didn't understand it, but there was an element of ownership to the contact that made her bristle at the same time her cunt opened for more.

"I see into your mind as surely as I see into your future," he replied.

"And you can grant wishes, like a genie. Is that what you are, non-demon guy? Is that what you're trying to tell me?"

The side of his mouth quirked. "Yes." Before she could say it, he replied, "Seriously."

"Great. Not just delusions of grandeur but delusions in general."

"You'd know a little something about that, wouldn't you?"

"Fuck you."

"Not yet." He pulled her hair back so that her jawline, cheekbones, the curve of her neck, the bend of her clavicle and her exposed sternum were all visible above the neckline of her peasant blouse. "Do you remember what you wished?"

"Wouldn't you know that, psychic genie?"

"You wished you could look like my Skeletons. You see in these reapers' bodies what you think you could be happier being. Yours is one of the few wishes that I hear with all-too-terrible frequency. If you knew how many pennies fell into the wishing well in the name of losing weight or achieving the perfect body, if you knew how many curses have been dispensed in the name of ephemeral beauty... And you *are* beautiful, Vivian. You're beautiful now, and you will be beautiful when you look like death. But I want you to know what death looks like."

"Just do whatever sick thing you're planning to do and get it over with," Vivian snapped, still unable to move, unable to look away. "Cut me. Hit me. Fuck me over even if you won't fuck me. I'm tired of hearing your voice."

"And I'll never tire of hearing yours, no matter how you sharpen your tongue."

"I thought you didn't like me."

"I don't have to like you to like parts." Bell tied her hair back then let go of her once more. "You have no choice in the clarity of what you will see. The only choice you have is whether you want to become the Skeleton all at once or slowly, so that your audience can be aware of the change."

"What? You're going to starve me? You can't do that all at once." What he said made no sense, but deep down where she didn't like to dwell, she thought he might make too much sense in all the wrong ways. Because if he was telling the absolute truth, it added up to something that had to be impossible, something as strange and unusual and fantastic as Arcanium claimed it was — as Bell claimed he was.

"I won't starve you. The wish will eat away at your fat and flesh and render you as close to skin and bones as I can make you without straining too many biological laws and people's suspension of disbelief. We will feed you everything you need, if not everything you'll want — of that you have my word. But you will feel such hunger that the emptiness inside you now will feel like a tree hollow in comparison to the cavern I shall make of your appetites. I could spare Sandra that, but I won't spare you, so that you'll finally understand what you wished of me. You will curse my name, Vivian, but only wishes have power here, and I'm the one who wields them."

"Because you're a genie."

"Now you're starting to understand."

"You're insane."

"I'm not insane, love. You are. But let's not quibble over insignificant details. I'll take away your delusion. It's up to you whether you want to see yourself diminish slowly or quickly. And you have to decide now. Don't make me give you a countdown."

Vivian shook her head, feeling even less tethered than usual, as though she were Dorothy and reality was flying off in a hot-air balloon without her. "Fine. If we're playing this game… I'd want you to do it quickly. Get it over with."

"Very well. Wish granted." He stroked her hot cheek with his knuckles then covered her eyes.

When he removed his hand again, the woman in the mirror wore the same clothes, had the same makeup, the same hair. Everything was the same, but how she saw it was so fundamentally different that Vivian nearly collapsed.

Where her stomach had pooched and bloated against her skirt waist, where cap sleeves had dented her arms and made them look bulging, where the lines on her throat had created a double-chin, where she'd noted the cherubic quality to her cheeks, the enormous thickness of her thighs and ass… She saw all these places untainted by the subsonic whispers lying through the echo chamber of her mind.

People would always tell her to eat a cheeseburger, that she needed cake for her birthday, a steak instead of salad—all those things that were really none of their goddamn business. And it was still none of their goddamn business. But now she saw what they saw—

the hollows under her cheekbones, her prominent chin, the lumps of her larynx, the contrasting shadow under her collarbone, the contours of her sternum. And her actual figure — with curves and folds, yes, but when she pulled her peasant blouse tight against her abdomen, her belly narrowed nearly flat under her ribs. She was a little skinnier than thin, though not quite skinny. None of her bones were as visible as the Skeletons'.

And she was pretty. She'd never been pretty to herself, never, as far back as she could remember. She'd stared at her Barbies as a child, hating their beauty with a black hatred no child was supposed to know. She would pull their heads and limbs off and paint them black and red, rendering them voodoo dolls or murdered whores — or whatever the equivalent was for a four-year-old girl who didn't know what either of those things were.

But for the first time, Vivian really understood why she could wrap men around her little finger, why she was always able to get away with the things she wanted to get away with, why she was never without a drink or a meal or a movie, why she could always go where she wanted, why the man at the microphone had stumbled away as though she'd slapped him with the boob she'd exposed. She saw everything she'd always been and everything more she could be.

"I'm sorry." And he did sound sorry.

The hollows under her cheekbones became gaunt like a mummy rather than a model. Her larynx became even more pronounced, almost to the point of an Adam's apple. Above the neckline of her blouse, the clavicle, scapula, sternum and the top sets of ribs were as noticeable as they were on any science room skeleton.

In a rush of heartbeat horror, she lifted her shirt and ran her hand over her abdomen as though she would feel something different than what she saw. But her already-flat belly sucked in into something like a caricature, an animated woman's exaggerated wasp waist. She could almost see the lumps of her organs, the slimmest margin of fat, muscle and skin to separate them.

The waistband of her skirt sagged over the violent jut of her hipbones as she lost several sizes all at once, and her numbers hadn't been high to start with. Her underwear loosened, threatened to fall off. Even her sandals slipped over smaller feet, feet that also resembled those of a skeleton.

Because that's what she'd wished she could look like.

She saw death in the shape of her skull. He'd kept some flesh. *Of course* he'd kept her breasts, because even when men drew or painted skeletons they intended to be female, they somehow all had breasts. He'd left her smooth face gaunt but not quite sickly. It was the rest of her that bore that title, with thinned-out tendons and ligaments, even fibers of muscle seeming visible through her coffee-stained rice-paper skin.

Vivian clutched at her skirt to keep it from falling and tightened a fist in her shirt, which also threatened to slip down her narrowed shoulders. Then she turned around, which was how she knew that he'd broken whatever invisible bindings had kept her there.

"What the hell did you do to me?" Tears — stinging, awful, shameful, not forced out of her but unable to be forced back in — slipped down her cheeks. "What kind of a monster are you?"

"I gave you what you wanted. Wisdom is what tells you that you don't want it, love, but now it's what you have."

"You gave me what I wished," she muttered slowly. "That means I can wish again. I —"

He covered her mouth the same way he had when he'd dragged her into the tent. "Look at me, playing Kitty when there's no one else here to advocate for you. In another life, I might have let you use all your wishes. Then I could keep you indefinitely. You are many things, Vivian, but you're not a fool. Do you think I'd let you take this back? Do you think there's any wish that I can't use to my own advantage? Save your wishes for when you think I'll actually grant them in your favor. I can promise safety, health and that anyone who tries to harm you will feel a god's wrath. But I cannot promise comfort or happiness. And I promise that, though I am often cryptic, I will never lie, no matter what lies spill from your own tongue."

"Why should I believe you, you...whatever the fuck you are?" Vivian scratched at her stomach, searching for the flesh that had disintegrated before her own unveiled eyes. The horrifying, grotesque, sick, freakish and fatal remained. But her heart kept racing, and she kept standing, more than she had been able to do when she'd first gone to the hospital — and back then she'd been more substantial than this.

"You will learn that I am a man of my word."

She stumbled toward him. "You're no man."

"I am no human. But I am still a man, and my word carries more weight than yours."

"I don't care what kind of tricks you're playing, but you *don't* know me. If you're a man, you're a fucking sick one. And if you're a monster, you should just be a monster without pretending to be a man." Vivian spat on him.

Phlegmy saliva struck his cheek. Bell raised his eyebrows and brought his fingers his face as though he hadn't anticipated her reaction.

"There is no truth to a shapeshifter's skin." He wiped away her spit. "Even my original form is a lie when I can look however I like. I've chosen this for Arcanium, and it is as true as any form I choose. And a monster may be a man. You understand that better than most. Now, must I bind you and render you unconscious, or will you be a good girl and do as I say?"

"Suck on drain cleaner. Look what you did to me!" Vivian lost her skirt as she lunged at him, but the only thing she cared about was how her long legs had halved in width and looked like they couldn't carry her to her car, much less take her on a marathon.

"Who could possibly have seen that coming?" Just as she clawed at his chest, he brought a hand to her brow and sent her down, down, sinking to the earth, pitching forward like a bad night.

Chapter Three

When she woke up, she had a bitch of a headache, and her stomach felt like it would grow teeth any minute and start eating her from the inside out.

From what she could see through the haze of her headache, she was inside a different canvas tent, accented with red velvet through the interior like some kind of harem. She lay on a cot. It wasn't the worst thing she'd woken up on, but it wasn't hers.

The ground underneath the cot was grass and dirt, but it had been covered by a thin traveling rug that reached to the edges of the big room, which was about the size of a fast food restaurant. Four other cots lined the edges, each with a few plastic tubs at the foot and rolling clothes racks behind them. There appeared to be another room in the tent accessible by a tent flap. In the center of the large room sat a kneeling dining table for six. Each spot at the table had been prepared with a cushion. There were napkins but no plates and no silverware.

Behind each cot was a standing full-length mirror.

Vivian sat up, holding her head. Underneath the quilt, she wasn't wearing her skirt, and her underwear was still too big for her. She clutched at it through her peasant blouse, which was long enough to cover the tops of her thighs at least, although it slipped down one shoulder. When she shrugged it back up, it slipped down the other.

Her body hadn't changed from the parchment skin and bones that Bell had left her in. It hadn't just been a horrible nightmare — not that her dreams had ever been that vivid. Life provided plenty of nightmares to make up for it.

A girl with short, sea-green hair stepped out from the closed-off room, towel around her head and face stripped of makeup. She looked freshly scrubbed, skin pink, although God knew what kind of bathroom accommodations even a magical monster could provide in the back of a tent. The girl wore a cotton dress that did nothing to conceal how terribly thin she'd become, bones knifing against her skin. It was all the more apparent without the skeleton makeup creating added illusion. Her thinness was stark, real, and Vivian saw her own body reflected, although the other girl's skin was pale and unevenly suntanned, and Vivian's bronze complexion seemed all the more golden in comparison. Strange how less surface area rather than more enhanced the differences between them, from skin and hair to eye shape to almost imperceptible differences in skeletal structure, like jawline, brow, cheekbones, collarbone and hips.

Vivian didn't move. She waited for the girl to settle on her cot, angled away, before she climbed out from under the quilt and crawled to the tub at the foot of her tiny bed. It contained clothing, accessories, a few books she'd never seen before and certainly weren't hers, but nothing had been used, and it all seemed arranged in preparation for someone new — *anybody* new. Anybody new who'd suddenly lost a third of their body weight and needed something to wear that wouldn't fall off.

Despite her distaste for touching clothes that weren't hers, since she didn't know how clean they were, she grabbed a plain pair of beige panties and switched hers out for the pair that fit. That was all she needed. An over-the-shoulder blouse wasn't going to kill her for now.

When she stood up from behind the tub, the girl turned around at the movement and smiled.

"Oh, hey, Vivian, right?" The girl stood up from her cot, hands behind her back as though contrite. "Bell was kind of abrupt about everything when he brought you in."

Based on her hair, Vivian guessed she was the backup singer. There was an almost mechanical quality to her tone, like she spoke into an Auto-Tuned microphone.

"I'm not sure there's anything like a welcoming committee around here, given the circumstances," the singer continued, stepping a little closer. "I'm Alicia, one of the actual Skeletons of the Skellies. I was brought in before Arcanium reopened, when Bell was out playing fortune teller on his own and had a wishing well outside his tent. Cheater."

Alicia came close enough to carefully sit on Vivian's cot.

"The wasting away was slower for me. This was before he'd conceived the Skellies and just wanted someone to replace his original Skeleton. He wasn't in any hurry to display me, so I just got to sit around and suffer, watching myself slowly disappear. Before I made the wish, I would have celebrated that. Hard to believe, isn't it?" She smoothed her hem over her bony knees, broader than the thighs above them.

"What are you doing?" Vivian said.

"What do you mean?"

"Talking to me. Why are you talking to me?"

Alicia's brow creased. "Just explaining how I got here. The girls here, we know what you're going through better than anyone in the circus, because we're the only ones he chose to replicate — unless you count the triplets, which I don't. I just mean he made more than one Skeleton for his freak show so he could put together the Skellies. And that's where you come in."

"Is there a *CliffsNotes* to the whole history thing? Because I'd like to fast forward to how we're getting out of here."

Alicia blinked. "We're not. People don't leave Arcanium unless Bell lets them. A whole bunch left soon after we were brought in, but that was different, and no one from before likes to talk about it. All we know is that people don't get out. If you run, the magic gets you. Then the Ringmaster whips you."

"Whips." Vivian laughed, but it wasn't funny. "He actually whips you? Like a whipping boy?"

"Yeah. And he doesn't hold back." Alicia touched her hunched shoulders as though there were scars, but her skin was pristine, unmarked except for ordinary blemishes. "He's a demon. Like, a real demon, more than anything else in the circus. You should see him smile when he goes after someone who broke the rules. He never smiles except when Bell lets him off the leash."

"There's got to be a way out," Vivian said.

"You think we'd be here if there was? You think we wished to be Living Skeletons dancing in his little puppet theater?" Alicia tugged at her dress as she got to her feet. "You try to run, you get whipped. You try to send up smoke signals, you get whipped. You put up a piece of paper that says 'Help! I'm kidnapped' in the window of the RV when we're traveling, you get whipped. You try to wish out too soon, Bell's got new ammunition to make your life even worse. Lily didn't start out in the Skellies. She saw me losing weight and accidentally wished in Bell's earshot that she could lose weight like that while eating as much as I did. Then she got the Paganini and *Thinner* curse going all at once."

"I heard my name." The lithe woman, who wore her skeleton with more grace because she'd clearly already been tiny, slipped into the room in nothing but two towels, one around her body and one over her hair. Given her petite, delicate frame, the large body towel covered her more than the sundresses covered Alicia, and certainly more than Vivian's shirt covered her.

"What? Is there a communal shower back there or something?" Vivian said.

"Actually, yes," Lily replied. "Bell makes the makeup endure all day then easy to clean off when everyone's gone. But it's still body paint, and it's still everywhere. I don't know where the shower and bathrooms *are* exactly, in the sense of time and space, whether we step into another dimension to get to it or what, but it reminds me of my old school gym locker room. If you're body shy, you're going to have to get over that. Bell doesn't give us a lot of room for modesty."

"If I never have to hear that name as long as I live…" Vivian said. That's all anyone kept saying. *Bell, Bell, Bell, Bell, Bell*, as though his name tolled.

"Bell is Arcanium, and Arcanium is Bell," Lily said. "In comparison to a lot of his other oddities, being a Skeleton isn't all bad. You'll either get used to it or you'll go mad. Trust me, you don't want to end up like the Tooth Fairy."

It seemed like it would be just the right amount of dramatic irony if the Tooth Fairy were to walk through the front door—Vivian assumed Lily meant Shane, their drummer—but instead, the keyboardist, still dressed as a skeleton belly dancer, jingled into the tent, the guitarist latched to her lips and backing her in.

Vivian curled her lip at the thought of kissing that thin-lipped mouth, knowing exactly where it had been. But the sight of the keyboardist kissing Lennon, her slightly curved abdomen pressing to his bare skin, because he'd taken off his skeleton shirt at some point… Vivian didn't expect the sudden pang in her abdomen, as sharp and painful as her hunger, but lower. With her new eyes, she saw the keyboardist for the beautiful, desirable body that she had, with curves that Vivian could have matched during certain points in her life, softness that seemed sexy instead of fleshy. The keyboardist wasn't as voluptuous as the Patchwork Pirate, but Vivian found herself staring in many kinds of envy as the woman simulated sex with her flexible hips against the equally eager guitarist, whose tight leather pants did literally nothing to conceal how aroused he was.

Neither of the other girls in the room appeared annoyed or surprised that the guitarist lifted the keyboardist up to wrap her legs around his hips and took her to an empty cot—presumably the keyboardist's, since no one protested when he crouched with admirable strength and slid the two of them onto the thin mattress, pushing her skirt up at the same time. She frantically opened the front of his pants, gasping as he kissed her neck and bit her ear.

Something about the light in that section of the tent played tricks on Vivian. She could almost swear that Lennon's skin was a sickly, sallow yellow-green, that his black hair writhed over his shoulders, catching and twisting over the keyboardist's fingers.

He sat up as the woman jerked his pants down over his hips and his cock bobbed out. As big as it had seemed while clothed, Vivian couldn't believe it was actually bigger, thicker in total circumference than any of the Skeletons' arms. Flushed with blood, it had turned an almost teal color, and his skin seemed all-the-more chartreuse for it.

He tangled his fingers in the keyboardist's hair and pulled her up to kiss her again. Her black-painted hands left little smudges over his slender, toned torso. Was every man here secretly sculpted by a Renaissance artist?

No, not with that cock, he wasn't. Michelangelo's David he was not. That was a monster cock, disproportionately huge in comparison to the rest of him. And that black hair definitely wasn't hair anymore. Vivian edged around the room, but whatever Bell had done to her perception didn't change with movement. She saw the guitarist exactly as he was — a yellow-green-skinned man with hair that moved of its own volition, like a bucket of worms or pit of vipers. It stroked the keyboardist's face, her hair, continued to pull in her fingers.

When the guitarist yielded her mouth, the keyboardist's moan filled the tent, especially as his long tentacle hair pushed down her bra to stroke the black-painted nipples.

"God, Lennon, I can't... I can't, I can't. Just..." She tightened her grip on the tentacles that had hold of her fingers and pulled him down over her.

Lennon laughed as she wrapped her legs around him and canted her hips up, urging him without words. He kissed her again, possessing her mouth in a way that should have been unpleasant, should have looked unpleasant. Instead, heat sank between Vivian's ungenerous legs, making her feel swollen against her briefer flesh. She wondered if she even had room anymore for a cock, especially one like Lennon's. The keyboardist certainly did, because her moan lifted higher and higher as Lennon slid himself into her, slowly but without pause.

Vivian tore her gaze away. Alicia hadn't moved from behind Vivian's cot, but she'd slipped her hand under her panties, watching intently. Lily changed out of her towels, but she kept glancing over, licking or biting her lips.

Well, it was a band. And the tent seemed to function like a band trailer. But when there was this kind of free love, the band usually had a much higher ratio of men, and the lead singer would be the one getting all the pussy. Lennon didn't seem to want to front a band, or else Vivian wouldn't be there, and the female-heavy band was all looking at him — whatever he was — like he was fourteen deep-dish pizzas in a male body.

Vivian's stomach growled.

Lennon broke the kiss to look up, but he didn't stop thrusting into the woman, his strong, frankly amazing ass and thighs flexing as he held himself up.

When he smiled, his teeth were sharp. He'd had a good smile before, certainly not what one would expect from a man of his age and that habit and devil-may-care attitude. But these weren't the teeth she remembered. They looked like something from a tiger fish — small, conical, interlocked like that of a wolf.

"Well, hello there, legs. Didn't realize you'd be bunking with the rest of the riffraff. Don't divas like you prefer their own trailer?"

She crossed her arms. She wasn't self-conscious about being called 'legs' or a diva. But the guy was just pumping away inside the keyboardist, the keyboardist moaning like she was getting fucked by John Lennon himself, and Vivian was back to not being sure whether the entire day wasn't just a dream. Women turning to skeletons, a man turning into an alien-monster-man thing, a woman with mouths all over her body, wishes granted, singing in front of a crowd for a circus audition... Was any of this really happening? Was her clarity the real hallucination?

Vivian took in the sight of the black claws at the end of his fingers, the long tongue he slithered from his mouth to lick his teeth as he looked her over.

"What are you?" she said.

"Demon, love. Now, I've no problem if you want a turn. There's more than enough of me for five as well as four. If you'll just give me a few minutes to take care of Nasreen, I'll help you with whatever itch you need scratched."

"Ew. Gross." She headed for the door. Not to flee, but if the room was going to turn into an orgy, she had better things to do, and he still smelled like fucking cigarette smoke, even from her distance. God, why did people—and demons—do that to themselves? She just wanted to take Febreze to his whole discolored body.

"That would hurt if I had a heart. No worries. I'm just fine with the girls I have. And they're just fine with me. Door's open anytime, though."

Lennon returned his attention to the girl underneath him, but as Vivian lifted the tent flap and strode out, she hit what might as well have been a glass wall.

She stumbled back, holding her nose, then fell onto her ass. She didn't have nearly the cushion on it anymore, so it jolted her straight through bone. When she drew her hand away, blood smeared near the knuckles and slithered down to her lip.

Lennon collapsed on top of Nasreen, still flexing to fuck her through her orgasm but laughing into Nasreen's shoulder. "Maybe I spoke too soon," he managed to say.

The other two girls covered their mouths, but the shaking of their shoulders and the mirth in their eyes couldn't hide their own laughter. Lily came over to help her up, but Vivian refused the offer, climbing to her feet on her own. She held her sleeve to her nose to staunch the bleeding. It wasn't like the damn shirt fit anymore.

She approached the door again, more cautiously this time, holding out her hand as though feeling around in the dark.

A few inches past the opening of the tent flap, she flattened her hand over a completely invisible wall. So it wasn't a piece of thick, clear glass, despite what her nose had told her, but something *was* keeping her in the tent.

Fuck that.

She turned around and headed instead toward the bathroom.

"Careful, now, love. Don't want to knock out any teeth." Lennon raised himself up from the bed. He didn't bother tucking himself back in or zipping. Alicia was beckoning him over, her dress already open, sleeves sliding down her arms. Seeing a skeletal woman nearly naked hit Vivian as hard as the invisible wall. This was several stages thinner than 'model'. And that's what Vivian was under her own shirt.

Lennon didn't seem dissuaded by the sight. He stroked Alicia's body like it was velvet under his hand.

Vivian raised two fingers in a salute Lennon would understand.

He grinned, snaking out his tongue in an equally lewd response.

She shook her head, scoffing, as he wrapped his arms around Alicia like a rock god, with all the swagger of someone who thought he was owed adoration and sexual favors. And Alicia just gave it to him.

Vivian tested the other side of the bathroom tent flap to make sure she didn't walk into another invisible wall. Whatever didn't want her getting out apparently had no problem with her going to the bathroom, which really was like a girls locker room. There were no doors to the outside and no windows, so as far as she could tell, the edge of the world was a cinderblock gym shower with half stalls for toilets. And mirrors across from the shower and over the sinks, because of course.

Vivian went to the sinks before withdrawing her sleeve from under her nose. She was stuffy and the sleeve looked gruesome, but the bleeding had stopped.

Carefully wiping the blood from her face, she studied her reflection with the care privacy afforded her. As soon as the blood was gone, Vivian stepped away from the sink. Her bloody shirt crumpled on the floor, the last vestige of the life she'd had before this…weird-ass dream.

She was taller than the other girls. The Skeleton wasn't so stark on Lily, but on Vivian, it looked like that wasting disease Bell had mentioned, and Lennon's 'legs' comment made sense. Without enough flesh, she looked like nothing but leg and ribs.

She slowly untied her braid and let her long, dark brown hair slide around her shoulders. Now she looked like a banshee or a wild wood witch who hadn't eaten enough babies before hibernation. Her cheekbones and chin seemed more pronounced, yes, but she hadn't expected how big her mouth would seem when she opened it or stretched it into a fake smile.

"Oh, I'm sorry."

Vivian glanced over her shoulder at the woman who had walked in. She tightened her fist but remained pleasant in case the Tooth Fairy was harmless. She didn't bother picking up her shirt to cover herself, though.

"Okay, so we're staying naked." In contrast to the freeness the other girls seemed to show when it came to nudity, the Tooth Fairy wrapped her oversized cardigan around herself and tied the belt. "I'm Shane, by the way. I know who you are and why you're here, but I didn't catch your name."

"Vivian Mendez. You human?"

"Straight to the point." Shane ran her hand over her scalp, stopping at the gash where the teeth began. The mouth there wriggled, teeth closing over nothing at having something so near. "Yeah, I'm human. I just lost all my hair and gained some teeth instead. You asking because of Lennon?"

Vivian nodded.

"You can't always believe what you see." Shane snorted and tried again. "Well, that's not necessarily true. You can believe everything you see around here. But don't think that just because someone looks like a monster, they are. Ironically, it's the demons that tend to look more normal."

"Is this real?"

Shane blinked. "I'm sorry?"

"Is this real?" Vivian covered her eyes, closing herself off in darkness, then parted her fingers. Shane was still the Tooth Fairy with a gash in her skull and down her throat before covered by the cardigan — even a small one at the top of her left foot. And when Vivian looked down at herself, she was still Anorexia Barbie's best friend. "Do I really look like this?"

"Skinny as hell? Yeah. And I look like the human answer to a Venus fly trap. And Lennon's a water demon. He's convenient, so the girls usually go to him if they get too horny to function. Sometimes he grows out all these other tentacles and takes care of all three at once. I usually steer clear of the orgies. It's unbearable. He's got a mermaid he takes care of, too, but don't feel like you're stepping on anyone's toes if you ask him. He can be a bit of an asshole but he's not cruel, and by all accounts, he's really good."

"But you never..."

"I can't." Shane looked away, rubbing her arms as though cold. "Bell seems to have made you a standard Skeleton, though. And judging from your performance this afternoon, he didn't have to do much to your voice. You're lucky."

"Lucky? Bitch, please."

"Luckier than most of us." Shane stepped around her, still avoiding her eyes. "Because you look human. You're possible. Some of us aren't so normal."

Vivian spun around. "Look at me. I should be dead."

"But you're not. And the makeup'll hide how extreme it is. But he doesn't let me hide. If you'll excuse me, I'm going to be naked now, too, before my mouths decide they like the taste of polyester blend."

Shane untied the cardigan and shrugged it off onto one of the benches across from the showers. The latex dress underneath required a bit more care, the material almost like skin itself.

Though she seemed self-conscious by the fact that Vivian continued to stand there in nothing but a pair of panties and hadn't looked away, Shane peeled the dress off, exposing more grasping mouths. The one across her concave abdomen was the largest, the size of a large deli sandwich with teeth as large as pennies. But there was one that the bandage dress hadn't been designed to display, because Arcanium let children in.

It started at the top of her mound then slashed down the path of her vulva. Vivian couldn't tell how far back it went, but with her clitoris, urethra and vagina completely taken up by the monster mouth, it was anyone's call.

"How does that work, exactly?" Vivian asked.

"You mean anatomically? It doesn't. I taste everything, and I sometimes even feel like I've eaten when they do, but it doesn't go to my stomach. I haven't peed in months. I don't know how anything works and I don't care. I just want to not be hungry anymore."

Shane took her place under one of the showerheads, which were arranged in an intimate circle, and stepped under the spray, closing her eyes as she used a facial scrub to remove the light makeup that marked her as one of the Skellies. Like Nasreen and Lennon, the association was strictly through accessory, despite the fact that Shane did look thin, too thin. Her hands were still beautiful to Vivian, though, the knuckles defined like Lily's.

As Shane washed herself, the mouths sucked in some of the water in before it could reach the ground.

Shane seemed aware that she was being stared at but she didn't glare back or preen, just went about her business with the weariness of any worker after a long day.

Vivian respected that. When she was finished inspecting the Tooth Fairy, she didn't linger.

She left her shirt on the tiled floor. There were white towels by the door. Vivian wrapped one around her before going back into the tent. She wasn't modest or nervous about being seen by the other women, but she had no desire to give Lennon another partial frontal.

When she stepped through the tent flap — incongruous on the bathroom side, placed into an otherwise solid wall — Lennon had moved on to Lily, who bit the back of her hand as he took her from behind. He was more focused this time, not looking up from the writhing back he stroked as he took her hard, snapping his hips, the sound of his thighs on her ass like a slap. She looked too little to take someone so big, but it didn't seem to get in either of their ways.

Vivian pretended she wasn't watching as she made her way back to her cot. Alicia had put her dress back on and now studied herself in the mirror as she tried on a series of necklaces with the dress. She'd had enough time to at least brush her hair, because she didn't appear particularly rumpled from whatever Lennon had done.

Vivian searched through the clothes set up on the wheeled rack next to her mirror. Despite the high hemline on a few of the dresses and skirts, they were practically innocent, hardly the wardrobe of a rock diva, which confused her. At least most of the colors were dark. She pulled out a little black dress and dropped the towel to step into it then zip up the side. The dress was a double zero, and it was loose, although her breasts pressed against the bodice and threatened to fall out from the loose neckline. As Vivian tried her best to adjust the dress so that she wouldn't flash everyone every time she bent forward, she kept an eye on Lennon and Lily in the reflection on the metal rack.

Lennon grabbed Lily's hair and pulled her upright as he growled his orgasm—an actual growl, like something from a wolverine. Lily kept her teeth latched to the back of her hand as she shuddered, shoving herself back. Lennon rubbed her clit through their climax, his smile feral.

When they finished, he whispered in her ear before kissing her forehead soundly and easing from her. She tucked one of the wet towels between her legs and actually thanked him, like showing gratitude to a waiter for service.

"I'm on my way, loves. I'd say you could visit me anytime, legs, but apparently Bell wants you to stick around here for a while, probably for dinner. Sure you don't want any?" Lennon asked, looking at her from behind as though aware she'd watched through the reflection.

She couldn't imagine getting close to his smoke-soaked skin or kissing his mouth, but to her own irritation, she was turned on and his cock looked damn tempting between the dampened placket of his leather trousers.

"I'd rather deep-throat bleach," she said.

"Suit yourself. Looking forward to our next rehearsal."

As soon as he was out of sight, Vivian turned around again. "I can't find my purse."

"Your things should be in the tub," Alicia said, meeting Vivian's eyes through the mirror. "If you're looking for your phone, though, that's been confiscated."

"The fuck?" Vivian flipped open the tub lid and pawed through the things inside. Underwear, bras, her wallet and keys from her purse but no trace of her phone.

"Involuntaries don't get phones. If you're nice, the voluntaries let you use their computers, but I wouldn't hold my breath. Bell doesn't like us to have any way to communicate with the outside world."

"How am I supposed to let people know where I am? What am I supposed to do about rent, about work, my boyfriend, my family?"

Really, only her landlord would care that she'd disappeared. Work was work and could always replace people like her. Her boyfriend wasn't actually her boyfriend, which was the tangle she was currently in with her friends. She'd never really been close with anyone except her little sister, but they'd fallen out of touch ever since they'd moved out of their parents' house. Angelica mostly couch-surfed between friends these days and wanted nothing to do with her. Vivian didn't blame her. For once, it wasn't anything Vivian had done.

"We're completely cut off," Alicia said. "Any attempt we make to communicate with the outside leads to the Ringmaster's whip, just like trying to escape."

"What's to stop me from using someone else's phone?" Vivian asked. "They're literally everywhere."

"The Ringmaster," Alicia and Nasreen replied together, Alicia visibly annoyed at having to repeat herself.

"Worth it to get word out." There had to be a way they hadn't tried yet. They were just *sitting around* a harem tent waiting for a water demon to fuck them through the boredom of not having Internet.

"Uh-huh. And what then?" Alicia finally settled on a strand of pearls and turned around again, looking like the Ghost of Future Housewives of Beverly Hills. "Say Bell doesn't stop the phone from working before you can do anything. Say you get word out to a friend. The Ringmaster whips you. Bell does whatever he needs to do to make sure it doesn't happen again. But now Bell has to convince whoever comes after you to leave. And sometimes he just lets the clowns have them or the sex demons feed. So, by all means, contact someone, if you don't care whether they live or die. Look... There are a lot of us in Arcanium, and not one of us has found a way out that isn't Bell letting us go. That's just how it is. You might as well start getting used to it now. And you might want to think about putting on earrings or something. Jonas likes us to look nice for dinner."

"Well, fuck Jonas, too."

Nasreen snorted, but she covered her mouth as though she didn't want anyone to hear. "Is Shane *still* in the bathroom? I want to get this paint off sometime today."

"It's a communal shower," Vivian said.

Nasreen shrugged. "She's skittish and doesn't like sharing. Usually it's fine, but Jonas is going to be here any minute with dinner. I don't want to be late."

"What does he do if you're late?" Vivian asked. "And who the fuck is Jonas?"

"Jonas is the odd chef of Arcanium," Nasreen replied. "He's the one who feeds us. But he doesn't do anything if you're late. He's not that kind of demon. I'm just really hungry, exactly like you."

"How do you know how hungry I am?" Vivian's stomach seemed to sense the question and exclaimed with a growl that had Lily snickering while she adjusted her dress and tucked the dirty towel away somewhere. She wore a pair of dangling golden earrings.

There was no trace of Nasreen's smile now. "We're always hungry."

Shane came out with her cardigan around herself again. She sat on the cot nearest the bathroom on Vivian's side of the room, her shoulders curled in and her eyes downcast, worlds away from the confident drummer that she'd been on stage.

"Thank goodness." Nasreen darted through the tent flap with her change of clothes in a tote bag.

"Sorry," Shane muttered after her. She wasn't wearing a dress like everyone else, but she still reached into her tub and pulled out long necklace with a crystal glass cluster pendant.

The main tent flap opened. Three people dressed in plain black that marked them as crew entered, each holding a cloche-covered platter. They set the platters equidistant from each other on the dining table. Lily, Alicia and Shane all straightened, suddenly attentive, but they didn't flock toward the table, despite the fact that Vivian's stomach wasn't the only one growling at this point. The mysterious crew ducked back out without a word or the barest acknowledgment. They were like mannequins who could walk, but she was more interested in the platters.

Vivian was used to being hungry, felt pride every time her stomach clenched, though she never talked about that with anyone any more than she talked about all the other things she did—like how much of her refrigerator she was allowed to fill, how much she was allowed to eat at restaurants so that people wouldn't know she was controlling herself, how she avoided people watching her eat at work by keeping snacks at her desk instead of taking a lunch. She'd always been hungry, but this was different. This was like when her mother had padlocked the fridge and Vivian had given the last of her snack stash to Angelica.

A man ducked into the tent.

Vivian hadn't stepped foot in the Arcanium food court, but given the number of people who had lined up outside his booth, the circus chef had some kind of reputation. From what little Vivian had seen in people's grubby paws, she was glad she hadn't stopped by the food court, because she could barely keep the controlled contents of her stomach down at just the thought of fried grasshoppers, spider pie, tequila worm meringue tarts, cricket doughnuts or whatever else insectile he'd managed to put in an oven or deep fryer.

The chef wore a black coat and something between a toque and a beret, small enough to not overwhelm his bald head. Unlike Shane, his baldness seemed cultivated to hide a receding hairline. Thick hipster glasses perched on a round, unremarkable face. Unlike most of the other men in the circus, the chef was soft, not a hard edge to be found on his body. His hands, though, were large, strong and somehow elegant, with flecks of burn scars.

Shane had said that the demons were the ones who tended to look more normal. He was as far from a demon as a person could be. Either this wasn't who Shane had been talking about or he had the best human disguise in the circus. Without the hat and coat, Vivian would never have given him a second glance.

But since he was from Arcanium and right there in their tent, Vivian gave him that second glance.

She could swear that the thick frames and lenses of his glasses were intended to conceal eyes that were dead black to the brim.

"Good evening, children." He gestured them in, smiling, although it didn't quite reach his eyes and his welcoming gesture was stiff and awkward, like a marionette.

If Vivian had thought she couldn't be more disgusted by how the girls had flocked around Lennon, Alicia and Lily crawling toward the dining table and cooing like actual children at his feet nearly made her vomit.

"We've been waiting." Alicia knelt on his right and wrapped her fingers around his leg. "What took you so long?"

Lily settled in front of him and took his hand. "What'd you bring us today?"

"Are you hungry?" Although his smile still didn't reach his eyes, he sounded genuinely delighted, like a cat lady about to feed her horde.

"So hungry," Lily said. "Please, please, we need to eat."

"I'm this close to eating my own fingers," Alicia said. "Please, Jonas, we're ready to eat. We've been ready. *Please.*"

If this turned into some kind of food orgy, Vivian was going to spend the night in the showers. She didn't move from behind her cot, refused to humiliate herself like that just because some demon liked girls to dress up for him and beg.

"I was putting the finishing touches on the pies." Jonas slowly drew them to the table, placing them at each plate with an affectionate caress to their face or hair.

The only one who didn't fawn was Shane, but she still crawled over and took her seat when Jonas touched the bare skin of her head. He lingered at the gash there, tracing the edge and making the mouth writhe. Shane closed her eyes and clenched her hands tightly in her lap, but when he stroked his fingertips down to her cheek, she leaned into his touch, and it didn't seem coerced.

Over my dead, mangled, desecrated body.

There were three empty cushions left at the table – one at the head for him, one at the other head and one next to Lily, across from Shane. When Jonas reached that empty cushion, he finally looked up at Vivian.

She clenched her teeth against a shudder – not in disgust and not from arousal, but the kind that stroked a wet, icy finger down her spine.

"I wanted to make sure the details were perfect for our new Skeleton. Please, Vivian, join us and I shall serve."

Vivian still didn't move. "What are you serving? Mrs. Lovett's meat pies?"

"Just ordinary shepherd's pie. At one point in my life, I did make it with actual shepherd, as they say, but I don't use human flesh in this circus." He gave a little bow, once again awkward in his performance, but it didn't seem forced…just uncertain.

"What the fuck are you, man?"

"Please, language. And I am as I appear – a chef of oddities and, as many can attest, an odd chef. Bell entrusts me to feed not just his cast with specific dietary needs but his Skeletons, include honorary ones." The chef nodded to Shane. Shane didn't beam at him like the others, but she managed a smile.

"You never asked me about dietary restrictions," Vivian said.

"You don't have any dietary restrictions." The chef continued to smile. Vivian didn't know why it continued to be creepy until she realized he didn't blink.

"I have plenty of dietary restrictions."

"No, you just have restrictions." Jonas approached her, not once taking his eyes from hers. "Even if you had food allergies or gastrointestinal malaise, Bell would have removed them when he changed you. He allows only a few exceptions when it comes to diet. Elizabeth was raised vegan and still ascribes to the ideology. Nasreen originally kept *halal*, but she has since succumbed to the law of necessity."

If he was trying to intimidate her by standing less than a foot away from her, he was succeeding, but she refused to show it or look anywhere but his distorted black eyes.

"It clearly doesn't make a difference when it comes to what we look like," she said. "So what does it matter?"

"It's missing the point," he said.

"Which is?"

"Dismantling your restrictions. I may use unconventional ingredients, but I don't hold back when it comes to feeding my children. I promise satisfaction, at least for the night."

He offered his arm, old-fashioned and just plain weird to the end. His smile widened when her stomach growled again, more loudly this time.

When she tried to go around him, he took her hand and tucked it in the crook of his elbow.

When they arrived at the cushion intended for her, he urged Vivian forward as though it was all part of the dance. The savory smells coming from under the cloches coaxed her the rest of the way down.

The chef slipped a pair of black latex gloves from his pocket and pulled them on.

No, not creepy at fucking all.

He lifted the covers from two of the platters. Underneath were plain, white ceramic plates, each featuring a meticulously layered shepherd's pie. The mashed potatoes had been sculpted like a tart base to hold the vegetables. Minced meat formed the domed top, on which had been poured a careful layer of brown gravy. Each pie included a cluster of crust baked into flower shapes to accent the dish. It seemed a lot more pretentious in theory than it looked, and it smelled delicious.

But Vivian could only see that the mashed potatoes and vegetables were too much starch together, the gravy might as well have been melted fat, she didn't know what kind of meat he'd used and the rosettes were basically buttered, refined flour. She could eat a little of it, but there was no way she could eat the whole plate.

Alicia, Lily and even Shane struggled not to fidget as Jonas placed a plate on top of each girl's place setting. Nasreen came out from the bathroom just as he knelt at the head of the table near the door.

"Welcome, Nasreen. Do join us. I would tell you to clear everything from your plate, Vivian, but I think you'll find that's no chore. If you subscribe to a deity, feel free to pray. Otherwise, dig in. I have fruit and cheese to vary your plates as well." Jonas lifted the cover of the last platter, revealing a snack plate of apples arranged like roses blossoming atop stacks of different cheeses. An array of cheese knives and crackers surrounded the pile.

"I'm not going to eat this," Vivian said. "I don't eat things like this."

"Things like what?" Jonas asked mildly.

"All these foods. All of them are…wrong."

"And how are they wrong, Vivian? How is eating wonderful, filling comfort food as exuberant and robust on the palate as it is to the eye wrong? You could eat four chocolate cakes in a row and nothing would happen. Bell would still keep you healthy and functioning."

"How is that *healthy*?" Vivian snapped.

"It's not. It's joyful. And it's freeing. I've been forced to starve before. I know your hunger. I know that when you look at that shepherd's pie, you long for it in your mouth. You long for its heat, its substance. You ache to swallow every last bit of it down and lick your fingers when you're finished."

"We're still talking about food here, right?"

The chef blinked—the first time she'd seen it, which meant it was deliberate. "What else would we be talking about?"

Lily snorted. She and Alicia shared a glance, smiling as though they were the only ones with a secret.

"Seriously?" Vivian said.

"Enough of this chatter. I know my children are hungry. Go on, girls. Eat to your heart's content."

All four women dug in with their bare hands, scooping up mashed potatoes, gravy and vegetables in makeshift spoons they created with their fingers. For a demon who preferred them in nice jewelry and in perfect order, his devotion to appearances apparently didn't extend to utensils.

"We had a tendency to use them as weapons against each other, fighting for food," Shane whispered, her mouth smeared with gravy. "We're not trusted with cutlery yet."

"Hands can be washed after use, but a butter knife in the wrong hand can end a life. Don't be shy. There's no need to be ashamed when you're in the same situation as everyone else."

"*You're* wearing gloves."

The odd chef stood again. The girls paused in their devouring—yes, devouring, as though they hadn't eaten in months rather than hours—to eye the chef as he made his deliberate way back to Vivian's side of the table.

He stood above her for a few seconds. Then he abruptly crouched, easing into a kneeling position with much more flexibility and grace than she would have given him credit for.

"You're going to cause me trouble, aren't you, Vivian?"

"That demon genie sucked me in here. He changed me. I didn't choose any of that. I'm not going to make your life easier."

"It doesn't serve you to cause trouble," Jonas said, almost gently. "I am here to make your life in Arcanium easier."

"Bullshit. You're here for the tea party. Aren't you a little old to still be playing dolls?"

"You're never too old to play." He slipped his hand into a coat pocket and pulled out another pair of black latex gloves. "If it's a mess you object to, there's no reason why you shouldn't wear gloves."

She leaned in, expecting him to lean away when she got to close, but he didn't move a muscle. "I'm allergic to latex."

"Who's lying now?" He brought the pair of gloves to her mouth, running a limp, deflated finger over her lips, then pushing in with a brief shove to pass them through.

Vivian turned her head and spat.

"I know everything you can take into your body. You have no allergies, no sensitivities. Your only obstacle is pride. I'm afraid what is on the table is all I have to offer you, child. If you decide to eat only apples tonight—or nothing—it will be on your own head. You'll crawl to my table tomorrow, too hungry to even sing for your supper."

"I don't crawl to anyone, and I never beg. Men beg *me*, motherfucker."

Jonas slapped her lightly with the pair of gloves. It didn't hurt. "Language. Really, Vivian, you're at the dinner table."

Vivian snatched the gloves away then let them flutter to the floor. "Is that what you like? You like watching your little girls crowd around like you're some kind of king? You want me to beg you to feed me like a baby bird? Is that what gets you off?"

"I won't deny enjoying well-fed women. I live to view the pleasure that my food gives. As for what gets me off, as you so crudely put it, I don't."

He stood again. Vivian was all the more aware of where her mouth was in conjunction with what they were just talking about. A glimpse suggested that he was either much less endowed than the other two demons she'd seen so far or was as uninclined toward arousal as he claimed.

"I serve, child. I want to satisfy your hunger. It doesn't please me in the least to have you beg me to feed you, crawling in desperate hunger. But if that is what you insist upon, far be it from me to get in your way. Should you change your mind, your pie is there in front of you. I urge you to eat it before it cools."

The girls watched them argue the way a family watched television during a meal, with big eyes and full mouths. Most of them were almost finished with their main course and kept glancing at hers with envy.

"You really think I'm going to eat something a demon gives me?" Vivian said.

"I think you'd refuse something a human gave you. You're giving me every excuse except for the one that's relevant." Jonas shook his head and turned away to return to his place. "You'll learn. Everyone does. You'll eat what I serve or you won't eat."

Something inside of Vivian jerked violently, as though there was more in there than flesh, organ and bone, although one could clearly see there wasn't room for anything else. She dug grooves into her palms with her nails.

Without another word, she picked up her plate and threw it down to dead center of the table.

The shepherd's pie exploded. Mashed potato, gravy, minced meat and vegetables flew, shrapnel from a culinary grenade. Each girl cried out as pieces struck their faces and chests. At the center, where the splatter was densest, it left the apple and cheese plate ruined.

"What did you *do*?" Lily snapped. But instead of wiping herself off, she leaned over the table to scoop whole chunks of Vivian's shepherd's pie into her mouth. Alicia and Nasreen didn't hesitate either. They moaned as they extended their meal with a portion of another girl's entrée. Only Shane didn't join in, but it wasn't out of respect or because she was full. Where food had splattered on her mouths, they slithered out prehensile tongues and eagerly slurped over her skin. Shane shuddered and shivered, holding her arms and breathing too fast, her eyes clenched shut.

Bits of shepherd's pie had struck the odd chef as well, stark against his black coat. He drew his eyebrows in over the bridge of his nose, slowly removed his gloves then tossed them onto the table with a certain finality.

"Do you know how long it took me to prepare that?" His frown deepened. "Shane, if you're not going to eat any more, follow me."

Without another word, he spun on his heel and strode out of the tent.

Shane kept her arms wrapped tightly around her, twitching with every movement of the many mouths all over her. She didn't look up, barely even opened her eyes, as she scurried out of the tent after him.

"Why'd you have to go and do that?" Alicia said, her mouth full. "You didn't have to destroy it. One of us could have had it. Or we could have shared. Now it'll take forever to get all of this. And the fruit and cheese are going to taste funky."

"As though it isn't already messy enough eating around here." Lily scooped up more gravy and vegetables with crackers. "I don't know what you hoped to accomplish. We don't get fed until late morning, and that's just a light breakfast. Then we don't get another chance until Jonas serves us dinner again. You're not even *allowed* to eat anything other than what he serves."

"All these rules, all these things we're not allowed to do, and *my* restrictions are going too far?" Vivian grabbed a few slices of cheese and apple roses then stood.

"That's not going to be nearly enough," Alicia said. "As the first Skeleton, I went through all five stages of grief, learning what I can change and what I need to accept. Each of us has been exactly where you are. But what kind of knucklehead throws a demon's food? What kind of child throws food at all?"

"What kind of adult acts like a little girl just to eat?"

"He's nice, okay? And he likes to see us enthusiastic for the meals he serves," Alicia said. "It's not much to put on a nice dress and jewelry and seem eager, especially since we are. We're hungry. He feeds us. What about this equation is off for you?"

Vivian sat on her cot, trying to convince her stomach not to growl again as she ate a piece of cheese. It was only the best piece of cheese she'd ever had in her life. She gazed at the cheese and fruit plate with longing, knowing she couldn't crawl back now, and she didn't even *want* to. "All of it. Since when are you a dog?"

Lily huffed. "Since when are you a bitch?"

"If you make our lives harder here, it's not going to end well for you." Alicia's fury was only somewhat muted by the apples and cheese she was chewing. "Arcanium's not a place to play around. The best thing you can do is just go with the flow."

"Oh, I've heard that before." Vivian was still hungry, but nausea threatened to push up what little she'd already eaten. "Fuck going with the flow. Fuck the chef. And fuck Arcanium."

"You can curse all you like," Nasreen said, gentler than the others. "It's not going to make things go your way."

"You'd be surprised." Vivian nibbled at the apple next. It had bits of mashed potato. The slight taste was so heavenly that she nearly cried.

This wasn't right—er taste buds, her hunger, her reaction, none of it.

"You do you," Alicia said. "Just don't include us in your shit. I don't want to get punished because you don't know a lost cause when you see one."

"You're not the only one in this," Nasreen said. "That's why we're all here together."

Vivian turned around on her cot, crossing her legs and trying not to look in the mirror. "I'd rather be alone."

"Oh, joy," Lily muttered. "We've had to take care of Shane and now we have to deal with *that*? I just thought we'd have to deal with a diva-tude."

"Cool it," Nasreen said. "It's her first night. Remember your first night?"

"And some people just don't listen," Alicia added. "They have to learn for themselves. She might have to learn it starving and under the Ringmaster's whip, but she'll learn."

Vivian kept eating her makeshift appetizer plate. When she was finished, she licked her fingers, contemplated chewing them off to get something *substantial* into her stomach. God, she was so fucking hungry.

Chapter Four

She went to sleep a good three hours before she usually wanted to, and when she woke up, none of the girls would look at her, much less talk to her.

That wasn't the terrible part. The terrible part was how the front of her abdomen threatened to pull back behind her spine. Her head ached and her tongue was thick and fuzzy. She hadn't had anything to drink, but this wasn't anything but a hangover.

Somehow, Alicia and Lily managed to keep from saying *I told you so.*

More crew came in with a small basket of breakfast tacos wrapped in butcher paper and tied in clusters of two — one cluster for each girl. Vivian fought not to fall on all ten like a single-girl pack of ravening wolves.

But when she started to go outside, she walked straight into the invisible wall again.

"What the fuck, man?" She clutched her nose and stared out at the sunlit field in indignation. This time Alicia and Lily didn't even try not to laugh.

Apparently, a bloody nose was funnier the second time. "I can't even go outside when no one else is out there?"

"Maybe he doesn't trust you," Alicia said. "Can't imagine why."

"Oh, bite me."

"Some days, that would be tempting." Alicia hooked her arm around Lily's. "Come on. Looks like we don't have a diva for the Skellies quite yet. Mostly bad karaoke it is. Please don't trash the tent, Vivian. It's a small world, and hungry people are vengeful people."

Vivian distracted herself by eating the pieces of tortilla still stuck on the butcher paper then considering the fiber content of that paper. But now that her mouth had been slimed with the grease of the best chorizo breakfast tacos she could remember having, she couldn't lose the taste of *bad* from her tongue. And the tacos hadn't made a dent in her hunger or her hangover.

Another hanger of clothes rolled into the tent, pushed and pulled by a pair of crew members. The Bearded Lady followed them in, her skirts swirling around her legs.

"Ready to play rock star?" the Bearded Lady said brightly.

Great, she's one of those *people.* "I thought I was grounded."

"Just until you're less recognizable. To facilitate that, I'm here to help you pick out your wardrobe."

"I have a few suggestions for what you can do with your wardrobe," Vivian said.

"I'm sure you do. But you can either lead the Skellies looking the part, or you can wear tea party house dresses. It's really up to you." The Bearded Lady barely seemed to notice the crew, ignored them even as they left. "I'm Kitty. I don't handle the Skeletons' makeup and hair, since it's so involved that Bell decided to automate the process, but I can help you glam up your look with glitter and rhinestones, if you like. And I'm the one who sews most of the non-leather costumes, so if I could get a sense of what kind of presence you want to put out there, I'll be in a better position to give you more variety." Kitty rubbed her hands together. "Where do you want to start?"

"Let's start with what you did to piss Bell off. I know what *I* did."

Kitty smiled, but it wasn't a good smile. "Sweetie, I was born this way. I joined the circus of my own free will over twenty years ago. I've heard all the hair jokes. There's literally nothing you can say that I haven't heard before, and none of it makes you sound clever. You already have a reputation for being prickly. The odd chef was devastated last night. Believe me, even for a demon who tears up at a perfectly baked macaron, it takes a lot to devastate him. But I don't have as much as patience as I used to. I'm more than willing to let you use your pre-picked wardrobe for your performances if you don't want to collaborate. You'll be done up in your Skeleton paint no matter what we do. I just thought that someone who has very few choices in Arcanium would appreciate having some say in how people see her."

Vivian crossed her arms, but she didn't throw the clothing rack across the room—mostly because she'd lost the strength to do so. "Fine."

"Good."

With some reluctance, Vivian eyed the rack. There was lots of black, with a pop of color here and there—an electric-blue sheath dress, a green mesh tank top that looked like something an alien would wear... There were skinny jeans that might not be skinny enough, yoga pants that would look like leisure pants on her, quilted witch skirts, lace floor-length jackets, bralettes, halters, tank tops, corsets, leather jackets, belts — all kinds of looks and none of it coherent.

"Anything can be tailored or made to order. This is just about finding you a few outfits. Sasha and I can take it from there." Kitty gestured for Vivian to look through to her heart's content.

Vivian wanted to spurn Kitty with every ounce of bile that always seemed to be waiting in the back of her throat, but she really liked clothes and she didn't have to pay a cent for these. Clothes and music. If that was going to be the only thing to distract from the bottomless pit that was her stomach, she'd just have to take it.

So awfully familiar.

She thought of the songs she'd sung at the audition and the songs the band had played before. Their eclectic sound ranged from symphonic and power metal to rock to punk, with a little pop thrown in, which meant she could really choose anything on the rack as long as the edges were hard and it went with Skeleton makeup.

"I have a screen back in my tent if that would make you feel more comfortable," Kitty said.

"You know what the others look like, don't you?"

"Nakedness is nothing new, even in a normal circus. But some of our people are more private than others — including me."

Vivian pulled her dress over her head.

She tried one thing after another, tossing the things she liked onto Lily's cot. The first time she let one of the things she didn't like drop to the floor, Kitty cleared her throat and glared. After that, Vivian started putting things back on the hanger and arranging them on the rack again. She'd make a fuss, but that was one of the few courtesies she afforded minimum-wage gremlins. She'd been a Kohl's sales monkey back in high school and college and still had nightmares about folding and hanging and the kinds of things she'd found in the dressing rooms.

"So I heard the first night wasn't the best," Kitty said.

"I'm not here to make friends or talk about my feelings."

"There are worse things than being a freak, Vivian. And worse places to be one than Arcanium. Otherwise, it's really quite simple. You learn the rules, follow them and things go more smoothly. It's best not to make too many enemies. You don't know how long you'll have to live with them."

"I still don't want to talk about my feelings."

"I'm talking about mine." Kitty sat on Lily's cot to go through what Vivian had selected, arranging them into an aesthetic collage. "So, based on the outfits, you prefer tight pants, short tops and leather accents. You should have a plethora of accessories at your cot, but I have more in my tent. If you want to go accessory fishing, my tent is always open. We also do a book club on Wednesdays, but since you're not interested in making friends…"

"Still not." Peering in the mirror, Vivian studied how clothes had changed on her. Her ass looked so much smaller. She had a thigh gap now, though someone of her frame and figure should never have had one. Kitty had mostly picked just the right sizes, but that couldn't always make the shirts tight enough under the jut of her ribs and breasts.

Kitty came up behind her while Vivian was trying to adjust the lace-cutout maroon crop top over her upper abdomen.

"I can fix that," she said softly, folding the fabric in the back to create the illusion of darts. "Alicia goes more cyberpunk with neon colors, occasionally rockabilly. Nasreen prefers bohemian. Lily's a bit of a dark pirate fairy, so more my style. You definitely run rock star. The Skeleton look is really noticeable with tight clothes."

"But not as severe when all the bones are covered." Vivian didn't look nearly as sickly with leather pants hiding her pelvis and knees, the crop top hiding her ribs and the riveted leather jacket hiding her shoulder blades.

Kitty gathered Vivian's hair over her shoulder. "I think we should keep the hair long, don't you? The whole head-banging thing. But I can color it in streaks or in whole if you want."

"No. My hair stays my hair." Vivian stroked her fingers through it, which called attention to how skinny her fingers were now, how much weight had been lost from her face. It was a lot of hair for her new figure, but she'd grown it ever since she'd left her parents' house at seventeen. With everything else taken from her, she didn't want to lose this.

"Okay, then. Let's work on making the lead Skelly glitter."

* * * *

Kitty warned her that though she could wander through the Renaissance faire if she wanted a change from the circus, she couldn't spend all of her time there, couldn't purchase any of the food and was expected to spend most of her time with the rest of Arcanium. Her voice would be limited. Bell would keep a close watch. A flight risk, Kitty had said, as though she were a criminal.

But Bell wasn't wrong.

"You'll know when the band convenes. They don't scrimp on a sound system," Kitty said.

"Like they scrimped on a stage?"

Kitty laughed. "Believe me. When they're ready for the Skellies to be a complete group and not just a karaoke cover band, does Bell seem like the kind of man to scrimp on a proper stage?"

Except for Vivian's dig on her hairiness, not much seemed to faze Kitty, and maybe Vivian recognized too well the drawn exhaustion underneath the fur on her face that made makeup an impossibility—so no concealer.

Something had happened to the older members of Arcanium. That's what Alicia had said. Vivian wanted to poke, prod, pick at the scab, but the tiny voice inside her that so rarely spoke up whispered that she should leave this particular wound alone.

It wasn't altruistic. The tiny voice never was. If she didn't poke someone else's unhealed wound, they'd be much less likely to poke hers. Everyone had wounds. Pain recognized pain, and pain knew how to cause more. Misery loved company, after all, but only when one could control the misery that bounced back. Vivian had lost control of it a number of times—with little regret but with consequences.

Kitty directed two crew members to take the remaining clothes back to her tent. The ones that needed to be altered had been folded into a bag for Kitty to haul away on her own, but that left Vivian with four complete outfits to mix and match as needed until her wardrobe could be supplemented. For now, she wore the maroon lace crop top — despite it being loose — faded black skinny jeans and a leather jacket with straps that belted around her waist like something out of a dystopian movie. *Post-apocalyptic rock goddess,* Kitty called her.

Unlike the other Skellies, she didn't go Skeleton all over. She wore a pair of bejeweled, silver skeleton hand bracelets, and with Vivian's help, Kitty had done her face paint as *calavera de azucar*. Kitty had apparently done it before, because once she'd had an idea of the coloring and style Vivian wanted, she worked quickly. She'd chosen the same ruby maroon as Vivian's shirt for her eyelids and lips, and among the lacy skull outlines, Kitty had carefully applied black and clear rhinestones.

With the face paint applied, Kitty had arranged yellow and orange fake marigolds around a rose-ridden headband. Kitty's expression had closed off as she'd smoothed Vivian's hair back and pinned the headdress in.

Now Vivian walked through the fairgrounds, with her new clothes, new face, new body — Arcanium's new Skeleton. She felt like a goddamned Disney character, all these phones pointed at her and people asking to take pictures. At first, when people had asked if she wanted to pose with them, she'd tried to tell them to fuck off. She'd learned that was one of the many things she wasn't permitted to say aloud. She'd only been allowed to smile with clenched teeth and nod, even though she could swear she wasn't the one doing it.

"You are more than capable of being distantly friendly, Vivian." Bell's voice took over for the whispering voice of her dried, decayed husk of a conscience. *"You know what I want from you, and you know I don't ask for much. The least you can do is smile. It's just a little attention, and you look delightful."*

The images Vivian thought in his general direction only sent his laughter down her spine, like hot chocolate pouring down her throat, which she suddenly craved with all the intensity of a drug addiction — although that was one of the few vices she hadn't tried.

"You're lovely, my little sugar skull. You are as lovely as a Skeleton as you were before, when you believed you had adequately hidden your ugly. I suggest you use Arcanium to widen your gaze to all kinds of beauty. If you need to walk the creepy-crawly tent, I'm sure the Spider would accommodate you trying new things. You could see how many 'fucks' the two of you can include in a single conversation."

"Get the fuck out of my head, fucking douchebag. I'm smiling, okay?"

God, there wasn't enough room in her slighter body to hold how much she hated him and everyone else in Arcanium right now. But she still smiled for all the cameras on everyone's phones, played the part of the Skeleton, flashed her pearly whites and the jewels on her skeleton hands, cracked her knuckles and popped her knees and shoulders to startle people into nervous laughter.

In the end, though, it wasn't *too* bad — the pictures, the posturing, the pretending. People wanting to be near her, complimenting the artwork. Her smiling as though she were happy and people thinking it was true. People not looking at her with disgust, although she felt even thinner in comparison to the normal bodies around her. She hated Bell all the more for the fact that this wasn't too bad.

But Bell had still found a few ways to torture her. The first was watching everyone eat while her stomach growled louder and louder. Guests told her to eat something or offered something from their paper basket, calling her too thin like they always had. But when she ate what they offered, it didn't make the deepening, broadening hunger any better.

She could stand the looks of appreciation, although she received fewer than she once had — curiosity now more than competition with other lovely people. She noticed it all the more when she was in the same vicinity as the snake charmer or the Patchwork Pirate, who attracted men like bacon candles.

No, the other part she couldn't stand was the girls and women who looked at her with envy — and knowing that she'd been the same just yesterday.

She wondered how many sternly worded letters Bell received about setting a good example for impressionable young girls.

"Not as many as you'd think," he whispered. *"I run a freak show, not a fashion show. Fewer people wish to emulate freaks, and none of my Skeletons are airbrushed to soften their angles."*

"I wanted to emulate, you bastard."

"I can't change the inclinations of thousands upon thousands of my guests, but the Skeleton isn't usually what they want. Still, between the fortune-telling and the infernal wishing well I used to keep outside my tent, I've had my fill of weight loss wishes. I'd like another Torso from such a wish,

but I haven't had the taste to create another one. You were lucky your voice left me in a good mood."

"*Lucky.* Lucky?"

"*Oh, my dear, if you don't already realize how fortunate you are, you will.*"

At that point, his Jiminy Cricket voice abandoned her, so she didn't know how much of her cursing him out again he heard.

As Kitty had promised, Vivian knew immediately when the band had come together. She could hear it sheer across the fairground, the bass notes in the keyboard thrumming through the earth like a minor earthquake.

Vivian took her time making her way back to the center of the circus, fighting the compulsion to return. It never got as keen as her hunger, though. She couldn't very well let the unwashed, tone-deaf masses take control of that microphone.

On the way in, she was momentarily distracted from someone doing a passable rendition of *Believer* by the smells riding the air. Granted, the scents of fried food, cheap beer at obscene prices, bad ale, turkey legs, roasted nuts, popcorn and cotton candy suffused the entire fairground. That was the nature of the beast.

But the nature of the beast took on a whole new dimension as she entered the food court, which she'd been determined to avoid. She hadn't wanted even a glimpse of the odd chef, with his blank human face and awkward posture, his black latex gloves, those stupid fucking glasses.

She'd rather he be more like Bell or resemble all the rumors she'd heard so far about the Ringmaster. Demons should look like monsters, and if monsters weren't demons, they should look like the kind of humans that demons would become. Jonas didn't look anything like what a demon should look like, and she didn't know enough about his behavior beyond its creepiness—but not demon creepy, ordinary human creepy. What the hell did he do with Shane after dinner anyway?

Vivian didn't want to get anywhere near him again, but the band was set up right next to the food court's picnic tables. She tried to go around, but smells carried, and Vivian could tell the second the smells stopped being those from the fairground and started being from the odd chef's booth. She'd thought her hunger had been unbearable before, although she knew how to smile through unbearable. It was one of her gifts that she'd give half of her brain and one of her kidneys to return.

But now she stumbled to her knees, gasping.

A random guest stopped next to her. "Hey, you okay?" He grabbed her by her arm to help her up.

Vivian still couldn't speak, but she wrenched her arm away.

"Whoa, sorry." The burly man with a beer gut held up his hands defensively. "Just trying to help. Are you okay?"

No. No, she was not okay. How had her stomach not developed teeth to chew through her like a parasite from the inside out yet? Because that's what it felt like—as close to pain as a sensation could get without actually being pain.

Vivian smiled, nodded, pacified in mime like the clowns. The man watched her stagger toward the food court with some concern, but he didn't follow.

She looked at the line of people waiting for the odd chef's food, thought of the brilliant display he had created for the Skeletons' dinner, the shepherd's pie she had ruined. The handfuls of apples and cheese she had eaten and the breakfast tacos from the morning that were little more than a memory, not so much as a taste of grease in her mouth anymore. Everything danced before her eyes like mocking ghosts.

Then there was the real food that actual people were eating. Because it was really there and within reach. All she had to do was snatch it away.

She still had her damnable pride — the pride that kept her leather jacket on even though the sun was warm in the cool mid-spring air. But when she came across the discarded remnants of food that guests had left behind, she learned she didn't have that much pride left.

People laughed. They laughed at her as she darted forward to shove pieces of pizza crust in her mouth, laughed as she licked at the butcher paper. There were a few worried glances, but most of them probably thought it was an act, some kind of performance art. Sure, such comedy, a starving person scavenging among picnic tables like a homeless woman.

They laughed at her as she fought tears when a few scraps weren't enough to satisfy and she pushed the butcher paper away to run to the next spot, where she didn't hesitate to dive face first into a basket of spicy pineapple buffalo wings. There were only bits left, but she nibbled at them until all that was left was bone. Then she broke the bones to suck at the marrow.

Mouth smeared and fingers dirty, she moved on to the next discarded tray. Really, trash cans were all over the place, and they had no idea that a Skeleton was going to go around clearing food from their plates. Was everyone raised by barbarians?

Everyone kept laughing at her, and she swallowed back a wail, because it wasn't enough. Bursts of flavor assaulted her tongue, triggering the strongest cravings for everything and anything she put in her mouth that she'd ever had, but she could only take in little pieces at a time from what was left over. Her stomach seemed to be getting hollower instead of fuller.

She wasn't supposed to cry, damn it, but she couldn't help it when people started holding out food, taunting her like she was an amusing stray dog performing for treats. And still she snatched at pieces of food she didn't bother to identify, barely chewed them before swallowing.

"Just like that other Skeleton, Daddy," a daughter said, wiggling the strip of pretzel under Vivian's nose.

"Ooh, someone go buy the fried ghost pepper popper."

"Guys, is she crying? Like, for real crying?"

She took a quarter-full plastic cup of margarita and downed it to stop the actual sob that threatened to bubble from her throat. She dropped the cup onto the picnic table and spun around in a circle, keen eyes finding food everywhere she looked – food in the trash, food that people held out for her, food that people intended to keep for themselves. The smells surrounded her. The taste coated her mouth like a grease and spice explosion.

Food was fucking *everywhere*. Everything she wouldn't or couldn't eat, everything she'd carefully portioned and controlled, everything she'd allowed or not allowed herself, everything she'd called bad or good – more bad than good in a circus like this. So much bad, and she wanted it all in her mouth, in her empty, empty body, in her deep-earth starving monster of a stomach. She wanted food more than she wanted freedom, more than she wanted sex, more than she wanted to be pretty or loved or ignored, more than she wanted dignity.

She'd sworn she wouldn't beg, and now what was she doing? Could the odd chef see her? Of course he could. The commotion was too strong and she was within the booth's line of sight. He was probably laughing at her with the rest as she ate the fried grasshoppers someone had been afraid to try, despite the exorbitant prices. They crunched terribly in her mouth, their legs prickling at her palate and tongue, but she groaned from eating something closer to a full portion.

People were cheering now, and it wasn't because of the brutal rendition of *I Don't Wanna Miss a Thing* from the stage. She'd ask why there weren't more decent singers taking the microphone, since she knew there *should* have been more, but she honestly couldn't care. She nearly impaled herself with the fried grasshopper skewers.

Vivian stumbled toward the man holding out a candy spider. At least she hoped it was candy, not that it mattered to whatever kept her eating.

Someone took hold of her shoulders and steadied her—another pair of big hands that had her wrenching away. God, would people stop putting their hands on her?

"It's just me." Jonas laced his gloved fingers through hers to keep her from tumbling back. "I know you're hungry. I know. Calm down. You're okay."

"Eat raisins, you son of a syphilitic jackal."

That actually earned her a smile, which had not been her intention.

He pulled a butcher paper package from his coat pocket. "I have something for you."

The package warmed her palms as she eagerly unwrapped it. The meat pie was just the right heat, which was good because she ate it in five bites. It was everything she wouldn't have allowed herself to have before, but for a second, she felt...

Satisfied.

The rumbling in her stomach quieted as it finally digested something substantial. She wasn't full—far from full—but she was briefly satisfied.

As Vivian ate, he retrieved a handkerchief from another pocket and dabbed at her eyes and cheeks then her mouth when she finished eating. He was thorough over her fingertips, insistent when she tried to jerk her hands away.

"Don't worry. Your makeup isn't smeared. Now..." He tucked the handkerchief in his pocket and took the empty butcher paper from her. "Don't you feel better?"

"Fuck you." Her expletive cracked on the sob she'd swallowed back.

"It should hold you until tonight. I'm not supposed to feed you outside of the scheduled times, but it was the first time you've had to contend with your appetite."

Jonas removed his gloves then touched her cheek, despite her face paint. "Just remember that no matter how difficult it gets, you're going to be okay." He cracked another smile. "And I like raisins."

"You would, you utter asshole."

"You sound better, sugar skull. I make those for Halloween, you know."

"You don't make anything like a sugar skull, white boy."

"There isn't a dish in the world I can't make," Jonas said. "It is my skill, child. It is my life. It is all the magic I possess. Go now. It's time for you to work your own magic. I hear you have quite the talent."

"You've already heard it. Must have really made an impression."

Jonas adjusted his glasses like a class-A nerd instead of the demon he was. "If you haven't already guessed, I can be rather single-minded. I'll endeavor to be double-minded today."

"Don't break a brain cell on my account." She backed away, reeling at her own mindlessness, the depths to which she had sunk and so fast, at how easy it was to break when she'd tried so hard to glue all her pieces together with cement. That she was still so easily broken and at the mercy of a fortune teller and his cook... If she could strike a match and set the whole place on fire, she would. But she wasn't sure she could even get her hands on a lighter without Bell knowing.

"Vivian..."

"What?" she snapped.

Jonas apparently thought better of saying anything else. He gave another short bow, his hand between his coat buttons like Napoleon, then returned to his booth, pulling on a new pair of latex gloves as he went.

"God, he is so *weird*," she muttered.

Vivian ignored the smattering of applause that followed her out of the food court. She hurried—walking, not running—away from the food and closer to the noise from the makeshift stage. She arrived among the cast just as the person in classy gender-ambiguous clothes made their way to the microphone. After the three-breasted drag queen's baritone, Vivian literally had no expectations.

Nasreen switched her main synth to a classic piano sound and introed something jazzy, Lennon's electric guitar wailing instead of a trumpet or trombone. Shane added a smooth cymbal beat line. The person at the mic held their cane in front of them and moved their hip and knee to the piano's emphatic beat.

Then, with a smoky voice as low, rich and ambiguous as Annie Lennox, they took on *I Put a Spell on You*. The electric guitar kept it from being too much like Lennox's version, and the person singing had moments where their voice went lower, with an easy growl to their tone that lacked Vivian's demonic edge — like cayenne in chocolate, roughness that emphasized the velvet of their voice. It did nothing to clarify the person's gender, but since that seemed to be the whole point of this particular cast member, Vivian wasn't sure if there was a gender to clarify.

Whatever. Vivian appreciated good voices. They made her less rage-y.

They got less applause than the drag queen. Gender ambiguity trumped talent in most people's estimation, if their confused expressions were anything to go by, but Vivian clapped and even gave a good howl. Maybe if she encouraged good voices, she'd get to hear more of them rather than endure rusty nails piercing her eardrums.

No such luck. Vivian shook her head and rubbed her temples as the next bad singer found the microphone. The headband headdress wasn't helping, with its pressure on the sides of her head.

"Weren't you supposed to save us from this?" the suited individual said, sidling between the drag queen and Vivian.

"Bell wants me to keep a low profile, so I have to let it go on for a while. I should just let everyone suffer all afternoon," Vivian replied. "It makes everyone enjoy the real gems like you and your friend."

"Aw, thank you, sugar. But they enjoy Miss Delilah more than they enjoy me."

"You know how people are when they can't figure out which box to put things in. It short-circuits their shortcuts."

"Oh, believe me, I know. Making people uncomfortable is what I do. I'm the Quandary—also known as the Awkward Introduction."

It was a special kind of relief for Vivian to still be able to laugh, although she'd never been an easy audience. "Do you think if you'd never seen me before, you'd still recognize my voice?"

"Depends on the voice you used," they replied. "You strike me as versatile."

"So do you."

"Thank you, sugar."

"Please, God, stop flirting and save us," the drag queen, Miss Delilah, said.

"Save yourself. You've got a voice, too," Vivian said.

"Save us before the Mountain decides to sing again," Miss Delilah begged, but she smiled as she nudged the mountainous man next to her.

Miss Delilah was at least six-foot five in today's heels, yet the Mountain still dwarfed her. He grunted from within his tiny head. In comparison to the Mountain, the Quandary seemed much more straightforward to Vivian.

A group of men from the audience went up to the microphone to good-natured cheers from the audience and demanded *Piano Man*.

Miss Delilah groaned. "Sweet baby Jesus."

"How often do you hear that one?" Vivian asked.

The Quandary shuddered. "Literally every time the band comes out to play. That and *Don't Stop Believin'*. It's embarrassing. And we don't embarrass easily around here."

"Well, you've convinced me. I think I'll go up there and do *Hit Me Baby*," Vivian joked.

"Please, oh, please do," Miss Delilah said.

The Quandary laughed, leaning on their cane. "Yeah, I don't think that was actually a threat."

"I always need to remember my audience." Vivian winced the more *Piano Man* collapsed into a pile of notes on the grass in front of the group at the mic. Some people enjoyed or even preferred bad karaoke, but she'd never been one of them, nor had she ever understood the celebration of obvious mediocrity. "You know, I'm tempted to just say Bell made his own hell and now he has to lie in it."

"Can I be there when you do?" the Quandary asked.

"Pretty please with a cherry, save us?" Miss Delilah pressed her hands together in supplication. "We have to be so polite to these people."

"What do I even sing?" Vivian said. "After last night, they'll probably start playing *My Heart Will Go On*."

"Sweetheart, I don't care if they play *Butterfly Kisses*," Miss Delilah replied. "We just want respite. A little peace."

"I don't do peace."

The Quandary shrugged. "A little quality, then. Something that won't make our ears try to self-destruct."

"Oh, I can do that, too. I'm the dangerous metalhead your mothers warned you about. I'll probably ask you to join Satan afterward."

Miss Delilah reached around the Quandary to rest a heavy hand on Vivian's shoulder. Vivian didn't jerk away, because this one she'd seen coming. The queen's nails were exquisite, longer than some people's little fingers. "I'll follow anywhere you go, honey, if you help us."

The group of men pumped their fists as they left the microphone.

Vivian turned her back on the band with a grin. "What exactly did the Mountain sing last time?"

"Oh, go *on*." The Quandary gave her a less-than-gentle nudge toward the stage.

"Good afternoon, everyone." Vivian took the microphone from the stand. "Although I stand here before you looking very much like I belong to the boneyard behind me, we haven't had a single rehearsal, and I have absolutely no idea what they're going to start playing. I'm hoping I know the words, otherwise this is going to be very awkward." She faced the rest of the band and looked each of them in the eye before covering the mic with her hand. "Do your worst. But remember, you have to get through it without your ears bleeding, too."

Alicia, Lily and Nasreen all shared a glance, while Lennon appeared thoroughly entertained.

Nasreen set up her primary synth and started a familiar intro in its delightful minor key. Lily joined in with her electric violin, but though Shane worked one of her bass drums, Lennon swung his guitar back and stepped toward the backup singer mic.

"That's what I'm talking about," Vivian murmured into the microphone before facing the crowd again.

She started *People Are Strange* by herself, but for the second verse, Lennon and Alicia took the harmonies, and after the bridge, they all ramped up the music to something wonderfully vicious, Lennon coming in with a power chord almost as good as the start of an orgasm. Vivian shook her head in excitement, whipping her hair along with her, brought her voice into a full metal growl then up to a shriek.

When the extra instrumentals fell away for the last verse, leaving it just the piano and her, Vivian stripped her voice of all the tricks—just a clear, dramatic sound that minor was so good at showcasing. It was a simple, repetitive song, all about execution. But once again, for a group who had literally made no plans, it was amazing how it all came together.

Could it possibly be magic? But Vivian couldn't even get mad about it.

After the applause—loud white noise in her ears— Vivian shouted with a defined growl into the mic, "Is that all you got? Come on!"

The audience loved it. They shouted louder, urging the band to do something harder. Vivian wanted a challenge. *Hit Me Baby* was starting to look really good right now.

"So she wants something more complicated, does she?" Nasreen purred into her own microphone. She pulled her boom mic stand over to the larger synth station. The table looked like a techno pipe organ. "Want us to try to give her something she can't sing? I think we've heard her range, haven't we, Skells?"

"Believe me. You haven't even begun to hear my range," Vivian purred right back, going even lower than Nasreen's sultry alto. Just like she hadn't practiced with the band, she hadn't warmed up her voice once in the last six months. She should have been rusty, less limber, shakier placement, breathing and support more unreliable than they used to be. But she felt like she'd been warming up for days, and her voice was as flexible as a possessed woman.

Lennon nodded to Nasreen then started in on the iconic strumming beat of *Barracuda*.

"Child's play," Vivian spoke into the mic before dancing to the intro. She made Lennon and Shane repeat it three times as the crowd cheered before she brought the mic back to her mouth and started singing.

Lennon hadn't made it easy for her. He'd put it right at Ann Wilson's key. But Vivian kept her voice clear for the higher notes, which resonated strong in her head. After the first chorus, she started pointing the microphone at the audience for the only word everyone knew. Even the rest of the band was getting into it, shouting "barracuda" right along with them. Vivian did her own riffs and runs when the pounding theme returned, bringing the notes up to the top of Wilson's range and higher, using the growl to keep the screaming from getting too shrill.

At Shane and Lennon's conclusion, the crowd erupted. The rest of the band couldn't help grinning at each other, but Vivian didn't need their accolades or validation. She hadn't changed her tune with them just because God, in his infinite wisdom, had blessed her with a voice that could sing circles around most.

Bell was the one to take the microphone from Vivian, but he placed a hand on her back to keep her there. "Sounds like our diva to me, doesn't she, everyone?"

More applause, whistles, even a few lighter apps in the air, though it was still bright out.

"I think I only want to hear one more song to solidify her place with the rest of the Skellies, although she certainly looks the part, no?" He said that, but for some reason he could barely look at her. "We've heard rock, some metal, but I'm wondering how symphonic that metal can be. I don't know whether you've heard this one. I hope so, because this audience certainly doesn't want to hear me sing."

"You mean Mr. Great and Powerful doesn't have a wonderful voice of his own on top of the rest of the perfect shit you sit in?" Vivian muttered.

Bell cupped the microphone with his palm. "There are many things I can't do. I wouldn't call myself tone deaf, but singing is not one of my many accomplishments."

"Will wonders never cease?"

"Don't encourage me." He looked over his shoulder opposite Vivian to signal the band, seemingly so he wouldn't have to glance at her on the way.

Vivian didn't mind being avoided, but she understood why the Skellies were avoiding her. Bell's reaction was a mystery. "Did I do something wrong?"

"No. You did nothing wrong, Vivian. At least not to me."

Vivian would have responded, but Lily and Nasreen had begun an impromptu collaboration, with Nasreen playing two different keyboards and Lily improvising with a dizzyingly complicated interpretation of the melody.

The music was vaguely familiar, so Vivian had probably heard it before. However, 'vaguely familiar' translated into having absolutely no memory of the lyrics. When Bell handed the microphone back to her, she experienced a moment of nightmarish panic.

"Don't worry," he whispered. "It'll come to you."

Shane and Lennon jumped in just as a sudden, almost organic memory Vivian knew wasn't her own surfaced. She brought the microphone back up to her mouth.

She favored rock-edged divas in symphonic metal, but Vivian knew how to shape her sound into something rich and classical, nowhere near the rasps and growls she usually peppered her voice with. As lyrics to *Walking in the Air* came to her, she switched to that more operatic quality. She certainly wasn't trained and her technique was probably iffy, but the average audience didn't care about technique. They cared about beauty, inside, outside, across every sense. And she could give them that, damn it. In spite of everything, she could be beautiful when she was singing—even she knew it.

Vivian closed her eyes to swim in the dreamy sound, in the synthesizer strings and the electric violin, in the hypnotic drums, in Alicia singing backup in a lower harmony to show off Vivian's soprano, in the electric guitar solo, in the sound of her own voice coming from the speakers a split second after she heard it in her head, reverberation added from whatever Nasreen had done to her microphone.

This was so much better than those garage bands. She didn't feel enchanted, at least not in her voice. It all seemed real instead of cheap, accomplished instead of cheating. They were *skilled*, a testament to practice they'd never had, a nod to talent they'd not necessarily cultivated.

This was what Bell had chosen her for, not the wish. He'd chosen her to sing. And now that she'd started, now that the screams were coming out controlled and ugly-beautiful or just plain beautiful, she didn't want to stop.

But when she did, everything else Bell had tacked onto her sentence in Arcanium entered her body again like demons.

Vivian smiled and tossed her hair, bowed for the audience. It wouldn't do to let any of them see it. She never let anyone see it. They could see ordinary. They could see bitch. But God help her if they ever saw beyond that. The tears in the food court had come too close.

It was the hunger. Hunger stripped away the paper-thin layers of armor to the soft underbelly. In addition to making her more acerbic than usual, it risked letting that underbelly show.

Stepping away from the center of the makeshift stage reminded her that just because the odd chef had given her a meat pie to quell her stomach, it hadn't been designed to last forever or even until the evening meal. Already the rumbling emptiness returned—not full-blown, but she knew it was a steep, slippery slope.

Bell stood next to Kitty, who was still clapping and grinning like a lunatic. Apparently, singing was just about the only time everyone liked her all at once. They all probably wished she were in some kind of opera — no book, no lines, just lyrics to make her far more likable. Fuck them, though. She didn't need to be liked the rest of the time.

"You're in, Skelly," Bell said.

"I thought I was already in."

Bell tilted his head and smiled tightly. "Just wanted to make sure you were worth it."

"Am I?"

"I guess we'll find out."

Chapter Five

Vivian wanted to throw another dish down on the table and ruin all of the odd chef's hard work — and possible throw Lily's dish at his face while she was at it.

But she'd already learned better.

The most normal pizza offered was the fettucine alfredo, with shiitake mushrooms, parsley, crab and alfredo. Another had arugula, grapes and Italian sausage and another cold sardines, capers and marinara. Then there was his specialty, a cricket-flour crust topped with crickets and meal worms sprinkled with melted mozzarella, and sautéed ants mixed in the sauce. At the very center was a dignified fried grasshopper. Lily said it was sometimes a hissing cockroach, other times a wolf spider.

Vivian had already eaten twelve grasshoppers during the food court frenzy, so she'd had every intention of leaving the bug pizza to the rest of the girls. But Jonas put one slice from each pizza on her plate, and after three slices, she still wasn't full enough. She plowed through the special with as much gusto as the rest.

It didn't taste bad. Far from it. But it was insects. Fucking insects. In her mouth.

There were a few thin slices left of each pizza. She grabbed the last sausage and arugula before anyone else could, since the fettucine alfredo pizza had already been reduced to crumbs. She cleansed her palate with just a few bites.

She hadn't even washed her face yet. It was surreal seeing herself in multiple full-length mirrors around the room, a Skeleton in face as well as body, eating as though she couldn't eat enough in five lifetimes.

"Are you going to behave?" Jonas asked as he uncovered a less esoteric dessert pizza. The man liked his themes — and his pizza oven. "Can I take Shane for the evening without any trouble here?"

"I promise nothing." But Vivian snatched the dessert plate he held out to her and groaned at the first bite of chocolate-drizzled, cinnamon-sugar pizza. Bug pizza aside — or maybe because of it — the man could have opened a pizza restaurant in the hipsteriest place he could find and made a killing on oddities. Why he chose a traveling circus of all places was beyond her.

"Alicia…" He raised an eyebrow at the equally ravenous backup singer.

"I got it. If she pitches a fit, we'll hogtie her in a bathroom stall until morning. We have it all planned."

"You and what army?" Vivian said as Shane left with Jonas.

"Don't underestimate a group of briefly well-fed, fed-up women."

"Believe me, girls, you aren't even close to being fed-up with me." Vivian took a sip of her wine. Because what went better with bug pizza than a sweet red wine?

"Bell may have changed your perception like he did for the rest of us, but you have no sense of proportion. Do you even realize that if you weren't actually good at what you do, you might have ended up dead?" Alicia said.

"What do you mean?" Vivian asked.

"What did you wish?"

"I wasn't exactly paying attention. Something about looking like the rest of you." She ran her finger over her plate, unconcerned with whether alfredo mixed with chocolate, as long as there was something else she could put in her mouth.

Everything — *everything* — tasted amazing, even the goddamn bugs. She didn't know whether something in her taste buds had changed to make everything taste a hundred times better or whether the odd chef was just that good. Given the fact so many people still came to his booth and ordered the weird shit, Vivian guessed skill was at least part of it.

But all of them scarfed everything down like dogs in a matter of minutes, sometimes seconds. She couldn't make it last, make it seem like more than it was, though he fed them much more than she'd otherwise portion for herself.

"Imagine you didn't have a good voice," Alicia said. "Bell works with the talents you already have whenever he can. So imagine he didn't need you. Imagine him just granting the wish you made and not sucking you into Arcanium. You go home with it. You end up looking like us. How long do you think you'd go before giving up the ghost?"

Vivian didn't answer. The way she'd seen herself before, her last thought would have been *At least I'm dying pretty*. "So what? Am I supposed to get down on my knees in abject gratitude that Bell cursed me into Arcanium instead of killing me?" She switched to a high-pitched, heavily Southern accent. "'Oh, thank you, kind sir. I know you tricked me into making a wish so that you could use it to steal me away, but thank you so much for not letting me go and killing me instead. Let me kiss your boots and the boots of everyone else.' You people are so fucking Stockholm. Bell isn't a savior for not killing me, and Jonas isn't a savior for feeding us." Vivian hadn't exactly lost her appetite, but her stomach churned, as though everything involved in eating had magnified from Bell's transformation, including disgust. "While we're on the subject, where does Jonas take Shane every night?"

Nasreen shrugged. "He takes her back to his booth. I think he sleeps there, like Kitty sleeps in her tent."

"She looks like she's going off to her execution. What does he do to her?"

"We think he keeps feeding her." Lily also used her fingertips to gather up as much as she could from her plate then from one of the pizza trays. Her cheeks twitched from more than chewing.

"Yeah, or he fucks her," Vivian said. "But at least she's not dead, right?"

"Hey," Alicia snapped, "if they're having sex, then it's because they agreed to have sex. That's one of the big rules in Arcanium. No means no."

"Doesn't seem to be a lot of no going on." Vivian's plate looked nearly clean. She could run her tongue over it, but she already felt enough like a bitch as it was.

"That's just the circus vibe," Alicia replied. "With the snake charmer and the strongman around, you'll start to feel it, too, if you haven't already—if you're even capable of feeling it."

"Feel what, exactly?"

"The urge to hump anything that moves," Lily said.

"No, can't say that I have." Vivian had squirmed in the shower that evening, knowing what Lennon was doing to the rest of the Skeletons all over again—as though they hadn't had enough the night before. The larger droplets down her body had felt like fingers. Desire didn't usually vibrate quite this much and so steadily inside her, but it wasn't like it was unbearable. Her hunger was more pressing.

"Then maybe you're one of the lucky ones," Alicia said. "Why do you get to be so damn lucky?"

"Why does Shane get more food than the rest of us?" Vivian asked.

Lily tossed the pizza pan back onto the table with a deliberate clatter. "I always assumed it's because she has more mouths to feed."

"Or maybe Jonas really does have sex with her," Nasreen said. "I mean, have any of you seen him with anyone else? How do you survive this place unless you find someone?"

Alicia shuddered. "She can't be. She doesn't like going. Bell wouldn't let Jonas do anything like that to her if she wasn't okay with it."

"But she doesn't get any either," Lily pointed out. "Whenever Lennon's here, she isn't. Has anyone seen *her* with anyone?"

"She can't. Every time something gets close to her mouths, they start biting," Alicia said. "As far as I know, she just doesn't have sex. Sometimes I hear her crying at night, but I don't know if that's the reason. Because...you know...we've *all* cried in the middle of the night."

Nasreen settled back on her cushion, showing off her sweetly curved figure to its best advantage, which was a slap in the face every time Vivian looked at her, so she looked away. "Maybe she does whatever she does with Jonas then skips away with one of the cast members. She's more private, and this tent is really not."

"If she were getting some, you'd think she'd be in a better mood when she got back." Alicia shook her head. "No, something else is up with her."

Vivian looked up from inspecting her nails. "Did you ever consider, I don't know, asking?"

"We talk about it when she's not here, obviously," Lily said, "but we don't pry."

Whatever. Vivian stood then clutched her stomach. It still roiled, twisted, sloshed, groaned at having food inside of it. Movement made the old, familiar nausea even worse.

All at once, she remembered every last thing she'd put in her mouth since picking, scavenging and desperately grabbing for anything edible in the food court. In front of everyone. Eating other people's food. Other people's saliva. Things sitting there in the sun, decaying petri dishes. The basket of fried grasshoppers. The special pizza. Four slices for everyone, an extra slice to rid herself of the bug pizza taste, plus two slices of dessert. Her abdomen still looked concave instead of bloated like it should, but she was so terribly *aware* of the food that had quieted her stomach again.

The hunger was still there, though. It couldn't be quenched, no matter what she ate, no matter whether it was good, bad or evil. She was only on her second night. Some of the other girls talked like they'd been here for months. Kitty had been here for twenty years.

Twenty years of this shit? Twenty years of fighting for control of her appetite? Twenty years of these stupid girls?

Twenty years of singing was nothing, but twenty years of this utter *hunger*?

Vivian ran to the bathroom, each piece of food running through her head in a dizzying loop. She knelt in one of the half toilet stalls, shaking her head against the prickling that shivered through her and conjured hot and cold sweat to the surface of her skin. She needed to get the insect legs and the contaminated remnants out of her body. She needed to get rid of whatever poisoned her, whatever made her this hungry, this dangerous. She needed it *out*.

She struck the toilet seat with her palm as the world swam around her but everything stayed down.

"You can't throw up," Nasreen said.

At least it was her soothing voice and not Alicia's, which was becoming like demon claws on a chalkboard for her.

"I need to," Vivian said. "It can't stay inside me. It can't." Fuck, did her voice actually quaver?

Really *glad it's not Alicia behind me.*

"You *don't* need to," Nasreen said. "I'm sorry, but you don't."

Vivian fell back onto the tile, leaning against the metal stall partition. "What do you know about it?"

"Why are you in here? Why are you in the bathroom trying to throw up? Why were you trying to excessively control how much — or how little — you ate last night?" Nasreen lowered herself to the floor, too, sitting across from Vivian with her legs crossed. Girl could keep her back straight while sitting on an awkward floor.

Vivian wondered if she did yoga. Wondering whether Nasreen did yoga was better than answering.

"If you're in the Skeleton tent, skeletal or not, you've got the same problem as the rest of us. Maybe Bell thought it would be therapeutic," Nasreen continued, unfazed by Vivian's silence. "We all have something, something that led us to make our wishes and get locked into Arcanium. Alicia was here first. Lily was next. Then Shane. I'm the newest. When we came to Arcanium, my friends encouraged me to dance while the band played. That was my audition. But I was already belly dancing semi-professionally, teaching classes and modeling and all that."

Nasreen closed her eyes. "The things I was doing to keep my figure that threatened to go fat at every turn… I counted calories, starved myself. Then I'd get so hungry that I'd eat everything in sight and order too much takeout. Then binge to get it out of the fridge. Then purge so that none of it would make a difference. Then I'd be back to starving, telling myself this time I'd manage to keep it up and I wouldn't see that needle on the scale go up again. I agonized over nutritional data, purged sometimes just for going over by a few calories…"

She opened her eyes and sighed, resting her elbows on her knees, hands clasped under her chin. "I think you know how it goes. Me and Alicia went this particular route, but Lily was a calorie counter, too. Her wish barely made her lose any more weight, but like you, she kept watching what she ate until the hunger took her over every time. And Shane has a thing about eating healthy, clean. She did all these cleanses, obsessed over where her food came from, to the point she sometimes ate nothing but homegrown vegetable broth for over a week at a time.

"She and I both wished we could eat anything we wanted, but I added 'and not gain a pound.' When I'm not the Skellies' keyboardist, I'm Arcanium's belly-dancing circus geek, which means it's fun for everyone else to see what I'm willing to swallow." Bitterness harshened her tone. "Sometimes it comes on like this abrupt need—makes me feel crazy, suddenly having the burning desire to swallow a handful of nails. None of it harms me, although even a bulletproof constitution can't stop nails from feeling weird going through my intestines. He keeps me less skeletal because belly dancing is meant to be done with curves, but it all looks too big to me, too fat. My mother and sister would always say I was too fat."

"What's your point?" But Vivian knew what the point was.

"It doesn't matter what you eat. It doesn't matter how badly you eat. You'll stay the same size. You won't die or get sick or have heart problems like Alicia was having. And because we don't get sick, we can't throw up. I don't know how it is for the rest of the cast, but the Skeletons can't. Bell won't let us." Nasreen straightened, although she appeared deflated, wan. "Sorry we didn't tell you earlier. We didn't know you were that kind of Skeleton."

"I'm not." And Vivian wasn't, most of the time. "I really feel like I need to throw up. I'm not making myself throw up."

"All the things you've been doing, trying not to eat, feeling sick from what you did eat... That's in your head, Vivian. It's not reality anymore."

Vivian bristled. "Doesn't sound like it's teaching us much healthier habits. You're still bingeing. We're eating as much as we possibly can because there's a black hole where our stomach should be. What's that going to do to us when we leave? We'll just keep eating whatever we want, ballooning up and hating ourselves all over again."

"It's not about being healthy. It's about letting go of the fixed, rigid patterns we followed before, because they no longer apply."

"You sound like my psychiatrist." It was as close as Vivian would get to a confession. She wasn't the share-and-hug-it-out kind of person.

Nasreen grinned. "I may have had one of my own. Anyway, I bring up my other job as an Arcanium Skeleton because one of the main things that helps during this kind of transition, dealing with your hunger and the other changes, is distraction. Arcanium unfortunately doesn't offer much of it. We have a lot of downtime between weekends, since we don't have to practice much. As you've probably figured out, most of the hard stuff has been eliminated here. We practice to try new things and play around, but we could twiddle our thumbs all week and still sound bangarang when the circus opens, not that I'm complaining. I used to be a decent pianist, but I've developed skills since that I'd only ever wished I'd had. Fortunately, I never said *that* aloud like Lily, so I still have two wishes left."

"It's three wishes, then."

"Bell's a traditional nontraditional jinni. Are you feeling any better?"

"No." Vivian grabbed the side of the half stall and pulled herself, shaking, to her feet.

"You don't still think you're fat, do you? Alicia sometimes has issues with that, even after Bell fixed her perception."

"It's not just about gaining weight. It's about..." Vivian brushed past Nasreen instead of finishing the thought. There wasn't enough time in the world to say all the things she wasn't interested in sharing.

"I understand. Believe me. And hopefully you understand now what Arcanium's changed for you, so you won't feel the need to portion or feel guilty about eating non-*halal* roadkill."

Vivian hesitated. "Seriously?"

"What do you think was in the shepherd's pie? Roadkill stew is another one of his specialties. It's not his only kind of meat, by any means, but for anything that involves obscuring what kind of meat it is, he isn't picky."

Vivian put a hand over her mouth and heaved, but again, nothing came out. She hadn't even eaten the shepherd's pie.

Nasreen shrugged with a sheepish grin. "You can't tell. He's that good."

Vivian looked away from Nasreen before rolling her eyes. "I bet his margaritas cure cancer, too."

"We really wouldn't be surprised."

* * * *

The invisible barrier kept her in the tent when the circus wasn't open until Arcanium picked up and moved from the fairgrounds where Vivian had been kidnapped. The tent became an RV while the girls slept. Vivian woke up in a tiny bunk bed, three to a wall. She hit her head sitting up, which made all four girls giggle madly. Vivian hurting herself seemed to never get old.

As soon as they arrived at the new fairground, the RV faded back into the harem tent, each girl in her own cot, seamless and disorienting as a dream.

Then she just had to wait for night to fall.

Vivian was impatient, but she knew how to wait.

It was easier to plan for things when no one was paying attention, so she played the good girl and ate whatever Jonas served. She still ended up back in the bathroom, nauseated again from the stew he'd ladled into her bowl now that she knew what was in it—not that stew, chili or goulash in general had ever appealed to her. They looked like someone had regurgitated them, more suggestion than temptation.

She waited until everyone had gone to sleep, except for Shane. She wouldn't come in until late, which was why Vivian wanted to leave before then.

She had no idea where Arcanium was when she stepped out of the harem tent. All that mattered was that she could.

They were in another open field, and the temperature was similar to the one they'd left, but the tent faced a different lightscape on the horizon. It wasn't a big city, that was for sure, and everything was terribly flat. That was all she could tell from the general blackened landscape in the middle of the night.

She didn't care where they were, though. She was in Arcanium no matter where she went, and aside from things in her apartment that she'd worked hard to afford, she didn't mind leaving everything behind. If anyone missed her, they wouldn't miss her for long. The same went for the people she'd miss. This was, for all intents and purposes, her new home, her new 'friends'.

It was time to get to know them better.

The flaw in her brilliant plan to follow Shane hit when she stepped into the food court.

The rest of the cast ate family-style at the picnic tables during days off, though Jonas continued to serve the Skeletons in their tent. Everyone else apparently knew to keep their food away from the Skeletons. When Vivian had tried to sleight a breakfast taco away from a woman with long black hair and deathly pale skin, she'd received three claw marks on her hand for her trouble. Bell had sipped his metaphorical tea as Vivian had staunched the bleeding with paper napkins.

In the middle of the night, the food court still smelled like dinner — not as intense as the usual circus fare, but it was enough to make her gag and salivate at the same time.

Curiosity overwhelmed both hunger and distaste. Vivian made it to the food booths without drooling, so that was an accomplishment of some kind. Now she just had to get into the odd chef's booth without anyone seeing her and without Jonas or Shane knowing that she was there, wherever they were.

With her luck, Shane really did have a fuckboy somewhere else in the circus, and Jonas was just tucked into his bed with some boring book like the boring human he pretended to be. Maybe he'd have an expensive, distinguished port or brandy that he could drink while sitting around in his socks.

If he was fucking Shane, Vivian wouldn't want to stick around, but at least she'd know.

There was a swinging half-gate that led into the serving part of the booth, which was about the size of a short bus, but there was another section behind a closed door — presumably the kitchen. It was hard to believe Jonas and a small team of cooks could do so much in such a small space.

The gate creaked a little, but thin as she was, she could slip in sooner than the average person. She crouched behind the counter for a few minutes after closing the gate. The door didn't open, and no one peeked over the counter. Vivian thought she heard animalistic sounds elsewhere in the circus, but they were far away.

Vivian crawled to the door and reached for the doorknob, praying that it would be unlocked and wouldn't squeak as she turned it.

The knob turned easily, and as long as she moved slowly, nothing clicked or squeaked. She peered in with one eye first.

It wasn't a small space at all. It was a full-sized industrial kitchen, with large refrigerators, preparation counters, open shelves, a pinboard of cutlery, hanging pots and pans, a spice rack to make a witch green with envy, several pantries and two walk-in freezers. So it was like the harem tent — bigger on the inside, everything needed with all the convenience magic could provide.

Insta-skills were nice, but this kind of felt like cheating.

"Just hold still, child. This isn't supposed to hurt."

"I can't help it. It's wriggling, and it feels so *weird* every time…"

"It'll feel less weird if you relax. You're always so tense. Would you like some tea?"

"No, just get it over with."

"We've been here for over an hour, Shane. Are you sure you don't want tea?"

"Tea will make it take longer. Just put it in and get it over with."

Vivian couldn't let dialogue like that go without investigating. She crawled in and shut the door behind her, though she didn't close it all the way in case she needed to make a quick exit.

The floor was tiled like the harem tent bathroom — the exact same kind of tile. Vivian suspected that wherever the bathroom and kitchen were, they occupied the same building. So it wasn't so much that the interiors were bigger than the exterior. The doors seemed to be portals to another place, a physical place. An abandoned school, perhaps, because not a lot of buildings had communal showers and industrial kitchens.

She slowly leaned forward to see around the prep counter in the front of the room.

A nook had been set up in the back for the odd chef's bed. It was very much a place of necessity — a twin bed barely better than the Skeletons' cots, with a few blankets, a plastic tub underneath with clothes and maybe a few other things. That was it.

Rather than lying on the bed, however, Shane had been arranged over a sturdy butcher block. And even though they weren't having sex, a health inspector would have a few things to say about the fact that Shane was completely naked on said butcher block.

At first, Vivian thought it was still a sex thing, because what *wasn't* sexual about a pretty young woman naked in front of an older man perving over the tight body spread for him? But in spite of the fact Shane held her legs open and the odd chef was bent between them, Shane's face contorted in what looked like pain. Her head was angled toward Vivian, but her eyes were clenched shut.

Vivian lowered herself closer to the ground and crept forward for a better vantage point.

When Vivian understood what she was seeing, she nearly laughed out loud. *This* was what they did late into the night? *This* was what made Shane miserable?

Jonas held a pair of chopsticks and patiently fed strips of raw meat and fish to the mouth between Shane's legs. The mouths all over the rest of her had their tongues out as well, licking the edges of the gashes and between teeth. A few pieces of meat trapped between those teeth suggested that the rest of her had already been fed. They'd saved the biggest and most awkward mouth for last.

Jonas brought a strip of red meat to the gnarly gash that had taken the place of Shane's cunt. Its larger tongue emerged, as bright red as the interior of the other mouths, and thick rather than flat. There was something terribly obscene about it, but just when it started to seem nothing but sexual, the tongue wrapped around the piece of flesh and pulled it in, and the huge, sharp teeth on either side of the mouth clamped down like a toothed clam.

It was almost a joke. Almost a pun. Almost hilarious. But Shane arched, writhed, looking for all the word like she was either in extreme pleasure or pain. She held her breath until she couldn't anymore, gasping out the air she'd held in.

This should have been Jonas' idea of a perfect wet dream. Hadn't he said that he favored well-fed women? Feeding one so personally—even if it wasn't his dick he was stuffing inside of her—*had* to do something for him. But as far as Vivian could tell, his trouser mouse still slept soundly, not so much as a twitch.

He was just...feeding her, like an enthusiast fed a favorite pitcher plant.

When Jonas fed the mouth a strip of sashimi, Vivian didn't think she could take any more unintentional hilarity. She carefully crawled backward until she was out of sight, then eased back out of the kitchen and into the booth. Both of them were too involved in what they were doing to notice the door closing again.

On the other side of the door, it stopped being funny.

They were all supposed to get the same amount of food. Shane had more mouths, but she didn't have more stomachs. She didn't even know where what the mouths ate went. So why was Shane the exception? Why did she get handfed by the odd chef while the rest of them were treated separately and differently, with amused detachment? It clearly wasn't because Shane was giving him something extra on the side.

Vivian wasn't necessarily mad at Shane. The girl's discomfort made up for the fact she got more. But they were all supposed to get the same amount — too much. They were supposed to be shown no favor, not even from the other members of the circus. And though Vivian had scavenged, the way it hadn't satisfied until Jonas had personally handed her a meat pie seemed to suggest something even shadier.

Vivian sneaked out of the booth. About halfway through the food court, she eased up her care and let her slip-ons crunch on the dead grass shot through with soft, new green.

She looked in one of the trash cans on the way out. Not for anything in particular. Just an idle glance — the way she looked in change carriages for discarded coins, never really expecting to find anything.

The bin was half full. Arcanium was new to the field, but it looked like there had been another event there before they'd arrived, maybe that weekend. Maggots and mold crawled over old fried chicken. Open Styrofoam bowls contained mashed potatoes, gravy remnants and bits of corn. Interspersed among the food were soda and beer cans that probably had a last swallow in them. A cup of cigarette butts at the top made everything reek.

Vivian held her stomach again, because she was pretty sure that without the cigarettes poisoning everything else in the bin, she might have actually reached in there and grabbed the chicken bones. If she had the constitution of a goat and nothing mattered, then a little mold and a few maggots wouldn't hurt her.

She thought of the powdery, sickly-sweet taste she imagined mold would taste like, the slimy soft texture of decay, maggots moving over her tongue. Clutching the side of the bin, she bent over the grass and retched hard, coughing. But true to Nasreen's word, nothing came up.

"I wouldn't stay out after dark without an escort."

Vivian straightened. The snake charmer was a few yards away, wearing a tank top. She looked a bit like Lara Croft, except for the king cobra wrapped around her shoulders and propped on her arms. Her eyes were hooded, eyelids heavy with suspicion.

"I thought the cast was safe from anything dangerous," Vivian said.

"You should be. But if the clowns don't immediately recognize that you're one of us, it could get quite ugly before it gets better. Best to have a demon with you if you plan to sneak around like someone up to no good. Are you up to no good?"

"None of your business."

"That," the snake charmer said, "is very true. Just be careful."

"I can take care of myself." Vivian wiped the back of her hand over her mouth then headed back to the harem tent. She sank into her cot and lay there until Shane returned about an hour later. Alicia had been right. She was crying.

* * * *

Literally the only time Vivian got along with the rest of the band was when they were practicing. Talent forgave a multitude of sins from both sides. It was also the only time Shane seemed to enjoy herself.

But one thing Vivian respected Shane for—she didn't complain. She was clearly miserable, but she didn't drag anyone else down with her. When asked to do something, she did it. She didn't whine, didn't cry except when she thought no one was looking and, though she clearly didn't like going with Jonas, she still did it because she knew she had to.

Life was misery, but a person still needed to go on. Shane got it. Vivian liked that. It was better than faking that everything was okay.

When the Skellies weren't playing, however, Vivian was dead bored. There were books in her tub and they were encouraged to ask for any others they wanted, but Vivian had never been much of a reader. A book club sounded more like hell than the rest of Arcanium. Bell permitted the harem tent to share a tablet with a few streaming services, but any other apps were complete locked, and no one trusted her enough to use their computers or phones.

Which left her with oodles of time on her hands. No work. She could only sleep so much. And there was literally nothing on her usual leisure docket that she could do.

It made her cranky as hell and that much more of a terror in the tent. She even annoyed herself. As soon as she got dressed in the morning in one of her prim tea party dresses that threatened to fall off in the absence of double-sided tape, she got the fuck out of there.

The only entertainment left to her was exploration of the circus and the new Renaissance fairground while avoiding anyone's attempt at conversation. People were far more interesting to look at than talk to.

Oddity Row was a meandering but somehow sensical path of canvas tents accented with red velvet curtains, each about the size of a gazebo. During the week, the cast didn't hang out in them, but Vivian still read their placards. The creepy-crawly tent and covered courtyard completed the Row. Though Vivian couldn't stand bugs where they shouldn't be, she didn't have a problem with them when they were in their own little habitats.

In the afternoons, many of the other acts practiced, and when she wasn't with the band, she watched them. Like the band, no one had to practice to keep up their skills, but what else was there to do?

Vivian knew exactly what else everyone was doing when they weren't practicing or doing book club or eating. Proper people-watching meant sneaking around, and sneaking was half the fun when people liked fucking each other inside and outside of their RVs and trailers. It was even better when people from the circus fucked people from the faire. The faire folk always had this expression of stunned confusion.

She wasn't a voyeur by nature, but sex interested her. When Vivian knew what someone liked in the bedroom, she could always use it outside the bedroom. Like, if a boss liked being spanked and told he was a bad boy, all a person had to do was use the same voice and look at them just the right way and they'd do whatever she told them, especially if they knew they weren't supposed to have been spanked in their office by an intern in the first place. She didn't even have to have been the intern doing the spanking — which had only happened once. She just had to have seen it.

'Find the people having sex in semi-public places' had turned into her favorite game. The best to watch were the Patchwork Pirate with the snake charmer and strongman — either or both. Not only were they insanely pretty, they were goddamn enthusiastic. And they had incredible stamina.

Watching them always got her hotter than anyone else she caught. When she'd leave them behind, even Lennon started to look good. But the feeling would fade, and she'd go back to being hungry in the normal way.

Still, even her favorite game was going to get dull fast.

* * * *

"No band today," Alicia said as Vivian started pulling on her usual post-apocalyptic rock goddess attire for Friday's opening. "And no body paint, thank God."

"Why?"

"Friday night is more about...indulgence," Alicia replied. "Sexier costumes. Flashier lights. Looser morals. The fairgrounds aren't open, so their people get a discount, and all the leather babies get to cut their teeth."

"I never thought I'd ever hear you say 'leather babies'." Vivian could stand never hearing it again.

"You should hear me say 'anal beads'. Friday night is about indulgence, which means an amateur eating contest—Skeletons versus all the fools who think they can keep up with actually hungry people who can't get full to save their lives, though the contests get us pretty darn close. You'll feel amazing afterward."

That wasn't the word Vivian would usually associate with eating contests—'heartburn' came to mind.

She eschewed skinny jeans and reached for one of the thin, dark dresses on the tea party side of her clothes rack, but she accessorized the sweetness away with a spiky, black diamond tiara and her leather jacket. "I take it participation is mandatory, or else you wouldn't be bringing it up."

"Yeah," Shane said. "Even worse, since the theme is indulgence, the odd chef doesn't do the usual contest food. He prepares aphrodisiacs—oysters, chocolate, chili..."

"Chili's an aphrodisiac?"

"Spicy things, apparently. We also have banana pudding eat-offs, and in the summer there's supposed to be watermelon-eating contests. I think Jonas does some naughty cake baking and fruit carving as well."

"Yep," Alicia said. "We had a dick-eating contest before you came in. Cake balls in the shape of dicks and, well...balls."

"What do you get if you win?" Vivian asked.

"House always wins, so we don't get anything but a full stomach, which is prize enough. There's supposed to be a cash prize, too. Apparently that goes into whatever fund constitutes our salary that we don't receive while we're here," Alicia said. "Sometimes other members of the cast join us, but no one beats a Skelly, even when Ciarán's on the mound. And his stomach's bigger than all of ours combined."

"So what if I just…didn't try?" Vivian said. "Bell can force me to be there, but what if I just didn't swallow down a week's worth of food in one sitting?"

Nasreen got up from where she'd been lying on her cot. "As long as you're there and eating, I don't see why you'd hold back. It's the one night of the week you aren't hungry going to sleep."

"And the sex doesn't suck either," Lily added. "I don't know if the food's really an aphrodisiac, whether Jonas adds something to it or the sex demons just turn up the noise. But God, you think this place can't make you any hornier. Then you eat a whole cake in less than five minutes and want to fuck the first demon to whip out his cock."

Vivian didn't get it. She enjoyed sex. She'd had plenty of it. It had sometimes gotten her into more trouble than it was worth. Yet everyone else seemed to get ridiculously worked up in Arcanium, talking about sex demons and pheromones and aphrodisiacs. Maybe it was a placebo effect of some kind — someone had told them Arcanium made them horny and that gave them permission to get freaky with freaky things. Still, it was hard to believe placebo effect could lead to three of the four girls in the tent having a torrid affair with the same man and not bothering to hide it — and acknowledging that they might have others.

"Remember what we talked about," Nasreen said as they left the tent, entering early darkness lit with strings of Christmas and bulb lights in red, yellow, green and purple. "There's really no reason to hold back from what you're eating."

"Unless I want to piss Bell off and don't want to perform like a circus monkey just because he made me food-motivated."

"I guess 'because I want to' is a reason," Nasreen conceded.

"Damn straight."

The circus still wasn't fully operational in terms of performances, but it went all out on a Friday night. The performers the circus did have were out in full force, dense in Arcanium's smaller space.

Chelsine did her fire-dancing routine, with fire fans in the shape of lotus flowers. She also had her own small booth in the food court, where she poured fiery cocktails and, for a sizable tip, swallowed or breathed fire.

Okeyo, the armless dancer and tumbler, had a tendency to get lost in the shadows and emerge to scare passersby if they weren't paying attention. He and Carlo, the legless Torso, weren't the only scares. May, the woman who had clawed Vivian for stealing her breakfast taco, played Japanese demon, walking around midway booths and oddity tents to freak out the guests. The contortionist, Selena, creeped around with her hips twisted one way and her head twisted the other, sometimes on all fours, sometimes upright, her latex body glove creaking in a way that Vivian assumed was supposed to be erotic. And the slender, faceless Gentleman from the haunted funhouse could sneak up on anyone, despite the fact he was as conspicuous as Ciarán.

Skinless, the human pincushion, and the Insane, a woman in a straitjacket with a cage around her head, abandoned the funhouse as well to join the clowns, Shane and the Serpent King, David, in frightening guests everywhere from the midway to the Row.

Most of the tents on the Row had been closed except for the creepy crawly tent, with the Spider tied in the center of her web, and the open courtyard tent outside of it—thinner, translucent red canvas draped over poles strung with more bulb lights. It was open to the night sky in the center, which let in a good breeze

The cast that was more oddity than freak, more weird than scary, tended to congregate in the courtyard. Here was where Nasreen played the circus geek, swallowing things from a selection of jars on the table before her. The armless, legless, heavily tattooed Torso, with his scarred-over mouth, eyes and ears, wriggled his way through a petting zoo enclosure. The Mountain sat on a tiny stool that shouldn't have held him. Both the Quandary and Miss Delilah preferred walking among the guests, but George, the Two-Faced Man, had whole creepy conversations with the face on the back of his head in the courtyard.

The albino triplets, who apparently weren't even related, looked ethereal, like Fates or white witches. The Horned God, the Fallen Angel and the gargoylian Creature were so still on their platforms that they could have been waxworks.

Before the circus had opened, Bell had passed out skull half-masks for the three Living Skeletons, leaving Nasreen to play geek and Shane to play Tooth Fairy. Vivian's skeleton bracelets were the only ones bejeweled, but the other two had their own silver hands, and Lily wore a necklace that looked like a human collarbone. Alicia had gone full-on Halloween in a pair of skeleton leggings and a retro skull-printed rockabilly dress.

Like the other Skeletons, Vivian was expected to wander around and look pretty for people to pose with in the strategic places set up with more lights, which she did everywhere except in the food court. From a distance, she watched the crew carry Gothic dining tables to the grass in front of the chef's booth. They also set up a sign. Arcanium liked its signs.

Aphrodisiac Eating Contest, $500. Can you beat our best?

She tried to wander to the far end of the midway, but before she made it halfway down the row, she fell to her knees, gagging and covering her mouth, confusing the painful heights of hunger for nausea once again. Bell wanted her at the food court.

Hating every step, she staggered to the food court, where the rest of the Skellies were waiting for her, alternating seats at the stretch of covered tables.

Bell personally escorted her to one end and placed her in front of a chair. He held it for her until she sat down. "We have our newest Skeleton at the dinner table with us tonight, folks. I wouldn't say she's shy, but she's not quite used to our unusual crowds. Is she a worthy addition to our little contest? You decide."

When he placed a hand on her shoulder, she covered it with her own, smiling to convince everyone around her that she was fine, even as she dug her long nails into Bell's knuckles. He didn't seem to notice.

"Now, this would be an entertaining contest with just our lovely Skeletons, the Tooth Fairy and the Geek Queen pitted against each other. But would anyone here like to challenge our reigning champions in addition to our newcomer, who has just as substantial of an appetite?"

Hands raised in the crowd, and Bell selected a few to come forward. As with the band performances, the crowd consisted not just of guests but other cast members, from Kitty to the snake charmer, from the strongman to Moss sitting on his usual perch on Ciarán's shoulder. But Bell selected only guests.

"Remember, friends, our girls are slender, but they're fierce. The only thing you should get your hands dirty on is the food. Please seat yourself between the cast and prepare for our odd chef's masterpiece of the night. Justin, the wine."

One of the crew poured red wine for each of the contestants. Red wine, black tablecloth, candelabras set in the center of each table... It wasn't your typical eating contest. But Vivian understood why they didn't have makeup now. They were probably going to be eating so much that it would smear even the best paint cake.

The crew brought each participant a plate of chilled oysters on the half shell, drizzled with lemon juice and sprinkled with sea salt.

Vivian hated oysters. They were like eating slime. But when the crew member put the plate in front of her, her stomach growled, as did those of the other Skellies across the table. The crowd hummed with indulgent laughter.

"Each plate has ten oysters. The first to complete twenty plates is the winner. Our crew is ready and able to replace plates at the moment of completion. Please feel free to avail yourself of the wine left at the table. Do you have the timer ready, Jonas?"

"It is prepared." Jonas hovered his hand over the button of a giant timer with green luminescent numbers.

"Are you familiar with eating shellfish, sir?" Bell asked as he passed behind the contestants at the table, milking the anticipation. He paused at the man between Alicia and Lily. "We have some women with us today who are quite adept. Are you an enthusiastic consumer?"

The fair-skinned man flushed florid and squirmed uncomfortably, but he licked his lips and nodded.

Bell bent toward the man sitting next to Vivian. "You don't want to be beaten by a Skeleton, do you, sir?"

"Depends." The man glanced down at Vivian's neckline, which gaped just enough to entice.

Vivian loosely wrapped her fingers around the wine glass, moving her fingers with the suggestion that he and Bell seemed intent on creating. Then she brought the wine glass to her lips. The man watched her hungrily.

If she let her dress gape more, there was no way he'd even come close to competing. Then again, it was already a foregone conclusion that the cast was going to win. There was no need to play dirtier than necessary. It did, however, feel good to have his undivided attention. It was easier for her to feel sexy when she still wore her leather jacket.

So, of course Bell took the lapels of her jacket and eased them back to pull it down her arms.

"Bastard," she whispered.

"The point is a Skeleton with an appetite, my dear. Believe me. No one will care."

"Looks like you need to fill your mouth with some good oyster, huh, honey?" the man next to her said as Bell handed her jacket off to Kitty.

"Oh, definitely on my menu tonight. No sausage, *esé*. Little pigs in a blanket aren't to my taste."

"Bitch." But he seemed to take it all in stride.

"Pig fucker."

"Rug muncher."

"Cow tipper."

"Do I look like a farmer to you?" the man asked. He didn't. He looked like a banker.

"Just means you have to be more creative."

"Peace, children," Bell said. "We'll fill your mouths with more than filthy words."

The audience loved each dirty joke more than the last, getting into the spirit with each other. Couples squeezed places they usually wouldn't. Groups of friends did the same, but with irony or just miming.

"All right, is everyone ready?" Bell asked. "If you absolutely insist, there is silverware provided, but we encourage everyone to enjoy everything as finger-licking good as it was intended."

The crowd laughed.

"Set...*go*."

Vivian hesitated, not wanting to put the squishy, snot-like substance in her mouth—though she already knew rotten meat started to look good when she was desperate enough.

She turned up her nose, twisting her head away.

Bell tsked in her head. *"Now, now, Vivian. You'll never win with that attitude."*

"Bite me."

"To the right person, I'm sure you'd be very tasty. Eat. All you need to do is put one in your mouth and you'll wonder why you never could before."

"Are we still making sex jokes?"

Bell smiled. *"If you like."*

"I hate even the idea of oysters."

"I could put offal in front of you and you would eat it as though it were ice cream. Don't you want to be full, Vivian? Don't you want to be satisfied? Don't you want to fall into your bed without any needs or desires, only satiation?"

"Really, are we still making sex jokes?"

"If you like. With another member of the circus, though."

"You don't want me?"

"You don't want *me. You* can't use *me."*

Vivian glared at him. She didn't like that he always seemed to know so much more about her than she wanted anyone to know. But he was a manipulative fucker himself, and in a circus full of sex, she wondered why he didn't use it. Why *didn't* he try to take her and use her, the way he'd said she couldn't use him? Was he afraid she *could* use him if she found his weaknesses?

"Any attempt to exploit my weaknesses will end badly for you. And I deny you from my bed because I have no interest in a pale imitation of women I have loved. I'd be no good for you. You don't even know what you ask. Now, eat at least one oyster, love. Participation is *mandatory."*

Vivian crossed her arms over her chest and sat back in her chair. The audience clearly noticed the tension between the master of ceremonies and the contestant, and as far as they were concerned, the woman refusing to eat was briefly more interesting than the ones scarfing as much as they could as fast as possible.

Bell raised an eyebrow. Then he lifted his chin.

Her stomach became a crater, an emptiness as vast as whole cities laid to waste, and her mouth watered so much it seemed like she was foaming at the mouth. She darted forward to take the shell between her teeth, snapping it closed and swallowing the oyster down whole, shell and all.

There were shouts and gasps and surprised laughter, but no one was more surprised than her.

"If you don't like the texture," Bell said into her mind, *"there are alternatives."*

"Your face is an alternative. I'll get you for that."

"You'll try." There was certainty in his reply, as though he knew her plans more than she did, knew before she'd conceived them how spectacularly they would fail, so why should she even start?

She couldn't linger on the thought, concerning or not. The odd chef had prepared this food, although it hadn't required much in the way of preparation. Her stomach had tasted meat, and it would not be satisfied with just one.

Vivian didn't eat the other shells. She tipped them to eat the oysters inside faster than she registered the awful texture, like swallowing a slickened slug. The lemon and salt made the aftertaste better, but the slimy quality of the oysters meant they slipped down her esophagus and settled in the base of her stomach like fish. For Nasreen, who sometimes ate live goldfish, Vivian was sure this was nothing. The other girls didn't act like it was any more difficult for them. Lily groaned as though she were being screwed with the best fucking machine in the business every time she swallowed.

Whatever aphrodisiac was in Lily's oysters, Vivian wanted some. Maybe if she could get something else out of it, that would make this humiliation less complete.

The man next to her had stood to close the distance between him and table so that he could eat faster. Another part of him stood as well.

Really, what it is about this circus?

Vivian was on her second plate now, Alicia on her third, Shane on her fourth, not even bothering to tip. She closed her nails in the awful flesh of the oysters and brought them to her mouth double-fisted, one hand after the other to maximize the speed. Her other mouths worked all over her body, teeth opening and closing over nothing. Their desperation drove Shane faster.

Vivian didn't think she could hope to catch up, but all she wanted was to be better than the man next to her, if just to keep him from trying to hit on her later. The faster she went, the faster he tried to go, but he was an amateur.

All the guests coming in were at a disadvantage, even with Vivian's late start. They had to deal with the limitations of a human body. For his Skeletons, Bell had removed those limitations.

The crowd started to clap to Shane's pace, which threw off her rhythm, but when she finally overlapped the rhythm of the clapping, she started going faster. No chewing. No tasting. Just swallowing. The odd chef was ruined on the eating contests, since the point wasn't to savor. Vivian wondered if he'd prepared the food as reluctantly as she'd eaten it.

When Shane was finished, she held up her hands. The odd chef buzzed the timer at two minutes even.

Vivian almost threw the oyster in her hand away — contest was over, so she didn't have to keep going. At the last second, she tipped the shell and sucked the oyster into her mouth. It was still unbearably slimy, but umami spread over her tongue, enhanced by the citrus and grains of salt.

Once she had the full taste, she couldn't stop. She kept eating, though the other guest contestants had already sat back, the one next to her holding his stomach.

The odd chef came up to Shane to raise her hand for her victory, but the other Skeletons still shoved oysters into their faces, Lily still moaning as though someone was tongue-fucking her under the table. Her thin white tank top had been covered with lemon and oyster juice, which treated her top half to wet T-shirt translucence, nipples perky and dark for everyone to see.

And Bell just watched them, arms crossed as he surveyed his handiwork with the pride of a dog trainer watching his charges walk on their hindlegs. Even as Vivian polished off her last plate, she kept glaring daggers at Bell, hating him more strongly the more her body wanted the oysters she hated.

She was third. Even though she'd started late, she was third after Shane and Alicia.

She threw the shells to the plate after she finished with the last ones, lest she decide to polish them off, too. She gulped down the rest of her glass of wine then stood up from the table, the top half of her dress as drenched as Lily's tank top, and strode away. She smelled like oysters, which probably contributed to the speed at which the crowd parted for her.

"Oh, dear. Either she's a sore loser or not a fan of sticky fingers."

Bell, always trying to get a laugh and a twitch of the boner at the same time.

Vivian went straight into the harem tent. If Bell didn't want her leaving the circus before it closed, he didn't care enough to stop her.

She shed her accessories on the way to the bathroom. The mask joined them on the ground. She was only in her dress when she stepped under the shower spray. It hit her skin hot, almost too hot. She didn't care. She still heard Bell's voice in her head, felt everywhere his hands had touched, but like he'd said, she wanted nothing to do with slipping into bed with him, the snake.

He'd made her do it. He'd made her hungry, hungrier, made her starving then made her put one of her least favorite foods in her mouth and swallow it over and over again.

Vivian rubbed her lips with the back of her hand before finally reaching for the liquid soap, lathering it in her hands to clean them, lathering more to wash her face. She tried to pull her dress off the normal way, but when the zipper wouldn't go down, Vivian jerked it until it tore and the fabric could slither down her wet body.

She'd rather swallow her dress than oysters, but he'd made her eat them, take them into her body, made them satisfy, made them good. It was just another straw on top of all the indignities he'd heaped on her — through the odd chef, the other girls, through the band and every reflection in every mirror.

She washed her chest, washed down her body to catch everything the dirty water spread over her until every last trace of the oysters had been scrubbed off, although that wouldn't do anything for her insides. She wished she could say that they made her feel nauseated, gross, like a bait bucket, but she couldn't deny that they had satisfied, as promised.

She brushed her teeth three times.

The real insult was that this place might not have been that bad without Bell going out of his way to make her miserable. But unlike Shane, she was more than willing to share the wealth.

Not tonight, though.

She walked out into the tent naked and slipped between her sheets, unfolding the quilt at the bottom of the cot to use that as an extra layer. She was colder than she used to be, but she used to sleep naked all the time, even when there wasn't someone else in her bed.

When the others came in, they noticed her sleeping and they were quieter, but not as quiet as they could be. They were drunk on their own satisfaction, and when Lennon came in, they didn't bother going separately.

Vivian faced the other way, but she watched through slitted eyes in her mirror. Bodies writhed and tangled. There were tentacles, so many moans. Lennon didn't invite, and she didn't ask. She stroked her clit but kept her legs shut. She wasn't turned on enough for that, and if Lennon realized what she was doing, he might try to use it against her in the future. She was satisfied enough for now.

But as they all went to their own beds and Shane's remained empty, Vivian stayed awake. Was she satisfied? Could she ever be? Would she ever give herself that satisfaction?

Chapter Six

It wasn't enough.

The eating contests weren't enough. The dinners weren't enough. The breakfasts weren't enough. She was this close to taking a complete stranger's partially eaten turkey leg from their greasy hands and devouring it like a whore handed a fifty.

The others were satisfied, so why the hell wasn't she?

Her only haven was during the performances, though she was still only singing about three songs an afternoon after listening to bad karaoke from guests and decent, surprising covers from other cast members.

Some days, Bell didn't even let her have that.

He didn't want too much scrutiny. He needed people to remember the surprise of her voice and not how skinny she was, in case people who knew her saw videos uploaded online. It wouldn't be until several months after her abduction that she would be able to take the gig full time — which meant more torture for her ears in the meantime, more times she had to fight against the smells coming at her from the food court and from people getting food from it and settling in the crowd. Every powerful scent hovered in the air like heavy perfume.

It was all she could do not to eat the microphone.

* * * *

A month after entering Arcanium, Vivian stepped in front of the mic to see the odd chef dead center at the back of the crowd.

He was always busy, especially in the afternoons. There was no reason he should have left his post, but there he was. He had his hands behind his back, chin lifted. His glasses glinted in the sun, threatening to boil his eyeballs, but he stayed as Zen as always.

Why, of all times, did Sarah McLachlan's *Fear* need to start behind her?

The band opened the song with just the synth and Vivian's clearer voice — simple, soft, almost waiflike — but once the second chorus hit, so did the electric guitar, and she turned on the rock growl and shriek for the final 'fall'. Anger and frustration intertwined, trembling inside her and clawing through her throat.

As she finished in the clear voice again, those glinting glasses seemed instead like magnifying glasses that made her scrutable. When she was singing, she felt the way she thought other people did — exposed, without the layers of coldness and bitchiness that usually kept her stitched together. It was bad enough that Bell could read her mind. The last thing she needed was the odd chef to see her like this, to *know* her like this.

"What next?" she spoke into the microphone, looking away from the odd chef. "If you want me to sing more, what's your pleasure?"

She closed her eyes at the suggestion she heard most clearly, possibly from the circus ranks. It wasn't Miss Delilah's voice, but Vivian couldn't help but suspect the drag queen was to blame for making her do *Total Eclipse of the Heart*.

The intro began, locking her in. If she was going to do *Total Eclipse of the Heart*, she needed to do it right. She let the vamp out hard and tried to put every other melodramatic interpretation of the song to shame, her flowing long sleeves setting the mood along with the rasp in her belt notes.

As thunderous applause followed—most common after eighties rock songs, which everyone seemed to love more than anything else—she glanced at the odd chef. Just out of sheer curiosity. Not because she cared.

God, was he crying? No, that had to be sweat or the angle of the light on his glasses trying to burn a hole in his cheek.

Vivian never quite knew what to think when people had emotions beyond admiration when she sang. A few tears were okay, but if the set of his mouth was any indication, he was more than the ordinary level of moved.

"All right, everyone. I think I'm done for the day."

"One more, Vivian," Nasreen pleaded. "Come on. They want more. They always do. Haven't you been wanting to do *Black Hole Sun*?"

Vivian shook her head and backed away from the microphone, turning her face from the audience, although that just put her at a better angle to hear their boos. Nasreen was right. Two had been enough for her first time, but now that she looked like she belonged in Arcanium, three seemed to be the balance that satisfied when she couldn't give them a whole set's worth.

As Lennon opened the song, the soulful minor key kept her from walking away. She'd almost made it, too, right on the edge of the group of circus folk who had also been cheering for her to finish the three songs they'd come to expect. Vivian would've thought they'd be tired of her, or at least used to her, but they applauded as enthusiastically as the people in the audience who had never heard her sing before.

As the mournful whine of the electric guitar snared her, Vivian held her head against a growing pressure headache.

It wasn't the same manipulation as Bell, but it was manipulation nonetheless. Lennon knew it would work because he knew good music was her weakness, while she didn't know any of his, other than his fetish for bandmates — which she still had no interest in indulging.

She backed up to the microphone again and almost angrily latched onto the first verse. It was a lingering song, one that she played up with a strong vibrato that transitioned into her usual rock goddess in the chorus. During the instrumental, she filled the singer silence with classical notes soaring an octave higher than the electric guitar.

It was a personal song for her, one she liked practicing during the week, but she'd always balked at singing it for the performances.

So of course Nasreen had to bring it out when that damn chef was in the audience. She was practically metal-growling by the end of the song. Anger wavered with pain she tried to hold back but couldn't, and it showed in the unevenness of her voice.

Vivian didn't smile when she was finished, felt the warm spring sun around her while a black hole pulsed in her chest, ice cold, sucking everything of light and substance into its orbit to be consumed. Black holes were only noticed by the absence of light, and here she was, a voice from a black hole, noticed.

Singing was supposed to be her haven, her moment of real satisfaction, of adulation. But performing her favorite song had only left her colder. She couldn't meet anyone's eyes as she escaped for Oddity Row, well away from the food court and the odd chef — in case he wanted to come up to her and tell her how her singing had made him *feel*.

But when everyone had left and most of the strung lights went dim or turned off, the compulsion to return to the harem tent drew her inexorably back to him, back to the creepy demon who had her wrapped around his little finger because she could only eat what he had to offer — and she didn't want to eat it anymore.

She wanted her notes. She wanted her food journal and app. She wanted the moment when she could go to bed and feel like she had everything under control, where discomfort in her stomach meant she'd done well.

She wanted to be in Simón's arms, making him pant, making him almost cry as she edged him with her pussy, telling him he couldn't come inside of her and couldn't leave her yet. She wanted to fuck him on the couch while Fernanda went to sleep early in the bed she was supposed to share with her boyfriend.

She wanted her own bed, where she could stretch out and be naked whenever she wanted. She wanted a world in which the only person in the shower was her and no one could see when she was in the bathroom. She wanted to go to sleep without other people's sex ringing in her ears.

That shouldn't have been so much to ask.

All she got instead was being able to eat without gaining weight, but nothing she did was ever enough to quench her thirst, fulfill her hunger, quiet her body so that her mind had room to think. And Jonas watched *every fucking bite*, as though her body's reaction to food was enough sustenance for the demon.

She sneaked into one of the empty Oddity Row tents and perched on the stage, holding her knees against her chest as the murmur of the cast and guests gradually faded into silence in the darkness. There would still be a few solar-powered lights at the food court, although the floodlights would have been switched off, but she didn't mind the dark. Any darkness outside of her old childhood home had been safer than what she'd come home to, so she didn't mind the shadows of the oddity tent—a birdcage covered with cloth to calm the bird within. Her stomach and her breathing were the only things to break the enclosed silence.

No one came after her. No one forced her out or made her go to the harem tent for dinner. But in spite of that, and in spite of the multitude of little choices she made during the day, she couldn't help but think that those choices were illusions, that everything about her life in Arcanium had already been decided, that the choices she was given were the ones that didn't matter.

She couldn't stay in the tent forever. She could stay until the next day if she really put her mind to it, but her butt was bonier than it used to be, and the wooden platform in the tent was unforgiving.

She waited a while longer. Then she stepped through the red velvet curtain onto the Row. The clowns darted between the tents at the sight of her, like a pair of coyotes going after a rabbit, but once they recognized her, they ran back into the darkness without a word.

The trouble was that there was even less to do in Arcanium at night than during the day. She could always play her usual game, but what she really wanted right then was to *eat*, damn it, and to know that if she ate, it would make any kind of difference. Already she was so freaking bored.

Vivian didn't want to go anywhere near the food court, so she wandered into the Ren faire instead. There was no guarantee that what she'd find would be the fair's food or the circus', so she made sure to rummage around trash cans at the edge of the fair as far from Arcanium as possible, just to have *something* to eat that the odd chef hadn't touched. *Anything.*

She shoved a half-eaten turkey leg in her mouth. She knew it wasn't from the circus because it looked dry as hell.

The meat turned to nothing in her mouth — tasteless, textureless. She might as well have been swallowing air for how it hit her stomach. She tossed the leg back into the trash, but it didn't get any better with the fried mushrooms or the French fries or the cups of bad beer.

Ashes and water, nothing more.

"It's not fucking *fair*." Vivian punched the side of the trash can then clutched her hand against the pain before sinking to the ground to lean against the rusty, curved metal. Not the most romantic place to settle, but she couldn't give two shits.

"What are you looking at?" she snapped at Carlo, the legless Torso, as he passed through the faire, presumably from the parking lot, which meant only one thing. Pity she wasn't playing her game and pity she couldn't go past the edge of the faire to inspect parking lots, because the Arcanium cast rocked more than a few cars on a regular basis.

"I was just making sure you were alive. Around here, it's sometimes hard to tell. Need help getting up?"

"I can get up just fine. Piss off."

Carlo mouthed 'okay', shrugged and continued toward the circus, powerful arms flexing.

She banged the back of her head against the trash can for a few minutes. It sounded like a dinner bell, adding insult to injury.

The emptiness in her stomach seemed to expand. Not like what Bell had done to her at the eating contest. This was just what she'd been created to feel when she denied herself. It was the hunger she had experienced after that first night, except her body had grown used to indulging since then, and it protested much faster now when it didn't get what it knew it needed.

Vivian climbed to her feet, wiping her dirty hands on her jeans.

She made her reluctant way to the food court, each step feeling inevitable, like she was a lab rat being coaxed by cheese at the end of the maze just to get shocked. How could a filthy outdoor half-circus make her feel so much like she was back in the sterile environment of the hospital again? Wind up the little white rat, poke her with something sharp, see how she runs. Then punish her if she runs the wrong way or does anything a little white lab rat shouldn't do. Put her back in the cage until next time.

She could only be so lucky as to find a piece of good cheese before she was shocked. She wondered if lab rats got the good stuff. Lord knew the hospitals certainly didn't, even to tempt her and the other anorexics to eat. If they'd wanted her to eat a burger, why hadn't they gotten one that didn't taste like veggie pulp?

Jonas probably made a hell of a good burger.

Seriously, though, all this place needed to make the cosmic joke complete was a goddamn taco truck. The breakfast tacos weren't the same. She was talking street tacos — carne asada with avocado, pesca with lime juice and queso fresca, fajita veggie. If her mouth watered any more, she was going to drool.

Vivian didn't waste any time side-kicking one of the food court trash cans. Without muscle mass, she'd lost strength, but frustration and desperation created its own. Food and drink spilled out. There'd be some faire food among the rest, but it was more likely that anything discarded here had come from the circus.

She lowered herself to her knees and sifted through every paper basket, every strip of butcher paper, every napkin, every cup, every glass and aluminum container, systemically eating everything and anything she could as she went. She crawled halfway into the trash can to reach what hadn't tumbled forward. Her knees ground into buffalo and barbecue sauce. She didn't know what kind of crap she had on her hands anymore, because her fingers were covered with residue from everything she'd touched, even if it wasn't edible. There was a wrapped diaper, but she wasn't that desperate — though it didn't turn her off the rest of the smells in the trash can.

When she'd reached the bottom, she huffed, groaning as her stomach clenched its impotent little fists and cried for *more, more, more.*

This didn't taste like nothing. Flavor exploded in her mouth every time, which told her that it was all from the food court, except for the cockroaches that she grabbed and thought were dead but weren't. She'd throw up, but they actually tasted good — maybe because they'd been feeding on the odd chef's meals, too. Or maybe that was just Bell's sick sense of humor again.

One trash can's leftovers wasn't enough. She scrambled to the next, knocking it over with another side-kick. She raked her fingers through the garbage to pull more of it out at once this time. The amount of food that people just threw away sickened her more than eating it. There was a whole chicken leg's worth of chicken on the buffalo wing bones she pulled out. She hated beer, but she was already a good way tipsy on the partially filled cups and aluminum cans that hadn't spilled from her kicking the bins over.

"Vivian?"

Vivian hit her head on the top of the trash can as she jerked up at the sound of her name. Shane had her cardigan wrapped around her, facing away from the booth with the odd chef's hand on her shoulder, which meant she was on her way back to the harem tent.

Vivian looked around, confused.

She'd have sworn she'd only been to two trash cans, but maybe after the fifth living cockroach, her brain had thought a blackout would be better. All six trash bins in the food court had been toppled over and scrounged through, as though a gang of delinquent raccoons had done their usual dirty deeds in the dark. And considering she didn't know what her face paint had turned into after shoveling so much food into her mouth, she might have even looked like a delinquent raccoon.

"Oh my," Jonas scrutinized the consequences of Hurricane Vivian on his food court. "I thought we simply had vermin knocking about or that someone had decided to use one of the picnic tables for an enthusiastic tryst. If I had known it was you, child, I could have offered you better fare than this."

"I missed dinner," she said, still holding a turkey leg that she'd nearly gnawed past the first layer of bone.

"Yes, I know. I was there. Is there a reason?"

"Yes, there's a reason."

"Care to share?" he asked patiently.

"It doesn't matter."

She was less upset by the odd chef seeing her as Shane, who stared at the mess at Vivian's knees in something like horror. Had she never been this hungry before? If not, had she ever really been hungry at all? Had all this squirming and groaning and sad eyes just been a ruse to get the odd chef to personally feed her more?

Vivian liked Shane — as much as she liked anybody — but hatred burned so hot that her face flushed and she was surprised her eyes hadn't bored a hole through Shane's chest. It seared Vivian worse inside, though, that she'd been seen doing...this, *choosing* to lose herself in other people's discarded trash as though she were little more than trash herself. She could imagine what she looked like, what she smelled like. To carry that knowledge was one thing — to share it another.

Jonas patted Shane on her shoulder and touched her upper back to propel her forward. "Go on ahead. I'll take care of this."

"Are you okay?" Shane asked, hesitating.

"I know what you do in the kitchen," Vivian said. "Don't tell a soul what you saw."

Shane reeled back at the venom in Vivian's voice. "I wasn't going to. Have you told?"

Vivian shook her head, nibbling on the end of the turkey leg.

"Vivian is somewhat vulnerable at the moment, Shane." Jonas narrowed his eyes at the revelation that Vivian knew what went on in his kitchen, but if he'd really wanted to keep that a secret, maybe he should have locked the door. "You know how my girls get when they're hungry. Return to the tent and don't worry."

Shane kept looking back at Vivian, but she was eventually swallowed by the darkness on the other side of the food court lights.

When Shane was officially out of sight, Jonas took off his thick glasses and folded them into his pocket. Without them, the blackness of his eyes seemed absolute, and it was suddenly difficult to believe that anyone could think he was human.

"I rather thought we were beyond these temper tantrums, Vivian."

"Screw you with a raw carrot. Screw Bell, too, but you're the one who takes advantage of what Bell did to us. You're the one who feeds on our hunger. Or do you feed on our satisfaction? That's the shell game here, isn't it? We're always hungry because you take away our feelings of being full, you son of a bitch."

"You ascribe much more power and malice to me than I have. I'm a demon, but not all demons are dangerous, child. We're just manifestations, really, of different desires, different appetites, different temptations. It doesn't please me that you are always hungry. Far from it. It pleases me to satisfy. If you were satisfied for longer periods of time, that would please me more. Please, Vivian, come with me to the kitchen."

"I've seen what you do in the kitchen." Vivian wiped her mouth with the back of her hand, which probably only made the mess worse.

"And we will address that in due course, but for now, I'm sure you have more pressing concerns." He didn't offer her his hand, which didn't surprise her, given how fastidious he was with his gloves, but he stepped back and gestured toward his booth. "I don't have much, but I have a shower, and I can make a quick dinner, if you're done with all of…this." He surveyed the knocked-over trash cans with distaste.

"What are you trying to do?" Vivian held the turkey leg as though it were a club, which appeared to amuse Jonas more than anything.

"I'm giving you an opportunity to clean yourself and eat more than scraps before you go to bed. It isn't nefarious. I just want to help. And I'll keep your secret, as I keep Shane's."

"Is that a threat?"

"Even if you stumble back to your tent rather than accept my hospitality, I would never divulge what I see now to another soul. But your fellow Skeletons will know what you've been doing. It's smeared all over you, and you're covered with the very distinctive perfume of a restaurant dumpster. Please, Vivian. Come with me. I offer you comfort."

"Sounds like something a demon would say," Vivian muttered.

He cracked a smile. "It does, doesn't it? Purely human comfort, I assure you."

"Assure your ass." But she climbed to her feet again, finally getting a good look at herself, at least from the chest down. She looked like she'd been in a food fight.

"I suppose I don't have to warn you about the surprise of what's behind the door," Jonas said, stepping into the kitchen and beckoning her in. "What exactly did you see?"

"Shane on the butcher block. You with a plate of raw meat and fish. Her legs were open. Her cunt mouth was eating what you fed it."

"It's a delicate procedure to feed her bigger mouths without including fingers on the menu. I learned that the hard way. I had to regenerate this one." He raised his left forefinger. "It's nothing shameful. She just prefers to engage in that particular practice in private, especially when it comes to the mouth between her legs. It's unkind to use that against her when you suffer your own embarrassment."

She wrenched away when he tried to take her jacket off. He held up his hands to show that he wouldn't touch her again.

"The shower is over there. Just toss out the dirty clothes, and I'll give them to one of the golems. The leather goes to Sasha, but it's best for me to send the golems to her rather than arrive in person. She's nervous I'm going to use one of her snakes for an exotic meal."

"You cook snake?"

"Almost every living thing is edible. It's a matter of separating the food from the poison." He nodded to the left wall, which Vivian hadn't been able to see from behind counters.

A large aquarium had been set into the wall next to the two industrial-size fridges. Three blowfish swam among a small sea of coral bed, rough clams, shrimp and other small fish. And next to the aquarium was a mushroom garden. But he wasn't cultivating shiitakes. Vivian immediately recognized death caps and toadstools, which made her suspect that the others were just as poisonous.

"Are those even allowed in a kitchen?" Vivian asked, momentarily distracted from her own state.

"The mushrooms? No. The blowfish are, of course. I'm licensed to serve fugu, though I haven't had a proper sushi party in a long time. We sometimes used to do them for our Funhouse events, but those…stopped." Jonas turned his back on her, futzing about the kitchen for ingredients—tomatoes carefully snipped from the vine, red peppers, onions, butter, cream, blocks of cheese, a loaf of sourdough.

"The shower, Vivian. Surely your keen sense of smell can't stand the filth anymore either," he said quietly, still looking away.

"It smells like your food to me, and Bell made that irresistible to us. Everything else might as well be ash."

"That was just extra motivation to stay in the circus rather than try to escape," Jonas said. "Though you actually don't taste my food any more strongly than anyone else does."

Vivian didn't believe it. But now that he had drawn attention to the scents coming from her body, she smelled other things besides his food. She couldn't remember everything she'd put in her mouth, but she remembered enough. She could almost feel cockroach legs on her tongue.

She coughed against the fruitless urge to retch as she fled to the small bathroom, as spare as the alcove that comprised his bedroom. Vivian did as instructed, throwing articles of clothing out the door as she removed them. She hesitated before doing the same for her underwear, but it would be awkward no matter where she left it, so she tossed it, too.

His shower had just enough room to maneuver, with no-nonsense shampoo that was nearly full—since he was bald, she guessed it had been a while since he'd used it—and a store-brand shower gel. Bare essentials. But at least she smelled clean when she got out of the shower. There was only one towel. She balked because she knew it was his, and she didn't know him well enough to share something that had touched him like that. But his was the only towel in the bathroom, so she had to use it.

It smelled like him, which was an odd thing to notice, since the man always smelled like circus food and whatever weirdness he'd concocted that day, yet the towel smelled nothing like food.

His robe hung from the hook on the inside of the door, and it smelled like him, too. Like the towel, it was terribly familiar to wrap it around herself. His masculine scent, untouched by cologne or scented bath wash, reminded her of memories locked in cages. Her chest felt tight, her skinniness weaker. He'd said she was feeling vulnerable, but she hadn't been until the terrycloth embraced her body.

It was like maggots under her skin, and the most terrible thing was that it *wasn't* the most terrible sensation. There was comfort in terrible, familiar things, a reassurance of the nature of the world. It offered a sense of balance that threw her off, because it brought her back to when she was a child and she was definitely not a child anymore. It didn't help that she practically swam in his robe, her tiny limbs all the more apparent in the clothes of an average-proportioned man.

She eased from the bathroom as quietly as she could, uncertain and sick with it, just as unable to assuage the discomfort as ever.

Vivian approached the mushroom garden. There were the telltale destroying angels with their white frills and the classic red toadstool with white spots. Death cap she was familiar with, but there were a few cap varieties she didn't recognize. She shifted to stand in front of the aquarium. It was deceptively placid. Between the mushrooms and the blowfish, the odd chef had the means to poison a whole city if he wanted to.

A kitchen was already a dangerous place, with cutlery and the risk of food-borne diseases and food poisoning from improperly prepared dishes. And there were all kinds of poisons available in the average household, usually kept in kitchens and bathrooms. It was just a matter of off-label use. But to keep things known particularly for their deadliness seemed arrogant, like some kind of challenge.

"Have a seat at the counter, Vivian. I'll have this ready in a jiff." He pulsed an immersion blender in a small saucepan while two pieces of sourdough simmered on the grill in a bubbling layer of butter while cheese melted on top.

"Tomato soup and grilled cheese. Really?"

"Sometimes it's the simple things that are deceptively difficult to make great. Eggs, for instance, or pan fries. I'm rather fond of tomato soup and grilled cheese, especially on a cold night." He slowly poured a little cream into the saucepan, stirring through before salting and peppering. He took the saucepan off the stove then used the spatula to bring the two pieces of bread together and pressed until the combination of cheeses oozed out the size. He ladled soup into a wide bowl then brought the wooden serving tray over to her.

"Eat." It was a short command but gentle, with no implicit threat if she refused.

It was her stomach that would accept no refusal. This meal was fresh, smelled amazing, and it was just for her. Here, no one else would watch her eat, not even the odd chef, who had poured himself the rest of the soup in another bowl for himself as he puttered around what looked like an espresso machine.

"You smell much better now, more like yourself," he said.

"Funny, I was thinking I smelled like you, with your soap and shampoo and your robe."

She could tell he smiled by the lift of his cheeks. "I smell that, too. But you're underneath it. And, like you, I've an exceptionally delicate nose."

"What exactly do I smell like, then?"

"Would you like a golden milk? Also known as a turmeric latte, it's an excellent nightcap. I can drink caffeine late without ill effects, but I know most humans can't."

Anything that would add something to her belly. "Yes, please."

As she finished her soup and sandwich, he used another saucepan to make her golden milk while he set up the espresso machine for his own latte.

He slid the mug toward her, nudged her a bottle of honey shaped like a bear to flavor the golden milk to her taste then sat across from her, hands cupped around his own mug. "That's what you smell like. Warm honey. Now, how about telling me why you thought trash would be better than my dinner."

"It's no big mystery. I don't like what Bell makes us do. And that includes the whole eating schedule, the way he makes us completely fucking dependent on you, the way that even when we do everything right, it's still not enough. I mean, when I'm done with the milk, I'm going to want to drink the whole damn bear of honey." Vivian indicated the honey bottle. "I just ate the contents of six trash cans, a bowl of soup, a sandwich and a latte, and I'm still starving. It's not right."

The odd chef took a sip of his latte. "It's what Sandra had to go through before she arrived at Arcanium."

"Who the fuck is Sandra?"

"The previous Skeleton, the one who left before all the trouble. She would eat and eat and eat, but her body used next to none of it. As the Skeleton, she could finally feel full, f healthy. As for the rest of Bell's Skeletons, you'll never feel full, coming in as you did. But I remind all my Skeletons that they'll never starve."

"I feel like I'm going to float away on the next stiff breeze. It's not just stomach-grumbling, haven't-eaten-in-a-day hunger. This is haven't-eaten-in-weeks, nearly-dead hunger. It's not enough. What can I do to convince you that it's not enough?" She drank the rest of the latte, mourning the last drop as it slipped down her throat. "What can I do to convince you for more?"

Jonas took their mugs and put them next to the sink to clean later. "That's not how it works. I was given strict instructions. I'm given leeway to bend those instructions if necessary, but I cannot show favor to one and neglect the others."

"They don't need to know. As long as we're keeping secrets, what's one more?"

"It won't help," he said, not quite meeting her eyes. "More food isn't going to fill you up any more thoroughly. You'll be as hungry as you were before."

"I know it's possible to feel full. That's the reward, isn't it, for winning the eating contests? But if it doesn't make a difference how much you feed me, why *not* feed me more?"

"It's time for you to go, Vivian. The golems will bring you your clothing." He tucked his hand in her elbow, guiding her back to the door with unassuming preternatural strength. No matter how she resisted, he pulled her with him across the kitchen.

"Please." She grasped the door frame, stumbling between the tile and the dirt floor outside. "You have to know some kind of secret. I'll do anything."

"The secret isn't in my hands, Vivian." He remained patient, but there was a line between his eyebrows that wasn't usually there. His reactions were always subtle, but without his glasses, she could see more. She caused him distress, although she wasn't sure what kind. "The best hope you have is to starve for a while then wish respite from Bell. I cannot change your appetites. My only task is to fulfill them."

As soon as he'd gotten her outside the swinging gate, she raised her arm to unhook his hand from her elbow. "I don't think you're hearing me. I'll do *anything*."

"And I'm telling you there's nothing you or I can do."

"You can give me more."

"It won't help."

"I don't care." She grabbed him by the collar of the chef's coat and maneuvered him rather suddenly away from the front of the booth and up against the side of the kitchen, out of the light. "I want *more*."

He blinked. Then he took her wrists and eased them back. "I don't."

"Well, that's a little insulting, but if you'd rather have someone else, all you have to do is close your eyes. Everyone's mouth is the same in the dark. You can pretend." She trailed her long, bony fingers down the off-center buttons of his coat. "I don't care, as long as I get what I'm asking for."

He didn't look distressed anymore. In the dim light, he seemed uncomfortable instead, squirming away from her fingers—and not in an aroused way. She didn't understand what she was doing wrong, but rather than dissuading her, his discomfort made her want to convince him more, spurred her beyond reluctance. The more he denied her, the more she needed him to want her.

"I didn't expect this from you," he said. "I realize you've had a bad night, but you said you'd never beg me for food. You were adamant."

"Begging is wanting something for nothing. This is an exchange."

Vivian eschewed being coy over his coat and instead brought her hand firmly between his legs to find his cock. That he was flaccid surprised her. That he was so large while flaccid also surprised her, especially since he'd never exhibited even the slightest bulge. For a moment, both facts made her nervous, because she wasn't sure how to handle either.

"No, Vivian, I don't do this. I don't feel… Oh. Oh my God…" He stopped with a choking sound as the cock that she'd been afraid was beyond her control swelled with alarming speed in her hand.

This, however, she knew how to deal with.

"Another part of you begs to differ." Her lower register purred over her lips. She hoped it felt half as good over his skin as it did on hers.

He sagged against the wall, his head falling back. With his demonic eyes shut, he seemed only human, an older man caught in the throes of a much younger man's desire. He continued to grow beneath his trousers as she stroked him, thickening and lengthening to an intimidating degree.

Knowing that she had him in hand, literally and figuratively, turned her on more than she thought she would for him, but controlling men had always been a potent aphrodisiac — much better than oysters.

"You don't understand. I foreswore these appetites. I shouldn't feel... Oh God, Vivian, please stop." His usually expressionless face contorted as though in excruciation, and his matter-of-fact speech shifted into obscene groans that her ears liked as much as her mouth relished his food.

"Are you sure? Because it doesn't feel like you want me to stop." She brought herself against him, letting the shoulders of the robe fall down her arms. It wasn't the silhouette she used to display, but her breasts were still full, small but lush to contrast with the boniness of the rest of her.

He kept his eyes closed, but when her breasts pressed to his chest, he shook his head again. His hips jerked against his efforts to rub his cock against her palm. "Please, stop... I'm not supposed to want this."

"But you do. Don't fight it. It's such a little thing to give me what I want." She ran her free hand up his coat to his bared neck and stroked the bobbing Adam's apple before standing on her toes to kiss his moaning mouth.

"No…" But he parted his lips when her breath struck them, his nostrils flaring. Whatever he smelled conjured a deeper groan as he met her.

A strong hand grabbed her by her drying hair and yanked. Vivian screamed as she practically flew back.

"He said no." Bell's voice was quiet, but anger came off him like shimmers from a boiler.

"He wants it. Just look at him." Vivian wrenched back and forth, stretching to claw at Bell, but he was never where she struck at him and he didn't let go. Hair ripped from her scalp like tearing paper.

"Fight all you want, Vivian. I make many allowances for your history, but you of all people should know better." He practically spat the last words.

"I wasn't hurting him. You think that was rape? *That*? You have no *idea*."

She grabbed her hair closer to her head than his hands, which made the tugging hurt less, but now that she had a grip on it, too, he stopped being 'gentle'. He pulled her so fast that she fell, and he dragged her right out of the robe, leaving her naked in the open circus. Even so, she shrieked, kicking at the ground and fighting to twist out of his grip.

Bell flung her into the sandy enclosure outside the food court that the clowns sometimes used for tumbling performances. "I have *every* idea. It is *you* who don't understand. My law was meant to protect the humans from the demons, not the other way around!"

Whenever she tried to get up, he raised a finger from his outstretched hand and something pulled her feet out from under her again.

"If demons can observe the simple law that permission must be given, to stop when told to stop, it is the least someone like you can do. And to make sure you remember it, the Ringmaster will strike the reminder in lines on your back."

Vivian tried all the harder to get out of the ring, but she might as well have been trying to run on slick ice.

"You sick fuck, let me go! Degenerate prick! Self-righteous bastard! He was begging. He was moaning. He wanted me. He was going to come in his goddamn pants. You goddamn sadistic little *boy.*"

Bell crouched down where she was practically trying to swim through the shallow sand to get out. He was a quiet totem to her flailing chaos. "And you are a damaged little girl pretending to be a tiger. But your kitten claws are no match for mine. Do you realize what you've done? Do you have the slightest comprehension of the crime you've committed? Be *still.* Do. You. Understand?"

"No," she snarled. But with her hair in her face and her fingernails dusty brown where the whites should have been, she stopped struggling, because it only seemed to bring her lower before him.

"He is the rarest gem — a fireborn demon who chooses to not just look human but whose soul burns brighter than many human souls I meet, day in and day out. Brighter than yours, blackened frail thing. That isn't your fault, but what you do to my people is."

He slammed his boot on her hand when she tried to pull down his trousers — not to do what she'd planned to do with the odd chef but to humiliate Bell as much as she felt humiliated at that moment, as humiliated as she'd been when discovered among the trash cans. Anyone could come across them and see her. With the commotion she'd made, maybe they already had.

Bell ground his heel against her knuckles before kicking her away. "When someone tells you no or stop, Vivian, you *stop*."

"Then fucking *stop*," she shot back at him, holding her hand to her chest. Three of her fingers didn't want to move, but she didn't think they were broken.

He shook his head. "Not this. This is the consequence, my dear, for failing to observe the most basic of courtesies in a sexually fraught circus. The Ringmaster is on his way."

"He *wanted* me."

"He was aroused, Vivian," Bell said, dangerously quiet once more. "Don't confuse that with wanting you. And don't confuse his generosity with your control."

As though Bell had anticipated it, Jonas came running to the ring, the bathrobe over his arm. "Bell, please don't do this to her. It was my mistake."

"It was *not* your mistake." Bell kept his eyes on Vivian, his clenched teeth emphasizing the hollows under his cheekbones.

"I don't want her whipped because I was startled. It is my prerogative to withdraw my denial at any time, as it is my prerogative to deny."

Bell finally looked up. "You're protecting her. You know how I feel about this."

"Protecting her is also my prerogative — and the task you've given me."

Bell lowered his gaze back to Vivian. His lips thinned. "Very well. Once. Once, I will respite her from the whip. Next time, even your generosity won't dissuade me. It doesn't matter whether human or demon, man or woman. I will not allow this in Arcanium."

He released her from whatever held her to the ground, and Vivian scrambled up in a cloud of dust.

As Bell passed her, he gripped her hair to say in her ear, "You don't deserve him. Tread very lightly, Vivian. You are not hidden from me."

"Perv," she muttered back.

As Bell left, presumably to cancel the whipping, Jonas handed the bathrobe back to her. "You should return to your tent. You don't need to worry about anything else tonight."

Vivian took the robe, but she just stood there, gaping, as he turned around again and walked back in the direction of the food court.

"That's it?" she said, spreading her arms. She jogged after him, as her breasts would allow. "I thought you..."

"I withdrew my initial denial, not my present one." Jonas kept walking, maintaining distance from her. Safe distance. What he thought a skinny woman could really do against a grown man was beyond her, as was the wariness in his demonic eyes.

"You're still hard." She didn't have to be coy. The tent in his pants would have been comedic if it hadn't been so large.

"I'm not supposed to be." Mild irritation crept into his voice, but she didn't think it was directed at her. "I'll somehow convince it down, I'm sure. It's not your concern."

"What the hell kind of demon are you?"

He stopped. Turned. "Excuse me?"

"A woman offers to get you off, and you say no?"

"What kind of a human are you, propositioning a demon in the first place?"

"I've always known I was going to hell. It's where I started, and it's where I'll end," Vivian said. "Please... You're still hard. I can still give you what you want."

"But I'm not going to give you what you want in return for this 'exchange', which I'm certain goes under another name."

"There's nothing wrong with using what you have, and as long as money doesn't change hands, it's not prostitution. Men and women have been doing this since the beginning of time. Being a whore just adds a money middleman into the mix. Why bother when you can go right to the source?" She stepped closer, this time mindful that she didn't touch him. The last thing she wanted was Bell to interrupt again, which she hated more than the promise of a beating from the Ringmaster.

"I can't give you what you're asking for." But Jonas didn't step back this time. She hadn't put on the robe, and she could practically feel the path of his gaze over her. His nostrils flared again.

"What if that doesn't matter? You like a well-fed woman, don't you? I hardly look well fed enough, sir. I think I need more. Wouldn't you like to feed me?" In case she hadn't made her innuendo clear, she lowered herself to her knees.

He stared down at her, almost glaring, though with his entire eyes black it was hard to tell, his expression blank once more. His nostrils continued to flare every time he inhaled.

"Why you? Why you, of all the others?" he muttered. Then he brought his hands to the front of his pants to undo the fastenings. "What is it you truly starve for, Vivian? Shall we see?"

Jonas' mild voice deepened, became harder, almost mechanical. He grunted a little as he wrapped his fingers around his cock and drew it out, as though just touching it was too much. Its width was greater than her wrist, and as he stroked himself, he grew bigger still. It was difficult to believe a man could hide so much in his pants.

He looked slightly ridiculous, clothed but for his exposed cock, but all men looked ridiculous that way. His size more than made up for it with intimidation.

"Is this what you're asking for?" he said. "Is this what you wanted? Because you'll get nothing in return if we continue this dance. I can't feed you any more."

Vivian crawled forward, but he made a fist in her hair to keep her from starting. He wasn't as forceful as Bell, and he was sloppier, grabbing a part instead of the whole. Dark brown spilled from his hands on every side, swinging in front of her face.

He backed out of the light, leading her on her knees to the side of the kitchen where she'd pushed him against the wall. This time he leaned there of his own accord, licking his lips as she obediently followed, awkward on her knees but mindful of how he stared at her as she did so.

Jonas softened his hold, combed his fingers through the tangles he'd made. He looked troubled again, but this time he didn't try to stop her when she slowly raised her hands from the ground to his thighs, stroking her thumbs toward the sensitive places on the inside as she leaned forward in his hold. She wanted to tell him that everything would become so much simpler if he just let her have what she wanted, if he just let her touch him. But after Bell, she was hesitant even to bring her hands to Jonas' erection.

"Yes," he finally said in that deeper, harsher voice that shivered like hot liquid metal down her spine, and he let go of her hair and his cock.

She slid one hand up from his trouser leg to his erection, stroked upward at the same time she sank her mouth down over the head.

"God." Jonas pressed his palms against the side of the kitchen and, curling his fingers, dug grooves into the wood with his nails. "Oh *Christ.*"

It was like he'd never been touched before, as though he'd lived like a monk and never even allowed himself the luxury of masturbation, both of which were completely foreign to her. She moaned, taking in as much as she could, but he wasn't like some of those other guys she could deep-throat if she pushed down far enough. He was too massive for her mouth.

Her surface thoughts were flippant because the thoughts beneath were anything but confident or dismissive, and they troubled her as much as the darkness in his voice and the expressionlessness of his face with every slow, deliberate, pressured pull of her mouth over the head of his cock.

She'd corralled inexperienced men before, made herself their goddess to whom they could to present alms and favors in exchange for what she did to their untried bodies. It didn't matter much to her if they weren't to her taste. She could get the kinds of men she liked, too, even when they technically belonged to other girls.

Teaching a man that a woman held his pleasure by the balls was her own greatest pleasure. She'd reveled in the power she had, but that didn't mean she'd liked it when lovers past had shoved their cocks against the back of her throat, humping her face like dogs. She'd held on to them while they rode her, fucked her every which way, because she had one hand on their scrotum and the other on their marionette strings, and that was the way she liked it, even if she had to fake her orgasm.

But Vivian took in Jonas' cock like it was something special he'd made for her, savored the length as it slid over all the different taste buds in her mouth. She wanted him deeper, kept taking him deeper, until she was choking around him with not even half of his cock in her mouth and pushing into her throat. She swallowed, coughed, but let out shaky, staccato breaths through her nose every time she had to relinquish him.

Finally, she couldn't stand it anymore. She grabbed his ass, dug her fingers in and pulled herself down, swallowing him all the way, though her lips cracked.

She had no gag reflex—no use for it when she was meant for eating contests and other such high-volume feasts—but she coughed and couldn't breathe when her lips finally nestled almost to the base, the curly hairs there tickling her nose.

He exhaled hard, knees buckling, and his groan was one of terrible pain, but he stared down at her with intensity that pierced her, heat that might have been the coldest ice. "Yes, God, yes. Take it. Take it all in. Fuck, Vivian…"

When she started to black out and struggle against her own will, she jerked back and gasped for breath. Hot tears stung the corners of her eyes at no longer having him in her mouth, and when she braced herself against the ground, she realized that her thighs were wet and cold where she'd dripped down from her cunt as though she'd used too much lube. But she hadn't used anything. She hadn't even touched herself.

His cock was a gleaming, aggressive temptation before her, bobbing as he shifted to spread his legs for more balance. There were fresher grooves in the walls, but his nails were blunt as he traced them along her jaw, over her cracked, swollen, saliva-wet lips. He brought his hips forward, not to fill her mouth but simply to slide his cock against her lips, watch it stroke her, leaving wet marks over her cheeks and chin.

"I know you can do it. I know you can take me in until I come down your throat. I know you want me to fill you, that you crave the taste of me, the weight of me on your tongue. I know everything that thrills you to taste and that I am now one of them." He traced her eyebrows with his thumbs. "Go ahead, darling. Take a deep breath and take me in. Feast, as only my Skeletons can feast. Swallow me whole. *God...*"

Vivian moaned again as she sank down around him, but this time she wasn't sure how much of it was only for him to think she was into it. Because her pussy clenched as though it were accepting him—all of him, the whole of his two-inches-thick, over-nine-inches-long cock. And how did one little girl fit all that meat in her mouth? With enthusiasm—sheer enthusiasm. She undulated her tongue over the underside as she swallowed, swallowed, swallowed him down, all the way to the root once more.

She had never taken something that big before. She worked her mouth over him like a snake, practically dislocating her jaw, but aside from the cracking of her lips, it didn't hurt. When it closed off her windpipe, she convinced herself that she had more than enough air because she wanted his cock more.

He slid his big hands—*I should have known, with such big hands, big fingers*—through her hair and pushed her down, pushed himself inside her, snapping his hips. The head of his cock pressed against the back of her throat and deeper with slight bruising pains like something hitting her cervix. But she dug her nails into his ass and moaned so loudly around him that she almost drowned him out, even though she was the one muffled. She rocked her hips over nothing, her cunt squeezing out wetness like juice from fruit.

She nearly blacked out, vision clouding over, but he drew his hips back to bring the head of his cock to her tongue. He fucked her mouth as he came, pulse after pulse after pulse of hot cum over her tongue, over her taste buds, and she tightened her mouth around him to suck and swallow every last bit.

Even to her distorted perception of time, in that extended moment of pleasure and hunger and feasting, she thought his orgasm went on much longer than other men—a full minute or more of his cum down her throat, joining with the other things that he had prepared for her. And like them, it gave her the same brief satisfaction, as warm and tingling in her stomach as her climax was between her legs. But she couldn't think about that part of it. She drank as much from him as she could, though he came so fast and so much that some of it spilled from her mouth and dripped down her chin and his cock.

When she could milk no more from him, she ran her tongue all over his shaft to catch the rest of it, her moans no longer muffled and her enthusiasm humiliating to her own ears—as humiliating as being found with trash in her mouth.

Once he'd been licked clean and she couldn't find anymore, she gathered what had dripped and drooled down her chin onto her fingers and sucked from them instead. Like his cock, her fingers themselves tasted tempting, but it was the cum she'd wanted from him all along. She dismissed the afterglow of her orgasm as the afterglow of victory instead, enhanced by whatever magic ran through this circus and by how difficult he'd made it to have him before he'd succumbed.

The ones who played hardest to get were the sweetest to conquer sweetly. And she could be sweet.

Vivian's legs shook as she stood, but she'd been kneeling, and before that, crawling. And before that, she'd been afraid of being whipped. She continued to lick the cum from her fingers and her lips as he stared, intent but expressionless, his hands still in her hair, his cock still hard and inordinately impressive.

She drew her fore and middle fingers in to suck deeply for the last little remnants, startling another brief groan from the chef.

He drew her naked body closer to his, tilting her head up to him. "Vivian..."

Against his lips, she whispered, "I told you I'd get what I wanted." She kissed the corner of his mouth. "You fed me more."

Jonas stiffened slightly. He withdrew his fingers from her hair and instead clasped her shoulders to push her back.

She licked her lips again, although there was nothing left to feed upon. "Thanks."

Her work done, she backed away toward where she'd discarded the robe, shook it of dried grass and pulled it on. She was dirty again, but this time it was literally dirt as well as sand and grass — things that she could rinse off in the harem tent shower.

When she turned toward her tent, he still hadn't moved from the wall, although the angle of darkness made it difficult to tell if he'd tucked himself back in again.

Chapter Seven

The tent was dark when she entered, with the girls already asleep or almost there. But Shane's bed was empty. Vivian wasn't surprised when she entered the bathroom to find Shane there under the spray, her toothsome mouths slurping away at the soapy shower water. She didn't turn around as Vivian came in, hung up the robe on one of the wall hooks and stepped under another showerhead. She didn't need long, just enough to get nature off of her and to soap up the places where semen had coated her skin.

When she turned off her side of the shower, Shane turned off hers, twitching against the movement of the mouths.

"How long have you known?"

"A few weeks."

"You didn't tell the rest of them, did you?"

"They've already guessed. It's not like it's a horrible, awful thing that your other mouths need to eat. I don't understand why it bothers you."

"God, I hate how girls talk." Shane ran her hand over her bald head, avoiding the side with the gash. "What have they told you about me?"

"What *haven't* they told me about you?"

The panic that passed over Shane's face was too perfect, but Vivian couldn't keep it there forever, not when the poor girl was so *serious* all the time.

"I'm kidding, Shane. Nasreen pulled me to the side and said we all have...an eating disorder of some kind." Vivian didn't like putting a name to her problem, which her psychiatrist had noted during her first hospital stay. "She said you're a health nut."

Shane carefully toweled herself off. "I prefer to eat clean."

"Clean, natural, organic... Most of those words are meaningless."

"That's why it's so much work. You have to research everything. You've got to visit farms. You've got to know the name of the cow you're about to eat, if you can even eat meat. No hormones. No antibiotics. No pesticides. No GMOs. Gluten-free. When I couldn't find it in the grocery store, I joined co-ops and went to farmers markets. I paid more than I could afford to get things that I was certain were healthy and could put into my body."

"Doesn't sound too bad to me," Vivian said.

"You'd think so. But when you're terrified of dirty food, you end up not eating much. Anything that wasn't healthy—stuff with MSG or flour or sugar or aspartame or soy—I visualized as a black toxic sludge invading my body. Frankly, almost everything had *something* wrong, and every time I put something that hadn't been completely vetted into my mouth, I felt cancer growing, felt my pancreas and my liver and kidneys failing, felt my brain cells dying, my skin cracking…"

Shane shook her head. "It hasn't really gone away, those thoughts. I feel disgusting all the time. My mouths will eat anything, but they need meat, and I was always more particular about meat than anything else. Now I can't control what kind of meat it is, where it comes from, and I need someone else to feed it to me. The last time I tried to feed the mouth between my legs, I lost the tips of my own fingers. When Bell grew them back, I asked him what the hell I'd done to piss him off. He just did his whole cryptic fortune teller schtick and didn't answer."

Vivian squeezed the moisture from her hair. "What do you think you did?"

"I don't *know*!" Shane tossed up her hands. "I thought maybe it was because he was really tired of weight wishes, but he pulled you in and didn't do anything extra to you. Maybe you're just special."

"How the hell am I special? Bell doesn't like me at all." Vivian didn't mention the near miss with the Ringmaster. "He actually said that to my face when he brought me in. That's okay. I don't like him either."

"You're special because you already had talent. If you hadn't wished yourself into a Skeleton, Bell would have found another way to bring you in. Alicia has a good voice, but it's not the kind Arcanium needs. Bell built the Skeleton band the way he wanted to, enhancing or creating talent as he went. Then you walk in, steal the microphone, flash the band and bring the house down without a drop of his magic."

Vivian wasn't going to lie — the envy in Shane's voice felt good.

"You should have seen him when he first heard you sing," Shane said. "Maybe not making you worse than me was your reward for being perfect."

"I don't feel rewarded, thanks. Have you blacked out while foraging through trash cans for food?"

"Does the odd chef have to play gynecologist just to feed you? We've all done stupid things for food, but if you don't want anyone to know about that, consider it forgotten. Just don't tell anyone what Jonas does to me.." Shane shivered, trailing her nails over her arm where gooseflesh had risen in sharp relief over her pale, blue-veined skin. "The worst part is, the mouth likes it...so much. And when he's feeding me, I want... I want more than strips of flesh and chopsticks. Damn sex demons."

"Why does everyone keep talking about sex demons? What sex demons, and what the hell are they doing?" Vivian felt like she'd been left out of an inside joke.

Shane gave a crooked smile. Her own teeth were small and perfect in comparison to the snaggle throughout the gashes. "Wait! Has no one told you about the sex demons?"

"I mean, I've heard about them, but I thought they were a joke. Then I wasn't sure why everyone kept bringing them up."

Shane sat on one of the benches in front of the hooks. "Lady Sasha, the snake charmer, is a succubus. Lord Mikhail, the strongman, is an incubus. They turn this place into a hormonal nightmare."

Vivian paused with her towel held against her chest, halfway through patting down. "Is that why they're humping the Patchwork Pirate all the time?"

"Yeah. They're not allowed to touch us, because if they fuck you, they kill you, but Neve is a nymphomaniac and immune. When the demons hold back from sex for too long, it's unbearable. Then when they're humping Neve, that's a whole different release of magic, and it's unbearable all over again."

Vivian didn't know whether she'd go as far as to call it unbearable. It was uncomfortable. Inconvenient. But not unbearable.

She shifted her towel lower, as though to hide herself, when she thought of Jonas' cock in her mouth and her cunt dripping down her thighs. "Hell, is *that* why Lennon's always in the tent, screwing everyone like it's 1999? *That's* why the harem tent is like a swinger's house in the sixties?"

"Interesting melding of timelines, but yes." Shane laughed a little. "Harem tent. I haven't heard it called that before."

"Between Lennon and Jonas, I'm surprised they don't call it a brothel," Vivian muttered.

Shane tilted her head curiously. "Lennon's a horny little tentacle demon, but Jonas doesn't do that. That's why I let him feed me in the first place."

"But you want him to, when he's feeding you. When the sex demons" — yeah, she wasn't going to get used to that — "are unbearable, you want him to."

Shane tugged her cardigan over her shoulders and hid her body, suddenly shy again. Her nipples pressed against the thin knit, although it wasn't cold in the bathroom.

"What about Lennon?" Vivian asked. "You're the only one I haven't seen swarming around him when he comes into the tent to be worshiped."

"It's not like he can fuck me. If I bite off fingers, I can bite off other things. Eating between my legs is...arousing." She looked uncomfortable at that confession. Vivian wondered whether she'd told the other girls or whether Jonas knew what he was doing to her when he fed the mouth with such clinical detachment. "But it doesn't satisfy in *that* way. It can't. Lennon's accommodating, but after chewing on the end of one of his tentacles, he sure wasn't going to stick his dick in me. I sometimes suck him off, but my actual mouth is hungry, too, and it's disorienting, wanting to swallow a cock for the purpose of digestion."

Now it was Vivian's turn to be uncomfortable, but she tried not to show it.

"It staves off the worst of it, but Lennon is usually so eager to make his rounds that he doesn't always ask whether I need him first, and I don't like giving him a blow job when he's already been inside the other girls."

"That's fair." For someone who didn't like filthy things in her mouth, a used cock probably qualified.

"And although it helps, it doesn't fix what's turned on *in* me. Sometimes I come, but it's not for *me*."

"Have you asked Bell, despite him being the devil?" Vivian asked.

"He told me there's always a way, and it was my task to find it."

"Fucking toadstool."

"In a nutshell, not to mix our metaphors."

"You must be the teacher," Vivian said.

Shane snorted. "Alicia's the kindergarten teacher. I'm a horse trainer. *Was* a horse trainer. If Arcanium ever get animals again, that'll come in handy, but the closest thing I get to a horse is Ciarán, and climbing onto his back is more Moss' speed. Are you feeling better?"

"Pardon?"

"You were gone an awfully long time after we stumbled upon you, and when you came in, you'd lost all color in your face and your lips were bleeding. You were quiet. I thought you were still upset."

"Oh." Vivian pulled on Jonas' robe. She'd rather go to bed without clothes again tonight. It really was her preference. "He made me dinner in the kitchen."

Shane nodded, but she still peered at Vivian as though searching for something else. "He's done that a few times. Like I said, we've all gone through an adjustment period. He has rules but makes exceptions when he needs to."

Yeah, he's a fucking saint. I wonder if she'd still think so if she knew whose cock got swallowed tonight.

Before she went out into the harem tent, Shane paused at the tent flap. "We don't have to be friends if you don't want to. I'm not the friendliest of people myself. But I like your voice, and I like what you do with us in the band. As long as we're keeping each other's secrets, I hope you know you can ask me anything. Don't wait another month to figure out why you're randomly horny all the time. It saves some serious angst. Now maybe you'll take Lennon up on his offer the next time he comes in."

It was Vivian's turn to snort. "Hardly. The man can play and sing like a rock star, but I can't stand the smell of cigarettes. My stepdad smoked like a chimney, and it got into *everything*. Into my clothes, my pores, my nose, my mouth…"

"There are other men…or women, human or demon, whatever's your game. Everyone's looking for someone, and not everyone settles on just one person to meet those needs."

Shane had trouble making eye contact on the best of days, but she couldn't look directly at Vivian, and her nipples still pressed against her cardigan.

Vivian would remember that.

* * * *

When Jonas brought dinner to the tent the next evening, it was just like every other night. The other girls crawled to him to fawn like Dracula's wives, he served them twice what an average person would eat and he gave no one Skeleton greater favor.

He met Vivian's eyes through his glasses, but there was no sense of greater recognition, of something shared — no sense that he saw her as a drug to hit at the first opportunity, like the virgins whose cherry she'd popped before had. She didn't think he'd been an actual virgin. Weird or not, he was still a demon. He'd just responded as though he hadn't been touched in centuries.

She tried brushing his fingers when he handed her the bowl of chicken and gnocchi soup and the accompanying warm, buttery croissant ham-and-Swiss sandwich. But he eased himself out of her reach as soon as he could. He didn't jerk away, didn't glance furtively at the other girls in the tent, didn't act like he was embarrassed, ashamed or overwhelmed — all reactions she could have used. And the line of his pants was utterly uninterrupted, as though his hungry moans from the night before had had the shortest shelf life ever in the history of sex.

Never, not once, had she fucked someone who didn't want seconds. Men fell to her feet just because she deigned to spread her legs for them without the slightest bit of resistance. They could call her slut to all their friends, but they were the ones crying when they came. Once, a whole group of guy friends insulting her to each other's faces were individually under her thumb at the same time and had no idea. There was power in that, too.

It rarely made her popular with girls, though, which was why living with four of them was something approaching torture.

She waited for Jonas to acknowledge her. He didn't avoid her gaze the way Shane did. But when he turned toward her, his attention passed over like it had a hundred times before. He could have been a better actor than she'd given him credit for, but she knew men's body language and what it indicated about desire.

He didn't want her.

Vivian looked down at herself — bird-thin bones, taut skin, clothes that didn't quite fit, drawn gauntness in every hollow a starving body could create. But that's what she'd looked like last night, except with less clothes. Did he want something sexier? Did he want nothing on? Did he respond better to desperation, some kind of vulnerability? Was it the fact he'd caught her doing something humiliating?

She racked her brain. He'd become turned on when she'd forced the issue, when she'd brazenly touched him. He hadn't given her a chance to touch him so familiarly again.

After Shane had ducked into the bathroom for her shower after getting the rest of her mouths fed, Vivian discovered that Jonas had locked the kitchen door.

* * * *

The next few weeks passed in a haze.

She'd been rejected before. It hadn't happened often, but offering to fuck plenty of people led to an inevitable number who said no. After all, sometimes the men were gay.

But there was something about Jonas' complete lack of reaction that squirmed through her mind — as though none of it had meant anything to him.

Sure, it hadn't meant anything to her, but that's the way things were supposed to be. She was supposed to make him hard just to look at her, pull him into his kitchen in secret and take advantage of him whenever she chose because it would never be enough for him.

Instead, Vivian had been dismissed.

She replayed that night over and over, looking for clues in something she'd done, something she'd said, but his every sound of pleasure, his every touch, every time he'd pushed his cock past her throat, every pulse of his cum, all said that he'd been utterly bewitched.

Then why wasn't he looking at her? Why didn't he stiffen at the sight of her?

Why hadn't he invited her back?

She tried. She wore looser dresses to hide her thinness in case that was what had turned him off. When that didn't work, she tried tighter dresses, ones that showed off her breasts as much as her skeletal figure.

Then, as the rest of the girls crawled to the cushions in their tea dresses and pearls, Vivian walked to the table and knelt on the cushion without a stitch on.

He didn't react, but Shane stared at her as though she'd grown a third tit like Miss Delilah. And Alicia looked like she'd sucked on a lemon, which seemed eminently appropriate with the lemon chicken that Jonas had prepared.

She didn't look at him while she ate, didn't try to touch him, didn't do anything but express her usual guttural appreciation for each burst of flavor in her mouth. Two could play at that almost unintentional innuendo.

When he served lemon meringue pie to her, Vivian thought the silver pie knife trembled. But that was it, and it could have been wishful thinking on her part — the worst kind of thinking in a circus like this.

* * * *

Bell still didn't want her to just take hold of the Skellies and run. On the contrary, he actually scaled her back. Instead of the perfect three songs, he sometimes only let her do one.

The cast members were a mixed bag when discussing whether to keep the karaoke going, but Vivian suspected it was Bell's way of punishing her after he couldn't let Ringmaster use his whip. Her sensitive nose close to the food court and her sensitive ears listening to the butchery of overpopular songs was indeed an insidious form of torment.

It was better when Miss Delilah and the Quandary had some fun at the microphone.

They were good as well as unusual, and that encouraged the audience to step up their game. Whenever the karaoke portion of the afternoon went well, though, there was no need to bring Vivian out for more than one hardcore number.

Vivian fidgeted as she listened to a decent rendition of *Paint It Black*, which reminded her of her beginning at Arcanium with an awkward mixture of nostalgic and disgust. The Quandary watched her reaction with their usual quiet amusement. Vivian liked standing with the Quandary and Miss Delilah, and although she didn't say much, they both seemed to like that she liked standing with them.

Bell came to the microphone, the consummate shirtless host. "Thank you so much, everyone. We hope you've enjoyed our modest musical efforts. Please visit our food court for performances in the ring all evening from our clowns, tumblers, acrobats, dancers and oddities."

"Fuck, wait." Vivian stopped fidgeting and straightened, holding her stomach against its usual grumbling.

"Were you not supposed to sing today?" the Quandary asked.

"I'm always supposed to sing. It's why I'm *here*." Vivian looked around in confusion and something approaching hurt as the crowd began to disperse. Her ego was saved only by members of the cast and even some people in the crowd showing the same confusion.

The band hesitated, but as Bell stepped away from the microphone, they withdrew from their own mics and started to unplug or turn off their instruments.

Vivian turned around where she stood, taking in other people's bewilderment amid her own and incensed with everyone else's indifference.

A still black form drew her eye. The odd chef had stepped away from his booth to see the band. To see her. To see her when he'd been wanting nothing to do with her. But Bell had cut the band's set short as though he hadn't known she was right there, anxiously waiting for her chance.

"Are you still punishing me, Bell? Did you change your mind? Am I just another Skeleton now?"

But Bell either didn't hear her or had no interest in answering.

It was bad enough that the odd chef wouldn't acknowledge what had happened, ghosting her to her face. But for Bell to take the only thing that briefly spared her hunger, something that other people could admire her for when they rarely liked her for anything else...

"I guess it's back to the salt mines," Miss Delilah said.

"Sorry, sugar." The Quandary rested a delicate hand on Vivian's back before turning to join Miss Delilah among the slowly dispersing cast.

No. No, this is not happening. He's not going to take this from me.

She went against the flow of the crowd, pushing through some of the other cast members with tears threatening—being hungry seemed to bring all the humiliating feelings to the fore, because she couldn't remember almost crying this much since she'd first left home.

She snatched the center microphone from a golem's hand before he could take away the whole mic stand. Her urgency failed to faze him. He just took away the mic stand by itself. She tapped on the microphone. It popped through the speakers.

"It's over, Viv," Lily said, jumping down from the backup singers' platform.

"No, it's not," Vivian said. "It's not over until this skinny lady sings. I don't know what's going on, but this is *my time*. This is..." There weren't words she could use that would describe what being able to sing with the Skellies meant. There was a barrier between those emotions and her tongue, but it was more powerful than almost anything else inside of her.

"Everyone's going back to the rest of the circus," Alicia said as she collected the rest of the microphones. "Bell dismissed us. We're done."

"Do you always do everything Bell tells you to do?" Vivian looked from Alicia to Lily to Shane. They all appeared unsure, but they were still breaking down the makeshift stage.

"Well, yeah," Lennon said. He was already halfway through dismantling his amp setup. "Kind of the whole plot, love."

Vivian lowered the microphone, but when the golem came back for it, she hissed at him like a cat without shame, and he placidly returned to other duties.

"Look, I know I've given you no reason to do this, but I want to sing. I'm supposed to sing. And as little as anyone likes me, you like my voice. I don't care what Bell says, whether he forgot or whether he's being a passive-aggressive asshat. Just one song."

"Big Man has spoken, kid," Lennon said. "If you want to busk in the food court, I'm sure Bell won't mind. But the band portion of the afternoon is over."

"It doesn't have to be complicated. We can just do piano." Vivian turned her increasing desperation, dizzying in its intensity, to Nasreen, who had a lot more to unplug. "Please, Nasreen."

Alicia paused with her handful of microphones, narrowing her eyes as she looked over where the crowd had once been. Vivian looked behind her. Jonas was still there, a motionless form against the fluid, chaotic movement of the guests spreading far and wide away from the band, away from where they were supposed to be when she sang.

But for a moment, it wasn't about getting the kind of positive attention she rarely received or being envied or having her art received. The odd chef had come out not to hear the band but to hear her. He was waiting for her.

She had his attention.

Vivian looked back to the band again. Nasreen and Shane were the only ones who'd stopped breaking down the stage, but they weren't rushing to put things back again.

"Fine. I'll do this myself."

She tapped the microphone again. Either the golems hadn't gotten to that part of the soundboard or they seemed to think that if she insisted on having the microphone, she intended to use it.

Vivian didn't look behind her, back toward the dispersing crowd, didn't meet Jonas' eyes, as she began *The House of the Rising Sun*. If the other members of the band were too cowardly or disliked her too much to stick their necks out, even for her voice, she knew how to make it work acapella.

Even so, with everyone returning to their circus activities, trying to sing without the band made Vivian seem as desperate as she was. They all had to be rolling their eyes, from the most ignorant of guests to the cast members who knew something had gone wrong or that she'd done something to piss off Bell. And now she'd shown everyone how much she needed this, how important it was to her, shown that they could weaponize it against her as effectively as Bell. And since they all followed his lead...

She closed her eyes and turned back to where the crowd would have been, to where Jonas had been waiting.

As she started the second verse, Nasreen added her synth, and Shane backed with a beat. Fuck, those were actual tears she was shedding — tears of relief, tears that arose from pouring hydrogen peroxide on an open wound. By the time she reached the second chorus, Lennon's electric guitar had joined the fray, so when they reached the instrumental solo, Vivian lowered the microphone and just let the music sweep over her.

Then it all fell away, but it didn't feel like an end, and she brought the microphone back up to sing the first verse again in the acapella she'd started with, but with every last dirty edge of her voice that moved through her throat like claw scratches over wood, so rough it could draw blood.

When she finished, she let the microphone fall again and opened her eyes to where she expected the odd chef to be.

But at least half the crowd had returned, obscuring her line of sight, and they all cheered, especially the guests who had been so reluctant to leave before because they'd been expecting her. She closed her eyes again, let it cover her like the music, and with the same relief. She was still here. They still saw her. They still heard — and it was still good.

Vivian kept her eyes closed as she brought the microphone back up. "Sorry, folks. It seems there was a little mix-up. But I'm so pleased to be here, and I've got one more for you, ready or not."

She sang the first few lines acapella again, but once the band had an idea of what she wanted, they proceeded into the song they'd rearranged in their traditional symphonic metal sound, using her more innocent clear voice for the verses and the wicked rock edge for the chorus. During the second chorus of *Toxic*, she found Jonas again. He hadn't moved, but as the crowd resettled in their standing places, he was easier to find.

He wasn't crying this time, but he barely seemed to breathe as he watched. With his black clothes, pasty skin and Coke-bottle glasses, he suddenly seemed alien, as though even his more human nature wasn't enough to counteract the demon inside of him. And that alien beam of intensity had fixed upon her, leaving her inexplicably lightheaded through her careful breathing.

At the end of *Toxic*, the applause was even louder. The circus cast had gathered on the edges once more, and Miss Delilah and the Quandary were her most enthusiastic fans.

But Bell stood behind Jonas now, and like Jonas, his expression was inscrutable. He hadn't interrupted or shut off the power, so even if it hadn't been his plan, Vivian assumed her hijacking the band again had been an acceptable outcome.

"Encore!" Miss Delilah shouted in her Wagnerian baritone. "Encore!"

"All right, one more." Vivian looked directly at Bell as she said it, searching for his reaction, but though he crossed his arms, the gesture didn't appear to be defensive or irritated.

With her first line into *Sally's Song*, there were cheers through the crowd—also some laughter, though not derisive. It was a simple melody, easy for less practiced voices to sing along with her. She switched into classical soprano for the instrumental solo but used her clearer voice for the rest of it. This wasn't the place for the rock goddess edge or anything that could scratch or shatter glass by the very sound.

"Thank you, everyone. Have a wonderful evening." She finally dropped the microphone and walked away. Satisfied. Applause followed, with cheers from the motley crew of cast, even as they dispersed for a second time.

Vivian walked the long way around so that she didn't have to get near the odd chef's booth, but he was still there at the back of where the crowd had been, and this time he was dabbing his cheeks under his glasses.

"Really, what kind of a demon are you? How do you even function?" she asked, but not as angrily as the last time. It was difficult not to be amused by a demon moved to tears by music.

"I feel, Vivian." He said it with a certain amount of emotionlessness, but despite his lack of affect, the handkerchief suggested much more went on behind those obscured eyes and obscure face. "As much as any human, I feel."

She hadn't the heart to tell him that he felt much more than she did. Wasn't that the point Bell had made? And for some reason, that hurt her now, while her brief feelings were still raw.

Bell came up behind her just as she was about to pat Jonas' shoulder in an awkward but semi-sincere way. She jerked her hand away. She didn't think the proscription against touching included a harmless 'there-there', but there was nothing wrong with being paranoid when that seemed to be Bell's intention.

"You own the direction of the band now. No more open mic," he said, "unless that's what you want to set your voice off as the lovely thing it is. And you may invite guests from the cast as you like. Please, don't misunderstand me. I orchestrated this rebellion. I wanted you to take ownership of your own volition so that I would know that the band matters to you as much as it does to me—but don't make a habit of it." He raised an eyebrow in implicit query.

"I understand." *Oh, I understand, you absolute troll.*

"I thought you would." The way his strange, beautiful eyes seemed to glow amber within the hazel as he left, he'd heard her thought. Whether the harshness of his face concealed amusement was left a mystery. Shane was right. He enjoyed being an enigmatic fucker.

Jonas touched her cheek lightly. "I must go back to the booth. But it is always a pleasure, Vivian."

"How much of a pleasure?" she called after him.

* * * *

It took all her willpower not to dig through the trash cans in the dark again while she waited for Shane to come out from the odd chef's booth, but this time Vivian wasn't starving. Hungry, always hungry, down to her marrow. But she'd had dinner. She could wait.

Shane came out alone. She noticed Vivian, because Vivian was all alone at a picnic table in an otherwise empty food court. But though Shane chewed on the inside of her cheek, she must have decided not to ask why. She nodded in acknowledgment but kept going, which made Vivian respect her all the more.

Even so, she waited until she couldn't see Shane anymore before going up to the food booth.

The kitchen door was already locked.

"Jonas, I'd like to come in."

"Kitchen's closed, Vivian, and I have tarts to make."

"I'm not here for food," she said.

"Yes, you are."

"I don't understand why you're resistant to this." Vivian pressed her forehead against the wooden slats, cool in the night. "It literally benefits both of us."

"And I don't understand why you don't understand why I'm resistant to this."

"It would help if we weren't talking through the door."

"I don't trust you."

Okay, that kind of hurts, too. She wasn't the most trustworthy person in the world, but when a demon said they didn't trust a human being... "Bell got his point across. I'm not going to take advantage of your virtue or anything. I just thought I could stop shouting through a door. You know I speak from the diaphragm."

Vivian sighed when her comments were met only with silence.

"Jonas, I'll go all *Moulin Rouge!* if I need to. If you tear up to *Nightmare Before Christmas*, how long do you think you'll last with *Your Song*?"

The deadbolt thunked. Jonas opened the door wide enough to put his head through, but he blocked the door with his boot. He'd taken off his glasses, which meant a little more of his emotion came through. "I can't put that much salt into the tarts. You play dirty."

"What about me ever suggested that I don't?"

"What kind of a human being are you?" he said.

"The kind that plays dirty. We do exist, you know."

"So do demons who don't."

"Can we talk?"

"Just talk?"

"I promise nothing, but I won't touch you." She struggled not to roll her eyes. "Deal?"

The shift of his eyelids suggested that he took in the sight of her in his bathrobe.

"I thought it was time to return it," Vivian said.

"You're not wearing anything under it."

"Those black eyes are awfully perceptive. Strange how they didn't notice me naked those other times."

"They noticed. I need to finish these tarts."

"I'll let you finish the tarts. But I don't like being ignored."

"I noticed that, too." Jonas sighed. Then he walked away from the door but left it open.

She slipped in. After a thought, she deadbolted the door behind her. Jonas heard it but he didn't comment.

Across the stainless-steel counters were parchmented trays of tarts. He'd filled about half of them with the tequila lime filling. There was an empty white bowl with a pair of chopsticks in them on the butcher block, so it looked like Shane had eaten all of her meat for the night.

"Do you have a dishwasher somewhere?" Vivian asked.

"Next to the sink. Leave the chopsticks there. They'll need to be hand-washed."

Vivian tucked the bowl into the dishwasher, left the chopsticks where he'd told her then used a warm washcloth and soapy water to scrub down the butcher block. He set a vinegar cleaner on the corner, which she used without a word.

Then she sat down on a barstool at one end of the block and watched him finish filling the tarts. He placed each tray in the clear-doored refrigerator before wiping down the counters.

"Aren't there golems to do that for you?" Vivian said.

"After hours, I prefer to do the work myself. And I do have more work, Vivian."

"You have to sleep sometime."

"Technically, no, I don't. Demons don't have to sleep. We just like to. And I have too much work to do during the weekends to justify sleep. I sleep during the rest of the week when not planning, prepping and sourcing ingredients for Bell to procure."

"Or picking up fresh roadkill from the shoulders when we travel?" Vivian asked, almost dreading the answer.

"No shame in using good meat. A culinary demon, like a cooking witch or a food fairy, is good luck to any kitchen. We keep things from spoiling. The meat in the walk-in freezer might last one of your lifetimes."

"Demons and good luck?"

"You sound skeptical, but if we couldn't do things that people thought they wanted, we wouldn't be very effective demons, would we?" That, at least, seemed to amuse him enough for the corners of his eyes to crinkle up, though his mouth stayed an even line on his face.

"I would expect a demon to do all kinds of things that you don't do," Vivian said.

"That's a choice I make. I *can* do them. I choose not to. I chose this kind of life a long time ago."

"Who would choose to live like a eunuch?" Vivian asked.

"Well, eunuchs, to start with." He went to his coffee machine and glanced back at her. "Would you like another golden milk?"

"I don't know. Is that too much extra food for me?" she said dryly.

"It's not much. It just tastes good and should help you sleep. I have cockroaches from my own cockroach farm, too, if you'd like a snack. Elizabeth won't let me use any of her American browns, which seems excessively protective."

"I'll pass." Her mouth watered anyway. "Just the golden milk, please."

He set the honey next to the mug of golden milk. "You're being nice. That's not a good sign."

"I'm nice."

"Vivian. You're *not* nice."

As usual, the golden milk had been heated to the perfect temperature. His attention to detail even for simple things could so easily be overlooked when she wasn't there to watch him do it. She was dismal in a kitchen herself.

"If you're such a sensitive demon and I'm not nice, why bother with this conversation, then?"

"Because you're persistent, and I have been avoiding you when you don't appreciate that treatment. But I haven't been ignoring you."

She squeezed a spiral of honey into the golden milk and stirred it in. "You might as well have been."

"It's not a good idea to treat any one hungry child with favor, because hungry children can be dangerous. You've seen what can happen when a hungry child doesn't believe she's being fed. Now imagine one is fed more than the others. The only reason the other Skeletons allow Shane to be fed extra meat is because she's so different from them. But you've been given the same curse as the rest, so you can't be given any more food. I simply can't do that for you."

"I accept that. What I want now is something different, something that feeds me more but isn't the same thing at all." She hummed as she swallowed down a good fourth of the mug. She bet his chai latte was devastating.

"Why do you want that from me?" He cupped his coffee but didn't drink. "Even Locke didn't think to use me in that way. I am eminently average, neither desirable nor undesirable, skill my only redeeming feature."

"I don't care what you look like."

"You care that I can give you what you want." His normally dispassionate voice became clipped and sour.

"What's your deal with quid pro quo in the bedroom?"

"Is that all you've ever had? An exchange?"

"All relationships are exchanges. A meal for a kiss. A necklace for a blow job. Everyone knows about it, but no one wants to admit it happens."

"I have not had my own arrangements in many centuries, but your conclusions are reductive and inaccurate. Perhaps all of *your* relationships are exchanges, as well as those of everyone you've surrounded yourself with to confirm your view of the world."

She laughed, incredulous. "How did you end up the romantic and me the pragmatist? Is this Backwards World?"

"It's Arcanium."

"Right. Arcanium, where demons can be human and humans can be demons, where demons make the whole circus sexual except in the kitchen? Who died and made you special?"

"You're a lovely girl. Why do you insist on pursuing me? All other men, demon and human, can give you what you're seeking now with me, much more willingly. Ciarán can fill a bucket."

Vivian sputtered into her mug, coughing, milk coming out of her nose.

He handed her a clean washcloth. This time he was smiling.

"Good to know. But I thought anyone else couldn't serve us," Vivian said, still coughing.

"You and your industrious nature have found a number of loopholes where I didn't believe there were any. Go forth and exchange to your heart's content. You no longer have to concern yourself with someone who will not allow himself to pay you greater attention."

Along with being ignored, Vivian hated being dismissed. And he knew that just as well.

She pushed the empty mug toward him then tugged on the tie to the robe. She didn't have much to hold it up. It took only a shrug for the thick material to fall away.

"Are you telling me you feel nothing? You pulled me closer to swallow your cock, to salivate over what you served me, but now we're back to being dispassionate and dismissive. What did I do? What *can* I do?"

He took the mug and turned away, his shoulders slightly hunched over the sink. "Why are you so eager to corrupt a demon? If it is conquest you seek, you have an endless supply, cast or guest, to conquer to your heart's content. If you prefer a challenge, the Gentleman has yet to find a lover, and he offers quite the unique experience when not distracted by feeding off of young fear."

Vivian stood. "What's wrong with wanting you?"

He spun around, almost hairless eyebrows drawn in. "Because you *don't* want me."

"And you don't want me?" she snapped.

"Of *course* I..." He threw the mug into the sink, shattering the ceramic, but it wasn't enough to drown out what he'd almost said.

Vivian took a tentative step toward him. Usually she'd know how to respond to a man who liked to throw things. It involved taking off her shirt or getting on her knees, but neither of those things seemed to work for him. "You *do* want me."

"I don't know why."

"Once again with the insults here, Jonas. I have feelings, too."

"No, I don't know why, after two hundred years of focusing all my skills and appetites on food, when I am finally at peace, my other appetites decided to rear up and take hold of me again. I worked hard to leave behind what I was, to discard the hungers with which I was born and the indulgences I shared to satiate them. I have no more use for sex or affection or similar creature comforts. I suppressed everything. But after years in Arcanium among the incubus and succubus with no effect, why did your touch undo everything? Why do I want to abandon the discipline I love to sink myself in the comfort you offer, a loveless, meaningless distraction?"

"I'm not seeing the bad here," Vivian said.

"It's not what I *wanted*. It's not what I came here for. I wanted to cook. It's what I love. It fulfills me. When the sex demons had no effect, I thought I was safe. I thought I was..." He slowly picked up the larger pieces of ceramic from the sink and tossed them into a bin underneath. "I thought I was free."

Vivian reached out to touch his arm through his chef's coat, but she remembered that she'd promised not to touch him. "I sound like a personal apocalypse. You say the sweetest things."

"You certainly set a romantic mood yourself, Vivian."

"I'm fucking romantic. I just need to know how I can make this more palatable for you. If sex itself isn't enough, what more can I do?"

"This is what I'm talking about. It's still the exchange for you. Sex is the transaction, my seed your payment, and you think you need to sweeten the deal in order to get what you want, which you don't even need from *me*. What is it that you can't find in my dinners, in the performances, in the trash cans, in the simple pleasures offered to you, in wishes fulfilled? What keeps you hungry, child?"

"I'm not a child. Do I look like a child to you?" She stepped back, her hip striking the butcher block. "What else do I need to do, Jonas? Light candles? Rose petals? A romantic picnic for a thick dick? What?"

"You're used to being given everything you want, aren't you?" Jonas stayed against the sink, his arms crossed. Unlike her, he didn't mind looking defensive. The chef's coat was like armor, thick and buttoned from neck to midthigh, and he still wasn't hard. If he wanted her, why wasn't he hard?

"Yes!" she replied in frustration. "If I want a good dinner, I wear a good dress. If I want a trip to Miami, I buy a good bra. If I want my friend's boyfriend to buy me a diamond, I do all the dirty things she's not willing to do. You hit the jackpot, Jonas, because I'll do anything if you just tell me what you *want*." She picked up the honey, flipped the lid up and turned it upside down to drizzle over her chest, over her breasts, over her abdomen. "You want a taste of honey, something sweet to sweeten the deal? I feed from you, you feed from me. Is this more fair?"

Jonas hadn't been moving, but he seemed to still even more, his head tilted down to watch the honey drip down her body as slowly as molasses.

Vivian paused with the honey bottle still poised above her body. "Is that what you wanted? Something that you can taste, too?" She brought the honey back up her body and poured a thicker line onto her breasts. The amber liquid sank with seductive deliberation down to collect on her left nipple in a heavy drop that threatened to fall.

"See? I can be sweet," she said softly, not wanting to break whatever kept his gaze on her breasts rather than on her eyes like a gentleman.

"You're always sweet," Jonas said. "You're just not nice."

"Nice doesn't pay the rent, sweetheart. And it certainly doesn't get you what you want."

"I give you that. If I were less nice, I would never have let you in, and you never would have wasted my honey."

"If you show me your spice rack, I'll waste your cinnamon sugar, too." She'd be his fucking sopapilla if that was what made him give in.

He lowered his head, turning away, but obviously trying not to laugh.

"Don't look away from me." She shifted from irritation and a bit of playfulness to the voice she'd used to finally convince Simón to kiss her with Fernanda in their bedroom, sleeping off an upset stomach. Vivian had versatility both when singing and not. Her voice could grate, but it could also purr, and when she spoke like that into a reluctant man's ear, sometimes she could practically see his cock jump in his pants. "You said you wanted me. I'm here. Just fucking take me."

She squeezed the honey bottle again. The buildup of honey on her breast weighed down the drop over her nipple. It grew pregnant then slowly dripped down suspended in the air, growing thinner. As bony as she was, with neither enough thigh or hip to stop it, the honey threatened to drip onto the tile floor.

Jonas lowered himself to one knee to catch the thread on his tongue, curling it in to snap the dripping honey from her breast, although it still gathered on and around her dark nipple.

He didn't touch her, but his arms caged her against the butcher block. He swallowed the honey from his tongue, licked his lips, closed his eyes. Then, his eyes still closed, he followed the next drip up to her nipple and took half her breast in his mouth to suck the honey from her skin.

Vivian gasped, her head falling back and her knees going weak at the sudden and unexpected intensity. This is what she'd tried to make him do, but she'd expected to be denied, expected the frustration now the way she expected the hunger.

He worked his mouth over her breast, pulling back slowly to draw in as much of the honey as possible. By the time he reached her nipple, the suction was almost unbearable, nipple aching and clit pulsing as her cunt squeezed like a cider press. When he moaned, it shuddered through her, joining the arousal that pooled in the cavity of her pelvis, thickening and warming everything between her legs. God, she'd forgotten how strong it had been last time, when all she'd been doing was pleasuring him. Everything about her seemed to melt, to drip like the honey.

Jonas released the butcher block to grasp her hips and keep her upright. He hummed into her skin, moving his lips against her. "Honey on honey should be redundant, but it's not. It's as though I taste what comes from you."

He found the honey wherever it was thickest, mouth hot and tongue broad and firm over the bony landscape of her body. Somehow, he managed to surprise her again at her other breast, catching his teeth on her nipple this time.

Her hand holding the honey spasmed and the bottle fell to the floor.

He slid his hands down her hips to her thighs, digging fingertips into the scant flesh. Then he grasped her hips and lifted her up as he stood again. His strength was as unexpected as the size of his cock. He didn't look strong, didn't look like much of anything, but even skinny as she was, he lifted her as though she were nothing. He gently slid her onto the butcher block, crawling without effort over her legs to crouch on his hands and knees over her honeyed body.

"What are you...?" Her question faded into another gasp as he continued to feed from her, cleaning as much of the honey from her chest as possible. He groaned like he had when she'd taken in his cock, but it had a different quality this time, more like the groan of someone who had just tasted something so terribly delicious that it made their teeth ache.

She ran her hand over his head but there was no purchase there. He was bald and smooth in spite of the late hour, no stubble to create friction, and his body over hers was suddenly so much bigger. The change in orientation made her understand how much smaller she was in comparison, how substantial his flesh against the wisp of hers.

He licked his way down her sternum, which was still sticky. She'd grabbed the first thing she could think of to put on her body, which meant she hadn't really thought through the repercussions. But he didn't seem to mind, because as he brought his mouth to the corrugated jut of her lower ribs and her concave abdomen, he slid his hands up to her breasts, taking the tight, dark nipples between his ungloved fingers and rubbing them until her hips lifted from the butcher block. His fingers and palms briefly stuck to her skin, as though the honey sought to glue them together, but as she grew warmer under his hot hands, beads of sweat thinned the stickiness, making it easier for him to gather it over his tongue.

He maintained the same thorough intensity as on her breasts, groaning his pleasure with every pass of his tongue. What surprised her now was the intensity not from him but from her.

Yes, she was getting what she wanted. Convincing someone to have sex with her was one of many conquests that turned her on. But even screwing Fernanda's boyfriend in her own house—sometimes daily—hadn't given her this kind of rush. Conquest was heady, but this arousal was everywhere—a mist in her mind, tingling over her skin, following his mouth and drawing down to defy gravity between her legs in a prolonged, profound ache. Her clit pulsed as though sending out a beacon. She'd come with Simón's cock deep in her ass while she'd muffled her moans in one of Fernanda's throw pillows, but her own orgasms had always been secondary, a pleasant accessory to her victory.

Whatever these sensations were, they were stronger than victory, so that victory became the accessory and pleasure her prize. And the closer he came to the pulsing, prickling center of her arousal, the more victory threatened to disappear entirely.

Jonas abandoned one of her breasts to gather some of the honey from her abdomen onto two hooked fingers, which he brought up to her mouth. She sucked his fingers eagerly, moaning from the sweetness that spread over her tongue and the taste of clean skin underneath, a potent combination that made her shake as she grabbed his wrist to push his fingers deeper. She held his hand to her mouth and his head to her belly, unaccustomed to so much attention lavished upon her and not sure whether she liked it, but if this was what it would take to get what she'd come for, what he would come for…

When he shifted his sucking mouth past the line of honey to the dark, trimmed bush over her folds, she twitched, her legs impulsively trying to cross.

Then he closed his mouth around the flushed, swollen bud of her clitoris — with softer mouth and softer tongue, but no less intense and with as much relish as over the honey of her body.

Vivian shot upright. The only thing that kept her from jumping off the table was the fact that he was still over her, caging her legs. He slid his fingers over her tongue once again, and she moaned in the midst of her confusion, but then she pushed his hand away from her and jerked her own hand from the back of his head.

The next pass of his tongue around her clit squeezed a cry from her newly freed mouth. It echoed against the harsh, cold steel and tile. Her head fell back, but she shook it from side to side, a no she wasn't able to articulate, so she shoved his forehead back. As soon as he'd withdrawn, his expression dispassionate despite the smears of honey and saliva over his mouth and chin, she pushed herself back and crossed her legs as best as she could.

A butcher block was hardly the most comfortable thing to sit or lay on, especially with her bony ass, but he seemed unperturbed by any pressure on his elbows or knees. He raised himself with the flexibility of a much younger, fitter man. From everything she'd seen and heard, she wondered how much she saw was as he actually was.

She panted as he knelt above her, alien at this angle, with the harsh kitchen light reflecting against his scalp and his pale skin grooved with shadow.

"Did I hurt you?" he asked quietly.

Vivian shook her head, but her tongue felt heavy and dull, her spine straight and hot, not with chocolate warmth but molten steel. She'd had men go down on her before, but it was rarely their favorite task, and toys in her solitary home had sufficed with far more effectiveness. It served no purpose for her, never had. It was a mouthful instead of a fingerful of honey — too sweet, too strong — and it jittered over her nerves like static shock. Too much. Too much of something that she couldn't even name.

"Don't do that," she said, sounding drunk and young, and she hated it, because in a room like this, there was nothing forgiving in either echo or reflection.

"Even though it makes pleasure course through you, thickening your scent?" He brushed his sticky thumb over the corner of her mouth to catch where a bit of honey had been lost.

"Yes." She turned her mouth away from him. "Don't do that."

"Perhaps you can understand now why I told you to stop before." He dismounted from the butcher block. "Are you okay?"

"I..." Vivian shook her head, but in uncertainty rather than denial. She uncrossed her legs now that she knew she was safe, then turned on the block and wrapped them instead around his hips to bring him back to her, on more familiar ground. "I'm fine. You just startled me. I don't need any of that. I just want this."

She tucked him between her parted legs and tried to bring his mouth back to her breasts but he resisted. Perhaps it was the stickiness of the smeared honey and saliva on her torso pressing to his chef's coat. Or perhaps it was the fact he still wasn't hard. She'd assumed from his groans of gourmand pleasure that he would be as hard and thick as before. But she felt nothing, nothing at all.

"I thought you wanted this." She pressed the heel of her palm over the front of his trousers. She couldn't feel anything. "What did you do? Did you get rid of it entirely so I couldn't do anything else to you? Then what use are you to me?" Vivian pushed at his soft abdomen and used her feet to shove at his thighs to get him away from her.

"I do want you, Vivian. And no, Bell doesn't grant such respite to anyone in his circus — part of the circus' dubious charm is the sex demons' influence. If you haven't been driven wild by their influence before this, perhaps you had some natural immunity and weren't prepared for the full measure of their magic, as I was not prepared. We are overwhelmed together, then."

"You certainly don't look like it." She nodded pointedly to the lack of interest showing in his pants.

"Since that night, I've had to bind myself. That's been a torment of its own, but it was the only way that I could walk into the tent with you there and not show you the kind of favor I swore my Skeletons would never suffer from me." Jonas undid the placket of his trousers and parted the sides to show an attempt to use bandages to tamp down his sizable cock into a clean, smooth front. "You tested my resolve, and the succubus tested it all the more with her magic, but I still tried to deny myself. You make that very difficult, Vivian. Because you make me want to be hard for you. You make yourself delicious."

He brought his mouth to her jutting collarbone, continuing to take in the remnants of the honey that had resisted being cleaned from her skin, and she tentatively touched his head again, returning to familiar ground once more.

He tasted her all the way to her sternum then worked his way up her neck where there was no honey for him to taste. Her hair had stuck to a few places where the honey had dripped, and he tangled his sticky fingers within the thick locks he gathered in his hands, but she could handle that. It all washed off in the end.

She hummed her own pleasure when the muffled sound of discarded cloth on tile signaled that the bandages had been removed. She wrapped her legs around him again to pull him in, pressed her lips to his scalp to reward him for the cock brought up flush and hot against her abdomen.

She had just reached down to cup his balls and stroke up the considerable and still-growing shaft when he used her tangle of hair around his fingers to pull her head back and kiss her.

He tasted of honey, and he smelled like her. Vivian jerked away, but both taste and smell drew her closer, irresistible to her appetites.

She abandoned his cock to grab onto his fitted chef's coat. That melting feeling had returned, that sense she quivered into weakness that she hated. He kissed her sweet as honey, his tongue as thorough and intense in her mouth as on the rest of her, his moans that of a man feasting rather than kissing. His cock grew harder and hotter against her belly, and he brought her closer, his closed eyes tight and his forehead drawn as though in pain. She kept her eyes open, because her mind was sliding, sliding, slipping as though down a hill of ice, and she didn't want him to pull her down with him.

She wanted to get down on her knees, wanted to wrest his orgasm from him so that she could take a shower and forget about the quicksand she'd escaped, but the longer he kissed her, the more she forewent his cock to wrap her arms around him to bring him flush against her, the more she felt herself sinking, lowering herself before him.

She'd never had problems kissing before, like she'd never had problems with a man trying to go down on her, but she'd never felt more control than when a man's dick was inside her, and she had to remember why she was doing this. She was doing it to make her body as addictive to him as his food was to her. She was doing it so that she, like Shane, could get more from him — pure and simple.

But this was neither pure nor simple, because she hadn't been pure in a very long time, and this wasn't going at all the way she'd planned.

When Jonas backed away from the butcher block, he took her with him to his small bed. He lowered himself to the quilt and drew her legs more tightly around him, continuing to taste her mouth as though it was the honey he'd licked from her body.

Vivian tried to find her way back to the scenario she'd set out to create. She changed how she kissed him, quickened the pace, tasted him back, sucked on his lower lip the way she'd suck on the loose flesh of his balls if she were kneeling between his legs, where she would prefer to be. She changed her moans, finding old rhythms, the ones that drove the men she'd ensnared insane, the ones that had them staring up at her with wonder in their eyes until she made them roll back.

She rocked over his cock, her folds spreading over his thickness. The arousal that had decided to drip from her at an embarrassing rate like before slickened the way to offset the stickiness of the honey. She tried to push him down on the bed, but he whipped them around so that she was underneath him, his body as hot and heavy against her as his cock was against her pussy. But he still didn't fuck her and didn't seem to want to let her to make her way down to take his erection in her mouth again.

"Don't you need me to take care of that cock for you?" she murmured as she guided his mouth down from hers to her neck again, although now that she was already worked up, that didn't help tame the sensations quite the way she'd wanted it to. She'd known about the connection between her tits and her clit, but she hadn't known that neck kisses could be anything but a nuisance. She bit her lip, swallowed hard, curled her nails into his scalp before she realized she was doing it.

He raised his mouth from her neck and looked up at her, poised and still like a reptile, which unsettled her all the more with those big black eyes not inches away.

"You've been aching so long. And I've been wet for you, wanting you all this time, touching myself in my bed, naked underneath the covers, just as naked as I was at the dinner table. Did you want me to pinch my tits for you then? Did you want me to press them together so you could fuck them in front of the others? Or did you want to pick me up like you just did and throw me onto the table, screw me from one end to the other?" She reached for his cock, bit her lip again when she found him as big and thick as he could become. Her mouth watered to consume him, and she tried to tug him ever so subtly to climb up her body.

He didn't comment, answer or move, although his cock twitched and pulsed in her palm. She wanted some kind of reaction, any kind of reaction, wanted more from his face than he seemed willing to give.

"Come on, baby. I want your cock in my mouth. I want it to fill me. I want you to cum forever down my throat. Fuck me with that great big cock. Make me come with you inside me. I can't wait anymore." She arched, rubbing the front part of her folds against his cock. She briefly looked away from him as her clit met his flesh, hotter and needier than her own. "God, you're so damn *big*. Don't you want my mouth feasting on what you serve, the way your girls are supposed to do? Don't tell me this never even crossed your mind before me. But I'll take everything you give me, no matter how deep, how hard you want to—"

"Stop."

"What the fuck, man?" She released him and pushed his chest again. This time he settled back on her legs, his cock free from its confines and folding up his coat. "What do you *want* from me, damn it?"

"Calm down, Vivian. I want you to calm down." He tucked his hands over her waist. With his larger hands, he could wrap them completely around if he wanted, but he slid them up to map each rib, her breasts, the knobs of her shoulders, her neck then framing her face. "And I need you to stop lying."

"I'm not lying," she protested, but he placed one large finger over her lips.

"You lie almost as much as you breathe. Sometimes it's as simple as your tone. But I taste every lie — every single bittersweet one. You're lying now because you want to get this over with, because when I try to feed the other appetites within you that starve for satisfaction, you stop me — which tells me why they're so starved to begin with."

"I don't know what you're talking about."

"Another lie. It's as pointless to lie to me as it is to lie to Bell. I'm not prescient, but my palate is tremendously sensitive."

With his hands still cradling her head in a way that threatened to feel like choking but without his hands squeezing down, he guided her to sit up.

"Whenever you try to regain your equilibrium, you resort to tactics that I assume have worked in the past. But every one of them tastes like ashes to me, as food from the outside tastes to you, because they aren't true. When my cock was inside your mouth and you drank me down, that was honest *in spite* of your efforts, in spite of the lies thick through your mouth. I won't do that again, Vivian. You don't need to manipulate me to get what you've come here for. All you need to do is let me serve you. The demon inside me wants to serve, whether my food or my body for your feast." He stroked over her lips with his thumbs, licked his own lips as though suddenly thirsty. "Your appetites call to me with honesty you are incapable of. Will you allow me to feed you?"

He dipped his thumb just past her lips. She tentatively parted them to run the tip of her tongue over the pad.

"Now, calm down, Vivian, and just feel. You'll have what you came here for in the end." He leaned in to kiss her again, withdrawing his thumb to replace it with his uninsistent tongue sliding over hers. "But I know what you really need," he murmured before taking her mouth and kissing her down onto the mattress, sliding his cock over her clit with purpose.

She couldn't calm down, but his efforts were nonetheless effective, pulling her from her own mind, her own plans, no matter how she resisted. It didn't help that he was a good kisser, not content to let her control the kiss, more controlled and controlling than she would have anticipated from such an otherwise passive demon.

When he pulled back again, she hated — *hated* — how she followed him with her mouth, her whimper caught between them and something she couldn't take back. She considered hitting him. Maybe her handprint would permanently flush his colorless skin.

But he brought his hands from her face and neck to her breasts and slowly but firmly pinched and twisted her nipples to harden them again, to remind her that she was aroused as hell and there was more she could take — evidenced when he pinched harder, lifting her one bit of softness and weight up by the nipples alone until she closed her eyes and squirmed with another whimper she couldn't take back.

"Are you salivating, Vivian? Sorry, wrong mouth. Are you wet? Remember that I'll know if you lie."

Her nipples were dusky purple from the blood gathered under the dark skin. He didn't stop playing with them, didn't let her get her thoughts together long enough to lie. She tried to shake her head, but she nodded instead at a particularly strong string of throbbing pulses through her clit.

"Good girl. Are you hungry?"

She nodded again. Always hungry. He knew that perfectly well.

He let go of her nipples. Her breasts rippled as they settled back over her ribs. She covered them with her palms to soothe the fading pain and keep him from doing it again, but he instead brought his fingers to the buttons of his chef's coat.

She tensed, and he paused. But when she didn't tell him to stop, he made short work of the tailored coat, shrugging it away and leaving it on the floor with the rest. He wore a plain undershirt underneath that showed off nothing, showed how unremarkable he truly was, unathletic, by all appearances without the strength he'd shown, the curl of hair over him like that of most older men to whom she'd made herself available.

The only thing of note was that he'd had his arms and shoulders tattooed — a full cornucopia across his upper back and parts of his arms and some kind of script on either arm, although she didn't have the patience to read it.

Something about him was almost like a hitman — someone who had once been on the frontlines and whose body might have impressed once, but who had retired from the shadows into a more sedentary life. There was something underneath, a kind of hardness unexplained by flesh alone, certainly not in the places where weight had accumulated into something softer, more comforting, skin silky but hair rasping over her palm as she slid her hands up his arms.

Usually she knew what to do, but she didn't know where to go from here if controlling him was off the table.

He was patient, though, with unsettling silence and stillness as she tested his skin and what was underneath it. She usually preferred more slender older men, men with the same boniness she liked in women, because it made her feel stronger. Men with muscles rarely came with the brains to try to manipulate her. The muscled ones *wanted* to submit.

Jonas' body was different than both of her usual preferences, and the shudder in her fingers scared her. *He* scared her, not his big hands and defined forearms from cooking, not his huge cock, not the tattoos that made her think of retired gang members or Mafia, not his demonic nature — whatever it was. She didn't want to pinpoint what about Jonas scared her, because then she wouldn't be able to go through with this.

"Don't be afraid. I won't hurt you. I *can't* hurt you." Jonas pulled his undershirt over his head.

God, she wished he were as strange as his face, as strange as his eyes, because he was so damn normal. He was any man and every man, and moving her fingers over his tattoos, down to his own small nipples, his soft abdomen, made her feel shaken loose, like cogs in a broken clock.

"If it helps, Vivian, close your eyes." He crawled back from her body to push down his trousers, leaving him naked. Strangely, she couldn't remember the last time she had been completely naked with a completely naked man.

Though she closed her eyes, she also found herself curling to the side. Why couldn't he just let her suck him off and get it over with? Why did he insist on these formalities that were so unnecessarily intimate?

She could gather the robe and run. She didn't have to stay. She didn't have to fear some unnamed shadowy figure looming over her in place of the odd chef, who she trusted to keep his word far more than he trusted her—both of them justified in their respective levels of trust.

Jonas didn't force her onto her back again, didn't push apart her thighs. He stroked over the wing of her hip. "You're safe here. Nothing will hurt."

"That's what they all say, hoping their dicks are too big. But yours actually is. Jesus, are all demons like that?"

"Almost all demons are like this, and most of us, even the dark ones, prefer to make it painless. But it's not my cock you're afraid of, Vivian."

"I'm not scared. Why the hell would I be scared?"

He sighed. But he lowered himself to kiss over the hip he had stroked then up her side, finding his way back to her breast—gentler, more tongue than suction. He raked his teeth against the underside of her breast, a caress rather than threat.

She turned onto her back again of her own volition.

Jonas licked a line up to her throat, closed his mouth over the center as though kissing her voice then slowly brought his body down against hers as he took her mouth.

Every movement, every choice, was deliberate, so much slower and considered that she was accustomed to. She was used to frantic and needy, used to that high she got from being so wanted in the moment that they dragged her into closets and bathrooms and spare beds, into backseats and alleys. She wasn't used to slow, and somehow it swept her up more than another man's need. He was a riptide—subtle, invisible, yet so very hard to fight as he pulled her under. He slid his cock over her abdomen, his pre-cum mixing with the sticky, heating honey and drawing it down between her legs as he shifted his hips lower.

"What do you hunger for?" he murmured against her lips, massaging her scalp through her hair, which in itself made her groan. God, how could one man be everywhere, and how could just the slight friction of his body be enough to set each point of contact alight like flash paper?

She wound herself around him, arms around his back, her legs parting to wrap around his, which gave him permission to spread them more and position the intimidating head of his cock against her pussy.

For a moment, she tensed.

But he pushed inside, filling her to the brim and squeezing out her wetness around him, and he kissed her as though wanting to eat all of her. Nothing hurt at all.

"Oh *God*," she moaned into his mouth.

"He's never been a part of this. He's never understood." Jonas slid a hand down her body to hook under one thigh, giving him something to hold as he braced himself next to her head and rocked his cock into her.

His simple little bed creaked with each thrust. It would almost be funny, cliched, except that creaking hit her like his groans. His eyes were closed now, the pained look on his face returned. He shoved into her hard, but every other movement was still agonizingly slow, savoring, the same way he kissed to consume, though she was now the one taking him in.

She curled her nails into him again, scratching down his back, squeezing her pussy as though to hold him in every time he thrust all the way to the base.

"More," she whispered. "I need more."

God, yes, she was swallowing him, taking him deep, deeper than anyone had ever reached, though so many lesser men had tried. It should have hurt, but it didn't, just like everything she ate should have destroyed her but didn't, and her mouth watered at the honey on his lips and chin, at the taste of it down on his chest. She bit his shoulder. *More.*

He roughened his thrusts. The metal headboard of the bed now struck the wall of the nook it had been tucked in, joining with the creaking springs and the sounds of their bodies, the sounds of their voices in the stark acoustics of the rooms. It jostled memories she didn't need, memories of darker rooms, a heavy body above hers, heavy breathing. She knew what she was remembering—all the things she'd tried to forget—but as much as she hated the memories and the helplessness within them, she couldn't tell him to stop.

Her arousal was much stronger now, unfazed by the turn of the screw in her belly, of the shadow that hooded her mind. Pleasure swam within the darkness as though it had always been a part of it, shivering her harder and making Jonas shout as she sank her nails in deeper, tearing skin.

It all tightened, heated, prickled with electricity, coiled like a midnight storm around where he filled her, where he fed her. Fuck, was she going to come like this? Was his cock alone going to make her come when she'd usually had to fake those orgasms, when she'd had to hold tightly to their trespass to bring herself to climax or just do it herself later with her fingers fast over her clit? She could insinuate her hand between them and stroke herself, but instead she dug more lines down his back, conjuring another low, pained groan. He nevertheless quickened his pace.

She closed her teeth hard over his shoulder. She could almost taste the ink in his tattoo, but strangely, it was the blood over her tongue that pulled her over, although she shouldn't have been surprised. If his cum could satisfy, why not his blood?

Jonas cradled the back of her head and rolled to bring her over him. He pushed up as she spiraled around him, and he came hot inside her, groaning like he'd eaten entirely too much at the feast. Every pulse of his climax was one more drop lost from her throat, but she was still coming, still rocking over him, her clit teased by the hair at the base of his erection and her pussy clenching, all out of her control as she nearly screamed through her orgasm.

And this was no lie, no carefully crafted expression of pleasure. Her hair surrounded them, some of it caught in her mouth, as she cried out helplessly through the strongest, trembling peak she'd ever reached. She'd thought people had lied when they'd told her how good an orgasm could feel, when they talked about fireworks and other explosions, as good or better than drugs. Sex for her had always been about control, not pleasure. The pleasure she had on her own was adequate—relaxing, but not explosive.

Vivian thought her head would burst, that she would lose her voice as she muffled herself in his bloody shoulder again.

"Yes, Vivian, ride it, feed upon it, *feel* it. Let yourself feel it."

With his back out of her reach, she clawed at his quilt. She might have actually torn a little hole in one threadbare place. Then she lifted herself upright and let gravity sink her all the way down his cock, grinding her entrance at the thickness at the base as she tried to raise herself away from the rolling pleasure. Gravity also seemed to pool the pleasure away from the headiness in her mind, but it meant the aftershocks were almost as strong as the climb itself.

"Did you think...?" Her words caught on one of the aftershocks. She forced her hips to still so that her brain could work again. "Did you think that you'd be able to stop me from getting what I came for by coming inside me?"

"It won't hurt you."

"Please. I'm not afraid of getting pregnant. Everyone around here's fucking like rabbits without being on any BC or cold-sore cream. Nasreen told me getting sick is impossible, and this doesn't seem like much of an atmosphere for a baby, especially with the clowns being promised stray kids."

She carefully lifted herself off his cock, fascinated by just how *big* it looked between her skeletal thighs. Her labia appeared taut to the point of pain, setting off her clit, flushed and shining under the dark hair above it.

From the sheer amount of cum he'd produced, it was only a matter of time and a few good pushes.

His semen trickled out of her to dribble down his cock. It looked as good as icing to her. She swallowed against the sudden hunger returning to hit her like a slap in the face, even though his blood still spread copper through her mouth. She'd expected demon blood to look different, something as black as his eyes maybe. But it bled from his shoulder like that of a human, dark red and thinner than honey. Little flowers of it bloomed on the quilt underneath him.

As soon as most of his cum had dripped from her onto his cock, Vivian crawled back, her eyes on his.

He raised himself up on his elbows, seeming more real than anything else at Arcanium at that moment, carnality in its rawest form.

Her stomach clenched like her cunt, and with the same kind of pleasure, as she lowered her mouth over the head. She felt like a starved vampire, drinking him in again, with all of his cum right there for her this time rather than something she needed to work for.

He stayed hard, pulsing, feverish over her tongue. And he was moaning again, moaning like a woman who couldn't get enough, but in that small, unavoidable space, there was no mistaking the shape of his body and the crude jut of his cock as anything but masculine.

He never would have been the kind of man she'd play with more than once on the outside. For that kind of man, she'd turn to someone like Simón, a hound with great abs, a hair regimen to rival her own and a car more expensive than he could afford. It wasn't about attraction. Most of the men or women she'd seduced, whether just a flirtation or sinking into their bed, weren't attractive to her. All that mattered was what they offered. They were just another person under her thumb, another notch on her belt.

Something about this man at whom she would never have looked twice, a man so normal that he stood out in a crowd of freaks... She wanted to eat him, all of him. She wanted to take his cock down her throat then just keep going, swallow him in her mouth and her cunt until everything was inside her. She didn't know whether that was attraction. It was so foreign to her that it might as well have been.

She bobbed over his erection, sucking every last bit of the seed mingled with her arousal that she could, although more slithered down her leg. His eyelids fluttered and his breath hitched as he fought to keep his hips on the quilt, but he no longer seemed weak, and his softness no longer seemed pliable. And though he was under her, she somehow couldn't make him lower, no matter how she tried to suck his soul from his cock.

"Vivian, I'm going to come. I'm going to... Gods above and below. I know why you tried so to control your food, to control Bell, to control me. When you let yourself go, this is what you become. This hungry...little...thing." He grabbed her hair and sank her over him. She coughed against the cockhead but forced herself to keep swallowing as he came, filling her throat once again, although not as much as she'd squeezed out onto him. She stretched her arms out to grasp the quilt in fists, holding herself down and moaning as she continued to swallow, until the only thing down her throat was intractable flesh.

As though in counterpoint to her own fists, he closed both of his in her hair to pull her up. Saliva dripped from the corner of her open mouth as she reached with her tongue to keep him inside of her. Her pussy twitched, thrumming with arousal that didn't feel new — just a continuation of before, unbroken.

He guided her until she leaned in of her own accord to kiss him. Her mouth tasted of blood, semen, flesh and salt, but though he had fed her more, she somehow felt even more unsatisfied, unable to tell one hunger from another.

"Come to me now, my hungry girl." He lowered himself onto the bed again and pulled her head up to draw her body forward. Then he let go of her hair to grasp her hips instead.

Uncertain but mesmerized by the raw craving on his usually neutral expression, she raised herself up on her knees to let him settle his head between her legs, his mouth under her pussy. He petted her thighs as though in reassurance then raised his chin and licked through the opening of her cunt, wriggling his tongue between her folds up to her clit again.

At her first whimper, she brought the back of her hand to her mouth, grasped with her other hand for something to hold, because his mouth was heaven and hell in one orifice — as feverish as his cock, firm but tender over the sensitivity that had followed her first orgasm. He caught her clit with his tongue, drawing it in with soft sucks, keeping her pleasure hard. He stroked over her sides, her back, her legs, caressing her as though his hands, too, could feast, meager though she was.

"Don't cover yourself. No one's watching. No one judges." He shifted away from her clit, sucking on her labia, sliding his tongue between the folds to places she didn't think should feel as much as they did. "This isn't about winning, Vivian. There is no winning, no losing.

There is no conqueror or conquered. There's just this. Don't block your pleasure from me. There is no need to impress. Just feel. Revel, child. This is why I am here."

He redoubled his efforts, not just on her clit but all over her, every part of her seeming equally delicious to him. Vivian shuddered over him, her thighs quivering to keep her up, though he might not have minded if she smothered him with her pussy, because he was doing it to himself. Never had she seen any man or woman so enthusiastic about going down on a woman, his moans vibrating in an intermittent stream through her.

Pleasure mounted higher once more, manipulated and nurtured not by herself, her own cleverness or pride, but all from him. She couldn't bite her hand, bite his shoulder, bite the blanket or do anything enough to stop each and every moan that he sent through her with his mouth alone. She grasped the headboard, clutched at the top of his head, but all that did was keep her upright and keep him feasting between her legs.

Sweat joined the dried honey over her body once more until its sweetness tempered the scents of sex, complementing them into something she thought she could breathe in every day.

Her tangled nest of long hair swung against her hips and along his chest as she braced herself on him, her head back from every heavy wave of desire sweeping through her. She moved her pussy against his mouth, silently begging as her own mouth expressed other things. The more she begged, the more he gave, the suction over her clit unbearable. She was back to feeling buffeted by a storm when she'd always had the sense before to stay out of the rain.

For all his words about no winning or losing, he was winning.

She pitched forward to grab the metal headboard again, threatening to warp the thin railing as she ground down over his mouth with no regard to whether he could breathe. But he was the one who'd brought her to this. He was the one who'd stolen her mind and left her with nothing but skin, raw and vulnerable and in the worst kind of danger if she lost all control.

Because she wouldn't really lose it. She'd give it to him.

And she did.

The pleasure in her clit spread to everywhere at once, rising to the top of her head and flowing down to the tips of her toes. She screamed, came so hard her face twisted, and when she shuddered and wrenched against the end of it, he shifted her just enough to feast instead upon the flood of her arousal. His sounds grew even more obscene, that of a glutton at his favorite table. He snaked his long tongue into her to draw more of it out, startling a small cry from her and another shudder at the sheer lewdness of the feeling.

He feasted on her pleasure, and Vivian kept falling and falling — or the world fell around her while she sat still. When he licked up to her clit for one last, lingering kiss then stopped, she sank even lower, far beneath him though she still straddled his neck.

Her heavy pants and cries shifted. The tightness of her face finally yielded in a different kind of flood. Feeling — powerful and just as dangerous as pleasure — crashed through her, and the worst kind of tears, hot and stinging, poured down.

She crawled off of him, almost fell off the bed as she tried to hide her face, push the tears and the expression and the feelings back in with the heels of her hands. She hated this, hated herself with the same kind of blinding fury she could hate everyone else. Hated that he'd gotten what he wanted more than her, that he'd made her this skinny, ugly wreck of a woman, ugly far beneath her skin even to herself — and it wasn't anything she could see in a mirror.

"Vivian, no." He sat up, his cock inexplicably still hard. She wished he would just look demon already so she wouldn't see his utter guilelessness and underestimate him every time.

"You don't get to stop this by saying no," she snapped.

But when he closed his hand around her arm and drew her back to him, she could barely see enough to try to get away, so she let him gather her onto his lap, holding her. She was all arms and legs, and it was perfectly awkward, but he propped them back against the pillows, half-reclined.

He ran his hands over her, grasping, stroking, but it no longer felt sexual. Sensual, perhaps, but it was more like he touched her for the sake of touching, massaging blood flow through her skin, soothing her muscles, soothing her. They both had all manner of sticky and slick things on them, but that just meant it didn't matter how messy they were anymore.

"You still hunger for more. You've been without for so long. Let yourself cry. It won't hurt you. All this discomfort, this impulse to run as far as you can? It's no longer needed. Don't you see? You can be satisfied if you let yourself be, if you trust that I know what you crave and trust my desire to fulfill you."

"I don't want to cry." She ran her knuckles over her eyes to force the tears away, but she probably already looked terrible.

"It's just emotion, my girl. It's nothing to be afraid of."

"What do you know about what emotion does? You're a demon. Do you bob for emotions like weird people bob for apples? Is that what you've been after this whole time?"

Again, she rolled to the edge of the bed to leave, but he turned onto his side and slid a hand up her abdomen to her breast, possessive but not implacable. His chest against her back, he was warm, solid. He pressed his lips to the nape of her neck.

"No. That's not the kind of demon I am. I satisfy appetites, songbird. To do that, I have to know what people want, but more importantly, I have to know what they need." When she didn't pull away from him, he tucked himself closer, his chin on her shoulder. "Another demon, one with an interest in destruction, would feed humanity what they wanted and deliberately starve them of what they needed. It makes them crave what they want more keenly. If what I serve you isn't enough, Vivian, it's because you've been trying to feed the wrong thing."

Despite his cock against the small of her back, he didn't try to push sex on her again. On the contrary, he seemed quite content with his erection pressed to her skin, not even rubbing it along her spine or ass.

"Or because Bell made us too hungry to spite us for making weight-based wishes," she said.

"Only one facet of his intentions."

"What do you know of his intentions?" She closed her eyes but listened.

"He is a mystery, even to me. But his intentions are many and often benign, if unpleasant."

She snorted. Her tears had mostly subsided. The low, mean feeling from which they had arisen had not.

"I have not begun to quench your appetites," he whispered. "There are so many empty spaces inside you yearning to be filled."

Vivian turned around in his arms to search his face, his opaque eyes. "Do you realize what you sound like when you say things like that? Because you say them a lot, and I'm not sure anymore that you notice."

Jonas cracked a small smile, tucking a sticky lock of hair behind her ear. "As simple as I am, I sometimes have many intentions as well."

He kissed the paths that tears had taken, his tongue comforting on her skin, like that of a cat. Tears had to add a dash of salt to the sweetness of honey. "You're no stranger to sex, but how starved you are for pleasure, for something as plain as contact. That you shun it so explains the emptiness."

"What about you, Mr. I Haven't Had Sex for Centuries? Pot calling kettle much?"

"Immortals cannot hunger as mortals do, because we have all the time in the world. Mortal cravings run deeper, keener, more painful." He kissed the corner of her mouth then deliberately settled back behind her. The entire bottom half of his face smelled of her arousal, but she couldn't throw stones with his blood crackling on her chin. "I can feed you so much more than what satisfies your stomach, child."

Vivian's obstructed throat kept her from replying. She turned away again. She usually left at the end of a fuck. She wasn't partial to the intimacy of cuddling, and most of her partners didn't mind having the bed to themselves.

Jonas was a cuddler. She rested, stiff and awkward, as he spooned her, stroking her again in silence, until she reached behind to slip his cock back inside to satisfy her once more.

Chapter Eight

Without windows in the kitchen and with the microwave angled away from the bed, she had no idea what time she finally broke away from him and he didn't pull her back.

Vivian turned toward the bed. Jonas' eyes were closed, his body settled and relaxed. She'd thought the places with honey residue that practically glued them together would wake him when she disengaged, but he appeared undisturbed.

She picked up the robe from the floor next to the butcher block. This time she didn't volunteer to clean it. They'd violated dozens of FDA regulations about kitchen contamination, but that didn't concern her and apparently didn't bother him either.

As she pulled on the bathrobe, legs weak, fingers shaking as though she'd drunk too much coffee, she eased over to the mushroom garden — a placid, passive, poisonous hooded collections of spores, as dangerous as the blowfish swimming happily through the blue-lit aquarium next to it.

Vivian scratched at her wrist, her mouth salivating but her throat dry. She glanced back at the odd chef again. Still asleep.

She left the garden, the aquarium and Jonas in the kitchen. He didn't stir when she undid the deadbolt. Since she was the one he'd been keeping out, it didn't matter that she couldn't lock it again.

The circus was all asleep at this hour of the early morning, a time she hadn't seen since college. The sky was gray, orange seeping through on the horizon. None of the girls stirred when she walked through either, although she felt like she made every noise possible short of drumming on the dining table.

She left the bathrobe behind her clothing rack and prayed no one would wake up as she went from her bed to the bathroom. She and Jonas had feasted upon each other's skin all night, but there was enough honey and semen still staining her body and tangled into the mess of her long hair that, in addition to the bite marks and bruises, there was no mistaking what they'd done.

She nearly tripped before reaching the bathroom.

The light in there was as cold and unforgiving as that of the kitchen. She switched most of them off. Only the lights over the sinks remained on. That left the showers in shadows—not dark enough, but she didn't want it pitch dark because she needed to make sure she cleaned everything off.

Vivian washed herself, shower gel and water, over and over again—not scrubbing until her skin was red, but just going through the motions of cleaning herself head to toe, head to toe, head to toe. When the water from the showerhead rinsed all the bubbles off, she squeezed more gel onto the loofah and start the ritual again. Once she thought she'd cleaned everything off, not to mention exfoliated, she pulled out the razor.

Another ritual. She shaved her legs under her arms, careful along her mound, where skinniness and protuberance of bone worked against her.

A pinch and a sting.

She pulled the razor away and turned toward the light. Bright red welled into the wet cut and followed the path of existing droplets like paint on a sodden canvas.

She watched it drip down between her folds. As soon as the blood thinned, she continued the ritual.

Vivian turned into the shower spray, rinsing out the razor and the lather off of herself. She stepped in farther until the water sprayed her face, in her open mouth.

The razor was free and clean now. She turned the blades toward her and struck herself across the hip then swung it over her thigh. It didn't cut deep, but it was another sting and pinch. Three thin lines appeared in the places she'd struck herself.

Not enough. Not even with the red sluicing down the water over her legs.

She brought the edge of the razor to her arm. She was all bones these days. It was easy to find a place to press. She drew lines from her wrist up her arm. Not the center. She had no interest in killing herself. There were always risks, but she doubted Bell, in his infinite sadism, would let her die.

Her old scars had faded a long time ago. These days, they were as ghostly as her memories, only seen from certain angles. The lines had been too clean to scar too terribly. She felt like she'd moved back in time, blood in the shower and staining the razor around the blades, pieces of skin caught between them.

She did it again. Six lines down her arm then nine. Blood welled to fill in the lines, much thicker and darker now. The high-pressure spray pounded down to sweep it away, but it returned just as fast. Her nerves shouted at the initial sting of the water upon them then settled into a steady throb.

More shallow cuts, over the bone of her wrist, up her hand to the knuckle of her thumb.

A clatter made her spin around.

Lily was there, bleary-eyed, too tired to pretend she hadn't seen anything. Instead, she seemed transfixed by the gradual glove of blood that covered Vivian's hand.

"Just needed to go," Lily said. Now she looked away. "Sorry."

Vivian stood there, daring Lily to stay, daring her to comment, making no attempt to shield her wounds or the razor in her hand.

But the trance was gone, and so was the brief respite from reality that came from hyper-focusing on bleeding skin. Now she was left with what had happened, the new mess and damage control.

Vivian already knew the girls talked about the other Skeletons when they weren't there. Until now, she hadn't cared whether they talked about her. But the last thing she needed was the girls telling each other and everyone else that she was just another screwed-up cutter.

Lily stayed in the stall a long time, which was Vivian's only vindication. It meant the blonde little pixie was scared. She'd rather the girls fear than pity her. But Lily eventually had to creep out from the stall to wash her hands.

"Lily."

The girl looked into the mirror to meet Vivian's eyes. She was fearless with a violin and outspoken, vivacious and enthusiastic in bed, but she had trouble raising her gaze. Maybe it was too early in the morning for courage.

"Don't say a word."

Lily didn't move at first. Then she nodded. "You tend to sleep longer than the rest of us. Shane doesn't get much sleep. She'll be the first to wake up. Then Alicia and Nasreen. You don't have much time."

Vivian didn't move until Lily had escaped back into the tent and left her alone.

She hurried to the sinks to grab a bunch of paper towels and hold them against her arm and hand. The closest thing to a medicine cabinet they had was less of a first aid kit and more a bath and body store, with toothpaste and soap and other cleaners rather than medicine or bandages.

After a few minutes, she plunged the paper towels into the trash can, trying to cover them with others crumpled up inside, though her blood seemed all the brighter among all the tan paper.

"Viv? Did you never come in last night?"

Goddammit. Vivian pressed fresh towels to her arm and hand. She couldn't hide it now, but she didn't have to face Shane either. "Just wanted a shower."

"You're bleeding."

No shit, Sherlock.

"Do you need any help? I think there's a first aid station close by."

"Sure you don't just want to get close enough to taste? Satisfy some of those raw meat cravings?"

Shane didn't respond. Vivian was afraid that if she looked back, she'd see hurt. Vivian usually didn't care, but Shane was fragile, and for some reason she'd attached herself to Vivian. It was poor judgment on her part, but Vivian gained nothing from causing her pain.

Backpedaling wasn't an option, so Vivian tried to soften the hard edges. "It's fine. It's already stopped bleeding so much."

"Your bed isn't slept in."

"It's none of your business." Vivian didn't snap. She needed to salvage this arrangement.

"It's not a bad thing to find someone else's bed to sleep in. I'm just concerned about the fact you followed it with bloodplay."

"I need you to let it go." Vivian lifted the newer paper towel to check the seepage. Still stinging and seeping. "You know I don't like to talk about it."

"No," Shane said. "You just sing about it instead."

* * * *

Out in the circus, Vivian smiled for the cameras when people asked, but she didn't make it easy for people to stop her. She stayed away from the places people liked to take selfies or congregate with other freaks, geeks and performers. And she definitely stayed away from the food court.

As soon as she heard the band, she stepped around one of the midway booths and leaned against the slats, arms crossed over her chest as though to hold herself back. The leather sleeves of her jacket pressed against the still-raw cuts on her arms. The ones on her hand were visible, but they weren't nearly as alarming. For all people knew, she had cats.

The music called to her, and something thickened in her throat, hurting when she swallowed. But Bell appeared to take seriously his charge to her to do as she liked with the band — including flake out. The discordant attempts at open mic told her that the band had gone back to what they were used to.

No one needed her for the show to go on. Arcanium had been going along just fine before she showed up. Sure, she'd saved the music, but though there weren't many better than her, there were plenty of people who could fill the position of lead diva in a second-rate circus's cover band.

Let's just be realistic.

Bell had brought her in for her voice, but he'd made her a Skeleton. That was all she had to be for him. If he wanted her there, he could fucking make her go, but she wasn't going to be his songbird anymore. Doing things Arcanium's way, she'd found herself in bed with the odd chef, crying and carrying on then cutting and getting caught. Things couldn't stay the same — but Arcanium seemed to be in the business of staying the same.

"I'd hoped we were past this, Vivian." Bell leaned against the corner, more casual in his posture than she was.

She spared him a single glance. "You knew better."

"Yes. But you know I like to be surprised."

"Surprise, motherfucker."

"You're only hurting yourself. I understand that misery loves company, but misery is not why I brought you in."

"Can't always get what you want."

"No, *you* can't," he whispered in her ear.

She jerked around, but he was still leaning against the corner. "You got a point, slick?"

"My point is that my path gives you all the things you need and an abundance of what you want. You continue to fight Arcanium, this will not end well."

She uncrossed her arms and pushed off the back of the booth to face him. "What if I don't want it to end well?"

"I won't let Arcanium be torn apart again, and certainly not by you. This is your home. Don't destroy your own home."

"You'd be surprised how much I do that."

"No. By that, I am not surprised. Please, Vivian." He slipped his hand into hers, the one with the cuts down to her thumb, before she realized how close he'd come. "You have all the attention in the world, everything to satisfy every appetite. This is what you've always wanted. Don't throw it away."

She slipped her hand from his as though he had syphilis. "I have no idea what you're talking about."

* * * *

After the circus shut down and the Skeletons had returned to their tent, Vivian laid on her cot and closed her fuzzy, blurry eyes, pretending to sleep when the odd chef entered.

"Vivian?" He sounded the same as he always did, detached but politely concerned when she wasn't doing what she was supposed to.

"She was up all night," Lily said. "She didn't come in until this morning."

"Who was she with?" Alicia asked.

"Beats me. She likes to hang out with the Quandary and Miss Delilah."

"She doesn't seem like the kind of bitch to sleep with queens, but whatever peels her potatoes," Alicia said.

"Should we wake her?" Nasreen asked.

Vivian's stomach growled. She shifted on the cot, hoping the creaks would hide the sound.

But she wasn't as hungry as she'd been the last time she'd refused dinner. Which meant that Jonas really was the loophole she'd been looking for. Goddamn bastards, both the demon and the jinni. They'd set this up perfectly.

She tucked the blankets tighter around her, teeth clenched as she listened to them eat.

* * * *

In the morning, she refused the golems' offering of breakfast tacos, downing a bottle of water instead.

"Are you okay?" Nasreen asked as Vivian tossed the plastic bottle into the recycling bin. "I thought we talked about this."

Vivian didn't respond, and she avoided meeting the eyes of any of the Skeletons.

"You going to be joining us at any point today, boss lady?" Alicia asked. "Or are we going to be fielding requests again?"

Still no response. Silent treatment wasn't Vivian's forte—her specialty was using every inch of her acerbic tongue or getting revenge behind people's backs, sometimes without them even knowing it.

"So we're sulking like a moody teenager again. Great. Let me know when you're going to grow up and realize you're not the only one here with a problem. If our diva doesn't have her head in the game, maybe we should start holding auditions again."

"Bell's not going to be okay with that. Everyone thinks she's perfect," Lily said, as though because Vivian wasn't talking, she also couldn't hear. "So perfect they think he made her that way."

"It doesn't matter how perfect she is if she's not going to sing." Alicia finished her second breakfast taco in record time and pushed herself away from the table in disgust. "I don't know what your childhood damage is, Vivian, but whatever you're doing isn't going to work. You can't not eat. It's not going to last, and it's going to get messy."

Vivian finally broke her silence. "I want it to get messy."

Alicia threw her hands up and started to leave, but she spun back just as the skeleton makeup appeared on her face. "What bug is up your butt? You spend the night with someone, and then you come back and everything has to go to hell with you? What happened?"

"Do you care?"

"I wouldn't be asking if I didn't."

With the skeleton makeup on, Vivian couldn't tell whether Alicia was being sardonic or just curious. "Nothing happened. I'm just sick of this place."

"You can be sick of this place all you want. It's not going to get you out." The edge to her tone had softened into something an awful lot like pity.

"Maybe you just didn't try hard enough."

"Maybe I didn't. But even the people who have it worse than us and tried to get out, they haven't gotten anywhere. There's no leaving Arcanium without Bell's permission, and making yourself more of a problem isn't going to do that. It's just going to make him double down harder."

Vivian stood. "You've only been here…what? Six months? Don't tell me what this place is like. You haven't been here long enough to know. And any place can change. You think Bell's the only one who can double down?"

"You're going to lose."

"With that attitude, maybe I would."

"Are you singing today?"

"Do I sound like I'm singing today?"

"Thanks for the heads-up, selfish bitch." Alicia tossed the butcher paper from her breakfast taco into the trash and flounced away. Since her skirt had tulle underneath it, she couldn't help but flounce.

"You're welcome, heartless cow."

Lily got up from the table, too. "Where exactly was she wrong?"

Nasreen didn't have anything to say, but she, too, left rather than linger with someone who was admittedly not very good company.

Shane didn't appear to notice any tension between the women. Her mouths were moving where her skin-colored latex dress revealed them, even though she wasn't dropping anything into them. Tongues slithered along carnivore teeth. She clutched the edge of the bench and stared at her empty butcher paper as though willing something new into it.

"Are you all right?" Vivian hated to do the same thing that everyone else did to her — and lived to regret — but Shane had a less caustic personality.

"It doesn't have anything to do with whatever you're going through." Shane glanced up, her knuckles white. "So it doesn't matter, right?"

Usually less caustic. "Take a long walk in a meat freezer, then. You're right. It doesn't matter."

Vivian spent most of the day under the courtyard tent, where Nasreen and Shane did their interactive performances for tips and snacks. She'd hoped that because they weren't eating the odd chef's prepared food that she would be less attracted to the scent, but the hamburger that people threw into Shane's mouths was cooked. And sometimes people fed Nasreen food that they'd purchased from the food court. They liked to watch her eat as she danced for them. Like the odd chef, some people just enjoyed a well-fed woman, and Nasreen was hardly going to tell them no when she was just as hungry as the rest of the Skeletons.

Vivian made it through the band playing. She made it through the guests' dinnertime. Then, once everything had closed down for the day, she hid not in the circus but in the faire. Food smelled good on this side of the fairgrounds, too, but she already knew that eating it wouldn't do any good. That much kept her from running. Alicia hadn't been wrong about that. Hadn't been wrong about anything.

The important thing was that she hadn't been right either. It wasn't about running.

After everyone had gone to bed, Vivian's stomach tried to eat itself, but she climbed into the front of Kitty's oddity tent, where the Bearded Lady sat and knitted while people came by to stare at her. Kitty's tent had a nice, big armchair that might have actually been more comfortable than Vivian's cot. It was the kind of thing she'd settle into to watch a movie on her tablet, if she still had one. But she wasn't granted that kind of diversion, and she knew better than to ask.

Hello, Bell, I know I want your circus to go to hell, but do you mind helping me entertain myself while I'm undermining the shit out of you?

She curled up, her legs over one of the arms, and she pressed her elbows into her belly in hopes that it would hold down the hunger that ached through every inch of her abdomen, not just her stomach. It didn't. She tucked her face against the corduroy, knowing that she'd wake up with their marks across her skin, and covered her head with her leather jacket, though it was already dark as pitch in the tent.

"Vivian." A hand on her shoulder.

The transition was seamless from midnight darkness to early morning brightness piercing under her fluttering eyelids, from being curled in an armchair to sitting upright at a picnic table.

She was no longer in Kitty's oddity tent, and Jonas was shaking her awake.

Her mouth was sticky, her hands covered in what looked like buffalo sauce, sea salt and bits of fried batter. Her entire torso and pants from the knees up had been smeared with grease, stale beer, ale and soda.

"Did you fall asleep after doing this, or did you do this in your sleep?" The odd chef lifted her chin to inspect her face and get a better look at the rest of her.

"Do what?"

Jonas stepped back and gestured to the food court. It was back to looking like a horde of angry raccoons had declared war on all trash cans, and this time it hadn't been cleaned up by the time everyone woke up. Golems waited on the edge near the odd chef's food booth, standing in such a coordinated line that it was clear they wanted to tend to the mess, but something kept them from doing so.

Some of the smears on her hands felt fresh rather than sticky or pasty. She might have been rolling around in trash right up to the point she'd sat down a minute ago at one of the picnic tables for Jonas to wake her. And someone had to have seen it. None of the Skeletons — they'd be waiting for their breakfast in the tent. But it was a matter of time before everyone who hadn't already risen for breakfast would know.

"*You win this round*," she thought in Bell's direction.

If he heard her, he didn't respond.

"*Me vale verga, pinche pendejo. Que te jodan.*" She had a few other choice phrases she was more than willing to mutter under her breath, but she also wasn't entirely sure what she'd put in her mouth, and that was more important right now than what she wanted to come out of it.

What concerned her most were the insect legs she couldn't place stuck in the shit all over her. It wouldn't be the first time she'd eaten bugs, but with a whole night completely blacked out, there was no telling what she'd gotten into. For all she knew, she'd broken into the creepy-crawly tent. She wasn't interested in adding the Spider to the list of people who hated her — not for something Vivian hadn't done on purpose.

"You weren't in the tent for dinner, and you haven't changed from last night. That's three meals missed. You're not designed to skip meals like this," Jonas said. "If you want to get cleaned up and have something that will actually sustain you, I can appropriate a portion of my kitchen for that."

"Don't go out of your way. I'm fine." Vivian swayed as she stood, her coltish legs shaking. She was covered in food — and things she was pretty sure weren't supposed to be food — but she was still hungry as hell, and if Jonas made something for her, she doubted she'd be able to walk away from it.

Jonas reached to steady her but jerked back when she flinched. "What are you doing to yourself? The Skeletons are concerned. Shane is concerned. I'm concerned."

"Please. They're not concerned. They're rubbernecking. And why not? There's nothing else to do here. But for fuck's sake, I haven't had your meals for only two days. I've skipped meals for four. It's nothing."

"That was before. That was when your body was different. That was when you weren't bound to Arcanium by this wish."

"Before I was bound to your food, you mean?"

Jonas tilted his head. "Is that why you're refusing what I serve? Because you're forced to eat it?"

"You're sharper than you look."

She turned to leave, but Jonas grabbed her by the upper part of her forearm. It was by far the most violent he'd ever been with her, and that included things they'd done in bed. This time, her flinch was more reactionary than deliberate.

"Who did this to you?"

The lines she'd made over her arm and hand were more livid now in their healing than they had been when she'd made the cuts, the new scabs yellow-brown, the edges dark pink and slightly inflamed. She'd taken her jacket off to sleep, and as far as she could tell, she'd left it in the armchair in Kitty's tent. Now everyone could see what she'd done to herself, too.

"This isn't from a knife or a piece of glass. This isn't an accident or an attack." For someone usually gentle,

Jonas had an immovable grip, nearly painful, and she didn't have much flesh to squeeze. "You did this to yourself."

"You mind saying it a little louder? I think the newcomers didn't hear you, *esé*."

"Why?"

"If I'm not slicing you up in my sleep, I can't see how it's anyone's business. Everyone asks why, but it matters to exactly none of them." She managed to extricate herself from his hand, but only because he loosened his grip of his own accord.

"That's where you're wrong. I care what happens to my Skeletons. I care what happens to you. Especially if you're self-destructing."

"If self-destruction is my goal, maybe you shouldn't get in my way."

"Is this because of what happened three nights ago?" he called after her.

"Really, Jonas, I think more people would hear you if you learned to speak from the diaphragm, too."

His eyebrows twitched together. As she turned away, she wondered whether she'd hurt him. She might still be able to use him again, but it would be better if she wasn't dependent on that. She didn't need another night in his bed, in his arms. She didn't need his kiss, his touch, his cock. She certainly didn't need his semen enough to risk going back for a good long while.

He was like Bell, except more insidious, because he seemed harmless. Sweet. Considerate. Kind. But he wasn't as he seemed. The demon grew poison, nurtured it, then fed hundreds of thousands, and who knew what he'd done to them over the course of time that no one could point back to him. Poisoning was so easy a child could do it. A trained chef could be all the more effective, and Bell would make sure none of it came back to rain down hell on their heads.

Because this *was* secretly hell. She'd figured it out. Arcanium was the best kind of hell, because no one suspected. Their friendly fortune teller told them it was a place where humans were protected and demons were God's little helpers, and the human cast just lapped it up, doing as they were told, happy enough not to question how Arcanium was tearing them down, disintegrating them like being soaked in mild acid.

It didn't have to be the literal hell. There were hellscapes everywhere if one just opened their eyes, and there were far more hells than heavens. She'd been victim in enough of them that she was more than willing to spread that hell around. She'd be her own demon.

She brushed past the Skeletons as they came out of the tent, perhaps because the golems were late with their tacos.

Nasreen and Lily stared at her, at the mess of her clothes, which she left in the pile with Jonas' robe.

Standing under the shower spray, her stomach and intestines shifted unsettlingly in her abdomen. She couldn't throw up and couldn't get sick, but it felt an awful lot like the introduction to food poisoning. What the hell had she eaten last night? She'd heard about sleep eating, but she thought this was more complicated. Namely, she thought this was Bell.

"You fuck me up. I fuck you up. You fuck me up. I fuck you up. Who do you think's going to blink first, Demon Lite?"

He still didn't respond.

* * * *

She avoided the circus all day, all night, hiding in the mostly empty fairgrounds, playing her favorite game at the edges. But the game had lost most of its luster now that she knew most of the players were just influenced by sex demons.

And every time she watched someone else have sex, she couldn't help but see herself with Jonas. Between food, booths and the rampant fucking, she was saturated with reminders. He'd integrated himself into every aspect of her life, just as Bell had planned.

She kept thinking she'd reached the end of hating Bell, but it turned out hatred quenched some of the boredom, because she always found a new reason to hate him and all of his minions, including Lennon and Jonas, as well as the naïve little groupies who didn't seem to notice that they'd become dehumanized circus bunnies for the mostly male demons to enjoy without much of an effort. For Vivian, all it had taken was a few mugs of golden milk and she'd turned herself into honey.

As the sun set, she snagged a piece of twine from a discarded hay bale in the fairgrounds and tied herself to a random railing. Leaning against said railing like a drunken cowboy outside a saloon wasn't at the top of her list of places to sleep, but the railing was as far as Vivian could get from the circus without going to the parking lot, and the fairgrounds weren't exactly rife with places to sleep. All the benches had been made to encourage people to keep moving along, not stay in one place for hours on end.

She woke up while it was still dark. The twine dug into her healing wrist deep enough to draw blood on its own. Her belly grumbled, growled and made other disquieting noises that seemed stranger in the dark —

like monsters in a cave. She was reminded again of Shane's gash mouths and their slithering tongues, the sounds they made as they opened and closed, like open wounds parted by deft fingers.

That just made Vivian hungrier.

She hit her head against the railing, getting a few splinters for her trouble, until she stopped thinking about Shane's mouths feeding. She managed to fall asleep again, but the sleep was troubled and she woke up again, prostrate on the grass with her tied arm pulled behind her and off the ground, as though she'd sleepwalked as far away from the railing as she could possibly get before collapsing. She thought she might have eaten some of the grass, too, because her mouth tasted like ashes.

* * * *

Four days. Eight meals. Everyone else got an extra partial share of food, because Jonas apparently still prepared meals for her that would go to waste otherwise. But Vivian refused to come in to shower or change until Shane left the tent with him.

Dark circles under her red eyes. Gaunt cheekbones that had begun to resemble the actual skeleton she looked like in the facepaint. But she didn't lose weight. She became hollow, but she didn't lose weight. Her body wasn't eating itself, no matter how painful the pangs of hunger, as though she'd grown Shane's gash mouths on the inside of her.

As though she were already dead.

She didn't want to leave the stall she'd tied herself to, but the person in charge of this particular stall, which housed the knife- and axe-throwing game, looked at her funny when he came in to get the booth ready for the next day. And why shouldn't he look at her funny? She knew what she looked like.

She stumbled into the tent late enough that the tacos would already be eaten, but she could still smell them in the air, could practically taste them through the smells.

There was a breakfast taco still on the table. Vivian stared at it intently, using every last string she had tied to her willpower. She felt like she'd starved herself for a month, not a few days.

"We didn't leave it for you," Alicia said. "What did you do to Shane?"

"I haven't done anything to anybody. What's wrong with Shane?"

"Seems you're quite the inspiration, Miss American Idol. She's not eating all her food either. More for us, sure, but she's the one who's always been hungriest. And we can tell she's coming in earlier at night, because at least one of us is still awake when she does. You're the only thing that changed. She started going off her meals when you did, after you spent the night somewhere el— Don't fucking tell me that you were with her."

"Why? Did you have your eye on her?" Vivian asked. As for her eyes, they were still on the breakfast taco. "You want some of that first?"

Alicia slapped her. Not hard, just enough for it to make a sound. "Tell me you weren't sleeping with her. Tell me you didn't use her and break her heart."

"I started starving myself first. Who said she didn't break mine?"

"You'd have to have a heart first."

Vivian finally looked away from the breakfast taco, though she had what seemed like a perfect taco-shaped hole in her stomach. "I have a heart. I've had it all my life. And I didn't fuck her. Whatever's going on with her, I'm not a part of it."

Lily folded her pajamas and set them on her cot. "Did it occur to you that she's having trouble because you're *not* a part of it? Because you went off and slept with someone else?"

Vivian opened her mouth. Closed it. Opened it again. "That doesn't make any sense." Shane's crush was harmless, not a pining-in-the-swamps-of-despair infatuation.

Nasreen shushed them, and not a moment too soon, because Shane stepped out of the bathroom in a thin white bathrobe instead of her tie-around cardigan.

"You look like shit," Shane said.

Vivian respected that. "You don't look too good yourself."

Shane lifted one shoulder, her hands in the pockets. "Lost my appetite. No, that's not right. It's more like I've lost my taste. It's just a phase. I'm sure it'll get better. It *has* to get better."

She didn't seem like a lovesick young woman, and Vivian couldn't be held responsible for someone else's feelings anyway. She wasn't going to pretend she liked Shane more than she did, especially since she already liked Shane more than about ninety-nine percent of the population. And she wasn't going to let her down gently, because she hadn't even raised the girl's expectations yet. If Shane was pining over something that had never happened to start with, what the hell was Vivian supposed to do about it?

Despite the weird looks from the booth boy again, Vivian went right up to the railing at sundown and tied herself to it, daring him to say something or tell her to scram. Maybe something about the way she looked at him scared him from protesting.

Because he was a hefty young man, and looking at him made her hungry.

She wound the twine around her chaffed wrist and sat her bony ass on the ground, her bathrobe acting as a makeshift blanket.

She wasn't as disturbed by her fantasies of consuming his flesh as she'd assumed she would be. The Mountain looked like a goddamn buffet. Only the Skeletons managed to avoid looking like movable feasts.

But Vivian kept catching herself watching Shane's mouths as they moved in their restless hunger, which probably didn't help with the perception that she was interested.

Vivian thought something else was going on with that girl—like her doing this hunger strike wasn't *just* because of the night she'd spent with Jonas. But the more Shane caught her staring, an odd, fey look on her big-eyed, skin-framed face, the more Vivian wondered if there wasn't something to Lily's theory, too.

Vivian did have a heart. It was cold and small and people probably needed a microscope to see it, but it was there. And knowing that Shane might be feeling bad because Vivian was sending unintentional mixed signals made Vivian feel bad, too. That wasn't something she could often say.

Chapter Nine

When she woke up, the whole shuddering world smelled like shit and her skin was on fire.

She didn't have time to investigate where she was or how she'd gotten there. She was surrounded by trash bags — some strong, some weak and leaking, some split from bottom to top to spill around her. The movement of her world had smashed the trash bags and their contents against her, nearly smothering her. But being crushed wasn't at the top of her concerns.

Thousands of burning needles burrowed into every inch of her skin.

Vivian wrenched away in any direction she could, trying to escape whatever had poured over her to burn and blister and boil, from whatever ate her away from the outside in. Something caustic from the trash bags? She was covered with plenty, but nothing she could see in the dim light seemed to be damaging her skin as much as it felt like it was.

There was nothing to wrench away from, nothing to escape.

Her world tipped her to the side then upside-down. The trash bags, loose trash and Vivian crashed down into a bed of more trash bags, just as pungent as the last, although Vivian landed on something with sharp corners that lanced her back. Again, though, it didn't matter nearly as much as what was immolating her alive.

Vivian screamed, cries coming from her throat that she had never heard before, not even in the darkest nights when she was younger and had had to muffle herself in her pillows.

There was more room in this new world. She thrashed and clawed her way up the pile, screaming as long as she had breath.

The world underneath her rumbled, screeched then gradually began to move.

Through the fire, she slowly gleaned pieces of what had happened and where she was. The world she'd been in was a dumpster. The world she was in now was the dump truck. She'd been in the dumpster sleep-eating when the dump truck had come to pick it up. Her tongue and face bore the evidence of a somnambulistic binge, as did her stomach.

The dump truck's compactor hadn't been activated. The truck was only half full, so there was no need to compress. That was probably the only reason she was still alive as the truck rumbled farther and farther away from Arcanium.

'If you try to leave Arcanium, you'll experience the most unpleasant sensations you've ever felt in your life, and I know you've felt plenty.'

She was out.

Getting out was all she'd wanted since Bell had brought her in. And now she wished the compactor would whirr to life and end her misery, because it kept getting worse and worse the farther she went from the circus.

Vivian slammed her fist against the walls of the truck bed, screamed, wailed, probably gnashed her teeth. She became a creature of the moment, an animal with her whole body caught in a bear trap. She couldn't climb up the walls, couldn't pull herself over the top of the bed, couldn't make the driver hear her, couldn't make *anyone* hear her through the thick walls of the bed and the cab. She was being taken God knew where, and she didn't know whether she was going to make it before the dump truck's next stop, much less wherever the truck was going to dump everything.

More trash bags sliced open, spilling and squishing their contents over her, as she tried to dig her way out. There was no room for logic. There was only here and now and pain.

The shuddering world shuddered to a halt.

A face appeared at the top of the bed. *Bell.*

Though logic wasn't her strong suit at the moment, but she could put cause and effect together. And Bell was the cause.

She threw whatever she could find at him, still screaming as though being stabbed by a serial killer. He clambered over the side, ignoring the trash pelting his chest and his legs, regardless of the stains they left. He dropped into the cushion of trash and nimbly crawled to her, avoiding the worst of the projectiles with maddening ease.

"I know it probably doesn't help things, my dear, but this was an accident. That's what I get for giving people their space."

Bell grabbed her wrist. Immediately, warmth far more welcome than the fire under the thin layer of her skin spread from the point of contact, eliminating pain in its wake.

Vivian slumped, but her muscles were still tense, twitching then cramping, and she whimpered.

The pain itself didn't even leave behind residual twinges or prickles, only the effects of her efforts to escape. Without the pain, though, she was far more aware of the *smell*, of what covered her. It was far more egregious and ripe than the trash cans in the food court and some of it not edible in the least, enough to make even her impossible-to-vomit stomach heave.

She swung back her arm then planted her fist dead in his eye. For a psychic adept at avoiding bits of trash, he apparently had trouble with fists aimed for his face, because there was actual surprise on the parts of his expression not obscured by her hand shattering his eye socket—in addition to her own knuckles, if that crunch and the new stabs of white-hot pain were any indication. But they didn't compare to what she had felt before, which gave her an immediate basis for comparison that horrified her so much that, as Bell rose from being punched, she grabbed him by the shoulders and shoved him back again. Even with her diminished strength, he fell off his feet and against the same piles of trash that had made her the worst kind of filthy.

"Geez, woman, I'm trying to help you." He seemed more put out by the interference than the smell around him or the swelling around his eye.

"Yeah, see where your help put me?"

"I didn't put you here. *You* put yourself in the dumpster by refusing to take care of yourself. The dump truck picked up the dumpster and pulled it and the trash outside of the boundaries of Arcanium, which triggered the spell that keeps my people from trying to escape. The spell worked *exactly* as it should. Unfortunately, the spell doesn't distinguish between someone escaping and someone being forced over the border. Now, if you'll come with me, I'll clean us as we leave the truck, and I should be able to handle your broken bones."

"Sounds like your spell's defective, you sick, sadistic measle." Vivian jerked away from the hand he offered and started climbing the trash bags to the back of the truck bed, where she now noticed a ladder she could reach if she made it up a few layers of trash.

"I see no reason to alter the magic to distinguish between runaways and accidents. Only two people have been forced over in ten years, and the border's been breached by accident only once. In your case, escape was not your aim, but your behavior has consequences, Vivian. When Skinless was trying to find the farthest edge of Arcanium and accidentally stepped over the border, she learned not to test those borders but to find peace within."

Bell didn't need the ladder. He jumped six feet without effort and clambered up to straddle the edge of the truck bed. The swelling around his eye was already going down, the burst of blood fading. That just incensed her more. She tried to push him off once she'd reached the top, but he swung his other leg over and dropped the fifteen feet back to the ground without so much as a wince.

He was true to his word, though. The filth that had slimed, smeared and crumbled over her and the pieces she had thrown on him just fell or slithered off of their bodies, as though they'd crossed through a wall that held everything else back. She still smelled like shit — or maybe she just still smelled it from the back of the truck — but her clothes and her body were 'clean'.

"Let me see the hand," he said, beckoning her for it.

"No."

"Don't make me force the issue, Vivian. I can't let one of my people walk around with a broken hand."

"I'm a hundred pounds soaking wet. What difference does it make if my bones are broken?" She wrenched away from him again and started back toward the circus. She could try to run while the spell wasn't harming her, but she doubted Bell would be as inclined to save her again when the spell came back in full force.

"You're a freak, and people expect that. A broken hand means that my circus is unsafe."

Vivian laughed, making no effort to hold back the hysterical edge. He ran a demonic circus and peopled it with slaves, but God forbid the optics look bad.

"Please, Vivian. I offer you every courtesy, every second chance in the world. You struck me in a moment of pique, but it was still an assault upon a member of Arcanium. I make allowances for your state of mind, just as I make allowances for the fact that you did not actively try to escape, but I'm well within the laws to have the Ringmaster punish you for the blow. Don't make me regret my mercy."

"You offer me every courtesy?" Vivian swung around to glare daggers at him. "Mercy? Are you fucking serious?"

Smiling, Bell raised a hand to the truck driver, who rumbled on his way with an apologetic wave. Then he turned back to Vivian, humor falling away. "Do you know how many times I've been lenient with you? For the stunt you pulled with the odd chef, I could have made you an Arcanium prisoner, your back reduced to ribbons under the Ringmaster's lash, as I have done to countless others. The only reason I didn't force the issue was because of Jonas' mercy, not mine. Instead of compelling you to perform as I have done to almost every other member of the circus, I gave you leave to use the band as you saw fit, and you spat my generosity in my face. You don't have to starve. None of the Skeletons even have to be hungry. But you insist on denying yourself every comfort. That is what has led you here. And it will lead you further and further down into a hell of your own creation, *not* mine. Now give me your fucking hand, and you can be on your way."

Vivian held out her swelling hand, hissing when she tried to move her fingers. "If you hate being lenient and making exceptions with me, why bother?"

"Because I'm a sap in love with perfect talent, of course. You disappoint me in so many ways, Vivian, but one."

Bell cradled her hand between both of his. The same warmth that had spread through her to dissipate the pain from the spell's punishment blossomed in her broken hand. She could practically feel the bones stitching back together.

When he withdrew from her hand, she flexed her fingers. There were no more pangs or little stabs of fire. The swelling had gone down as effectively as Bell's swollen eye.

But before she could stalk away, he grabbed her arm, the grip edging on more pain. "You're a problem child, but I've had problem children before. I beg you. I'd get on my knees if I thought it would help. Don't keep doing this. Accept my boundaries, take the gifts I have offered and make something wonderful from them. You have so much potential."

Vivian tried to jerk her arm from his grip. "Why don't you just let me go? Let me go back to the way I was, where I got to decide where I ate, what I ate and with whom — where I couldn't see myself right but at least I could do whatever I wanted with what I had."

Bell scoffed. "Where you had to poison your best friend in order to sleep with her boyfriend? Where she figured out at least the sex part and told every last one of your so-called friends, the people you surrounded yourself with because they got off on your drama and were occasionally useful? Where what was left of your family fled you as much as your parents? Where you couldn't keep a job to save your life? I give you a world where you don't need to concern yourself with what you eat, where you can see things as they are and where you can do the one thing in the world that you love." Bell finally let go of her arm, releasing her with a curl to his lip as though she disgusted him. "I do understand it's quite the imposition, but try to contain your gratitude going forward."

"You really do think you're generous, don't you? You think I should be thanking you on my knees, possibly with your pants open at the same time. You think you've given me so much."

"Perhaps, like pain, you simply need a basis for comparison." Bell stepped back. "I can only learn from my mistakes the way you don't learn from yours. No more. If you're not going to use the talent I brought you in for, there's no need for me to soften the blows or cushion the falls. The spell's punishment is your last warning. You know what resisting your hunger will do to you. If you cross the boundaries of Arcanium again, by accident or design, you will be punished by the Ringmaster, five lashes added to each subsequent event. And if you break any of my other laws, Skeleton, the Ringmaster will rain blood from your back. Do I make myself clear?"

"And you can go fuck yourself, too. You're not my father, my fucktoy or my friend. The only reason you're my boss is because you chose that job. Just take away the hunger and let me go."

"You have two wishes." As brittle as she was, Bell somehow matched her, the warm colors of his body and eyes icing over as he spoke. "Go ahead. Try to wish yourself out."

"I'm not wishing myself out just so you can manipulate it." Vivian crossed her arms as she backed across the invisible threshold into Arcanium. She could feel the difference, like walking into fog. Bell followed her in. There were circus members all along the edge of Oddity Row, investigating the commotion.

Vivian continued as though she couldn't see them and they couldn't see her. "You're going to let me go."

"You're not even close to doing enough for me to let you go," Bell said. "Your only hope for that is to do what I say long enough to please me."

"If you wanted a blow job, you could have just asked."

That was a definite curl to his lip now. "You're not nearly as good as you think you are."

"How would you know?"

"The odd chef desires different things than I. He is more easily satisfied. You take his abundance for granted. In denying his feasts, you hurt him the way you hurt everything you touch."

"Cry me a bloody river."

"You can't starve yourself forever," Bell said.

"Watch me."

"No, you actually *can't* starve yourself forever. Tonight is an eating contest."

"I'll just stay away again."

"Not this time. I forced the Spider to take her place every day when she started with me. I won't break my promise to you about the band, but I've made no such promise about your obligation as one of my Skeletons. I expect you at the table at sunset."

In view of the rest of his circus people, he plastered a smile on his face to hide his contempt before leaning in to kiss her cheek.

"At the very least, you won't end up in a dumpster tonight," he murmured against her skin. "You're welcome."

"Eat shit."

"Oh, I'm not the one who did that."

* * * *

When Bell called her, a subtle pull at first, Vivian kept riding the carousel's skeleton horse. Kids seemed to love it when she was on the nose like that, and it kept them from bugging her.

"You'll end up at my table, no matter what. There's nothing you can do to resist me when I take over your body. What's the purpose of resisting me now?"

She wrapped her arms around the horse's neck, resting her forehead against the golden pole. "To piss you off," she whispered.

"You piss me off just by being awake, Vivian. There's no point to this."

"It's kind of an end in itself."

"You're as maddening as the Spider and nowhere near as charming."

"You're welcome."

He jerked her off of the horse, sprawling her on the moving carousel floor.

"Whoa, are you all right?" A woman in a group of twentysomethings dismounted to help her up.

Bell kept a tight hold on her tongue. Vivian nodded, her limbs a pile of sticks for her to untangle on her own before Bell tightened his control once again.

As soon as the golem stopped the carousel, she jumped from the platform and walked quickly and steadily to the food court she so despised.

Scents surrounded her once again, much more appetizing than anything she could get from a trash can or dumpster. After five days of restraining herself from a proper meal, her entire abdomen a collapsed star, Vivian thought she would actually break down the closer she came to the source of those smells.

"Hello, love. Good to see you didn't lose your way." Bell stopped her with a hand on her shoulder and pulled her hair back, tying it with a strip of leather embellished with beads at the end, something more suited to his ensemble than hers.

"I hate you," she said through gritted teeth.

"You never had to like me to be a part of my circus, and you don't have to love me to love your life here." Next, he stripped her of her jacket. In her Jameson crop top, there was nothing to hide the cavern her abdomen had become.

"I smell chocolate."

"I think you'll find yourself quite pleased with the odd chef's talents, as you have been before. We do provide a glass of milk to cleanse the palate between each decadent slice of cake."

"Sounds healthy," Vivian said.

"And if any of your control issues were borne of health, that might actually mean something. Now, go to your place and enjoy yourself."

To an outsider, Vivian was sure their banter appeared affectionate. Visitors watched her with Bell from the corners of their eyes, as though viewing something meant to be private. Their regard crawled over her like the cockroaches from the dumpster.

But she didn't sneer, didn't wrench away, didn't say anything more as Bell sent her to the opposite end of the table from Shane, where her tall black throne waited and a golem pushed her in. Vivian stared sullenly at the fine silverware and china plates, at the vast expanse of table that had been left unarranged in preparation for the sheer size of the food that would be set there for her to consume.

When she thought of the size of cakes her childhood friends had sometimes provided during their birthday parties and that her mother had punished her for eating, Bell whispered in her head, *"Bigger."*

Vivian wrapped her fist around the fork, but he kept her from stabbing anything with it.

"You could eat five of his cakes and still be hungry for more, and at this point, you have only yourself to blame. Now eat your dessert before dinner like a good girl."

She'd intended to stab her own arm and let blood turn the audience off of the food, but now she wanted to stab him in the eye she'd tried to break.

The odd chef brought the first cake out and set it in front of Shane. As he straightened, he caught sight of Vivian. Hesitated.

But Vivian was more focused on the chocolate cake, because it was the circumference of a large pizza and three layers deep, with chocolate buttercream whipped into meringue-like peaks. Vivian could smell it all the way from the other end of the table.

Shane groaned, gripping the sides of her chair as though holding on for her life.

Between each Skeleton, a brave guest readied themselves upon the sight of the giant chocolate cake they were challenged to consume. The guests who volunteered to join the contest were almost always male to set off the all-female Skeletons. As Vivian tried not to look at the cakes the odd chef brought out, she couldn't help but notice that the men were noticing the girls quite a bit, from their perky nipples to their short skirts. Despite their excessive skinniness and men's frequent declarations that they didn't want to fuck sticks, Vivian knew that most men didn't give a damn one way or another, as long as they had something warm and welcoming to slip into — and sometimes they didn't need welcoming.

The man next to her was no exception, although he himself was not exceptional — a college or just-out-of-college bro with cargo pants and a T-shirt that he probably hadn't even looked at before coming to the circus. There was a barbecue sauce stain near the collar. She could tell by the scent, her already-sensitive nose working overtime to convince her to eat. The man sensed her attention and grinned, flexing to impress as he took in her exposed skin.

"Think you can take me?" he goaded, the innuendo as intentional and subtle as a penis hitting her cheek.

"I think none of you have any idea what you're up against."

"You've clearly never seen me at a buffet." The man continued to puff himself up like a rooster. "I play football. There's not a refrigerator I can't empty."

"Are you starving?"

"Do I look starving to you? You're the one who looks starving."

"Exactly. You don't have a chance, pigskin."

His grin broadened. "I like a challenge. And I like watching a skinny girl eat."

"Yeah, you and everyone else," she muttered, lowering her eyes as the odd chef slid one of the chocolate cakes in front of the man next to her. It was all she could do not to pounce on it, just climb right onto the table and bury her face in the chocolate icing.

The man held up his fork and knife. "May the hungriest eater win."

"You ain't got nothing on the Skellies, friend, and you ain't got nothing on me. It's barely even a competition." She quieted, though, as the odd chef brought the last cake to her section of the table.

"That's the fun part," the man said, not losing his good cheer.

Jonas slid the cake in front of her. Vivian ran the back of her hand over her mouth. Saliva threatened to drown her tongue.

"Let me make you dinner tonight, Vivian," he said quietly. "Even with the cake, you should eat something of substance."

"I wouldn't be here if I didn't have to be. I'm not stopping until I'm out of this goddamn circus."

"I don't understand what I've done to contribute to this unhappiness. I thought I gave you what you asked for, what you needed."

Vivian was aware the man next to her was trying to hear their conversation, and she turned away from both of them. "No, you don't understand."

"Help me understand. Tell me what you need, and I will provide it."

"I need to get out."

"You need to eat," he said.

"What do you think I'm doing here?"

"This is quantity. You need quality, although you pretend not to care."

"It's not pretend, *esé*. I really don't give a fuck. I'm hungry because Bell makes me hungry, and I'm here because he forced me to be here. Don't read too much into it."

Jonas sighed, but as Bell took his place standing next to Shane to announce the contest, the odd chef shuffled away to let the golems slice the first pieces for the plates. When Lily leaned forward to smell the fresh sponge, the slice was bigger than her whole head.

Bell brought a microphone to his lips so that he could use his phone sex voice. "Welcome, friends, to the notorious Arcanium eating contest, a labor of lust, love and lascivious appetites. Before you are nine giant chocolate cakes, five very hungry women and four brave souls intent on plowing through these rich, luscious cakes faster than my rich, luscious women."

Elbows nudged ribs, and lewd grins were shared among groups of men and boys over the heads of girlfriends and wives.

"Chocolate is both a symbol and stimulant of love and one of the most recognized aphrodisiacs among the varied buffet our chef has to choose from. The assignment to our challengers is simple—the first to finish the entire cake is the winner. If someone who isn't one of mine wins—which has never happened, even when we are graced by professional competitive eaters—they'll walk away with five hundred dollars. My hungry girls, however, only get the taste of good chocolate over their tongues. They're happy enough just to be fed."

He was laying on the innuendo much thicker than the man next to her, but everyone around them seemed to love it, cast and guest.

The crowd for the eating contest wasn't as large as for the band—the food court wasn't designed to hold as many people—but the keen expressions on people's faces were somehow meaner. What was an eating contest but the ultimate celebration of gluttony in a society that prized it? It was even better when the gluttons showed none of its ill effects—like a skinny girl who could eat the football player under the table, in more ways than one.

"Remember... The first to finish the cake with no large chunks of cake or icing left on the platter is the winner. Can you conquer the Skeletons of Arcanium? Begin!"

Vivian resisted at first, but with an arch of his eyebrow, Bell's control wrapped around her like bandages. It was only for a moment. All he needed to do was make her take her first bite. After that, she was lost.

She stuffed chocolate sponge and dark chocolate buttercream into her mouth as though she breathed it instead of air, groaning in both pleasure and discomfort, her stomach happy but overwhelmed by the amount she suddenly provided it. Before she knew it, the golem standing behind her sprang forward and sliced another giant piece as soon as the one she'd been working on had disappeared.

The man next to her laughed, because he was just a bite behind, and his golem dropped the next slice on his plate just a beat after hers. But he'd only been through one piece, and cake wasn't like pizza. Pizza had variations in its flavors. A chocolate cake was chocolate, chocolate, chocolate. Taste boredom would set in quickly...for the average person.

Vivian wolfed through the second piece then the third.

By the fourth slice, the man next to her started to slow down, although he kept a good eye on Vivian on his left and Lily on his right, consuming their cakes with single-minded fervor.

Shane had abandoned her fork and instead shoveled fistfuls into her mouth, barely chewing. Her forehead furrowed, creating worry lines. Worry lines. Red eyes. There might have been tears, too, but who could tell with the icing all over her face?

All four men slowed down. The one between Nasreen and Alicia eventually had to bow out, struggling not to vomit into the bin graciously offered by the golem behind him.

The golem put the sixth slice on Vivian's plate. Sixth slice on Shane's. Vivian was keeping up. It had only taken starving herself for a week to put herself at the same desperate pace, although Shane was still half a slice ahead.

Just two more slices to go.

The odd chef watched them, holding his hands in front of him almost primly, though his shoulders were tight. She doubted the issue he took was with the men who couldn't finish his cakes or the one who wanted to throw up. Jonas glanced instead from one Skelly to the next, concerned, but Vivian couldn't figure out why.

One more slice.

Shaking her head, Shane nearly inhaled the last slice, her eyes closed except to make sure that all the food made it into her mouth. Vivian still had half of her last slice left when Shane slammed both her hands on the table and Jonas stopped the clock to mark her the winner.

Shane lowered her head to the table and panted, smearing icing and catching cake crumbs on her forehead.

Vivian was second. That didn't get her squat, certainly not the sense of true satisfaction that the winner received, although the people inexplicably rooting for her cheered.

She'd beaten the man next to her by two slices. It was the closest she'd ever come to winning. She'd eaten an entire eighteen-inch, three-layer chocolate cake, and because she hadn't won, it hadn't been enough.

The man next to her had already lost, and he didn't even want to continue, so she stood from her seat and started grabbing whole handfuls of cake from his platter.

"Hey!" He laughed as he drew her back, and she stumbled into his lap. She couldn't reach the platter from there, so she took what was left on his plate.

"Uh-oh. Looks like one of our Skeletons went rogue," Bell spoke into the microphone. "Wonder how much she can fit into her mouth?"

Fuck him. He wasn't going to make her bottomless stomach part of his attraction. She ate as much as she could with the man underneath her snagging pieces with his fork until the plate was clean. With his arm around her waist, she still couldn't reach the platter, so she turned around and kissed him, his startled groan muffled as she licked his mouth for whatever was left inside of it. He'd already been partially erect when he'd pulled her onto his lap, but now his cock seemed to jump, swelling too fast to be natural. The sex demons had to be somewhere close in the crowd, because her hunger translated seamlessly into arousal, and it was just as powerful.

But it gave her a new idea. She licked the icing and crumbs from his face, sucking on the skin, as she rocked over his erection. His groans were no longer muffled, grunts wrenched from him as though he were being punched, but he tightened his arms around her and his hips jerked to meet hers as she gave him what basically amounted to a lap dance.

She'd never done this publicly before — unless a large party counted as public. But when it came to things like this, where she was the one in control, she had no shame. The man beneath her, with his broad footballer's shoulders and his decent abs, would do anything for her now. If she asked him for a diamond to swallow, he'd give her his own engagement ring. She hadn't even thought to look, but no one was pulling her off in a jealous rage, so Vivian decided she didn't care.

When his face was as clean as it was going to get, she kissed him again, practically having clothed sex with him now. She thought she heard Bell again, but anything beyond the taste of the kiss and the remnants of chocolate cake was only so many strung-together words.

As his hips jerked faster and his groans became rougher, she shoved her hand down his pants and took his hard, hot cock in her fist. In comparison to the odd chef, it was significantly smaller, but all that mattered was what it could give her, and the man was so close. She pulled him with everything she had.

"That's going too far, Miss Vivian." A fist closed in her hair, lifting her up and off of the man. She tugged a little too hard on the man's cock, which made him yelp, but Bell shook her like a kitten to make her let go. He dragged her onto the grass away from the table before hauling her to her feet. For someone who claimed not to want her, he sure did enjoy pulling her hair. "During circus hours, this is a family-friendly venue. There will be no sex in view of the young."

"Try to stop me." She grabbed where he held her hair and pulled against his grip. She didn't care that it hurt. She just wanted something in her mouth. If not cum, she'd take cake. There were three other men who still had both.

"You can't get away from me," Bell said with a touch of impatience as she fought his grip.

She slammed her heel on his foot. If she had to guess, surprise more than pain opened his hand.

She slipped through his fingers, with the exception of a few locks of hair that tore away when he tried to claim her again.

Vivian darted to the man between Nasreen and Lily because he was the closest. She snatched the cake from his plate first, but he was definitely interested in the kissing instead, slobbering all over her neck. She ate the icing around his lips before giving in, smearing cake on his pants as she grasped his cock through the denim to gauge his readiness. Oh yeah, this one was going to blow any minute, too.

"Vivian, what the hell...?" Nasreen said, scooting away. Lily was laughing so hard she had to cough.

But as soon as Vivian slipped her hand under the waistband of the new man's jeans, Bell grabbed her by the hair again.

"Goddamn it, Vivian."

Despite Bell's insistence that she not get sexy with the customers, the guests seemed to love it. Their cheers got louder every time she kicked or tried to reach another man or another cake.

Shane still rested with her head on the plate, panting, the definition of her shoulder blades and ribs more delicate than that of the actual Skeletons, as though she'd been carved from ivory. It was enough to pause Vivian for a moment, an image that almost struck a chord.

But the memory faded before she could place it, and the taste of chocolate in her mouth reminded her to try harder to escape Bell. Here she was, trying to get more when he'd told her to eat, and he wouldn't let her do that either. She had to eat what the odd chef served, but only what she was allowed. And Bell was okay with her dry-humping the hell out of a customer, but God forbid she try to jerk him off for the cream.

"Give her to me." The odd chef held out his hand, not for hers but for the hair that Bell had wrapped around his fist. "I'll take care of it."

"You're losing control of your children." Annoyance wove through Bell's otherwise composed reply.

"I'm not the one who chose their circumstances." It was the first time Vivian had heard that kind of coldness from the odd chef. The tension in Bell's fist around her hair and the stillness of his body suggested he'd heard the difference as well. "I will take care of her."

"Just take her away," Bell said. "If I don't see her for the rest of the night, it'll be too soon."

Vivian struggled as hard against Jonas as she had against Bell, but the latex gloves added another level of difficulty, since her hair stuck to the material. And though she'd thought he would be gentler, he dragged her just as determinedly away from the contest. When she tripped and fell, he kept dragging her through the grass as she kicked and screamed at him.

The crowd cleared a path, still cheering. She was sure it seemed appropriately dramatic and *Texas Chainsaw Massacre*-y. Only the cast would know this wasn't a performance.

Jonas didn't drag her far. The golems still selling snacks at the counter of his food booth deftly moved out of his way as he pulled her into the kitchen.

Golems worked every surface like the obedient, efficient automatons that they were—stirring stew, decorating tarts and gateaux, assembling specialty pizzas, shoving every manner of detestable things in the deep-fat fryers. The kitchen was a bustle of clanking activity, but it was strange without anyone talking or shouting orders to each other.

As soon as Jonas shut the door from any prying eyes, he yanked her up and shoved her back.

"Stop this pathetic tantrum! What on Earth has gotten into you, Vivian?" That was the closest the odd chef had ever come to yelling, and it was enough to startle Vivian into not kicking or punching out at him. "I can't help until I know what's wrong. Was it something I did? Was it the night we shared? Were you still unsatisfied? There's more yet that I can offer. And after all these nights of not eating to the point that you sleepwalk into one of the dumpsters to have my food, I'll make you whatever you want if you'll just eat something real."

"What? You don't make real cake?" she snarled.

This time she tried to kick him where even demons could hurt, but he grabbed her thigh in one of his big hands that were definitely stronger than they looked. He shoved it back against the door then grabbed her wrist before she could claw his face.

"There's a difference between trying to eat as much as you can of one thing and sitting down to a warm drink and warm meal, which you haven't allowed me to give you in days. Don't you want something better than anything you can get, discarded, secondhand, cheap, just to fill the hole—"

Vivian stopped him with a kiss.

But it seemed to be something they both did at the same time, his mouth on hers more important than anything else he had to say. In the middle of a bustling kitchen, she wrapped her free arm around his neck instead of slapping or scratching him, and he pushed her up the door with his warm, soft, strong body.

He feasted on the cake that had made its way over her cheeks and chin and even down her neck. Every time he returned to her mouth, she swallowed chocolate again, compelling her into deeper and deeper kisses, from him, from her, until it was as though they consumed each other.

It was messy, lacked every kind of finesse she had in her repertoire, but she'd since abandoned the tricks of her trade. She just wanted to taste as much as she could, take as much as she could inside her, bring him off so she could swallow that down, too — the only thing of substance she could consume from her present position, despite the fact they were in a kitchen full of food she could eat instead.

She didn't need anything else to eat. She just needed what Jonas could offer — the taste of his food, the taste of his flesh. She could eat him right up, from toes to his smooth head.

And she was turned on as hell. If she had a cock, she'd worry she would make a mess everywhere, but as it was, her underwear felt damp between her legs, and his cock felt enormous where it pressed against that dampness.

She needed... God, she needed something so big and deep that a cock wasn't enough, but it was as close as she was going to get.

Vivian didn't want to *need* it so much and so badly, but since when did Arcanium give her any choice in the matter? This reached into her, slithered like serpents through crevices that were supposed to be closed.

His need fed hers and her need fed his until they rutted against the door.

Without breaking the messy kiss, she jerked open his trousers and yanked down the zip. He didn't bother pulling her leggings off. That would force him to put her down. He tore at the leggings until they ripped, pushed her underwear aside.

He tried to stroke over her folds, over her clit, to prepare her, but Vivian positioned his cock and pushed the head in. That was enough for Jonas to abandon anything beyond shoving himself in the rest of the way, his body plastered against hers and his groan music to her ears.

Her head fell back at the sound. She moved herself over his cock with shallow rocking movements, acting by instinct rather than conscious decision.

"Fuck, Vivian. Look what you've done to me." Despair mingled with the desire in his roughened voice as he thrust into her. "A demon shouldn't dream, but when I sleep, I dream of you and wake up hard as this. I shouldn't sense your hunger, your need. I shouldn't sense anything. I shouldn't want more than what I have. Yet the farther you run from me and the emptier you become, the more I wish to fill."

"Then do it," she whispered, her reply more a moan than the voicing of actual thought. "Fill me. Damn it, fill me. Just…"

She tightened her legs around him, bracing herself on the shelf of his hips and clinging to his shoulders to ride him, even as he quickened and strengthened his thrusts. Out at the tables, she'd been fucking for a purpose, the sex itself incidental. But she couldn't make sex incidental with Jonas. It was why he could reach so deep inside, deeper than his cock filling her where she *needed* so damn hard.

This was sex, pure and simple — using him, yes, but he used her just as much, and there was as much giving as taking, a more equitable exchange of power, which only made her feel weaker, vulnerable, as delicate as Shane with her subtle bones and red, wet, exposed flesh.

Two golems holding trays of meat pies and fried tarantulas patiently waited for the door to be available for them, faces blanker than the odd chef's. Though the pies would likely cool and the batter on the bugs would go moist, Jonas seemingly didn't care enough about the food he was supposed to serve for him to get out of the way.

Yes, yes, fuck yes… Her orgasm rolled in like close thunder, and she released his shoulders to slam her hands against the door and the wall next to them, squeezing her cunt so hard around him that he shouted and came without warning through her climax. She pounded the wood and screamed through clenched teeth.

Then she hit the wall and door again, this time out of pure, unfiltered fury as raw as her lust. "Son of a *bitch!*"

Jonas breathed like a dragon against her neck, his cum squeezing between her walls and his erection to spill along its length. She wasn't angry enough to miss the opportunity. She reached between them to gather the semen from around her entrance then sucked it from her fingers while he watched intently. It took a few more swipes to get most of it, but she was still turned on and didn't want him out of her. Her cunt, like her stomach, couldn't seem to be filled enough.

"Sir, we need to take these out," the first golem at the door began. There was a line of five others behind him now.

"I know!" Jonas snapped, startling her again.

He pulled her back with him against the wall opposite the door, which gave the first golem a little room to squeeze out, but not the next.

Sighing, Jonas hitched her up to get a better grip on her thighs. Then he eased them through the crowded kitchen, avoiding the fires of stoves and the heat from ovens, avoiding the raw meat on the meat counter.

He finally collapsed them onto his bed to cover her once again, his slicked thrusts rough and insistent. He drank her cries until she could drink his cum straight from his cock on his next orgasm.

* * * *

After the circus closed, the golems cleaned up their various stations then left the odd chef and Vivian to their own devices.

They'd managed to pause long enough to get Jonas out of his clothes, but Vivian still wore her torn leggings, underwear and her T-shirt, her arm hooked around his neck as he lay partially over her.

Make a demon come enough and eventually even the sleepless ones went under.

Salt had dried on her temples from when he'd brought her to tears once again with climaxes so sweet that they'd shaken her foundation, when he'd feasted upon her the way she would have preferred to solely feast on him.

Every time she thought she was tightening the noose, he'd slip the rope around her neck to join him beneath the gallows. He'd said that he was helpless to want her, but she was still the one to come first.

There was something about the sensations he squeezed from her like water from cheesecloth. They were physical, but they felt like they came from somewhere else, an amorphous other that left her with tears drying in her hair, holding him even while he slept.

This was how low she'd sunk. This was the pit into which Bell had tossed her, with Jonas as the demon to torment her with everything she hated, everything that made her powerless before someone who seemed like nothing but a man.

It had been only a week of resisting the appetites Jonas tried so desperately to fulfill. She could keep going like this just out of spite—and she would—but she already knew it would backfire. From dumpster-diving in her sleep to jumping the nearest guest, it all brought her back to the odd chef's kitchen, feeding and being fed upon.

Vivian eased herself from under him, telling herself any tenderness was just to keep him from waking.

Her askew panties and torn leggings were massively uncomfortable. She kicked off her shoes, her leggings, her underwear, and since walking around in a crop top and nothing else seemed silly, she shed the shirt, too.

After rummaging through his clothes—all of them the same—she pulled on one of his undershirts. It smelled like him, the way everything of his did.

She stood in front of the bed for whole minutes, staring at the man who slept naked on the top of the sheets without any of the same vulnerability a human might have had. Nothing about him was pretty or handsome or much at all, but she stared anyway, although it accomplished nothing and she came to no further conclusion about him that was any less disturbing than the ones she'd already reached.

She forced herself to turn away and started to leave the kitchen to do the Walk of Shame once more. This time everyone would know who she'd been fucking. Unless she'd boned a golem, there was only one person who had disappeared at the same time she had and apparently destroyed all her clothes in the process.

Would that be juicy enough gossip to satisfy Alicia, or would it just be one more notch in the belt of her general dislike for Vivian? Their late dinner, which had yet to be served, probably wouldn't help. And what about Shane, who'd looked defeated by her victory? She'd go to sleep full, but would Vivian coming in without her clothes make whatever bothered her worse?

God, when did I start caring?

Vivian stopped at the door and turned back to the kitchen. The gleaming knives. The cleaning supplies. The swimming blowfish, one chewing on a mussel.

Purple light poured onto the deadly mushroom garden.

She stepped in front of the garden, not entirely sure how she'd gotten from the door to there. She had no memory of going through the kitchen. Everything felt frayed, unraveled, temporary. It was a familiar and unfamiliar feeling at once, and like most aspects of Arcanium, familiar and unfamiliar, she didn't like it at all.

Vivian dug through Jonas' chef's coat until she found a pair of those black latex gloves he liked so much and pulled them on as quietly as she could.

She picked six of the toadstools and six of the death caps.

Moving to the butcher block, she chopped the mushrooms as fine as she could get them then took a mortar and pestle and ground the rest. Some of it turned into paste, some of it into powder. She separated the loose, powdery part from the paste.

Vivian was methodical, patient but efficient. She was more accustomed to crushing pills and opening gel packs, but this was still within her wheelhouse, chef though she wasn't.

Every so often, she looked up to movement in the corner of her eye. The blowfish were active in the quieter kitchen. She would have caught one of them, but she couldn't figure out how the aquarium worked, and she wasn't sure how to guarantee something she used would have tetrodotoxin in it. The mushrooms were easier, more reliable and much more accessible.

The golems had left some of the roadkill stew in the refrigerator for the next day, but there was still a pot of it simmering on the stove, which told her what the Skeletons' dinner was supposed to be that night. She remembered the stew was always a little different but always tasty. Mushrooms would barely be noticeable through the aromatic, flavorful broth.

Vivian put a fourth of the paste into the simmering stew and stirred it in. The rest she put into the stew in the fridge intended for the guests.

Next, she opened the meat freezer.

Some of the meat was packaged in wrapping plastic, but especially if it was going to be used soon, they kept it bare. Vivian sprinkled the mushroom powder over a few racks of ribs, over cuts of meat she couldn't identify but were within her reach.

Then she went back to the fridge where they kept the pizza dough and sprinkled the rest in as many containers as she could, folding the mushrooms in so that they were indistinguishable from any other spice in the dough.

When she was finished, she washed the pestle, mortar and both containers that had held the mushrooms. She didn't know whether they'd contaminate anything else in the dishwasher, but it wouldn't matter anymore at that point.

She threw the gloves into the trash then washed her hands for good measure.

Nothing stirred but her as she considered what she'd done.

Vivian wondered if she had enough time to salt the edible mushrooms in the vegetable drawer with some of Jonas' poisonous collection and whether the golems would be able to tell the difference. Just as she turned from the sink to pick a few of the mushrooms she couldn't identify that might be confused for edible, Jonas grabbed her wrist.

His expression like that of a carving in a glacier, he maneuvered her without effort to the meat freezer. Then shoved her in.

Vivian fell hard against the shelves of loin, butt, shank and bacon. She crumpled to the floor.

With black eyes empty and evil as he stared down at her, Jonas slammed the door shut.

Chapter Ten

Vivian pounded on the thick metal door and jerked at the handle but the door wouldn't budge.

"Open this door! Goddamn it, Jonas, open this door!" She hadn't minded the cold or the slick floor when she'd been in here for only a few minutes, but her feet were bare and all she had on was the white undershirt.

"Let me out of here!" Her pounding increased the sense of doubling, the feeling she'd been here before, although she'd never been locked in a freezer. It was expansive, but the longer the door stayed locked, the smaller the freezer became. Her breath ghosted out in front of her, reminding her that there was a finite amount of air. She wasn't claustrophobic by nature, but the combination of elements brought her to the edge of panic then right over.

"Jonas! Jonas, please! Let me out of here!" She added a level of hysteria to the sound, but as the sob came through, she realized it wasn't artifice. She thought of being found dead with tears frozen on her skin and pounded on the door harder.

"Let me out! Let me out!" Both fists now.

"But should I?"

That wasn't Jonas. And the words weren't muffled at all by the thick door. Bell might have been standing right in front of her.

"Bell, you nauseating slime mold, you let me out of here right now!"

"I'm tempted to leave you in there all night."

He opened the door.

Vivian tried to dart around him into the warm kitchen, but he raised his leg and slammed his boot against her chest. She swore she heard a series of cracks before she struck the shelves of meat again behind her. Her feet slipped on the floor, and she knocked her head against one of the shelves as well. Her vision blacked out, world spinning. She was unable to do anything as Bell strode in, grabbed her by her numb feet and pulled her out onto the terracotta kitchen tile.

He didn't give her a chance to warm up or for the pain to fade. He hauled her up from the floor by the undershirt and shoved her hard against the counter, pinning her to the metal edge.

Every fiber of muscle under his exposed skin was taut, his lantern eyes burning, not with warmth but with the same pain that had spread through her with the spell's punishment. For the first time, she fully understood that he wasn't the annoying, unassuming, pretty, prancing owner of the circus. When Jonas had caught her, he'd shut down, his human exterior all she could see, like a golem. But Bell was furious, a thundercloud to her valley-bound fog. Every last fury of her own seemed petty in comparison.

"Do you realize what you almost did?" He spoke softly, but Vivian wanted to cover her ears against it.

"I'm—"

"If you tell me you're sorry and attempt to justify what you did, I will tear out your tongue."

His tone, when coupled with his expression, convinced her that his threat was neither idle nor exaggerated.

"Do you realize what you almost did?" he repeated, this time slower, as though to strike each word into her head with a rusty nail.

Vivian leaned away from him, but there wasn't anywhere she could go.

Finally, she just said, "Yes."

"You put poisonous mushrooms into food intended for both the cast and customers of Arcanium. Fatal poison. This is far beyond the laxatives and emetics you used against your friend or the rat poison you used against your stepfather. If you had succeeded, they wouldn't have had quiet, peaceful deaths. It would have been Jim Jones at a county picnic. Pray tell, who do you think they would have blamed?"

Bell stepped even closer now, his hips against hers, his words practically spitting into her mouth. There was nothing remotely sexual or sexy about it.

"They wouldn't have blamed you, you bony bitch. They would have blamed Jonas, since it was the food that was poisoned. What do you think it would have done to him—the man you refuse to acknowledge as your lover—to know that his mushroom garden killed people in his care? His life is feeding Arcanium, feeding his Skeletons. He has devoted more of himself to you than to anyone. And you repay him by implicating him in the deaths of hundreds, perhaps thousands, in the deaths of those whom he loves as his own?"

Bell filled the room. Jonas was almost inconspicuous, still and small, in front of the blowfish aquarium. He couldn't look at her. She wanted to be nasty. She wanted to snarl, snap and sneer at him for being soft and gullible, for being unbearably naïve. But his body had become a shell. She couldn't find him in it.

"Do you even have the slightest conception of the destruction that you would have wrought? Is your tantrum really worth other people's lives?" He shook her hard enough to chatter her teeth then pushed her to push himself back. "Don't answer that. For the love of everything in this world good and holy, don't you dare open your mouth. Because I know the answer."

He took another step back, glaring her into silence and stillness, though the space he gave her would have been enough to escape him if he were an ordinary man.

A plain water glass flew into his hand. He raised his other hand, fingers moving in little jerks. The refrigerator door opened in tandem with the freezer, and the lids lifted from the stew pots. From every direction came a crinkle of plastic and the sound of sand rustling over glass.

No fucking way.

Each grain of powder and smear of paste from the mushrooms made their way to the glass in Bell's hand, like ants following the lure of sugar through the air. Anything that the mushrooms had poisoned by moisture and proximity came with it, until everything had settled into the glass, leaving it half full.

Bell turned away from her to bring the glass to the sink. He turned on the water until it was a three-quarters full. Then he took a spoon and stirred.

Vivian still didn't try to escape. She was actually paralyzed in fear of what would happen if she tried.

Bell set the glass next to Jonas. Without blinking, Jonas took the glass and brought it to his lips.

Vivian started forward. "Don't—"

Bell raised a finger, as effective as raising a gun. Vivian could do nothing while Jonas downed the whole thing in four swallows.

"He didn't do anything, but you're punishing him instead of me?" Vivian asked, incredulous.

"I could blame him for trusting you, for knowing what you are and still taking you under his wing as though you were nothing but a broken bird. I could blame him for bringing you into this place and making its dangers and poisons accessible to you." Bell stepped toward her again. "But I don't."

"I grow the mushrooms for me," Jonas explained in a deadened voice. "In addition to my own culinary creations, I consume poison, you see. Like poison dart frogs, blowfish, xanthid crabs, I absorb the poison I consume. Venom, poison, toxins, parasites... They're what I was made to eat all along. Had the poison been disseminated, I would have remained unaffected."

"And the immortals would have recovered. So, in the end, had the cast received the brunt of your petty retaliation, you would have left yourself the only living human in a circus of demons." Disgust was what Bell had exhibited outside the dump truck. This ran several miles beneath the surface of disgust. "You selfish, thoughtless *infant*."

Jonas set the empty glass on the counter, his lips still showing signs of the liquid he'd drunk. "Would you like a kiss now?"

Vivian had nowhere to back away to, but he didn't come after her. She fought the impulse to slap him, make him look at her, make the slackness in his cheeks tighten. She wanted the dull glaze in his eyes to become less like that of a shark or the spores of a mushroom.

"I'm —" she began.

"What did I just tell you, Vivian?" Bell snapped.

She shut up.

"I see every crevice and cranny of your mind. I see your past and future and your present. I see what you were thinking when you did it and what you're thinking now. And there's nothing you can say." He jumped back to sit on one of the counters, deceptively casual, though that tautness was still in every last muscle. Movement only exacerbated the impression. "Please leave, chef. I think it's time to deal with Vivian my way. Take care of your other Skeletons."

"What of her punishment?" Jonas said.

"If there is to be a public punishment, you'll hear of it. You don't have to attend — I know it is distasteful to you — but your girls will."

"What do I tell them?"

Jonas wouldn't look at her, but Bell wouldn't stop, those hazel eyes gleaming golden like an Egyptian idol.

"I think this is best kept between the three of us, don't you? After all, they were in no real danger. She's just a little girl."

Vivian tightened her hold on the edge of the counter, but she didn't open her mouth this time. He would rip her tongue out. He really would.

Jonas took the simmering stew, made safe by Bell, from the stove and left the kitchen without another word.

"What are you going to do?" Vivian asked.

"A year ago, I would have put you in the funhouse as my prisoner to pay off the debt you owe to this circus. But to tell the truth, Vivian, I've lost my taste for that, and I've lost my taste for you. I've tolerated too much for that voice, that gift you certainly never appreciated, perhaps because it came to you too easily. Even those who wish for a skill know how precious that skill should be to them because they'd tried to achieve it on their own and failed. But you were born with your voice."

"I can sing for you again. You were always able to force me," Vivian said.

"Your voice isn't enough for me to expend the energy. Alicia and Lennon will do well enough for me until I find another singer, and Dom and Delilah are a good enough variety to supplement their efforts."

He jumped from the counter and approached her, each step like the sound of an axe on a wooden block. He stopped not four inches from the bend of her knee. "You betrayed your lover, cracked his spirit when I told you to spare him. And if I were a lesser man, you would have killed countless of my people. You no longer deserve to be called mine. You don't deserve him, and you don't deserve Arcanium. I'm done with you. You win, Vivian. You're free."

Vivian brought her brows together, narrowing her eyes in suspicion. *There's no way it can be this easy.*

"Oh, I suppose it's as easy as stepping across the threshold." Bell touched her cheek with the crook of his finger. Vivian half expected that her cheek would be more frostbitten than what the freezer had done. But his finger was just that of a man. "Easy. All you had to do was become a killer, Vivian. A murderer."

"No one died," she said, barely more than a whisper.

"They would have. Do you know what it would have been like for them? No, you don't, nor do you care. You're nothing but a child with a magnifying glass disturbing an ant pile."

"And you're nothing but a child with a terrarium on every shelf." Vivian found strength in her voice again now that she knew he wasn't going to kill her. "And a stick to poke your pets with."

"I take care of my pets. I love my pets. Every terrarium is clean, every animal is fed and tended to and every environment is according to their needs. But when an animal's gone too sick for me to tend, there's only one thing I can do." The threat of his finger against his cheek broadened into his entire hand, a caress that felt like fingers around her throat. "Oh, yes, I'll set you free, like you've wanted all along."

He stepped back again and gestured to the door. "The spell won't keep you here. I never want to see you again. I never want to so much as hear one metal scream from the microphone. Leave Arcanium and never come back."

Vivian inched to the side. He'd cracked her ribs, she was still aching from being thrown to and fro and her feet might have been frostbitten, but he wasn't stopping her.

When she reached the kitchen door, she rushed out of the booth and into the circus proper then into the fairgrounds.

But as she reached the knife-throwing booth where she'd been sleeping, she glanced back.

Bell was following her, quiet as a fairy in the woods. He stayed about twenty-five feet back. In the darkness rather than the bright kitchen, the glow in his eyes seemed all the more malicious.

She turned back toward the front of the fairground, where the ticket booths had been set up for the weekend. But she looked back again before crossing that invisible threshold, the hollowness in her stomach twisting like a knife.

It's too easy.

Vivian turned completely around to face Bell again. "What's the catch?"

"If you had done your time and embraced this circus, my dear, you would have walked out free, healthy, with meat on your bones and your hunger slaked. But you're poison, Vivian. I knew that from the beginning, although I hoped for a better outcome. As much as Jonas loves his own poison, as much as Sasha loves her venom and as dangerous as the Spider when she plunges her teeth into your flesh, you are the greater threat to Arcanium among all my cast by far. I won't keep you here to punish. I'll let you out like you wanted, but I won't take what I did away."

Bell hooked his thumbs in the waistband of his leather pants, traced dirt with the toe of his boot as though he already didn't have to concern himself with her. "How long do you think your body can support itself with the consumption I gave you? You might as well walk yourself right into a hospital. They'll poke and prod you, hook you up to a saline drip, force-feed you, but nothing will work. Soon you'll be nothing but the skeleton. The real skeleton—nothing left of body fat, your muscles paper thin, your brain gasping for air. And even then you won't understand why this is happening to you."

"You're killing me."

Bell stepped into the beam of the parking lot lights. "Yes."

"There have to be other genies out there, other people I can make a wish to," Vivian said.

"We're hard to find, and not all of them are as kind as I am," Bell replied. "That is your future — your carved-in-stone future — should you step over the threshold of Arcanium."

She narrowed her eyes. Bell didn't mince words. If his reply was conditional, it wasn't by accident.

"What if I don't step over the threshold?"

"If I want you over that threshold, I can ensure that you can never enter Arcanium again."

"And if you don't force me?"

He blinked as slowly as a cat, not in surprise but in consideration. For a long time, he didn't say a word, just stared as though reading her like a novel. "This would be the last chance. No more resisting. No more tantrums. You'll eat what the odd chef feeds you and you'll sing when the band sets up. I believe you're capable of obeying, but only with the right understanding of what you've done."

"But I didn't do anything. You stopped it. Nothing was *done*." Vivian resisted the urge to stomp her foot, throw something at him, just to make him get angry in a way she could understand.

"I stopped it because I'm prescient, silly girl, and because Jonas could smell the disturbed spores. If we were the mere men you delude yourself that we are, you would have succeeded. After all, you've succeeded before. It's your modus operandi."

Vivian crossed her arms. "What do you want?"

"Someone like you doesn't understand the pain you cause. You only understand consequences — fifty of the Ringmaster's lashes in the ring for all to see." He slowly stepped forward, hands behind his back, again with the deceptive casualness of any apex predator. "That's what you owe Arcanium. What you owe me is this."

When he brought his hands from behind his back, he held a large coffee mug filled to the brim with the same mushroom mixture that Jonas had drunk to the dregs. It had been mixed in hot chocolate, lumps of mushrooms instead of marshmallows.

"If you want to live, you will drink what you tried to serve. You will suffer what you would have made others suffer." He held up the mug as though raising a toast. "That is my condition for you to remain here."

"You can't be serious. I'm not drinking that. I'm not poisoning myself just because you get off on it." Vivian took a step back, but a shudder shivered up her body, and she nervously glanced behind her to make sure she wasn't close enough to the ticket booths for it to matter — like checking that she wasn't too close to the edge of a cliff.

"That would be your choice."

"It's a hell of a choice!"

"When you royally piss off the owner of a demonic circus, I'm afraid this is the consequence. You can die two months from now in a hospital bed, stuck with more needles than Skinless but your own woman — with no friends, with family who won't come to your side until you're buried and not enough money to cover the treatment you receive. Or you can poison yourself now and submit to me. You won't have family or friends here either, but you would have your understanding, and you'd have me. I would still be your keeper, and I take care of what I keep."

He held the cup out to her. "You won't taste it. You'll only feel the effects. If you intend to follow the path of malignant self-hatred that you've been on since you were young, then leave. But if you want to live, then drink the poison and come with me."

"I haven't been on a path of self-hatred. Everyone else can go to hell, but I don't hate myself."

"Everything you hate about everyone else is something you hate in yourself. Every choice you make that leads to another job lost, another friend with their back turned, another family member who barely remembers to call you on your birthday? That's you sabotaging yourself at every turn. Oh, some of it is in your blood, and some of it is in your past. But at a certain point, you are responsible for your fate, and you crossed that point a long time ago. So, which is it? Do you want your freedom, or do you actually want to live? You don't get to have both. Think about it, Vivian. I have all night to stand here waiting for an honest answer, if you're capable of one."

She'd never liked Bell, but it hadn't been because he didn't like her or because he insulted her at every turn. She'd preferred how he didn't sugarcoat how he felt. But in the quiet tension between them, that bald honesty soured.

He didn't insult to be nasty, the way she did. He truly thought she was a vile, disgusting, manipulative, lying whore-bitch, as repugnant to him as a turd on his bare foot. Each insult was spoken with complete and utter truth—not the kind of truth that was a matter of opinion but with the weight of fact.

She thought of the way Jonas had looked at her, as though she were dead to him. Alicia, her disgust rife with envy. Simón had looked at her like a meal, Fernanda like lice in her hair. She remembered the way her friends had looked at her every time she'd stolen someone's man, when she'd flashed ice she'd earned in bed. She'd always thought they hated her because she had the guts to do what it took to get what she wanted. But with their sneers, the subtle shakes of their heads, she wondered.

The way Angelica had looked at her when Vivian hadn't been able to hold her stepfather off. The way Arturo had looked at her when she'd first called her brother a freak, although she hadn't meant it with the same malice as their parents.

Vivian wanted to cover her eyes, cover her ears, but the images and words rushing through her were memories, and there was no stopping them once they started.

If she got out of Arcanium, Bell was right. She had nothing, nothing but a little time and no amount of dignity. If she stayed, she had nothing but all the time in the world, and Bell would strip what dignity she had left away anyway.

She reached for the cup.

He held it away. "This is it, Vivian. Your final chance. If you try to harm or kill anyone in my circus again, I'll feed you to the clowns. There's not much to you, but they're fond of organs. Are you sure?"

She wasn't sure. That's what scared her—and not much did. She wasn't sure which hellish end she should choose—which meant that death was an option to her, and she hadn't known that.

'Go ahead, little bitch. Go ahead and slice your throat open from end to end. But if you're gone, you know what I'll do. Your freak sister gone. You gone. There'll be no one left to protect sweet little Angelica. You go away and I'll have no fucking choice, will I? So go the fuck ahead and do it.'

She hadn't sliced her throat, and she hadn't sliced his. She wished she had, but she didn't say that aloud. Instead, she beckoned for the cup. "Give it to me."

Bell handed it to her.

Vivian chugged it down like it was Greek Week then dropped the mug to the grass. The handle broke off. Bell conjured both pieces into his hand and merged the broken pieces together until the mug was whole once more.

The poison had tasted like earthen hot chocolate, and for a moment, Vivian found herself craving more.

"Oh, there's more where that came from." Bell passed the mug behind his back again. When he brought his hands to the front, they were empty for him to hold a hand out to her. "Come with me."

"If you think—"

Bell didn't have to stop her. She stopped herself. But he arched his eyebrow, as though daring her to finish her automatic refusal. When she didn't, he gestured again for her to take his hand.

She wasn't the hand-holding type. But that wasn't what this is about.

"That's right, Vivian. You belong to me now. It's time to go to the ring."

"Everyone will see," she said, her voice far away.

"They'll see the whipping, not the poison. The poison is just for you and me. It's not such a terrible thing for me to see you, my dear. I see everything."

She wasn't used to voluntarily doing things she didn't want to do. But she also didn't want to die.

Vivian slipped her hand into his. Without another word, they walked together, side by side, through the Renaissance fair and into the crescent of the circus. When he'd said he'd take her to the ring, she'd thought he meant the one set up near the food court, but he took her back to his fortune teller's tent instead.

Bell lifted the flap and flourished her into the pitch darkness within.

It didn't smell like it had the last time she'd been there — of sandalwood and other dark, woodsy scents, of candle wax and cedar and smoke. This time it smelled of sawdust, animal hide, popcorn and roasted peanuts.

Spotlights, bright as interrogation lamps, switched on with a series of thunks. Vivian stood in the middle of a sawdust ring delineated with red-painted wooden partitions.

Bell lowered himself to sit on the edge. "This is where I've been keeping the ring since I had to close Arcanium a year ago. It's just waiting for its moment again. Really, with all the new talent, I think we've been ready for a while. I'm the one who isn't ready. I'm the one with performance issues. All my adversaries know I'm strong, but they know that Arcanium has been taken from me once, and that makes them believe there are ways to take it again."

Vivian didn't know why he was telling *her* this, of all people. He should have been talking to someone he actually liked rather than giving her this ammunition.

"All the people I like were taken from me when Arcanium was stolen. They have their own pain," Bell said quietly. "And none of this is ammunition. If I liked you, perhaps. But you used the last of my good will, and you don't have and never will have the means to exploit what I tell you today, much less take Arcanium from me. Center stage, please."

"Oh, now you're all polite. My dears. Please and thank you." Frankly, that panicked her more than the ferocity he'd shown in the kitchen.

"Remove your clothing, *please*. You'll have to strip eventually for the Ringmaster. You might as well do it now, before the side effects of the mushroom poisoning make themselves known."

Her stomach churned as she removed the undershirt, but she wasn't sure whether it was from the mushrooms or her own raw nerves. The spotlights focused on the ring seemed to get brighter, masking Bell in a layer of shadow right outside of their reach.

She put the undershirt on the partition. Bell pointed her back into the ring. She returned, her legs shaking.

"Mushroom poisoning can take effect over days or weeks. I will condense those effects into a few hours. You won't die. You'll just wish you would. Then you'll wish it all over again when the Ringmaster lays into your back. But you chose life, my dear, and I'll hold you to that for the next few years."

"Not the next few hundred?"

"You won't need that long to decide whether you want to escape again."

She shrugged, raising both shoulders and hands. "What now?"

"Any minute. Do you know why you chose to live after choosing to die when you poisoned the food?"

"I didn't choose to die. I chose to kill other people." She'd never said what she did so candidly, not even to herself.

"This wasn't something small that you could keep in the corner from prying eyes. You chose a dramatic death that would get my attention, and you knew I would take my revenge."

"Not everything is about you."

"You wanted to get caught. There's a word for people like you."

"Psychopath?" She'd only heard it once, at least from someone who was qualified to say it.

"Self-destructive. And that's not solely the province of a psychopath, my dear, if that's what you think you are. Self-destruction has led to so many being brought into my circus. You just self-destruct more spectacularly than most, maximizing the collateral damage. That is what I cannot allow, Vivian. I won't let you send shrapnel into more vulnerable flesh."

"What do you mean, what I think I—"

She was interrupted by a full abdominal cramp that curved her spine like a pill bug trying to close. She fell to the ground with a loud groan, wrapping her long, unnaturally thin arms around her long, unnaturally thin belly. The cramp pulsed inside her, but it didn't subside. She retched, clenched, pushed her hips up from the ground, but there was no escaping it. She'd put it into her body herself.

The poison hit her system like a freight train to a wooden pallet—headache, dizziness, visual auras, fever, chills, cramps, irresistible waves of nausea so much stronger than those of her little anxieties that she forgot they ever existed.

"Oh God, I think I'm gonna…" She managed to roll onto her hands and knees, but she couldn't brace herself in either direction.

"Don't hold back on my account," Bell said quietly. "The poison will do what it will."

It started with vomiting blood.

* * * *

When it was finished, Vivian lay in the midst of her own sickness, barely able to twitch. She was disgusting and disgusted herself, but she couldn't move out of it. Her body was smeared once again, coated with a layer of sawdust that dried out what it could, but it was no match for the damage that the mushrooms had done.

She'd cried her eyes dry. She couldn't anymore.

Bell stood from the shadows and approached her. Not many people would approach someone who looked and smelled the way she did now, but he crouched just outside of the mess she'd made.

"This is what you do to other people," he said. "This is what you make them feel."

"No." All she could manage was a whimper of a whisper.

"This is what would have happened to my cast, to my guests, except it would have taken longer. It would have been agony extended well beyond what you experienced, followed by death."

"No."

"Yes. Now, Vivian, do you understand what you have done?"

She turned her head to peer into his impassive but not dulled expression.

"You understand some of it," he finally said with a sigh. "I suppose asking you to understand all of it was asking too much. I'll just have to show you the rest."

"No. Please, don't. Please."

"That's the first time I've heard you beg," Bell said. "You only fear when you're afraid someone is going to see you for what you are. You don't like seeing it either, do you, Vivian?"

Her vision flashed and she could see the past from all perspectives this time, not just her own.

She was in Fernanda's house, on Fernanda's couch, underneath Fernanda's boyfriend, her nails making lines on his back as he shoved himself inside her, grunting his pleasure into her shoulder. He couldn't see anything, so he hadn't seen that Fernanda had picked herself up from her bed, where she'd been resting after throwing up all afternoon from the ipecac Vivian had put in her soda. But Vivian could see her just fine in the opening of the hallway, mouth open, eyes wide, anger surfacing under the dark circles.

Vivian had laid claim to the man she'd chosen to seduce because she could, and because he bought her nice things and said even sweeter things in her ear when his girlfriend was right there in the same room.

Simón felt guilt. He felt guilt every single time. He hadn't confessed to a priest yet, couldn't bring himself to claim to repent, because he knew he wasn't going to. He was getting away with it. He didn't know what was wrong with Fernanda all the time. He just knew that when she felt gross, that's how she was to him and his desire for her had faded.

He still loved Fernanda in his own way. She was familiar and convenient. But Vivian was spicy as hell, always up for whatever he wanted, showing him things he hadn't even known he needed until he got a taste of it. Vivian was a warm pussy and a sloppy lay, and he buried himself in the whole mess because he liked it. He liked getting dirty, and no one in their circle was dirtier than her.

All his friends had warned him about her, but he'd half hoped she would come on to him so he could have a taste – just one hookup. But she'd hooked him instead, and though he felt covered in a layer of slime every time he took her, coming inside her was one of the best of all the worst things in the world, like dying. It had never been like that with Fernanda.

He'd fucked her knowing that Fernanda could come in at any time. That had just made it better.

302

Which only made it worse for Fernanda when she finally did, when she saw who her man was, who her best friend was.

Vivian actually smiled at her. Because as sweet as it was to get away with stealing a man, it wasn't nearly as sweet as getting caught, when the woman realized her man had been taken away.

The fact that Fernanda was her best friend didn't matter. It was the same thrill.

Vivian felt it again, but there was also a tightening in her chest like a fist, shaky numbness all the way to her fingers. Something that wasn't physical — but might as well have been — exploded like a solar flare in her head as she saw herself through Fernanda's eyes, fucking her best friend's man. A virtual wave of feelings Vivian couldn't recognize, much less handle, flooded her all at once.

She was back in the ring, crying out as though in pain, but she knew pain, and this wasn't pain. Yet it was.

Vivian's vision flashed again, sending her back, sending her into someone else.

"No," she whispered.

She swept to when she was a baby, to when she was a child, to when she was a teenager. She saw herself through the fear when her mother held her in her arms as they sat alone in an empty apartment. Marisol had barely been able to take care of herself, much less two little girls.

Why did they have to be girls? Why couldn't she have had a boy? Though Anamaria had been an easier baby, she'd grown up into a sullen child who refused to wear her hair in pigtails, had to be punished into her dresses and wouldn't wear lipstick, even if Marisol paid her.

And it got worse when Esteban came into her life, with his broad shoulders and his grand romantic gestures. A man who liked a woman with kids, the best surrogate father, until Anamaria started withdrawing even more, wouldn't come home, wore her best friend Julio's hand-me-downs, chopped her hair off herself when Marisol wouldn't let her.

Marisol knew. She didn't want to know, but she knew. And she let it happen, because if Esteban was preoccupied with Anamaria, he wouldn't come after her. So she let Esteban do what he did behind closed doors. She found solace in what control she had – every calorie counted, each rib visible on her daughters' sides.

When Anamaria insisted her name was Arturo and ran away at fourteen, Marisol called her first daughter dead. She still had two more left, including the one product of her unholy union.

Esteban then turned to Marisol's second chance.

Vivian was stronger – a strong-willed, cold young girl with a violent streak, though she loved her younger sister and the one she called brother. She wore the pretty things that Marisol bought her, wore the things that showed her beauty, and Esteban was smitten.

Marisol looked away again, afraid of her husband, afraid of a life without him, afraid of dark little Vivian, with her accusing black eyes and a steady stream of boyfriends and angry parents telling Marisol to get her daughter under control.

But Marisol couldn't control Vivian. She couldn't control Esteban. And she couldn't control Angelica. The less she could control, the more she withered and the more Esteban told her what her reflection should be.

More than Anamaria's abandonment, more than Angelica's quiet hatred, it was Vivian who was the true reflection of what Marisol had done.

She loved and hated her middle daughter, loved and hated her so much that she sometimes vomited with it. Loved her strength, hated that Esteban kept comparing mother to the loveliest daughter. She blamed Vivian for the blight in her husband because it was easier than blaming herself for bringing that blight into her household, feeding it with every terrible thing that tumbled from her mouth. The only thing she wanted to say was that she loved her daughters, but nothing she did was of love.

And when Vivian followed the path of her brother and stole her sister away as well, there was no taking it back, no other buffer to put between herself and the man in her bed who preferred her daughters, including the one he'd made.

She was left alone, with bruises to mimic the hollows in her thinnest places, and the taste of stomach acid in the back of her throat every time her husband looked at her and said, "Wanna make another one?"

"Please. Stop." Vivian turned away from Bell, but that didn't make him stop. His magic transcended something as basic as eye contact.

She saw herself from behind, singing in front of the main microphone. Before Vivian had come to Arcanium, Alicia had been a serviceable lead, but she couldn't ignore how clear it had been that Bell was searching for something else. And that something else had come in the form of a woman who just walked up, flashed a karaoke singer away, grabbed the mic and screamed the house down without breaking a sweat, a woman who still remained ridiculously pretty in her transformation to a Skeleton. One who didn't know a thing about appreciating what she had and instead sulked around like a teenage boy, complaining, picking fights and destroying everything she laid her eyes upon. Destroying everything that had been working before she came.

Yet when she sang, it all fell away, and it was as though the woman — who Alicia was half-sure was a demon or witch — could be human after all. It was beautiful — more beautiful than thinspiration, more beautiful than a Victoria's Secret runway, more beautiful than an empty kitchen and a new scale, more beautiful than skeletons. It shivered over her skin and inside her head like cold water, like an orgasm, but it wasn't sexual.

When Vivian stopped singing, Alicia always felt so ugly – with a voice that needed oiling, all parts of her body that didn't show bone needing to lack more. She couldn't make herself prettier. She couldn't make her voice better. And she'd always be standing behind the woman everyone fell in love with when she sang. Lily had the electric violin, Shane had the drums and Nasreen had the keyboard. Alicia just stood there, second-rate in every way.

Alicia had wished first, so she was only a Skeleton. Vivian was the one Bell had really wanted. And she couldn't blame him. But she could blame herself.

"I don't. I don't want to know. Please."

Vivian already knew. Bell wasn't showing her anything she hadn't already known, but he showed it to her with a depth she couldn't bear. How did other people live with these kinds of *feelings* all the time? Anger was hard enough to handle, and it was nothing in comparison to the anger of others. Her anger was that of a miniature tyrant, a dehydrated facsimile of the fury Alicia felt when she looked in the mirror and saw Vivian behind her, perfect, yet somehow perfectly unhappy in spite of everything she had.

She saw her sister Angelica during every time Vivian didn't come home but Esteban did, especially once Angelica had crossed the threshold into puberty. Esteban had resisted the lure of his own child as long as he could, because even he felt there was a line he shouldn't cross. But whenever Vivian stayed out, that just put Angelica closer and closer to the line of fire.

At first she hadn't known how different her father was from other fathers, but with Arturo gone and Vivian getting thinner and meaner and Mother pushing Angelica to be a woman before she was ready, Angelica started to sense the difference. Esteban had been doting. He'd spoiled Vivian and Angelica when they were younger, but he'd spoiled Vivian more. Angelica had been jealous at first that her father, flesh-and-blood father, had been spending so much time with a daughter that wasn't even his. It wasn't until Esteban had started to stare at Angelica at the wrong moments, and for too long, that Angelica had understood why Vivian had gone distant, and how far she'd been willing to go to protect her sisters when their mother wouldn't.

But that realization came with a wave of impotent rage that was safer to apply to the sister who was her only buffer. Arturo had left them, saved himself. Vivian was going to leave eventually. She'd already started. Then there would be nothing left between Angelica and her father.

That rage didn't subside when Vivian had kidnapped her away. She couch-surfed with friends, sometimes with Vivian, sometimes didn't couch-surf at all but stayed in abandoned houses or buildings overnight, until she was eighteen. She hated Vivian as much as she loved her — for helping Arturo out of the house but not taking her away sooner, for not turning Esteban in, for taking it instead of fighting the way Angelica knew she could have, for being the kind of person who would use her own stepfather in the same breath she protected her sister.

Vivian looked like Marisol but she felt like Esteban. And Angelica couldn't stand the sight of her anymore.

Vivian threw up again — nothing but bile now, but at least it wasn't bloody. "Don't show him to me. Please don't."

"I won't."

Vivian didn't know whether he'd meant to, but there had been compassion in his response. Vivian recognized the weakness, but she also recognized more than ever that Bell's weaknesses were far stronger than her strengths, and she couldn't hope to use them.

"One more," he said.

She flashed into the odd chef's kitchen and watched herself go through the mechanical motions of poisoning the circus and its inhabitants.

Because Jonas had watched her the entire time. Every moment, he'd hoped that she would change her mind, that she would do the right thing, that she would step back and stare at her hands in shock. He wondered if maybe she was doing it in her sleep, the way she'd crawled into dumpsters and knocked over trash cans.

She didn't stop. She wasn't asleep.

And the deep, dark place that had survived Locke's Arcanium, had survived Socrates, Cleopatra and Heaven's Gate, that compelled him to be what he had no desire to be, raised its foul, venomous head.

No longer dormant, it pulsed with a burst of malevolent radiation to eradicate the qualities he had prized and strove to keep like a well-tended garden. He watched her poisoning Arcanium, and he wanted to join her, to take all the mushrooms, grind them down or put them in the food processor. Sprinkle them into the stew, rub them into the meat like salt, poison the spirits and the tarts and feed it to the grasshoppers and tarantulas in the room she hadn't yet seen. Gather the blowfish and cut them into fine, fatal pieces to serve to all and sundry.

Because the impulse to feed those who starved, to satisfy those unsatisfied, was the same impulse to feed them what they didn't need and satisfy them with things that made them emptier. He saw in Vivian everything his demon wanted, everything his demon was. He wanted to lay waste to Arcanium and the whole town beyond it and fuck her in the midst of the dead and the dying. Maybe then she would…

It was her emptiness that called to him, her longing to be satisfied on every level that she had denied herself from such an early time that she didn't recognize that she was empty.

She craved that emptiness more than fulfillment and called it control.

Some demons derided his love for humanity, but it was something that made him feel more in his own skin than that dark fire he had been forged with. Then she'd come into the circus like a demon born in human form, an agent of destruction in the guise of humanity, her broken pieces more solid than iron. He'd fed upon her drowning, fed her until she was full to bursting in exactly the way she couldn't stand because she'd awakened the demon, which confused the difference between satisfaction and desperation – and he pretended to himself that it was out of the goodness of his black heart.

Until she'd poisoned those he'd sworn to protect and his first impulse hadn't been to throw her into the freezer but to tear his shirt from her body and eat poison from the valley of her spine before making her come so many times that those who consumed the poison would also consume the salt of her pleasure.

She made him feel like himself, the very self he'd suppressed for hundreds of years because he hated it, because the joy he derived from good cooking was so much cleaner and brighter and sweeter than the joy he got from doing what he was designed to do. He wasn't like the Ringmaster, who satisfied himself with the pain of others and indulged the single sliver of humanity inside of him with one person. Jonas preferred the full breadth and depth of humanity that he was inexplicably capable of. And she'd destroyed that in a matter of moments, just when he thought he'd finally be able to show her her own humanity, buried as deeply as he'd stored the demonic inside himself.

Instead, the whole of him rose to the surface, and he hated that she made him want to destroy what he had created, render it little more than debris after a storm, that he would strike the Ringmaster down and bring Bell low again for the demon to walk free.

He tamped it down with every last bit of strength that he had, his hatred dark and swift and complete, wanting so much more than to throw her into the freezer.

She'd been lucky he hadn't bashed her head in like overripe cantaloupe.

When she came back into herself, the ring was clean. The mushrooms were out of her system, but she was shaking as though shivering through a fever, and she'd somehow found more tears to cry, because her face was wet and her eyes burned.

Bell sat next to her, legs crossed, holding her head in his lap. He brushed his fingers idly over her hair. She twisted from his touch, and he pulled his hands away, but she was too weak to shift from his lap.

"I can make you feel that all the time, as I do." Bell touched her cheek. "All you would have to do is wish it."

"Why would I want that?" she whispered, trying to get a hold on her shudders and the still-steady stream of tears. "Why would I want to feel like that all the time?"

Bell smiled wryly. "True, I was made to withstand the weight of time, the breadth of emotion. You made yourself incapable of feeling those emotions, not that you could feel them greatly from the beginning. You burned them out because you needed to. But that same hardness you created in yourself, that same fire, will only cause you to crumble now. That's why you're self-destructing, Vivian. You set yourself up to fight then had to go looking for wars when they didn't come to you."

"What exactly do you expect me to do? Change overnight to keep you from killing me?" Vivian tried to sit up, but her exhausted muscles were having none of it. "Because people change so easily, like blinking. What if I don't want to change?"

"Death should be its own motivation, yes. I'll have to be exceedingly clear what I need from you. I'm usually more flexible, but flexibility in your case has led to where we are now." He brushed the tears from her face. "Perhaps find new wars to fight, because fighting me, fighting the Skeletons, fighting Jonas, fighting yourself... None of those things seem to be working for you, are they?"

"How do things seem to be working for *you*?" she retorted, still trying to sit up. The harder she tried, the more her entire body felt like chicken noodle soup.

He was silent for a few minutes, neither helping nor hindering.

"Not as well as I'd like," he finally said. "But it's not to blame for your mistakes. Nothing's left to blame, Vivian, except yourself. Are you still willing to live? I can still end it. Put you down like a rabid dog—with kindness. Or will you submit to the Ringmaster's whip and to my every wish? I won't take advantage of that submission. My desire for you is simple—that you serve my circus. That's all I ever asked of you."

"That's not entirely true, is it?" She finally managed to get some headway pushing herself up by her elbows. It got her head out of Bell's lap, at least.

"No, it *is* entirely true. That's all I ever ask of anyone in Arcanium. Serve my circus and eventually the circus will serve you." Now that she no longer needed him, he got to his feet. "Are you ready for the Ringmaster?"

"Just get it over with," she replied before she could talk herself out of going along with Bell's punishment.

Bell pulled her to her feet then hooked his arm around her back and her ribs. If he'd been anyone else, she would have thought he was trying to grab her boob, but he just led her to a smooth, plain bench, where he lowered her to the wood. Her long arms and legs draped over the sides, bent where they met the ground. She was aware of the fact that anyone behind her would have a lurid view of her pussy, but this was hardly the arrangement of a romance-novel heroine, and she was too exhausted to try to hide it.

Bell moved out of the spotlight, far enough into the darkness again that she couldn't see him even when she strained her eyes. Then the lights in the rest of the room turned on, and she realized she wasn't in the fortune teller's tent at all, but a big top that could hold a good five hundred people in its metal and wooden bleachers.

People filed in, some still wearing costumes, others in pajamas or house clothes or nothing but a robe. Most came into the arena in groups. Jonas herded all four Skeletons in with him.

Vivian didn't give them an expression, although the sight inspired a quick, violent flare of anger that they always had to see the worst of her.

Shane started to climb over the partition, but Bell emerged from the tired crowd to close his hand over her shoulder and pull her back. He said something unintelligible. Shane looked back as she left, but she didn't try to climb over again.

Jonas certainly didn't. He was still more expressionless than she, his face and eyes more dead to her than those of the crew. He hadn't needed to come, but he'd chosen to sit with his Skeletons, paying special care to Shane, who seemed the most distressed.

There was already an air of judgment, a weight to the stoniness of their faces—old, new, demon, human. Their ignorance was the only thing that prevented outright hostility, but she didn't know how long that was going to last.

The Ringmaster entered behind Kitty. Kitty was sober-faced, but the Ringmaster grinned in a manner that could only be described as wicked.

Just as there was something fundamentally wrong about the way that Jonas looked in his human skin, there was something wrong about the Ringmaster. Lennon, Lord Mikhail and Lady Sasha, Ciarán and Moss all appeared perfectly comfortable. She wondered whether the difference was just how bad the demons were to start out with. She found that difficult to reconcile with the Jonas that she'd thought she'd known. But then, the Jonas she'd thought she'd known was the Jonas that he'd thought he was, too.

"I apologize for disrupting your evening, your rest, your other activities," Bell said. "But the situation arose that Vivian was in need of public punishment. Tonight, she has been sentenced to fifty lashes from the Ringmaster's whip."

There was a quiet uproar among the cast, murmurs among the groups, furrowed brows, demons incensed.

Kitty stood from her place at the front, her simple skirt swinging under the more elaborate corset she'd worn during circus hours. "Fifty, Bell? For her first time? She's not a demon. Are you sure…?"

"I'm dead sure, Kitty. Please take your seat."

Kitty turned her attention from Bell to Vivian. Then Kitty slowly lowered herself back onto the bench, troubled contemplation making her young face appear old.

Apparently, fifty lashes were not common among the mortal crowd. That didn't tell everyone what she'd done, but it gave them a good idea of how bad it had been.

As the Ringmaster entered the ring, Bell stopped him with a hand to his arm and murmured, "Do your worst."

Her arms twitched reflexively as the Ringmaster approached. He shed his jacket, exposing an action-figure-level body. Everything about his strength seemed natural rather than cultivated, and he moved with the grace of a dancer that belied his size.

His whip hung from a loop off his belt. He pulled the whip out and shook the fall loose. He stared down at her with hunger she'd never seen on the Ringmaster's face, hunger that was almost sexual, carnal in its simple intensity, as though he saw her bare skin and desired it bloody.

Oh fuck.

The whip was black leather, like his pants, and the fall was at least twenty feet, the end knotted to crack. It skittered over the sawdust she'd disturbed as he brought it behind him. Then he sent it flying in an arc.

It was as though he'd pressed a fire-hot poker across the length of her back. She registered the severity of the blow before she'd even registered the pain. Another rib cracked, and she screamed, jerking on the bench. The way her legs straddled the wood, she was secure there, but her torso jerked to the side.

Without a word, Bell sat on the end of the bench, took her forearms and held them against his thighs, giving her a direct view of his crotch. Once again, she thought somewhat blearily how sexual all of this seemed while not being sexual at all.

The Ringmaster brought the whip down again.

Bell tightened his grip around Vivian's arms.

Chapter Eleven

There was something off about the way the whip slithered over her back. Vivian couldn't look behind her, but she suspected the reason was because it moved over organs, not skin or muscle. She couldn't move anything lower than her shoulders. Muscle fibers had been snapped, and she thought the Ringmaster had cracked her vertebrae — but not her spinal cord, because she could feel everything that the human body was not meant to feel, was still alive through pain and damage not intended for a person to withstand.

The audience had disappeared around her. The world had narrowed to the pinpoint of spotlight, as though the universe had been destroyed but for this moment and this pain. Bell still held her as the Ringmaster draped the whip around his arm in loose circles to put back on his belt. There was blood on it, of course. It flecked the sawdust in the ring around her and had splattered in red paint drops on Bell's bare skin. But there was also flesh, black with blood, stuck to the leather.

Her vocal cords had seemed to shred apart at one point, or perhaps they'd just paralyzed. No sound came from her but she was still screaming.

Bell loosened his hold on her arms to slip away. His jaw was clenched, his temples twitching, the hollow of his cheekbones gaunt, as though he were the one starving himself.

She wanted to think that he'd enjoyed himself, that he was like the Ringmaster, who smiled beatifically as he walked out of the ring without a word, his task finished and relished like the finest of feasts. But the corners of Bell's mouth were turned down, and once he stood, he looked away.

"Vivian has had a difficult night. She will not be able to take care of herself, and I would prefer if she had someone to keep an eye on her and help her heal. Will anyone take ownership of her tonight?"

Vivian didn't know why he had to salt the wounds like that. Fifty lashes like this didn't come out of nowhere. He had to have known that when he asked someone to take care of her, after he'd all but told them that she didn't deserve it, no one would step forward — not Jonas, not Alicia, not Lily, not even Nasreen or Shane. Vivian's gaze moved from one to another. She met the gazes of hundreds of reflections.

Bell crouched next to her, brushing her hair behind her ear. "I'll do it then," he said quietly, "little though you want my company."

When he pressed his hand between her shoulder blades where some of the lashes had raised welts, she twitched again, but the warmth of his magic returned, spreading from his palm and down her back like hot summer rainfall. It didn't fix everything, because the tearing, ripped pain remained. But pops and crackles she heard through her own flesh suggested that the broken bones resumed their original places and at least nominally stitched together. The muscles the Ringmaster had destroyed restrung themselves. She could move her back and hips, and it didn't make the fire in her body go supernova.

"We'll take her, boss."

Vivian slid her cheek along the bench, unable to lift her head, and strained her eyes to see. They were just out of her vision at first, but the Quandary, in loose house clothes rather than their gender-ambiguous suit, entered the ring, followed by Miss Delilah, still in drag but only wearing her wig cap. The Quandary stopped where the blood began, but when Bell banished it, they stepped forward, beckoning Miss Delilah.

The Quandary wasn't in any kind of physical shape to lift Vivian, light though she was. But Miss Delilah was a giant in go-go boots. It wasn't the most stable thing to wear while carrying someone, but she didn't seem concerned as Bell helped raise Vivian upright for Miss Delilah to lift like a toddler into her arms. Her three breasts felt even weirder against Vivian's two, as though the third had been made to settle into cleavage. Sequins weren't comfortable against bare skin, but Vivian allowed herself to be clutched tightly against the queen's body, because she couldn't wrap her arms or legs around her.

"We good?" The question was straightforward, but the Quandary seemed to ask something completely different.

Bell nodded, handing the Quandary a bottle of something electric blue.

"Okay, then." The Quandary patted Miss Delilah's arm like someone knocking on a car to let it know it could leave.

The stillness in the bleachers broke. A few people went up to Bell, likely to ask what she'd done, but he just shook his head.

Neither Miss Delilah nor the Quandary said anything as Miss Delilah carried Vivian from the big top. It sat in the middle of a part of the field that had been empty before. Vivian had a feeling it wouldn't be there tomorrow.

Cast emerged like colorful ants into the night, most of them headed in the same direction as Miss Delilah and the Quandary — for the Christmas-light-lit caravan. The harem tent was situated away from the caravan, near the midway. She wasn't entirely sure why — maybe to keep it closer to the food court.

Vivian had never been near the caravan — a patchwork collection of trucks, RVs, trailers and a few semis. A few of the trailers and RVs were junkers or tiny enough that Vivian was pretty sure they were used for sleeping alone, but the trailer Miss Delilah carried her to was relatively new and large, the kind one might see in a mobile neighborhood, closer to the size of a decent tiny home than a chest of drawers. Given Miss Delilah's size even without the go-go boots, Vivian figured she was the reason.

The Quandary opened the door and held it for Miss Delilah as she made her ginger way in. She had to duck, which was a strain on Vivian's wounded back, but she straightened as soon as she could at Vivian's whimper.

"We're almost there," Miss Delilah said in her deep baritone rumble. "Where do you want her, Dom?"

"She'll probably be better on the sofa until we get those wounds handled. I'll get towels."

The Quandary came back with three large bath towels to spread on the small sofa in the RV's living area. It wasn't too shabby of a home at all, with modern finishes, and it was roomier than it appeared, although not in the same way as the harem tent and the odd chef's food booth. The RV expanded when the vehicle wasn't in motion, which meant the living room was nearly the size of the one in Vivian's apartment. It had the tiniest of dining areas, but the living space in the middle of the vehicle was maximized. A decent full-sized bed had been tucked above the cab. On the other side of the kitchenette was a small bathroom and a queen-sized bed in the back room.

Miss Delilah lowered Vivian onto her knees on the towel-covered sofa then eased her onto her stomach so that none of her wounds pressed against anything. Vivian buried her face in the towel and silently screamed again, frustration mingling with pain like tears in blood.

"Sorry. There's just no good way to do that." Miss Delilah backed away from the sofa as the Quandary sat on the coffee table in front of Vivian.

"This is going to hurt some," the Quandary said, "but it's going to make you feel better quickly. We have to be circus-ready tomorrow, so we'll be tired as hell, but at least you won't look or feel like you've been whipped. Physically, anyway."

Vivian nodded, her face still in the terrycloth.

"It's a salve we use for any major injuries. It'll completely heal the wounds, and once it's absorbed, it'll get into your system and help you heal from the inside. But it needs to be applied topically to begin with, and we've got a lot of places to apply it."

Vivian nodded again, biting back the impulse to snap at them to get on with it.

"You go ahead, Delilah. You have more to undo than I do."

Miss Delilah made the RV groan and lean everywhere she went, but she closed what Vivian assumed was the bedroom door behind her.

"Bell helps with getting everything on in the mornings, but it's up to Del to take everything off at night. That's a production in and of itself," the Quandary said. Vivian vaguely remembered Miss Delilah calling them Dom.

Vivian bit the towel when Dom put their hands on her back. Their hands were cold and wet, but Vivian quickly felt the warmth that she now associated with Bell's magic. But maybe it was just healing magic in general, warmth like that from a heating pad or electric blanket.

It hurt, but not anywhere near what the mushrooms had done or the lashes themselves — closer to pouring hydrogen peroxide or lemon juice on an open wound. After a few minutes, though, it dissipated as quickly as it had hit. She was still weak, but the flesh on her back, scant though it was, filled in to become healthy and whole.

After the salve had been spread over most of her wounds, Dom poured the rest of the bottle on her back and rubbed it in, this time less gently — more massage than applying topical medicine. Dom's hands were strong, and they dug their fingers into the muscle, but as far as Vivian could tell, the effort was therapeutic rather than a come-on. Dom probably put those insistent hands to equally therapeutic use after Miss Delilah had to walk around a whole circus all day in stripper shoes.

Dom wiped their hands on the towel. "Stay there. I'm going to wash my hands, then I'm going to help wipe the mess off your back."

Dom didn't wait for a reply this time. Water running in the sink was followed by a wet washcloth on Vivian's back. Dom did what felt like a one-sided spot bath then dried her off.

"You strong enough to sit up on your own now?"

Vivian tried to move her arms. It felt like swimming through a swamp, but at least she could move. However, she didn't quite have the strength yet to push herself upright.

Dom helped her by holding her shoulders and lifting her up until she was on her hands and knees. Then they helped Vivian to her feet to clear off the dirty towels. One-handed, Dom opened up new ones to put on the couch and eased Vivian back down.

"I can see why Bell thought you'd need someone to look after you." Dom glanced over at her as they gathered the bloody towels then threw them out of the door. "You need something to eat? I can get the golems to bring something. I'd offer what we have in the fridge, but..." Dom shrugged awkwardly. Everyone knew not to feed the Skeletons.

Vivian shook her head again. When she tried to speak, it came out a gasp. "No."

Dom turned at the open door to greet someone Vivian couldn't see. They spoke for a while in hushed tones, the kind one used with a sick invalid. Vivian supposed she qualified, but she was already bored with it and ready to move on her own, maybe go back to sleeping in the knife-throwing booth or whatever it would be at their next stop.

"Looks like you don't have much of a choice." Dom climbed back into the RV, shutting the door behind them. "Kitty came with dinner. Bell says eating will help with your strength. She says it's nonnegotiable and that you'll know what that means."

Dom held out a foil-wrapped burrito the size of a premature infant.

She wasn't hungry. Actually, she *was* hungry, the cherry on top of the whole cosmic joke sundae. She just didn't want to eat, and not for the reasons she'd not wanted to eat before.

"You promised," Bell whispered in her head.

Vivian sighed and held her hand out. She nearly dropped the thing. Dom actually had to help her get both hands on it. They also unfolded the top part of the foil so that she could bite. Vivian half expected to have to use their help to chew and swallow, but she managed that much on her own. She belatedly wondered whether the burrito was safe to eat, considering who had to have made it, but it was too late now.

That could have been her hell for the rest of the century — forcing her to eat her own poison over and over again — but the heavy ingredients of the burrito the odd chef had made didn't unsettle what the mushrooms had nearly destroyed and Bell had put back together again. There wasn't so much as a sickly gurgle in her intestines. Steak, pinto beans, rice, avocado, tomato, onion, and cheese in a thick tortilla — Vivian ate the whole burrito baby.

Dom appeared to be trying not to stare as they made their own dinner at the kitchenette.

Well, they did have a naked woman eating a huge Mission burrito in their living room while her stomach stayed perfectly concave. Vivian was pretty sure there was a subgenre of porn for that.

The food helped. Her body strengthened as she ate it—likely more from the salve than the food, but the food did what most food didn't do for her anymore. She couldn't remember the last time she'd felt full.

When Vivian finished her burrito, she rolled up the aluminum foil into a ball, chucked it onto the coffee table then laid her head back on the sofa with a sigh.

Dom ate their apple and peanut butter, crunching contemplatively. "You don't seem too concerned about it, but do you want something to wear? You and I are about the same height. Most of what I have should fit you, if it has a drawstring."

Vivian glanced down at herself. The truth in her perspective disoriented her like it had the first time. She'd gotten used to being a Skeleton, especially with clothes to cover herself, but in such a small place where she was the only one naked and the only one skeletal, the extreme level of her skinniness hit her even more.

She looked like she'd eaten the mushrooms months back and this was what was left of her. Vivian looked away from herself in distaste and nodded at Dom's offer.

Dom tossed her a long white tank top that looked like something a tourist would buy at the beach as a coverup. The graphic was sunnier than Vivian would usually choose for herself but she pulled it over her head. It was loose, though clearly made with a slender woman in mind.

"You're welcome to sleep on the couch, but the bed would be more comfortable. And I can stay down here if you'd prefer— Okay, then."

Vivian didn't waste time. She was still shaky, but she managed to climb the ladder to the bed over the cab. The bed was definitely more comfortable. Vivian grabbed Dom's sleeve to urge them up, too.

Dom continued eating their evening snack with their legs crossed between them as Vivian tucked herself under the blanket. Dom watched her quietly, and she watched them. It really was uncanny how, with their feathery hair and beard and the shape of their face, they seemed feminine from one angle and masculine from another—like looking at a holograph.

"You want to talk about tonight?" Dom asked.

She was the first to look away.

"Okay. Then are you gonna ask?" Dom said.

"Ask what?"

"Oh, good. I was worried you'd blown that out."

"I did. Salve's working. Bell wouldn't destroy his money." Vivian hesitated. "Thanks."

"No problem. Anyway, I usually get two questions, and only one of them's polite."

"Let me guess. 'What are you?' and 'What's your pronoun?'"

Dom grinned. They looked older when they were dressed up for the circus, but it occurred to Vivian that Dom might not be much older than she was. "I guess you know the drill. Which one would you rather ask?"

"I've been using 'they' pronouns in my head until told otherwise."

"You've done this before."

"You remind me of my brother. Our mother called him Anamaria when he was born."

Dom nodded. "You're an old pro, then. 'They' pronouns are fine. Like Del, it tends to be 'she-her' when I'm presenting feminine and 'he-him' when I'm presenting as masculine, 'they-them' when people aren't sure, but I'll answer to anything — Dominique and Dominic." They wrinkled their nose. "I'm sure it's just so precious. Dominic's on the birth certificate, but my parents thought it could be pronounced both ways, and they always called me Dom for short. I was the Awkward Introduction from the very beginning. 'Is it a boy or a girl?' And my parents would say, 'We're hoping for an anarchist.'"

In spite of the evening, Vivian smiled.

Dom glowed when they smiled back. "They were crunchy before it was cool, though like most parents, they sometimes got it wrong. I know the doctor thought so after he pulled me out. Mom and Dad don't like to talk about it too much. It had to be a confusing time for them. It's not every day doctors want to remove the female bits and sew up the vagina because the male bits are so well formed, all before they even bring the baby home. But Mom and Dad wouldn't have it."

In the absence of Vivian speaking up, Dom warmed to sharing. They spent so much time with Del, Vivian wondered whether they spent time with anyone else. Because here they were, revealing something deeply personal to someone who'd just been punished for some unknown crime. It didn't make much sense, but at least Dom didn't annoy the fuck out of her. Quite the opposite.

"The doctor said I'd have to deal with confusion about my gender if they didn't make it unambiguous from the start." Dom shrugged. "Given where I ended up, I probably would have had to deal with it anyway—somewhere around the time I started growing a beard and breasts at the same time. Kitty knows a little something about that, but I'm pretty sure descending testes along with periods probably didn't happen to her."

"So you're here voluntarily." Vivian pushed herself up, propping up the pillows so she didn't have to work so hard to sit.

"Del and I followed the call."

Vivian raised an eyebrow.

"After whatever happened with the previous cast that made Arcanium shut down for a while, Bell had to build his cast back up. So he put out a call—for mystiques and freaks of all ages, colors and sizes, the weirder the better. Del and I never really fit in much, even among a bunch of outliers and outcasts like us. Del takes drag a bit further than the average straight cis man—like, black market surgeon further. The queens let him sit at the table, but they all consider him a bit weird. As for me, I'm a unicorn."

"A pretty bisexual interested in a threesome?" Vivian asked.

She surprised Dom into a burst of laughter.

"Not that kind. Although yes, sometimes, if you think I'm pretty." They winked, but as they stopped laughing, Dom considered her with more than mere curiosity. Like Shane, it wasn't anything more than Vivian had already guessed, and she considered whether she wanted to do anything with it.

"Anyway, no, not that kind of unicorn. More like *Last Unicorn*. Genderqueer is a thing, but there are pictures of baby me in medical books. There are only a handful of us with both trunks of junk, and as far as I can tell, I'm the only one who's gotten a girl pregnant and been pregnant, too. She took the morning-after. I had an abortion." The laughter disappeared from Dom's face. They looked down at their snack bowl as though the contents had gone over. "I obviously wouldn't change myself, but I'm not sure I would want to put someone else through it. And Lord knows I wouldn't know what to do with a kid who was one thing or the other instead of both."

Vivian turned her head slightly, almost suspicious. "Why are you telling me all this?"

Dom fiddled with the peanut butter then licked it from their finger like icing. "Why am I giving you shit you can use against me, you mean?" Dom glanced up. "I'm not naïve, and your reputation precedes you."

"What reputation, exactly?"

"Prickly. And a bit mercenary."

"Mercenary?" That was new one. She was well-acquainted with 'raging psycho bitch' and 'pathetic attention-seeking whore', but 'mercenary' was a gentleman's description.

"You like the quid pro quo, I hear. And you like finding ways to control the people around you, one way or another."

"Who told you that?" As far as Vivian could tell, she'd only homed in on the odd chef, but old habits did die hard.

"No one told me. It's what I observed. You, my dear, are someone who likes an angle. And I know you're wondering why I stepped up to take you in tonight when no one else would—right up there with wondering why I'm telling you my life story when I'm usually kind of tight-lipped about the whole thing, especially since I usually get asked the wrong question. Then people get pissed that I'm pissed about it."

"So why'd you save me?"

Dom shrugged, making a noncommittal sound. "I like you." The grin was back, closer to the one they wore during circus hours.

Vivian crossed her arms. "You have no reason to like me. You know what I did."

"Nope. Haven't a clue."

"You know it wasn't good."

"Okay, maybe a *clue*."

Vivian was silent for a while. Dom didn't seem to mind.

They all knew she'd done something terrible. How terrible would it be, really, to admit what it was when everyone else already hated her? Dom had promised Bell to watch over her, and Bell would hold them to that promise. So what if she had to sleep on the couch instead of the bed?

"I tried to kill everyone."

Dom paused, a peanut-buttered apple slice halfway to their mouth. "Everyone?"

"No one in particular, just everyone."

Dom set the bowl down in their lap. "Why?"

"To get out of Arcanium, one way or another."

"That's cold, sugar."

"It wasn't personal," Vivian said.

"That's why it's cold. Was it poison?"

"What makes you think that?"

"You strike me as a poison kind of woman. Also, with the odd chef pulling you back into the kitchen, it seemed logical. They don't keep a nuclear weapon back there, and you'd only get so far trying to kill everyone with a frying pan."

Dom had been paying more attention than Vivian had thought. But they hadn't kicked her out of bed, and they weren't trying to stab Vivian with an apple slice.

"Why aren't you running?"

"Bell's the one who's pissed. Maybe some people are taking it personally, like you said," Dom replied, "but I don't live in the reality where you succeeded. What kind of poison?"

"Mushrooms."

Dom nodded. "Easy to blend, especially in the odd chef's weird foods. Aiming for an indiscriminate poisoning?"

Vivian nodded, wary, waiting for some kind of reaction beyond curiosity.

"Not your first, was it?" Dom slowly picked up their apples again.

"Why do you ask?"

Dom shrugged. "People don't usually become mass murderers overnight. I think you've poisoned people before, and you've tried to kill someone before. That's how you figured out you could. Most people can't imagine that."

"Can you?" Vivian asked carefully.

Dom smiled, but it wasn't the kind that glowed. "No. But people like me tend to attract all sorts, and I tend to be attracted to all sorts — sometimes those sorts aren't very nice. I've got the scars to prove it. Those scars were personal. I take them personally. But I've never been attacked like that by a woman. I've been hit by some, but knives weren't involved."

"You think I'm not nice."

"*You* think you're not nice. I still like you anyway, whether it's healthy for me to or not. A demonic circus changes things for a person. Most of the demons have

Aurelia T. Evans

been kinder than people in my life, and not all not-nice people have been cruel to *me*. Del's a teddy bear, but sometimes nice is overrated. You won't shock me, Vivian. When you're a unicorn, nothing shocks you anymore."

"I…" Vivian tucked the covers around her waist, not so much as a shield but to buy herself some time while she considered just how raw she was willing to be with someone she wasn't sure she understood. Dom had already shared some things that Vivian might be able to use, but in Arcanium, anything Vivian said would be worth more.

"You don't have to tell me." And now Dom seemed older again. It was the holograph all over again. They resisted any attempt to categorize.

"I sometimes poison women when they have men I want," Vivian said quickly, the words falling out in a rush before she could put them back in again. "It's usually a one-time thing, but before Arcanium, I was exiled from my squad for poisoning my best friend to fuck her live-in boyfriend while she was sick in bed. I just wanted her out of the way. It's usually laxatives or emetics, both something that any self-respecting anorexic might have in their medicine cabinet, and you don't get flagged for buying it. Really, other than my best friend, I didn't do it much. What girl wants to share her meds?"

Vivian tucked her hair behind her ears and played with the ends. She'd always had trouble using the words the doctors had given her. They reduced her. They put her into boxes and tried to tape down the lid. She'd already established how little she liked to be trapped.

"Just your best friend, huh?" Dom finished her apples and tossed the bowl with uncanny accuracy onto the sofa below.

"The ones you know best think they're safe."

"Mm-hmm. Or maybe you just have a bit of a self-destructive streak."

"Geez, what are you? A psychologist? A psychic? It's déjà vu all over again."

"Well, why else would you try mass murder in a circus run by a psychic? Which I am not, by the way, and my psychology never got much farther than armchair. But come on, sugar. Do you really think my granola family didn't have me talk to every shrink under the sun about my little problem? You talk to enough shrinks, you start to absorb it all. The jargon. The cadence. The suspicion. Frankly, they didn't know what to do with me either. No one ever did, including me. The unicorn gets 'em every time."

Vivian tilted her head curiously.

Dom shrugged, their shoulder lifting to create an almost-elegant shape under their shapeless shirt. "People keep wanting me to be one or the other, and they lose their shit when there's such a physical manifestation of both. The same people freaking out over the presence of a penis when they expected a vagina—and vice versa—only get angrier when they realize that's just the way I am, not something I did to myself. With a trans person, people can go, 'She's a woman' or 'He's a man', and only one of them is right. But you bring in an intersex person, the ones who think they have a right to assign gender get flummed. The genderqueer community is really welcoming, but they don't really know what to do with me either, just because my particular kind of intersexuality is so rare."

"*Last Unicorn*," Vivian said.

"Exactly. I don't want the doctors poking at me, don't want the therapists prodding at me and if people are going to debate about which gender I am to my face, I'd rather them do it invited. And I like the fact that the sex in Arcanium is so much safer. Knuckle-draggers still come along on occasion, but Bell keeps them effectively neutered. If anyone gets too handsy, it's to the clowns or the sex demons for them. And there are plenty of places to duck if someone actually strikes my fancy. It doesn't happen a lot these days. People fetishize me for what I think are all the wrong reasons. But I have Del when the sex demons get frisky."

Vivian relaxed a little. She'd been given enough informational meat that her own revelation felt paid for, if not quite balanced. "How does Del feel about you bringing me in here?"

"He thinks I'm being reckless, but drag queens appreciate a good performance."

Vivian sighed. "Yeah. Everyone loves me when I sing."

"So who'd you try to kill before?"

The question came out of nowhere, deceptively casual. Vivian didn't like that Dom kept doing that. It felt like a journalist doing a sneaky interrogation by keeping the subject off-kilter.

"I told you, Viv, nothing will shock me. I've been arrested for solicitation — charges were dropped, by the way — assault and battery for defending myself and I was once put through the court system for fraud, if you can believe it. The assault and battery required anger management classes, because the problem there was clearly my anger." Dom's cheeks twitched as they clenched their jaw. "And that's just me. We're not even talking about the people I dated — or the people I screwed or who tried to screw me over."

"You said you had therapists. Have you ever been institutionalized?"

Dom nodded. "Court-ordered during the fraud case. I was fighting for my right to be not one thing or the other, fighting to just be. It was exhausting. I didn't handle it very well."

Vivian ran her fingers through her hair, leaning forward to rest her head in her hands. "My sister and I lived a few months with Tio Luis, Tia Carmen and Abuelita. That was when I was starting to fight back against my parents and accuse my stepfather of the shit he'd been doing. Mamá compromised to shut me up and sent me and Angelica to her sister's and her mother. Tia Carmen and Abuelita had me with them for a week before they realized my mind was screwy with food and the way I looked. They pooled money and probably guilted Mamá into contributing as well to send me to an eating disorder rehab facility, which was a wing off of a psychiatric unit in a hospital."

Vivian pushed off the covers, suddenly hot, face flushed, although she couldn't pinpoint the emotions that roiled in her stomach with the burrito. "I stabbed a nurse with a syringe when they tried to give me a saline drip. Then I found a scalpel. She lost a lot of blood, and I wouldn't let anyone touch me or come into the room until they got these burly, pissed-off male nurses to restrain me. They lost some blood, too. They had to break my arm before I'd let go of the scalpel. As soon as they'd sedated and fed me then made sure there was nothing sharp around, a psychiatrist sat me down and told me that though I'd been brought in for anorexia nervosa and some purging behavior, he'd be working with me one-on-one for my violent tendencies."

He'd been a small man, under five feet, with curly hair like a hobbit and a calm but officious voice. He'd somehow found a way to look down on her, because he was the doctor and she was a patient strapped to a wheelchair for her own protection, surrounded by IV tubes.

'"You're fortunate you've been remanded to a stricter ward's care rather than Nurse Carr pressing charges. I hope you realize that. Challenges to obsessive behavior, such as your eating disorder, have been known to result in fearful violence, but yours is excessive, brutal and quite disturbing for a young woman your age."'

It had been a few more weeks of tests before she'd overheard 'psychopath' from one of the nurses, one not as compassionate and forgiving as the woman she'd almost killed. In truth, she hadn't been *trying* to kill Nurse Carr. However, if the doctor hadn't told Vivian that the nurse was all right, Vivian wouldn't have cared enough to ask.

But after Nurse Carr had had to get over fifty stitches and several blood transfusions, Vivian realized she'd gone too far. All things considered, she'd been lucky Nurse Carr hadn't pressed charges, but she'd been extremely lucky that the woman hadn't died on the operating table. Otherwise, Vivian might never had left that hospital.

Reacting so violently had made her noticed in all the wrong ways. So she'd learned to lash out more subtly. And she'd learned why she didn't mind killing all the spiders in the house, while Angelica couldn't stand to even see one. She'd learned why her mother cried at telenovelas and rom-coms while Vivian preferred true crime and horror, where the gruesome deaths never bothered her.

And she'd learned why her stepfather hadn't broken her, unless being a psychopath was being broken. But Vivian didn't think so. Being a psychopath made her hard.

Or she'd thought it had.

Vivian had been picking at her fingernails — and old nervous habit from the meds they'd used to sedate her, which had made her strangely wired while they took effect — but she glanced up at Dom. Two could play at their game. "What dark deed did you do to get stuck here?"

Dom smiled uncertainly. "What do you mean?"

"It doesn't matter that you joined Arcanium of your own free will. Bell wouldn't just take any freak because they wanted to be a part of his circus. He had to have a place for you. Even the humans have demons, don't they? So what demon did he see in you that he wanted here?"

"I'm a unicorn for him to show off. That's all."

"Bell doesn't do one-trick unicorns."

It was the first time Dom had seemed truly uncomfortable. "Identity's a tricky thing. Everything's boy-girl, either-or, and everyone's trying to make me one or the other and doesn't like either way I do it. I may not be the most mentally stable freak in the world, but we can't all be Kitty or Carlo, you know. I make bad decisions. Before Del, I made a whole lot of them, almost as many as other people made on me. If it weren't for him, I'd probably still be making them. But who would have thought a sequined giant with three implanted breasts would be the solid foundation I needed? Then again, a straight cis male who looks like he does on purpose would have to have a solid foundation, wouldn't he?"

"Okay, I'm going to be that person now. Are we sure about the straight cis male thing?" Vivian said. "Really?"

Dom brightened a little. "Yep. Just because he wants to look a certain way doesn't mean he's that thing he looks like. Just like Troy isn't actually a ringbearer just because he has a lot of rings. Drag is presentation, and it's not always connected to identity. You don't always want to be seen as what you are, do you?"

Touché.

"People wear masks all the time," Dom added. "Some people's masks are a little weirder. The drag community was perfectly fine with him, but everyone looks sideways at extreme surgeries like his. His weird found my weird, and when we were weird in the same room together, somehow we didn't stand out as much. That's what it's like in Arcanium. Fewer people take offense by my very existence when they see me here. Because I'm a voluntary, I can leave for a short time. You know, visit a mall, go to a restaurant or a coffee shop or a bookstore. But though Kitty leaves a lot, I don't really feel the need to. If I want food, I go to the food booths or order in. I like it here."

"I don't." Vivian sighed again, as though she hadn't exhaled enough the first time. "But then I don't really like it anywhere. Even my apartment was just kind of...there. But I *really* don't like it here. I don't like that I'm hungry. I don't like that what I eat is controlled by someone else. I don't like that what I see in the mirror is exactly the way I am. And I don't like Bell. Or Jonas. Or Alicia. Or anyone. I kind of like Shane, and I kind of like you right now."

"Sleep on it. It'll fade," Dom said cheerfully. "I thought you liked the odd chef, though."

"Why? Because everyone knows I fuck him now? 'Like' isn't a prerequisite for that."

Dom laughed. "Oh, believe me, I know that. It's clear he's way more into you than you're into him, but when you're in the same area and you both notice each other... I don't know what it's like when you're alone or what he looks like when you're with him in that tent the Skeletons sleep in."

"The harem tent."

That got Dom to snort. "That's...one way to describe it."

"You have to be there. Lennon does the rounds after the circus closes then they're all cooing and sweet and shit when Jonas comes in to feed them. I don't know who started it, but they're all suck-ups."

"But you're the one who found the jackpot, didn't you?"

Vivian searched Dom for their reaction, for some kind of judgment or permission, but Dom stayed annoyingly neutral, and not the way that Jonas did or the way Bell schooled his expression. Dom remained open and seemingly sincere without giving anything away, which suggested there was nothing to give. But there had to be *something*.

"I didn't like it," Vivian said softly.

She'd shared more with Dom than she'd shared with that smug psychiatrist, and she'd been more candid with Dom than with Bell. Bell could see all the answers, but it wasn't the same.

Saying things aloud... That rawness wasn't going away. If anything, it was getting worse. Freedom and road rash apparently went together.

"Didn't like what? The sex?" Dom blinked. "Is it even possible to have bad sex in Arcanium?"

"I don't..." Vivian didn't know how to vocalize what had only ever been true for one man, who was apparently a lot more demon than he let on. "I don't have sex the way other people do."

"Oh, do tell—upside-down, standing on your head and with a hula-hoop?"

Vivian made a face, but she also smiled. "No, you goofball. I mean that before I came to Arcanium, I thought sex was fun because you controlled the other person's physical reactions, and in doing that, you..." Vivian tried to mime the way sex had felt before, curving her fingers for the illusion of claws and digging them into an invisible person between her and Dom. "I got turned on, but it was..."

At Vivian's series of harsh sighs, Dom crawled across the bed and sat next to her instead, so the confrontation wasn't so direct. "Take your time. I'm not going anywhere."

"It wasn't physical. I mean, some of it was. I'd get excited about owning the person I was with, and I'd get wet. I fuck hard, fast and I never have to worry about lubrication, and God knows I don't need sweet. But about ninety percent of my being turned on was mental. I sometimes orgasmed, although I was much happier faking it. Something in my head, though, would seem to have its own orgasm once I...captured them. You convince a man he's the best lay in the world and his dick feels good, you make him feel like a king, then you own him. And that...that made me come, but not always physically."

Dom almost couldn't blink. "This is so fascinating that I want popcorn. But I get sex being good for reasons other than the sex. Kind of."

"Then I come here, and everyone's having sex everywhere, and I don't know why, because I'm not feeling any kind of urge for it."

"Mmm, must be nice. It's hella distracting for the rest of us."

"Then I come up with my plan to get more food and control the odd chef, because he seems simple and easy enough to control if I can make him come." She sighed again in frustration. "Every time I have sex with him, I sink my claws in, but he sinks his claws into me and I *feel* sex. I get turned on when he kisses me, and not just in my head. And I don't know what to *do* with that. I don't like it. I don't like that the harder I try to top him, he just turns the tables and does exactly what he wants to do to me instead, and we both end up satisfied, but that's not what I *wanted*."

"So you're pissed off at him because the sex is too good?" Dom bit their lip against a grin. "That's...new."

"I was perfectly fine with the way sex was before. I *liked* it before. It's not that it's good or better. It's that it's... Fuck. I don't even have the words for it."

"It's because it isn't just you giving someone else what they want to make yourself feel powerful." Dom looked away, peering through the picture window next to their bed. Apparently, they preferred to rise with the light. "If he's getting his claws into you, too, you're getting something you wanted — maybe something you didn't know you wanted...or needed. If you've never connected before, it's probably more intense than you thought it could be. Do you understand now why you were always able to exploit people's weaknesses?"

Vivian thought of the way the odd chef felt when he'd watched her pour the gasoline to light herself on fire as much as everyone else. She thought of the exquisite emptiness he longed to fill and make emptier. Of the way he wanted to cook for her, feed her, watch her eat and eat and eat and eat then fuck her on a pile of fruit bursting with juices to coat her skin. Eat choux pastry off her honey-glue belly then watch her devour the whole pile beneath her. He could watch her eat forever and never be filled, and he could fuck her forever and never satisfy her. One was caused by Bell, the other simply a part of her.

She'd felt the full breadth of his desires for her, even from that brief moment that Bell had shown her. He carried those desires with him every time he saw her, and when he'd looked at Vivian in despair, he'd seen an emptiness he could fall into, darkness that could surround him, a hole without a bottom.

Vivian traced the scars that she'd left on her forearms — new, pink scars on top of older ones. Dom had to have noticed them. Everyone had to have noticed them. Apparently the salve didn't smooth out scars, because they were still there.

"Why him?" Her heart beat hard against her chest. "Why does he reach where no one else does? Is it Arcanium? Is it because he's a demon, and I'm — ? Or is it because he's not like a demon at all?"

"Are you sure it's just him?"

Vivian glanced up.

Dom looked over Vivian's arms with a clear understanding of what they saw, but as usual, the understanding yielding no reaction. Dom understood what it was like to be taken advantage of, and they'd still chosen to be next to Vivian right now. They could have scars of their own under those long sleeves they usually wore, and that wouldn't surprise her. But Dom wasn't like her. Somehow, they'd gone their separate damaged ways. Vivian had become hard, and Dom had... Had what? They hadn't become softer. They had their own brand of manipulation, but Dom had to know they were being manipulated, too.

Yet here the two of them were, each playing right into the manipulation of the other. And for what?

Vivian lifted Dom's chin and leaned in to kiss them.

Dom let out a muffled sound of surprise, but they kissed her back, holding her face between their hands and hardly missing a beat. The kiss was neither slow nor sweet. She kissed Dom like she kissed anyone she wanted in her pocket, angling her head to take them deep then let them in when Dom pressed closer, smoothing their hands down Vivian's neck and nudging the tank top down Vivian's shoulders.

She shrugged the straps of the tank top off. The shirt fell halfway down her arms and chest, with little more than her boobs to hold it up, but it would be easy enough to remove the rest of the way, and Dom's clothing was loose. Loose meant that when Vivian took control of the kiss again and climbed over them to straddle their lap, she felt where Dom was undeniably aroused, though the size of the clothes had hidden the extent of their erection. They couldn't hide anymore when Vivian stroked over the front of their pants, squeezing the length of the cock underneath through the fabric.

Dom broke from the kiss, their head hitting the window behind them as they lifted their hips to meet Vivian's unhesitating hands. "Oh, fuck. I didn't expect... *Fuck.*"

The feelings were...different.

She still experienced arousal that shot like sparklers through her head at being able to leave Dom gasping from how turned on she made them. Those mental places of arousal were stronger than they once were — bigger, somehow, less in Vivian's control and much how she'd felt when she'd first gone down on Jonas. But the arousal between her legs...that was more familiar. It was stronger as well than before she'd come to Arcanium. But it didn't feel beyond her capacity for reason.

The feel of Dom's erection in her hand made her hungry all over again, though unlike Jonas, Dom couldn't feed her the same way.

The hunger still went downward, desiring them inside her, filling her, satisfying her, but not as...much? It was less needful, less desperate and far more in her control.

And she liked Dom — as much as she could like anyone. They turned her on enough, too, more than most of the men or women she'd conned into her bed or theirs. Whether that was because of the sex demons or because Dom knew better what they were getting into was difficult to say.

Vivian was uneasy, though, with the fact that she could like someone enough that they got her off fast and hard, too, uneasy with the fact that Dom had chosen this, had waited for Vivian at her most vulnerable then just let her kiss them and jerk them off like this.

Dom made another muffled sound of reluctant protest and tore their mouth away, pushing at her wrists. "Vivian, Vivian...stop."

"You goddamn manipulative *bastard.*" Vivian slapped the window, which was indifferent to her suffering and didn't even crack. Now she was aroused — more aroused than she'd thought she was — but yet another Arcanium cast member had told her no. Was it something in the fucking water? Demons fell over themselves to fuck the other Skeletons, but the two people she'd chosen to give her body to had to have all these second thoughts? "I thought this was what you *wanted.*"

Dom burst into loud, somewhat out-of-breath but genuine laughter. They leaned their head back with a little less tension, subtle Adam's apple bobbing every time they swallowed between laughs.

"I'm sorry, sugar. I really am. I'm not laughing at you. Well, a little bit, but not mocking you or anything." Dom stroked her hair with both of their hands, looking over her with a less-measured gaze. "I just told myself I wasn't going to try to have sex with you tonight."

Vivian sat back on Dom's thighs and crossed her arms over her partially exposed chest. "Do I seem like a delicate fucking flower to you?"

"You looked half-dead *before* the Ringmaster flayed half of you away. Magical fixes aren't as complete as you think. Your back is solid, but you're still healing and you're..." Dom ran their fingers through their feathery hair. "You *are* a delicate fucking flower. I wasn't supposed to do this tonight."

"What? Take advantage of me in my delicate fucking state?" Vivian pulled the tank top over her head, leaving herself naked again, and this time, Dom wasn't in caregiver mode. If the lack of flesh shocked them, they didn't show it. Their gaze seemed distracted by Vivian's breasts anyway, and she still had those just fine. "Let's call this what it is, Dom. I'm taking advantage of you, and you're taking advantage of me. What's wrong with that?"

"You just had to almost poison me to do it?"

Vivian blinked. Dom hadn't taken it personally before. There wasn't any reason for them to take it personally now. "That's kind of my trend, don't you think?"

Dom glanced up with a crooked smile.

"Look... I've had a *really* bad day." Vivian slid forward over Dom's thighs to settle closer to their cock and wound her arms around their neck. It had been a while since her breasts had been so familiar with another pair. "Whether it was self-inflicted is up for debate, but that doesn't mean it wasn't a spectacular shitstorm of a day. I'm solid enough, I'm horny and I could stand a little normal tonight."

"And normal to you is a murderous bitch doing the bump-and-grind with an intersex unicorn in a demonic circus?" But Dom found the jut of her hips with their elegant long fingers and slid their hands up her repaired back, as though drawn to her skin.

"I'm human. You're human. We're as normal as a demonic circus gets."

Vivian waited until Dom pressed their lips to her neck, a moan in the back of their throat. Knowing that Dom couldn't help themselves, that they were agreeing to this even though they'd promised themselves they wouldn't... It filled Vivian with all the flush of power she needed, more effective than the healing potion at infusing her with her old strength. She stroked the sandy beard along their jaw then threaded her fingers through their hair again—soft and fine in contrast with the beard's coarseness.

Vivian brought her mouth to Dom's ear. "Fuck me."

"God, yes."

If the poor baby regretted it in the morning, that was their problem. Vivian would stroke them through the tears if she had to, because she wanted to keep Dom on her side of the line in case she found herself flayed again. Although if she reattempted mass murder again, she wouldn't be flayed. She'd be demon food.

A stab of cold fear joined with the arousal that had gathered hot and thick in her abdomen, and she lifted herself up onto her knees to escape it, pressing herself tightly against Dom's slim but solid body and grinding back down on their erection. Pressing their cock against her clit created far more sparks than she was used to, but it still wasn't as strong or dangerously explosive as what the odd chef had done to her on his butcher block or in his creaking bed.

This time, when she took Dom's cock in hand, it was underneath their pants.

"Oh, fuck yes." Dom pressed their forehead to Vivian's, panting again as she stroked them from base to tip.

They were a good thickness, substantial in her grip, with a small sac behind, and when she reached farther back, her fingers met wetness against the folds that extended from the sides of the scrotum. Dom adjusted her hand back up to their cock — not as hot as Jonas' but still feverish in comparison to the rest of their body.

"My cock doesn't get nearly enough love these days. Most of the guests I bring back here are men who just want my ass or my cunt, and Del's too straight to do much more than a basic reach-around. I don't mind. He's a beast. But sometimes I want..."

Vivian yanked their pants down over their hips and lifted herself up again, pressing the cock against the entrance to her pussy.

"You ever consider asking?" Vivian said over Dom's low, prolonged groan.

She didn't waste any time, because Dom didn't seem like they were going to last very long, and Vivian had no interest in feeling this level of arousal more than she had to. She relished the ride, tugging at Dom's shirt until they both helped pull it off.

Vivian rolled her hips against theirs so that she could bend down and lick one bare breast then take it into her mouth. The push-up bra they usually wore enhanced them some, but in volume, they were around the same size as Vivian's, with a good heft when Vivian lifted one by her teeth on the bud of the nipple.

"God, you *are* damn fast. This isn't the first time you've fucked someone with breasts, is it?" Dom took hers in hand, circling the puckering areolae with their thumbs as she continued to take him.

"This isn't even the first time I've fucked genderqueer, fam. Don't think you're special."

She grinned as Dom took her in their arms and flipped her down onto the bed.

"Do tell."

"How detailed do you want me to get while you're trying to get off?"

"If I weren't balls-deep inside you, honey, I'd wonder if you were getting anything out of this at all." But with Dom over her and slowing the speed down, they could bring their hand down to her folds and stroke over her labia and clit to the rhythm of their cock entering her.

The pace wasn't as breakneck as she wanted — as she needed — to keep from thinking about how good it made her feel in more ways than just her need for control. Vivian bit her lip when a moan she hadn't choreographed threatened to push through her throat.

"My auto mechanic was trans. I fucked his strap-on and fingerfucked him until he screamed. I didn't have to pay, and he made me breakfast."

"Why the fuck is that hot?" Dom groaned.

"Vicarious thrill?" Vivian lifted her hips at a shift in their fingers that hit her clit in just the right way. "The thought of just taking what you want and no one stopping you? Just take me, Dom. Stop trying to be gentle. I'm skinny, but I'm not going to break."

Dom stopped stroking her, but they also stopped fucking her. "You know, you don't have to do this to have me in your corner."

Vivian shoved Dom flat on their back so that she was astride once again. "Why are you still coherent?"

"Look, I get it, Vivian." Dom massaged the jut of her pelvis. For the first time, they showed concern but didn't let it get in the way of visibly enjoying the sight of sliding their hands up to her breasts, heavy over Dom's face. "You use me and I use you, just a quick nasty to get off and feel good again. But you don't have to do this to pay me back for agreeing to take care of you or to ensure I'll do it again. I already liked you."

"Dom, shut up." Vivian lowered herself onto their chest, their noses almost touching. "I use sex to get my way and wrap people, usually men, around my little finger. But even if you weren't going to stand up for me again, I'd still be doing this. This isn't an incentive or reward. Now stop being sensitive and fuck the shit out of me."

Dom needed a moment, but no more than that. They pulled her down to close the gap between them, grasped her ass to urge her to take them harder as she resumed fucking herself on their cock. There was no more stroking her clit to make sure she'd follow them. She was following them just fine, making the whole RV rock as though they were as big as Del, even though their combined weight couldn't hope to match his. And the harder she fucked them and the less they cared about hurting her, the more her arousal intensified, the harder she kissed them, and when Dom rolled them back over to take her instead, she dug her nails into their back as she came.

Dom cursed, bit the base of her neck as they followed her over the edge.

Vivian smoothed her hands along Dom's back as though to soothe where she'd scratched them. They were both warm over the sheets, with a fresh sweat. Dom rocked their hips to shift their cock inside her through the last of their climax, but Dom didn't act quite like the men she'd been with, falling on top of her, the whole ordeal over when they were.

Vivian wasn't sure what she thought about the way Dom looked at her. If she'd seen any trace of falling in love in their eyes, she would have shoved them off then cuddled close until morning, when she'd let Dom fall all the way to the ground to shatter — not that that plan had worked with a demon. But it wasn't love that Vivian saw in Dom's subdued expression. Just as their attempts to manipulate her while she was manipulating them threw her off, the vision of hunger hit a little too close to home. It wasn't sweet, wasn't gentle, wasn't caring in the least.

That was what Vivian had asked for, and it's what had gotten them off, but her cunt was still sensitive and achingly awake as Dom slid from her.

"I don't need you to fingerfuck me until I scream," Dom said, "but I've been turned on like hell since that stunt at the cake-eating contest. One time isn't going to be near enough. And if you don't want me to care...I kind of want to know if *you* can scream."

Dom ran their hand down Vivian's body to stroke through her folds again. They slid two fingers in, and as their thumb found her clitoral hood to stimulate her through her post-climactic sensitivity, they probed her cunt until they found the place that made Vivian twitch and whimper. It only took them a matter of seconds to find it.

"Is it like being with the odd chef?" Dom asked as they beckoned her physical pleasure without any coinciding mental pleasure at her own power.

Vivian couldn't dismiss that arousal as mercenary alone, which left her with that same rawness that had led to her confessions, the rawness left behind by the Ringmaster's whip, the mushrooms' poison and the brutal attack of other people's feelings that had peeled away the rind of her soul, if she had one.

Dom couldn't reach as far as the odd chef, but Vivian's uncharacteristic vulnerability meant they could reach farther than any other partner she'd ever taken before. That left her making fists in the sheets and whimpering to keep from moaning — because Dom wasn't falling apart and she didn't want to fall apart all by herself.

"It's okay if it's not," Dom continued, peering down at her with that hooded hunger. It wasn't malicious, but it was...off, like Vivian was off. But Dom wasn't like her, so Vivian couldn't put her finger on what was wrong — or if it was wrong at all. "I only see you look the way you do with him when you sing. Whenever you stand next to Del and me, you finally relax. But when you're with him, everything about you becomes *aware*, and when you sing, it doesn't matter what makeup or mask you're wearing. You're more alive than anything else around you. Your heart actually starts beating. That's why you love it. It's like getting hit with a defibrillator, and everyone feels it. You're the Phantom and Christine all in one. That's where your real power lies. Although you're a hell of a lover, sugar. When you scream out there in the microphone, it's almost as good as the sex. What happens when you scream in bed?"

"Oh, you fucker," she spat, drawing her legs up as Dom' rubbed their fingers more insistently over the spot inside her, over and over, faster and faster, forcing the pleasure to climb. She couldn't turn it off now, even if she wanted to.

When Dom smiled, that hungry quality disappeared—although Dom had talked about masks, about people not wanting others to see what they were. Dom was eminently disarming with that smile, which was why Vivian suspected they didn't use it when the circus was open.

"Obscenities don't count as screaming." Dom played her the way Lennon slayed the electric guitar, with professional-quality coordination and skill. "It doesn't matter to me if you love him, because I get it. I'm used to the friends-with-benefits zone, and I'm happy with it. Just getting close to something like you...that'll satisfy for a long time."

"What the actual fuck, Dom?" She writhed, the moans grating through her throat in spite of herself now. She grabbed the pillow, trying to move her body to set Dom to her own pace, but they weren't having any of it.

Dom laughed, quickening their fingers even more. "I know it sounds a lot creepier than I mean it. I promise, Viv, I just like you and you seem to like me. I don't get that as much as you'd think, with my utterly unawkward and sparkling personality. So tell me honestly, is it the same or is it just him?"

Vivian planted her heels on the mattress as the second climax ripped through her, barreling at the speed and harshness that Dom had set, completely out of her control, a storm through her already-ravaged system.

They'd been concerned about doing this while she wasn't fully healed, and now she knew why. The barriers she'd reinforced for so long crumpled away from the gigantic crack that had already formed. Vivian shook her head as the orgasm joined with the flood of anger, fear, hatred and every last bit of poison that had built up behind that wall to use only in controlled, inadequate doses—like using an eyedropper to empty a lake.

Walls could be rebuilt, and she was still healing, but for now, she felt destroyed, utterly incapable of controlling herself, whether it was her rage at being so affected by another human being, the pain that she'd worked so hard to pretend had never touched her or the complete, toe-curling pleasure that Dom fucked out of her. As Dom had wanted, she screamed, struggling to get away from them while also impaling herself on their fingers, hitting the window then her own face.

When Dom realized how hard she was hitting herself, they abruptly sat up and grabbed Vivian's wrists.

"Shhh, shhh. Jesus, Vivian, I'm sorry." Dom forced her hands to the bed, which made it all the more embarrassing when Vivian started to cry again. "Vivian, stop hurting yourself. This is… I just wanted to make you feel good after feeling so bad. That's all it was."

"Yeah, you all want that." Without use of her hands, she couldn't even wipe the tears away. "Did you get the screaming you were looking for?"

"Well, sure, until you started punishing yourself for it," Dom said. "I didn't know your kind did things like that."

"And what's *my* kind, Dom? Psychopaths, you mean? You think psychopaths never cry?"

"You're not quite all psychopath, sweetheart, and even if you were, you could still cry. Psychopaths feel plenty of self-pity, believe me. I mean punish yourself. You just got brutally beaten by a demon, and you think you still have to beat yourself?"

"Seemed like the thing to do at the time. Let go, damn it, or do you want to wipe the snot away yourself?"

Dom released her, cautious as Vivian sat up and wiped her face. "Still can't stand good sex, can you?" Dom said.

"The first time was fine," Vivian snapped.

"The first time, where you wrapped me around you instead of the other way around. Control issues much?"

"I think we established that. You're still hard."

"I got distracted by the tears — I don't go for that — but yeah, I'm still hard. You're still hot. And you do scream in bed like you do in a microphone, so I get to be uncomfortable."

Vivian brushed under her eyes again to make sure she wasn't still leaking. "My singing makes you hard?"

"Do you actually realize how many people get one off after you perform? It's like you're half-siren, I swear."

Vivian snorted. "I'd think I'd know if my mother or father were a siren. Believe me, they couldn't sing to save my life. My stepdad could, but I'd rather put an airhorn in my ear than ever hear him do it again."

"If you want to control me to feel better again, I won't stand in your way," Dom said, holding up their hands. "Or we could, you know, sleep. That was kind of on my original agenda for the night."

"Please, with the way you were looking at me, you probably would have woken me up in the morning with an erection against my back." Vivian used the tank top to clean the rest of her face then caught Dom's cum before tossing the mess to the floor of the living area. "Hope you weren't attached to that."

"It all washes." Dom crawled back a little when Vivian turned back to him, so there must have been something in her eyes that telegraphed the emotions that boiled through her compromised system.

"So you like the sound of my voice when I sing as much as when I scream?" She shoved Dom onto their back, pinning them there with her hands over their collarbone as though she would slide her fingers up and squeeze at any moment. She wouldn't, but the feeling that she could made her fingertips tingle with residual arousal. "Shall I sing 'Happy Birthday' to you, Mr. President?"

"Holy fuck," Dom groaned as she sang her breathy way down their chest, their abdomen, to the cock that seemed to seek her mouth in its own mindless way. She hummed the rest of the song as she sucked them off. When she slipped her fingers inside and found Dom's spot with the same familiarity as they'd found hers, Dom didn't have a chance.

Dom didn't scream, but tears sprung to their eyes for different reasons as Vivian made them come for a second time, swallowing it down from their cock and drawing it from their cunt. Their cum didn't do anything for her — not that she was hungry tonight. But Vivian didn't care. She'd gotten what she'd needed, felt back on shuddery footing when Dom pulled her up to kiss her after she'd swallowed everything down. The kisses were gentler now, expressive rather than foreplay.

Weird vibes or not, tears or not, she still liked Dom in spite of herself — which was, in itself, a little scary, because she didn't need Dom. Arcanium made it difficult to use anyone except to forge alliances, but Dom had already established that they didn't need sex for that. Vivian still liked them anyway and would punch someone's jaw crooked if they mocked Dom for any of the things Vivian's brother had had to deal with, and that was… If not new, then it had been a long time since she'd felt anything like it. Or wanted to feel anything like it again.

But she was comfortable in Dom's arms for now.

"Is that true? Do people really get a quick one after the band plays?" Vivian asked idly, stroking Dom's fingers where they rested on her abdomen.

"God's honest."

"They might not anymore," she mused.

"Maybe not for a little while." Dom tucked closer and yawned. "But it won't last. I guarantee it. That's how you'll slay them, not with the poison." Their words were slurring. Dom was falling asleep already. "Your voice is better poison than anything. They come back to die again and again. Even Bell. That's why you're alive, Viv. And that's why you want to live."

Vivian wasn't sure how much Dom was actually aware of saying, because they fell asleep really quickly afterward, with the slightest snore that Vivian didn't even mind was right next to her ear. She stayed awake a lot longer, calm and still on the outside and tempestuous within, waiting for the walls to heal and waiting for the hunger to return.

Chapter Twelve

She woke up with morning wood against her ass and without the hunger that had plagued her ever since she'd been sucked dry by the wish Bell had used against her.

"I still expect you to eat, Vivian – the same meals as before, and from the odd chef's table. Or else the hunger will return."

"Made a little mistake, did you?" she muttered under her breath so she wouldn't disturb Dom.

"The hunger worked perfectly until you came."

"Should have seen that one coming."

"I did. I had hoped that it could be avoided. You make things difficult, Miss Mendez. You always have. Where there is room for free will, you frustratingly choose the less desirable path almost every time. Avoid breaking my Quandary like you have my chef, please."

"Fuck you. They're just fine."

"You know better," he whispered. *"And there are precious few in this place who would choose to accept you as*

you are, mortal sins and all. If you hurt Dom, do you think Del will carry you away again?"

Vivian stayed silent, closing her eyes. Bell didn't speak in her head again, but she still sensed him. Perhaps he'd always been there, like the hum of an amp when no music was playing, and she just hadn't recognized what it was.

When Dom shifted against her, she turned around in their arms. Despite the morning breath and the fact the curtains were still open in broad daylight, she kissed Dom like she hadn't seen them in weeks, the raw sense of desperation terribly close to the hunger she'd known before. Dom didn't comment, just let her take them as fast and hard as she chose, riding them under the sheets until their muffled moans caught between them and they both came, Vivian first and Dom second, though it all took less than five minutes.

Dom looked up at her, combing through her hair with an inquisitive arch to their eyebrow. But Vivian just sighed and shook her head, settling on her back next to them. She didn't care that the sheets had shifted down to her waist and her breasts were bare for Del to see when he came out from his bedroom.

Del didn't do a double-take at the implication — she and Dom hadn't exactly been as quiet last night as they had been this morning — but he paused outside the bathroom. When Dom propped up on their elbow, Del made an expression that Vivian couldn't read, although it was almost as though Dom had woken up with a tiger in their bed.

"We're fine," Dom insisted. "It's nothing. We're *fine*."

It wasn't nothing. Even Vivian could tell it wasn't nothing. It wasn't love, but it was *something* — something that could remain as therapeutic and cathartic as most of the night before or something that could turn dangerous. It was fine, but it wasn't nothing, and they'd have to be careful.

No. *She'd* have to be careful. Bell hadn't told Dom not to break her. Even if she grew bored, she'd still have to guard Dom's heart over her own, and that gave Dom more power over her than she'd anticipated. With those unsure moments… Vivian would have to be so careful.

"Now you're beginning to understand."

* * * *

Dom and Del joined her on the way to the food court for their breakfast, when she'd join the other Skeletons for whatever the golems served.

After some side glances and glares from the cast while she passed through the food court, Dom and Del decided they should probably accompany her on the way to the harem tent, too.

Vivian would have told them it was pointless and she could probably do just as much damage as the two of them combined, especially since she wasn't wearing heels on uneven ground. But Del was a gentleman and a giant and didn't feel comfortable leaving her to fend for herself while her back still looked scarred instead of healed over.

"The Ringmaster really cut deep." Del's rich voice resonated with concern as he touched the place on her back above the neckline of the dress Vivian had stolen from Dom. It was too big, of course, but she'd needed something to cover her until she got to the harem tent.

Vivian glimpsed ropes of scar tissue on her shoulder, but she didn't reach behind her to feel it over her back. "I wear the leather jacket."

"This looks healed, though. I'm not sure it's going to get any better."

"Bell must want it this way, then." Vivian shrugged, but she was more upset than she let on. Now she was a scarecrow *and* scarred? How exactly did that serve his Skeleton vision?

If he was listening, he decided not to answer.

Nor did he comment when they reached the harem tent and found all of Vivian's things outside on the dewy grass. Her cot was folded up on top of the plastic tub that contained most of her possessions. The clothes rack and shattered full-length mirror stood next to them.

Dom looked at Del.

"We have room for her," Del said with a sigh, "but that rack is going to push the limits of my wardrobe. You're gonna have to share the place with a big guy sometimes, and I hog the bathroom."

Alicia ducked out through the open tent flap. She stood at the entrance with her arms crossed. She didn't have to say anything, and Vivian didn't have anything to say about it either. What was she supposed to do? Stomp her foot and say it wasn't fair?

"This is her home," Dom said.

"Not anymore," Alicia replied. "If you want to share space with someone who earned fifty lashes for her first time, that's your choice. Jonas wouldn't say what happened, but he was cold as hell last night, and Bell wouldn't have had you punished like that if you hadn't done something unforgivable. We don't want you here. We don't want you trying to stab us in the night or doing whatever bitchy thing you're doing to Shane anymore."

"*Dios mío*, I'm not doing anything to Shane," Vivian said. Del had taken the tub and Dom had taken the cot, so she grabbed the rack. The mirror could go in the dumpster for all she cared. "I do a lot of things, but I'm not taking shit for something I *haven't* done."

"She's hasn't done anything to me." Shane ducked out behind Alicia. "Cool off, Alicia. She got punished already. Is this really necessary?"

"You feel safe sleeping with her in the tent?" Alicia said.

Shane didn't answer.

Dark circles bruised under her eyes. A grayish cast dulled already pale skin and the flesh of the monster mouths lacked their richer red color. In the light of day, Vivian could finally see what Alicia was talking about.

"How hungry are you?" Vivian asked.

"We're always hungry," Alicia said impatiently. "What part of 'you're not welcome' did you not under—"

Vivian interrupted. "You're still hungry?"

Alicia started to answer then stopped, bewildered.

"Of course I'm still hungry. It's fine. We're always hungry," Shane said. "Look, Vivian, you can come back in. Jonas'll be by with breakfast in a bit, and we can all just calm down..."

"No fucking way," Lily said, joining the rest of them outside the tent. "Majority rules. It's not like you've been sleeping here anyway. You can curl up in one of the booths and cry to someone who cares."

"Does it look like I'm staying?" Vivian tugged at the rack, but it didn't want to budge over the grass. She doubted the other Skellies gave a shit that she wasn't at full strength, and she was lucky to have someone to carry the other things.

"But Jonas is coming soon." Shane's distress sent another knife through Vivian's inexplicably sensitive heart. "We need to eat what he serves us. That's the rule."

"He can serve her at the food court, little sister," Dom reassured her. "She's out of the tent, not out of Arcanium."

"I don't know why Bell didn't just let the clowns eat her," Alicia muttered. "Didn't know her voice was literally that good."

She brushed past Shane a little too close to one of her mouths, which immediately tried to take a bite out of Alicia's side. If Alicia had been more substantial, it might have been successful.

"Ow! Goddamn it, Shane!"

"Sorry." Shane glanced back at Vivian, but she ducked back into the tent to follow Alicia. Lily pulled the tent flap closed again.

"You mind sharing what you did?" Del said as he helped her pull the rack along with them.

Dom glanced at Vivian. They wouldn't share something she'd told them in confidence, but they appeared less certain of Del's reaction than their own.

"You might not want me around after I tell you," Vivian said.

"Might not want you around if you don't." Sequins, heavy eye makeup and a wig cap did nothing to diminish him. He was a beefy dude. He had some serious leg muscles from all the dancing in heavy, sky-high platform heels.

"Del..."

"Dom, far be it from me to judge, but your own judgment might be a little impaired here."

"Delilah Grey, you take that back."

"You can sleep with who you want, but *moi* aside, you don't have the most discerning taste. Let's just admit it."

"I tried to pull a Jim Jones," Vivian said quickly, quietly, in case anyone else was around.

Del stopped walking.

"It won't happen again. Bell all but guaranteed that if I lose it again, he *will* feed me to the clowns. You're safe from the skinny bitch, okay?"

"Seriously?" Del said.

"I feel like I've had this conversation already," Vivian said. "Twice. Yes, I seriously tried to poison everyone. No, it seriously didn't work. Yes, it seriously won't happen again. Next time, I'll self-destruct unselfishly and in relative peace, quiet and privacy. And if I have to find someplace else to store my shit, now's the time to tell me I'm not allowed in your trailer."

Del narrowed his eyes, considering her as though he could laser straight through her unskullified face and see the truth etched on the skull underneath.

"I don't need much space," Vivian said. "It's just to sleep."

Del still didn't say anything, and he didn't move.

"I'll sing *Phantom of the Opera* with you."

Almost mass murderer or not, Del couldn't help the grin that cracked through his attempt to look serious and suspicious.

"Did you know about this?" Del asked Dom.

"She told me."

"Before or after the screaming?"

"Before."

"You screwed-up madperson. You need to stop taking in the psychopathic strays, Dom."

"But I'm so good with them," Dom replied, adjusting their grip on the tub. "It's your veto, Del."

"You try anything, Skelly, and I'll crush your bones to make my bread. You hear me?"

"I get it. I didn't slit anyone's throat in the trailer last night, did I?"

"No, but you didn't try to poison everyone before last night, either."

"Delilah, she isn't going to kill anyone," Dom said. "Bell didn't let her last night, and he won't let her again. Did we take her in last night, knowing she did something bad, just to kick her out now when she doesn't have anywhere else to go?"

Del let out a sigh of exasperation. "Don't get too attached, Dom." But he tightened his grip on the rack and continued to haul it toward their trailer.

"Thank you." Gratitude didn't come naturally to Vivian, but after all the nights she'd slept outside with nothing but a blanket and a length of twine, sleeping in a bed with someone else had been a lot more comfortable. And if the black-hole hunger was gone, she might actually be able to get a good night's sleep again.

As long as she was still alive the next morning — and the next, and the next.

* * * *

She sang *Phantom of the Opera* with Miss Delilah not just one time but once a weekend, because it turned out that, between Del's classical baritone and Vivian's rock voice mixed with the judicious use of the classical — not to mention their disparate appearances at the microphone, a giant man in a dress and a skeleton woman in leather pants — they had a hit.

Vivian wouldn't say all was forgiven, but getting the blessing of the alien drag queen and the Quandary ensured that the cast allowed themselves to enjoy the Skellies' performances again. Bell had taken away her choice in the matter. He kept the karaoke but expected her to do what she'd done before — interrupt amateur hour with something spectacular. He didn't require that she rehearse with the Skellies anymore, since they barely even acknowledged her, but she was expected to do whatever they played — which meant she got hit with *My Immortal* a lot more often than she would have preferred. The joke was on them. She still slayed it every time. She'd brought Nasreen to tears at least once.

Lennon didn't seem bothered one way or another. Most of the demons didn't react much differently to her now. If anything, she might have earned grudging respect after surviving the Ringmaster's punishment — whether she had the help of magic or not.

But Jonas still wouldn't talk to her, wouldn't even look at her.

What he served her every day from his booth, his lips a thin line and eyes downcast, worked just fine to tame the rabid hunger that preceded mealtimes. That hadn't changed and neither had the hunger before the eating contests. The only difference was that food quelled that hunger much more.

Vivian didn't need him like before. So why did eating what he made for her by requirement alone, rather than with affection and care, feel like eating ashes every time? And when her stomach was calmer, how could she still hunger so much? But Vivian knew better than to come to him for anything more than the minimum two meals, and all he had to give her was the absolute minimum of those minimum meals.

From whispers Del and Dom heard from the rest of the circus, everyone thought she'd tried to kill him in his kitchen. They didn't know the full scope of what she'd tried, and to their credit, both Del and Dom kept their mouths shut so that the rest of Arcanium didn't shun her completely. Del had decided Bell's decision to keep her around was enough for him, and true to Vivian's word, she hadn't tried to kill either of them in their sleep.

Whenever the odd chef wouldn't look at her, Vivian knew better than the rest of Arcanium why, and it had nothing to do with taking the poisoning personally. She felt it every time she looked at him, remembered with uncanny vividness what he saw in her. And she understood why he wouldn't let himself see it again.

But she didn't understand why she kept wanting him to. Because she knew what he saw, and it wasn't a sweet, nurturing, comforting, satisfying future. It would be as lean and hungry as she'd been before Bell changed her. It would be different than the explosive but somehow comfortable satisfaction that Dom gave her now that she was more susceptible to the sex demons' magic. Regular contact seemed to have that effect, to Vivian's combined annoyance and pleasure. Dom was officially attached, but in their defense, Vivian kind of was, too—the way normal people tended to get attached to kittens and puppies, the both of them. Dom still hadn't fallen, but damn, they sure held on tightly when they were unconscious.

The scars didn't fade—a perpetual reminder of the external punishment she'd endured, and whenever she thought of resisting Bell's requirements for her, she tasted mushrooms on her tongue. Feelings toward her were chillier than ever from the rest of the cast, but she had Dom and Delilah in place of the Skellies, and she was still singing and enjoying it. And she wasn't raiding trash cans and dumpsters in her sleep. It wasn't like the Skellies or anyone else had liked her much before, except Shane.

She kept telling herself that it was better this way. She didn't need Jonas or the harem tent or anything more than what she had now. She didn't need anything more than food in her belly and regular good sex that didn't make her feel like the entire world was cracking apart. She'd managed the food in her belly part.

She hadn't lost her entire line of defenses, but Jonas, Bell and Dom had broken through most of them. If the walls were broken, and walls were the only thing that had kept her going, what was left of her when those walls couldn't be built back up again? She could scream in the microphone all she wanted, but whenever she had to leave Dom and Del's trailer, she was as fragile as the skeleton everyone else could see. For fuck's sake, she'd teared up during *My Immortal* once or twice, too.

The way she clung to Dom during the evenings she fucked them hard and fast as well as when she let them go slow made Dom happy, but Vivian didn't know how much longer she could take feeling like she was on the edge of a mental breakdown. Not when Dom was as fragile as she was and Delilah was just a man, neither of whom she was allowed to break in the process.

She hadn't wished to feel like this. She hadn't wished to feel. But it was happening anyway, just more slowly.

Tears just behind her eyes. Chest pangs. Memories shot through with emotions she didn't remember having or that were supposed to have faded with time. Nightmares she'd thought she'd left behind after leaving that hellhole. Missing Angelica and wondering whether she'd saved her soon enough. Missing Arturo more often from all the time she spent with Dom. Hell, missing Fernanda every time she saw a Latinx couple or heard Spanish in a woman's voice. She'd turned into a goddamn cheeseball, as Bell had probably planned, the emotional vampire bastard.

The Skellies tolerated her when the band was on, although Vivian could practically feel all the knives Alicia wanted to throw into the scar tissue on her back. They cold-shouldered her at Antarctic levels the rest of the time. They were easy to avoid when there was so much ground to cover and plenty of guests to split their attention. But the Skellies were also expected to spend some time in Oddity Row to justify it being there, particularly in the courtyard, where everyone was guaranteed to get a good picture with a spider, a snake or a Skeleton. That's where the town simply wasn't big enough for the five of them.

Vivian didn't mind being ignored, but Shane actually seemed miserable. Vivian noticed it more and more. And she noticed that the rest of the Skellies noticed, because sometimes they forgot to hate Vivian when Shane would whine as though in serious period pain, doubled over as she waited for *someone* to throw meat into the mouths, and even then it didn't seem to make a dent.

Vivian couldn't ask the other Skellies what was going on in the harem tent and what Shane was like after getting hand-fed by the odd chef, so all she could do was keep an eye on Shane while she smiled on the photo platform. She was so tired of smiling, but that was just another thing she no longer had a choice on. At least the people she smiled with liked her, if just because she was cool to look at and made their snaps gold. She'd smile through the pain for that little bit of validation, shallow though it was. Shallow had never bothered her before.

She wasn't in the courtyard, though, when she heard a scream ringing through Oddity Row. Screams weren't unusual in Arcanium, with surprises — not to mention clowns — around every corner, but when that scream was followed by more and not by embarrassed or nervous laughter, Vivian looked up from the shared selfie she was taking with a seven-year-old.

"Sorry, sweetie. I need to go see what this is. Stay scary."

Lily ran out of the courtyard tent just as Vivian reached it. Any anger was forgotten, replaced by drawn, white fear. Lily nearly collided with Vivian as she grabbed her by the lapels of her leather jacket.

"Shane collapsed. She's bitten through her freaking arm trying not to scream. There's blood everywhere, but we can't get near her because her mouths keep moving her to snap at our hands.

"Fuck." Vivian ran into the diffused red light under the courtyard canvas, past Nasreen's belly dancing platform and the Spider's and Sasha's menageries. Alicia and Nasreen were both next to Shane's glass box, trying to keep the crowd back at the same time they tried to figure out how to grab Shane without a mouth biting them.

"Has someone called Bell?" the Spider asked from her web above the spiders and insects.

Vivian pushed through the crowd. "Back up. You can go viral just as well five feet back." When she reached the box, Vivian grabbed Alicia by the shirt. "How long has she not been eating?"

"She's *been* eating, Vivian. She eats when the golems bring in breakfast, and she eats when the odd chef brings in dinner. She's the eating contest champion almost every time."

Vivian yanked her closer and whispered harshly in her ear. "Not her regular mouth, you moron. How long hasn't she been feeding her other mouths?"

"What are you talking about?" But Alicia's eyes widened.

"Oh shit." Apparently Nasreen had overheard.

"Stay here. Don't let anyone touch her."

"What about Bell?" Alicia said.

"Fuck Bell!" And Vivian didn't care who heard. Because he'd taken away most of the Skeletons' regular hunger, but he hadn't from the rest of Shane's mouths. And surely the odd chef, Bell, *someone* had noticed. It wasn't like Vivian had been the biggest distraction since her big night. Someone else had to have known — and no one had done anything.

Vivian ran from the courtyard to the food court, shaking her head against the assault of smells that reawakened her cravings. That hadn't changed and wouldn't change until dinner. But her cravings paled in comparison to the clam-pink flesh of the mouths that had once been bright red, the way they seemed to jerk out of Shane's skin, threatening to tear themselves out completely. And that couldn't be put on Vivian. That was all Bell, long live the fucking king.

"Coming through! Coming through!" She darted between people standing or getting in line, using her size to her advantage.

The odd chef looked away from the customer he was serving, surprise managing to find its way through the usual courteous mask. "Vivian, what — ?"

She wasn't interested in rehashing the past or discussing their feelings. She pushed through the swinging door to the booth, grabbed Jonas by the collar of his chef's coat and pulled him toward the kitchen door. "We have an emergency."

The customer was not happy that the person serving him was being dragged away by a punk-rock skeleton. "Hey, I was — "

"I'll take care of you, sir," one of the golems said, sliding into the place that the odd chef had vacated. They apparently had a system.

"What's going on?" Jonas managed to ask before Vivian pulled him through the kitchen door and slammed it behind him. "This isn't the time for — "

"This isn't about me." She couldn't count on one hand the number of times she'd said that. "Shane's in trouble. You stop feeding me and suddenly no one else gets special treatment either?"

Vivian hadn't stopped just because they were talking. She dragged him to the meat freezer and yanked it open.

"As you're well aware, I can't *make* anyone eat more than they choose. Or rather, I can but I don't. While it pained me to watch Shane starve herself, I wasn't going to tie her down to the butcher block and force her. Why?"

"She collapsed in the courtyard, and I don't think the mouths are taking no for an answer." Vivian grabbed whatever ground meat she could find. The last time she'd been in here, she'd nearly frozen to death, and the freezing floor under her bare feet wasn't helping right now, but action distracted. "Buckets. Do you have buckets?"

The odd chef left the freezer. When he returned, he brought four five-gallon buckets.

"This needs to be thawed." Vivian stripped away the plastic and dumped the first few packages of ground meat into one of the buckets. "And you need to bless it — or whatever the hell you do."

The odd chef didn't protest. The ground meat in the first bucket poured out of its frozen shape to take the shape of the bucket instead. He thawed each subsequent chunk of meat she put in. When all four buckets were filled as close to the brim as Vivian dared, she tried to lift one, but it was five gallons of densely packed meat and it took two hands just to barely lift them with her diminished muscles.

Without a word, the odd chef beckoned one of the working golems, who jumped out of his lineup to take two of the buckets without any effort at all. Jonas seemed to have no problem with the other two buckets.

"Follow me." Vivian pushed her way through cooking golems, cashier golems and the crowd once again, power-walking so that Jonas and the golem could keep up. But she didn't know how much time they'd wasted already.

"Coming through!" Vivian shouted, using every bit of her diaphragm support to make herself heard over the crowd in the courtyard, which had grown with guests and cast alike. The Spider had climbed down from her web, and Kitty had managed to find her way as well. Ciarán loomed over the rest, Moss on his shoulder. They all stared at the writhing figure in the glass box.

"Out of our way!" When her voice didn't suffice, Vivian didn't hesitate to use force. She was a bony-ass bodyguard, shoving through the crowd to "Hey!" and "Bitch!" Jonas and the golem followed in her wake.

Vivian didn't waste any time when she got to the box. She looked back at Jonas. "Are they good to serve?"

The odd chef nodded. "Yes, but… Oh my. Oh, Shane, what did you do?"

At least he's not blaming me.

Vivian took one of the odd chef's buckets and hoisted it with embarrassing effort to the edge of the box.

"What are you doing?" Alicia said.

But Vivian had already tipped the bucket over, pouring five gallons of ground meat all over Shane.

The crowd around them who didn't have a clue what was going on went "Ewww!" Then they pressed closer.

Shane released her arm, which she'd bitten through — and it looked like she might have eaten some of it, too. She jolted out of the meat, but Vivian didn't think it was to get away. She thought it might be to get closer to the source of it — which was her. The scream lowered to cries, wails through her bloodstained mouth. But there was an element of relief to it, like the first cries after jamming fingers in a door. Though Shane arched out of most of it, the protruding mouths on her hip and her back both grabbed chunks of the meat and gulped them down.

So Vivian took the second bucket and poured it in, too.

The glass box was about the width of a small kiddie pool and reached Shane's waist when she was standing. Two five-gallon buckets barely filled the box, but it managed to cover more surface area of Shane's body and made it harder for her to get away from the meat. More mouths found something to bite.

Vivian poured in the third bucket. Shane held up her arms to keep the meat from striking her face, but the mouth on the side of her skull jerked her head so that the meat poured right onto it. Vivian also made sure to pour around Shane's thighs. The latex skirt was skintight, and she wouldn't be able to part her legs much, but Vivian noticed meat disappearing there, too, as Shane's thighs kept jerking open then closed again.

"You're going to smother her," someone called out as Vivian brought the last bucket to the rim of the box. Shane was almost completely covered in the indeterminate ground meat. It could be gallons of roadkill for all Vivian knew. But the kind didn't matter, and no one but the odd chef would be able to tell.

Vivian tipped over the last bucket, covering Shane completely. All anyone could see was where her arms reached out of the meat as though searching for something to hold on to and where her feet pressed against the side of the box. Then Shane wiped the meat away from her face, gasping, but not just because she'd reached fresh air. Her writhing had slowed, the pull of the mouths less frantic. Everywhere she moved, there was more meat to consume. As her mouths fed heartily, the relieved sounds that escaped from her own mouth were practically sexual—a fact that didn't seem to escape some of the people around the box, especially those with shorter companions who had delicate ears. Mothers hurried children away from the courtyard, muttering explanations and blushing.

But some people pressed even closer, pushing against the efforts of Arcanium cast to hold them back.

Everyone in front could see plainly that Shane's body was taking in the meat. They strained to watch more closely and muttered to each other, asking how she was doing it. Was there a funnel under her back? Was it some kind of trick skin over an even skinnier body? There were all kinds of bogus theories, but Vivian wasn't interested in the truth or whatever fiction Bell would spin about what happened. She put the last bucket with the rest of them and leaned against the edge of the box, her arms like noodles.

Shane wasn't screaming anymore, and she'd be satisfied, perhaps more than she'd been since before Vivian had come into the circus, now that Bell had taken away the persistent, perpetual hunger.

It was also kind of fascinating to watch Shane's mouths suck in the meat, which disappeared like water draining from a bathtub. And through it all was the vicious but carnal sound of teeth sinking into flesh and slurping it down. Shane didn't need to be moaning for what she was doing to sound obscene, like hundreds of mouths going down on someone. Listening to it made Vivian hungrier in a way she now recognized as a particularly Arcanium quality of horniness.

Finally, with nothing but small slimes of meat left in the box, Shane's body slumped, and she closed her eyes.

Vivian didn't let her relax. She grabbed Shane by the wrists and hauled her to her feet.

"Whoa, what—?" Shane stumbled like a woman drunk, trying to close her fingers over Vivian's arms, but the angle Vivian held her kept Shane from getting a grip.

"There's nothing underneath," someone from the crowd. "There's no hole. Where'd it all go?"

"Vivian, what are you doing?" Shane even slurred like she was drunk.

"Helping you take care of yourself, since that doesn't seem to be important to you."

"I didn't know it was important to you," Alicia said.

"No, but it should have been more important to you," Vivian snapped. "Come on, Shane. Out of the box. You're covered in salmonella."

That got people making an aisle in a hurry.

"How much meat did you pour on me?" Halfway through the crowd, Shane finally stopped stumbling and Vivian could curl her arm through the elbow to help her out of the courtyard.

"Twenty gallons. You ate almost all of it and didn't gain a pound. What the fuck, Shane?"

Vivian glanced behind her to make sure that none of the guests were trailing them like amateur paparazzi. It appeared they'd got the video they wanted — someone suffering was much more interesting than someone recovering. Then again, they still thought it was fake.

The odd chef had locked step five yards behind them. He revealed nothing of what he felt and kept his eyes on Shane rather than acknowledging Vivian. It was strange how well he could do that when Shane and Vivian were close enough for one of the hip mouths to nip at Vivian if it were still hungry.

"Do you really have room to judge me for not eating?" Shane said. She tried to walk on her own, but when her legs crossed and she nearly tripped, Vivian forced her arm back into the crook of Shane's elbow. Vivian was smearing raw meat juice all over her precious leather jacket, but apparently the golems worked miracles, and she could go jacketless for the band this afternoon if she had to.

"I have all the room to judge. I'm the fucking cautionary tale."

Shane and Vivian split from the odd chef near the food court. Jonas had to return to his booth, and Shane desperately needed a shower and a new dress.

"What difference does it make?" Shane shook her head, wiping stray bits of meat from her scalp. "I eat and eat and eat and I'm hungry all the time. I eat shit and feel like crap. I eat like a queen and feel like crap. The only thing I enjoy is the drumming, but even once the rest of the Skeletons stopped holding their stomachs all the time, *I* still couldn't eat enough. I'd have your share of the breakfasts and the dinners, but it didn't help."

"That's because you were feeding the wrong mouth, you whore." Vivian shoved her with her elbow.

"Do you have any idea how humiliating it is to have to lie on a butcher block while a man stuffs meat into your crotch-pocket?"

"Well, it didn't go *exactly* like that, but yeah, actually, I do," Vivian said. "You're supposed to be better at this than me."

"Better at what? At eating? I have an eating disorder, too. Better at doing what Jonas wants me to do? The dinners are where he shows his love. The feeding is just...pellets to a hamster for him. And that's what it feels like. Do you know how agonizing it is to watch the other Skellies lose their hunger, to watch them fuck Lennon every day, while I get hungrier and no one can get close to me? What's even the point, Vivian?" Shane pulled her arm away, and this time, she was able to walk a straight line. "Why are we eating just to starve? If nothing we eat matters, why does it matter if we eat or not?"

Shane lifted the harem tent flap. Since the rest of the Skellies were out, Vivian followed her in. It hadn't changed much. There was just an empty space where Vivian's stuff used to be. They hadn't filled it up with anything else, as though it was waiting for her. She'd never forgive herself under the same circumstances, so the idea that the other Skellies might had never crossed her mind.

"Isn't that just the way life is? You eat then you need to eat again then you need to eat again?" Vivian said. "Even if you want to control what you're eating and how much, the body still needs something eventually. Your body always needs something, and so do the mouths."

"They don't need anything." Shane gestured to herself, standing in the center of the tent. "Look at me. The meat didn't *go* anywhere. It's not feeding *me*. Why didn't Bell just make the mouths without all the extra crap? Why do they actually need to be fed?"

"I don't know where the meat goes, but it *is* feeding something. You've got, what, eleven mouths to feed, like you're carrying around eleven pets all the time. Just because you don't like them or because it's embarrassing to feed them doesn't mean they don't need to get fed. Bell made you responsible for them. He's an asshole. We can both agree on that. But this isn't an eating disorder thing. You're feeding yourself fine. Maybe it's a matter of figuring out how to feed the rest of you in a less humiliating way."

Shane crossed her arms, but she seemed to have calmed down a bit. "What's less humiliating than people throwing meat in your holes like a weird carnival game or a chef playing chopstick gynecologist?"

"Take a shower." Vivian removed her dirty leather jacket and threw it in her space. The golems would find it somehow and get it back to her. If not, she'd ask Kitty or Sasha for another one. "Wash yourself off, get dressed, drum the shit out this afternoon and avoid the hell out of Bell Madoc. Let me think."

"I thought you didn't care." Shane's arms were still crossed, but it felt more defensive now.

"Who said I did?" Vivian replied, but she refused to leave until Shane stepped under the showerhead and turned on the water.

Shane glanced back at her as she peeled off her bandage dress, suddenly shy.

Vivian could take Dom, but Dom was a manipulative bitch in their own right and perfectly aware of Vivian's inclinations. Shane was somehow more innocent, and Vivian sensed how easily she could slip her way into Shane's head right now, especially after what she'd done in the courtyard. She could so easily make Shane worship her, and there was an element of the old thrill in that.

But where had her old thrill gotten her? Without a single friend, without family, even the ones she'd wanted to save, and stuck in Arcanium on her last life. Everything she'd done had been to make herself feel better, more powerful, more in control, but she still felt miserable, numb and ugly, and what power and control she had was granted to her rather than taken.

Vivian wanted to strip the rest of her clothes, go into that shower and take advantage of Shane's vulnerability. She was attracted enough. The power of it would act its own aphrodisiac. But she'd be terrible for Shane, and choosing to be with Shane for the purpose of owning her would be terrible for Vivian, because she'd inevitably break her promise to Bell not to break any of his things.

Vivian forced herself to close the bathroom door and walk out of the harem tent. The disappointment in Shane's expression would fade. Maybe she could let Shane work out this little crush one day when Vivian had a better reason for letting her — or no reason at all.

She suspected that she was growing as a person and she didn't like it.

As Vivian walked back out into the circus, she was overly aware of her exposed skeletal arms, and she thought other people were, too. It was one thing to believe a woman was rocking sugar skull makeup and another to see how thin she actually was. But she couldn't let that bother her right now. She had a mini concert to rock.

The odd chef hadn't taken his place behind the booth counter. He waited for her at the edge of the food court where he'd stood before to watch her perform. As awkward as he always was, he seemed particularly so when surrounded by normal people moving around him, talking animatedly to each other, while he just stood there with a face as blank as the golems after everyone went home.

"What?" Vivian didn't bother being polite, because they both knew she wasn't polite, but she tried not to snap. He'd listened to her when he'd had every reason not to trust her in his kitchen again.

"Is she better?"

"Yes, she's better. She's showering to get ready for the performance. I told her she'd be on the stage this afternoon whether she wanted to or not. She wants to, though. She likes the music."

"You both do."

"Yes, we have *so much* in common."

"You have more in common with her than you might think."

"Sure. I suppose we're both bipeds in a band."

A twitch of his mouth. His expressions were barely the tip of the icebergs of his emotions. She'd known that before Bell had given her a first-row seat to his mind. She didn't understand how she could still amuse.

"More than that."

"Crazy bipeds in a band."

"You have more in common with other people than you believe you do. You aren't inhuman. You make yourself what you believe you are. I'm all too aware of what you believe. But it's not what you are unless you continue to choose it."

"What do you know?" Vivian peered around the odd chef as Lennon started his sound check and Nasreen practiced her keyboard with him.

"I know what it's like to change what seems immutable."

"What has Bell said to you?" she asked, trying to keep her voice and expression neutral, though her first impulse was to run.

"After that night? He has said things, but not about you. I don't need him to tell me what I already know."

"Yeah, well, you're immortal. You had time."

"You're in Arcanium. You have all the time you need — if you want to change."

The singers were at their mics. She needed to get ready. "I don't have a choice."

Jonas grabbed her bare upper arm before she could pass him. She immediately flashed back to when he'd caught her and shoved her into the freezer.

Then the flashback went farther back than the odd chef, shredding her ability to stay neutral.

He released his hold on her at whatever he saw on her face. "There is always a choice. The consequences may make the choice feel impossible, but there is always a choice."

"There isn't always a choice." Vivian backed away. "You didn't change. You buried it, covered it with a mask that you preferred, but you didn't change. So don't stand there and tell me I can be what I'm not. All I can do is know the reason to pretend. I can accept that for now. Can you?"

The quirk of light in his blank face had disappeared. He tilted his head, but though he didn't seem troubled, there was no way to tell what was going on behind those black eyes hidden by his thick glasses.

"Are you free after dinner? It's not for me," she added quickly. "It's for Shane. I have an idea."

"The kitchen is always available for Shane after dinner. And your last idea worked. For that alone, you are welcome, too."

Vivian nodded then slipped through the crowd to stand near Delilah and Dom.

She waited through a particularly horrible rendition of *Piano Man* that made her want to put Billy Joel's head on a pike next to stage as a warning to all potential singers. Then she snatched the microphone away from the next person, who tried to ask the band to play Lady Gaga's *Born This Way*.

Vivian ignored the man's semi-drunken protests, because he'd either go away or take a swing at her, and she'd dearly love to take a swing back with the mic stand. But at the applause from the audience — specifically the circus audience — the potential performer found something elsewhere to occupy his time.

She couldn't concern herself with him, because the opening notes of the song Lennon started were from nothing she'd practiced, nothing she already knew. It was another nightmare moment. All that needed to happen was for her clothes to disappear and everything she was hiding to become visible to more than just the cast of Arcanium. But whenever this happened, she could usually trust Bell to give her the lyrics after the initial panic.

The minor key didn't make her disquiet any better when the words didn't immediately come to her. Vivian looked back at Lennon and Nasreen, indicating confusion. Lennon shrugged and Nasreen tried to mouth something at her, but Vivian couldn't lipread anything but 'poison', which made her blood run cold.

The other members of the band glanced at each other, confused as to why she hadn't started singing— especially Shane, who'd wrapped herself in red latex instead of ivory, which set off the healthy redness in the flesh of the mouths and her choice of deep red lipstick. Vivian had been so distracted by the odd chef that she hadn't noticed that Shane had joined them. She'd never worn the red before, and it looked stunning on her, so stunning that Lennon had to take them through another run of the introduction before Vivian could convince herself to turn around again.

Only to see the odd chef still there in his place right outside the food court instead of doing his goddamn job.

After the fifth run through the introduction, the lyrics came to her in a rush, and she hated Bell all the more.

But she began to sing *Familiar Taste of Poison*, as though it had been made for her to sing at that moment — to Jonas, to Shane, to Dom, to everyone in Arcanium watching her now — in a place and state of mind where she could really feel it.

She tried not to look at him. She tried not to see him when she did look. But in spite of the fact that there was a crowd between her and the food court, she couldn't unsee him as she tore through every last lyric Bell had chosen for her.

It didn't help when the band followed up with Lennon power-chording into *I'm Not an Angel*, a Halestorm song she did know that was just as apt.

The odd chef didn't leave. He didn't spare her a moment of anger, lust, hatred or pain that Bell forced her to confront through her voice. The audience loved the tears and the rasp brought to her sound at the height of the final chorus.

At that point, Vivian would have been fine calling it a night and riding Dom until they couldn't take it any way Vivian could give it.

But no, Bell had to finish her up with Sarah McLachlan's *Ice*, as though it had been Bell's aim all along to reach too far inside her chest, where feelings were connected to memories and where the walls she'd tried to rebuild crumbled all over again. She couldn't hide behind the rough qualities in her voice with only Nasreen and Lily playing that haunting melody. She'd overpower them and the song wouldn't work. In stripping that away, Bell dared her to bare what soul she had left.

When the song was over, she stood there at the mic and didn't smile, didn't move. The crowd applauded, but she couldn't hear it. She was vaguely aware of whoops and whistles, the usual response to closing a set, even if she'd ended it on a slow, dark song. In Arcanium, no one expected anything different than that.

But Bell wasn't going to bring her here and end her like this, not when he'd left Shane to starve and let Vivian pick up his mess, not when he'd made his mistakes with her and with the other Skellies, not when he'd left her naked in front of everyone like the very goddamn nightmare she'd been afraid of.

She held up her hand for silence. She didn't need the instruments. And she sure as hell didn't need Bell Madoc.

Vivian looked back at Shane and nodded to her. She'd know how to proceed soon enough.

Then Vivian ripped into Emilie Autumn's *I Know Where You Sleep*.

Nasreen started to join her on the synth, but Vivian lifted her hand again and Nasreen stopped. It was just Shane's manic drumming, the background vocals and Vivian's rapid-fire snarls, with metal growls where they were needed. If she was going to tell the truth, she might as well tell her own, in her own way — not her truth according to Bell.

God, she wished her stepfather were here to see this. She'd growl his eardrums bloody if she could. If he were here, she knew what she'd wish for — but she wouldn't wish for it unless she could see, even if it was at the old man's deathbed. She wanted to be the reaper. And if Bell wanted a piece of her soul, he could have it if he gave her that gift.

When she was done, Vivian raised her hand again, but this time for the crowd, to say goodbye. She still couldn't smile for them, but her skull makeup smiled enough on its own.

Chapter Thirteen

Vivian ate in the food court so she would know when Shane was coming to the kitchen with Jonas.

She'd just finished up her five-mushroom pizza — offered to her without a slice of irony, since it had also been served to everyone else who came up to the food booth for their late-night dinner — when Jonas stepped into the light, followed by the unmistakable winding red of Shane's dress.

Vivian tossed her tray and joined Shane behind Jonas.

It wasn't until they were in the kitchen and standing by the butcher block that Jonas broke the silence. "After this afternoon, are the mouths still hungry? They were denying food by the end."

"They're not as hungry. Most of them got their fill, but one didn't quite get as much as the rest." Shane played with her thumbnail and couldn't look up as she responded. She was already a slight, slim woman, but next to Jonas, she looked like a scolded child — except for the press of her breasts against the latex and her still deep-red lips.

"Which one?"

"The one between my legs."

As Vivian had suspected, the tightness of her skirt hadn't allowed the mouth underneath as much access to the meat as the rest.

"Are you sure it's that kind of hungry?" Vivian asked.

Shane laughed nervously, letting go of her thumb before she could damage it. "Vivian, this is embarrassing even without you here."

"I told you I had an idea. Is it just hungry for meat?"

"It's..." Shane sighed, closed her eyes. "It's still hungry for meat, yes. And it's been hungry for other things for a long time. You know it has. But everything that used to be there is gone. I wouldn't know where to begin."

Vivian wanted so badly to take that insecurity and uncertainty and close a collar around it. Didn't Shane know how ripe she made herself? The fact no one had sucked her into their trap yet spoke more to the dangers of her vagina mouth than her vigilance.

Instead, Vivian edged toward Jonas, gauging whether he would let her close to him. When he didn't move away, she whispered in his ear what he should tell Shane to do.

He stilled more than usual. But after a few beats, he turned back to Shane.

"Take off your dress and get up on the butcher block." His particular brand of emotionlessness made the command sound even more disquieting than if Vivian had said it.

Shane jerked her head up. Her gaze went back and forth between Jonas and Vivian in quick succession...

confused, suspicious. But when she settled her attention on Vivian, Shane nodded.

She stripped the dress away from her body. Without the red, the mouths were all the more of a contrast. She let the latex pool on the ground then hoisted herself onto the block with decent strength for her height. She kept her thighs closed, but her nipples had gone hard.

"Lie down," Jonas said, at Vivian's prompting, "and spread your legs."

"*Fuck*," Shane whispered. But she lowered herself to the wood, adjusting her spine against its rigidity. Then she parted her thighs.

"More," Jonas said, again with Vivian's whisper in his ear.

Shane brought the crease behind her knees to the corners of the block.

Vivian took her ankles and shoved them back until Shane's legs draped over either side of the block instead of in front of her. Then, careful of the mouth on one thigh, she pulled Shane as close to the edge of the block as she could.

So close, the mouth where her vulva should have been seemed freakishly large, extending back to her ass on one side and almost completely over her mound on the other. With her thighs open, the mouth took its opportunity to spread its teeth, the dark red, wet flesh leading to the smaller opening of its throat. The tongue slithered out from the hole, reaching for Vivian, but she wasn't close enough for it to grab, just close enough to see that there was, in fact, a throat.

"Now, stay." Vivian left Shane, her face flushed pink and her hands over her eyes, along with a perplexed Jonas standing there holding one of Shane's knees to keep her legs parted.

She went to the meat freezer again. This time she went for the sausages strung like garlands in the back. They weren't covered with plastic, so Vivian used a sheet of butcher paper to pull a full length of links from the hooks. There were twenty-five sausages to a string. Vivian wasn't worried she didn't have enough. There were four other strings in the freezer.

Jonas looked down at the bundle of links in her hands. Understanding dawned in his difficult face.

She passed the sausage to him. "Thaw…then feed."

"How many?"

"All of it."

"You've got to be kidding." Shane propped herself up on her elbows and stared at the pile of linked sausages.

"I said lie down." Vivian closed her hand over the shoulder without a mouth and shoved Shane back onto the butcher block again. Based on the sigh that escaped Shane's lips, Vivian didn't think she minded the rough treatment or the commands. This was what Vivian had wanted to avoid, but Jonas wasn't getting the hint that he needed to take charge. Not for the first time, she wanted to scream at him, 'What kind of a demon are you?'

"Are you crazy?" Shane asked. But she didn't push herself back up again.

"It's just an idea."

"It's a bit…literal."

"So is the mouth," Vivian replied.

Jonas tilted the sausages into a smaller bucket than the ones used to feed Shane that afternoon. As the sausages thawed, they slithered down and gathered in loose spirals. Then, instead of using chopsticks, he chose a pair of tongs to lift the end link up and bring it to the mouth between Shane's legs.

It was much bigger than what he usually fed to her, each fat sausage link almost two inches in diameter at the widest and about seven inches long.

It *was* awfully literal. But Vivian wouldn't put that kind of irony past Bell Madoc.

The tongue wrapped around the sausage, poking at the tongs as though to test whether they were edible as well. It jerked at the metal, but Jonas pulled the sausage back until the tongue decided it would rather have the meat in its mouth than the hand on the other end of the tongs.

As the sausage crossed the threshold past the teeth, the mouth closed hard over the first few inches of the link.

"That would hurt in the morning," Vivian muttered.

"This is what always happens," Shane said.

"Just give it a few minutes."

The teeth weren't made for chewing. They were made for ripping and pulling food deeper into the mouth with the help of the tongue. The mouth took the meat down its throat inch by inch until the entire first sausage link was gone.

Shane reached for Vivian's hand, but Vivian slipped out of her reach. Shane opened her eyes, her forehead furrowing in confusion and clearly a little hurt.

"I'm not good for you," Vivian said softly.

"I don't need you to be good for—"

"For Christ's sake, I'm trying to do the right thing here. You have no idea how hard that is for me. Maybe another time…when it doesn't matter as much. It matters to you right now." She tilted her head to Jonas. "*He's* the one feeding you."

Jonas pushed the second link toward the teeth. They snapped it up just as fast as the first, pulling it into the throat.

"Oh God." Shane shook her head, gripped the edges of the butcher block until her knuckles turned white. "That's..."

The mouth drooled onto the treated wood and down the side — or at least it looked like drool.

Jonas pushed the third one in, but after that he took a small step back, because the mouth had figured out that meat was there, meat was coming and meat would keep coming. The teeth chomped down with a violent sound every time, and Shane's breath hitched with every swallow.

Around the fifth link, Shane bit her lip against the moan that whined through her throat.

Vivian indicated to Jonas that he should step closer to Shane again. When he didn't, Vivian went to him again. "If I didn't know better, I'd think you wanted me here," she whispered.

"What do you want from me?"

"Look at *her*. She wants everything you give, and she won't make you feel like a monster when you do."

Shane released the butcher block to bring her hands over her thighs to the edges of the mouth, tracing the curved flesh that was almost lips. The mouth was on its seventh sausage link and still going strong, still filling her to the edge of the throat that constricted around the meat with every swallow.

"God, it's like sex. It feels so *weird*, but I need..." Shane arched up, urging the mouth to eat faster, and it did, swallowing down a link every few seconds.

"Touch her," Vivian whispered to Jonas.

"Her mouths are dangerous everywhere, even the one that's full."

Vivian hit him on the arm. "Are you telling me that after everything you've done for them, they won't purr if you tell them to? Are you a demon or aren't you?"

He turned his head just slightly, as though he was about to look at her but stopped himself. Then he stepped forward and slid his big hands over Shane's knees. He smoothed them up until one covered the large gash on one of her thighs. It tried to bite him, but he leaned in to whisper into Shane's skin near the edge of the gash. Shane shivered as the mouths over her body seemed to loosen, tongues emerging but with no urgency in the set of their teeth.

Fuck, they actually did purr.

As Jonas stroked over Shane's thighs, up her abdomen to her breasts, the mouths he passed on the way slithered their tongues out to greet him, not with a tug but a caress.

"Oh, *fuck*." Shane clutched at his arms, her fingers slipping on the fabric of his chef's coat. "What are you doing to them?"

"I've told them that if they're good, they shall be satisfied. All of you shall be satisfied." Jonas bent between her spread legs to lick a path to just beneath the mouth that was her navel, where he kissed her. "If it is your will to allow me."

"Are you kidding? Don't stop. Please, don't stop. It's been *months*, and I can't…" Shane grasped at the chef's coat as she lifted her hips from the butcher block. Her thighs flexed and the mouth worked over three sausage links in quick succession as Shane came.

Jonas remained inscrutable, but he petted her and her mouths through the pleasure as the mouth between her legs continued to take in the meat.

She'd gone through twenty links before the mouth started to slow down. The meat dangled over the bucket, jerking and swinging with each swallow.

Finally, with two sausages left to go, the mouth opened wide, letting the rest of the sausage fall to the bucket.

"Oh, *please*, don't stop," Shane begged, still lifting her hips.

Vivian brought her mouth back to Jonas' ear. "Now fuck her."

Jonas stilled. "I don't do that."

"You did it with me."

"I shouldn't have. I told you, Vivian, I foreswore such appetites."

"Screw that. You foreswore nothing. If I built walls, you dug graves, but it didn't stay dead, did it? Don't pretend you don't want this. You're hard again, and you can't will that away." Vivian brought her hand to the front of his trousers, stroking over the length of him and willing herself to stop salivating — with about as much success as Jonas willing away his desire.

He abruptly swung his head around, bringing his mouth to her ear instead. "It's your fault."

"Well, you don't want to take it out on me. She's willing. She wants you. She *needs* you. *She's* the one with the monstrous appetite. *She* was the one made for you that you've been ignoring. She's been unsatisfied all this time, and you can do for her what you do best." Vivian jerked open his trousers and took him out, but she didn't linger, didn't stroke him, didn't do anything but give his cock room to grow, room to stretch for what it desired more than the demon that owned it.

"You're the one meant to satisfy your Skeletons. Do your job." Vivian stepped back and crossed her arms.

Jonas slowly brought his cock to Shane's open mouth between her legs, but his black eyes were on Vivian with every inch that entered the monster's throat. As he reached the end, though, he turned back to Shane with a low, desperate groan, closing his eyes against the sensation. Vivian could only imagine what it was like to feel a strange creature's throat rather than a cunt.

It seemed to be just his taste.

Shane whimpered, lifted her legs to wrap around his waist and clutched at the front of his coat to pull him all the way in. "God, yes. Don't stop. It's ready. Fuck it hard. Fuck me, *please*."

"I'll fuck you hard, but I won't fuck you fast." Jonas stroked over Shane's head, as bald as his own, petting along the edges of the mouth that gashed through her scalp. He pulled himself even closer to her, covering her body as he kissed a gentle path up between her breasts. "When you come, it will be enough for every orgasm you haven't yet had."

Vivian didn't stay for the climax. Watching Jonas lose himself in the kiss, Shane's small body subsumed under his own without any teeth sinking into his flesh, was enough. Her work was done.

It wouldn't make up for the mushrooms, but hopefully it put a few points in her favor, setting Jonas up with the woman he should have been with the whole time, the woman who would make him feel more human, not conjure his demon. And they would satisfy each other, rather than each satisfaction triggering deeper despair in its wake.

* * * *

"What's gotten into you tonight?"

Vivian let out a long sigh, moving her hips over Dom's already softening cock. She didn't blame it for being unable to keep up. Dom had already come twice before and had had to ply her with toys until they could get hard again. She, on the other hand, couldn't seem to reach high enough. She'd never used to have this problem back when the kind of orgasm didn't matter.

She dismounted and flopped onto the bed in frustration. "I did the right thing."

"And that made you horny?" Delilah opened a Dr Pepper. "Does it inspire you to more altruistic acts?"

Del didn't make a point to watch—unless Vivian invited him to—but this was his trailer, too, and his presence wasn't distracting. He could sometimes sit in the living room, reading a book—or pretending to read a book—while Vivian and Dom were fucking right next to him, and he didn't touch himself once, which meant he either had ironclad self-control or his tuck job was the best in the world. Vivian didn't doubt, however, that he jerked off later. She'd hear him sometimes afterward—although Vivian had heard masturbation didn't scratch the itch. Dom probably helped scratch it when Vivian wasn't around.

The Quandary certainly had their needs met these days.

"It didn't make her horny. This isn't horniness." Dom sat up and propped themselves against the window. "What the hell is it?"

They still kept the windows uncovered, no curtains or blinds, so God knew who saw what was going on when the lights were on in the trailer. Vivian couldn't bring herself to care, especially since she'd seen everyone else having sex back when she'd made that her game.

"If I knew, do you think I'd keep riding you?" Vivian said.

"So this 'right thing' you speak of... Care to share?" Dom asked.

"I taught the odd chef how to feed and fuck Shane."

Dom raised their eyebrows. "Why would you do that?"

"Because she needed it. And I can't give her what she needs."

"A dick?"

"A beating, bleeding heart," Vivian said. "And meat. Lots and lots of meat...in the literal sense. Only Jonas can give that to her. All I did today was figure out that's what she needed and tell him to give it to her. He can figure out the rest on his own. And now that Shane's figured out how she can have sex, she certainly doesn't need her little crush on me anymore."

Dom bit their lip, but they couldn't hold back a smile. "You think that's why she crushes on you?"

"Don't tell me it's my voice again."

"Oh, I'm sure that's part of it. But you don't think she digs the hot, bad-girl vibe?" Dom asked. "Girls go for bad girls, too, you know."

"Not everyone has your masochistic streak, Dom." Vivian sighed again then sat up.

"No, but a surprising number do," Del said. "People like the idea of being with someone who doesn't give a fuck. Short-term, at least. It's what makes one-night stands and impulse control issues exciting. Bad is intriguing to people who have always been good. She's a nice, shy drummer, if that tells you anything. Don't think that just because you gave a reformed demon and a hungry little girl the happily ever after you think they need, it's going to be over. Dr Pepper?"

"Now." Vivian accepted a can and drank deeply for three large swallows before the carbonation set her teeth on edge. Unlike food, she could accept drinks from her roommates. It wasn't like she drank them for the nutritional value. "Why?"

"Because people don't always want what they need or need what they want," Del replied. "And sometimes you can want one thing and need another. Just because you gave Jonas and Shane a meet-cute doesn't take you out of their equations."

"I'm not allowed near Shane. It's not like she's so pure I'd taint her or anything, but I know better. And Jonas doesn't want me anywhere near him. The only reason he let me back into his kitchen was because we were there for Shane, not me."

"I can't speak for the odd chef, because he's...well, odd. And I'm the one saying it, so it must be true," Dom said. "But you, my little torte parfait, are frustrated as hell because you handed someone you want to someone you need, and where does that leave you? With a pair of crazy queers, that's where."

Vivian would punch Dom, but she had a drink, so she kicked them instead.

"We can talk about this until we're blue in the face, but I'm walking the high wire in Arcanium. I can't afford to have an affair with Shane the way I would outside of Arcanium. And Jonas will barely look at me."

"Do you want him to look at you?" Delilah asked. Dom always sounded like they didn't take anything seriously, as though just under their voice was an ironic twist, but Del made everything sound meaningful and solemn. He possessed natural gravitas, which was the only reason Vivian thought he pulled off his entire look, even out of costume. And he sang a mean baritone Christine to her Phantom.

"No... Maybe... No."

"You're allowed to have complicated feelings about him," Del said. "I have complicated feelings about you." His ambivalence was no secret, but to his credit, he didn't force Dom to make a decision one way or another. He tolerated her in the trailer as a lover, enjoyed her body from a distance and loved her as a singer. For someone who had changed himself so dramatically, he was brutally honest in all other things. And for someone who lied like breathing, Vivian liked it more than one might have thought.

"It doesn't make a difference," she said. "Not after what I've done."

Dom pushed themselves down the bed to tangle their legs with hers and bring their hand to Vivian's cunt. They slid their fingers inside—between arousal and cum, Dom didn't need any help and didn't need to wait—to stroke her inner walls until Vivian couldn't help but groan. This would be orgasm number seven. Her record was still with Jonas, damn him.

"Screw what you've done." Dom used their lower register in the purr they knew she responded to. "What's done is done, and that's for Bell to judge. What matters is what you do. So why don't you take that altruistic streak you've developed and put it to some good use?"

"What did you have in mind?" Vivian set her drink on a shelf and crawled over Dom's thighs so that she could raise herself up and down over their fingers while they fucked her again.

"Far be it from me to tell you how to seduce a man — or a woman. You seem to have it mostly figured out. But you might try doing something that, I don't know, *he* really likes. Taking care of one of his Skellies scratched the surface. Introducing her to him dug a little deeper. When he's seen you, back when he was still looking, what did he want most from you in this world?"

"To satisfy. Then rip away that satisfaction to make me desire more in a vicious, never-ending cycle."

Dom stopped fucking her for a moment, but Vivian grabbed their wrist until Dom kept going. "I thought he didn't do that sort of thing. I heard he was a weird, awkward sweetheart."

"Yeah, well, he's supposed to be celibate, too. I guess I bring out the worst in people."

"Not the worst." Dom brought her down for a rough kiss. "You're sandpaper, darling. You abrade them long enough that it shows what people try to hide, and most of what they hide is something they're ashamed of. But don't think you're creating anything that isn't already there. Besides, you'd tempt a saint to fall."

"I still don't get that." Vivian slowed her efforts over Dom's fingers. "My voice only accounts for so much. My speaking voice is hardly pretty. I got men into bed before just by offering them sex and being attractive. But ever since I got here, what gives? I'm hardly the baddest person in the circus, and I'm hardly the sexiest. I know what I look like. Bell used my first wish to make sure I knew good and well what I looked like as objectively as possible. So why do you fucking look at me like that, both of you?" Vivian pushed at Dom's shoulder when they and Del laughed. "What?"

"You may be objective, but the way other people see you is still colored by their feelings. We're *not* objective, far from it," Dom replied. "And Jonas is a demon, so who knows what gets his motor running? Except we all know it's you. So put aside the whole hell-on-earth scenario, honey. What does he love most in this world and what about *you* made him first want to love you? Then you give it to him. Simple as that." Dom ground their fingers into her cunt to the rhythm of their speech until Vivian dug her fingernails into their back. "Who knows? Maybe demons gone good like the bad girls, too. Are you a bad girl, Vivian?"

"Show me," she whispered, shuddering toward her climax.

Chapter Fourteen

'*Simple as that.*' But it wasn't simple at all.

Vivian lifted the flap to the fortune teller tent and found Bell, even though the circus wasn't open. Her stomach sank even lower. She'd hoped he wouldn't be there so she'd have longer to talk herself out of what she considered doing. Vivian couldn't tell whether Bell waiting for her was a good or bad sign.

"Hello, killer." Bell leaned back in his chair, his boots propped up on the parlor table in front of him.

"I haven't killed anyone."

"Not for lack of trying, which is why you're here."

"Why are you? The circus isn't open."

"If the circus isn't open, why search for me here?" Bell asked.

"Where else would I look?"

Bell conceded with a slight nod and kicked his feet off the table, the chair rocking him forward into a more formal posture. "I knew you'd look for me here, so I made sure I wouldn't disappoint you." The smile in the corner of his eyes suggested he knew perfectly well she would have preferred not finding him. "What can I do for you this afternoon?"

"I want to make a wish."

Bell gestured to the chair on the other side of the table. "Please, sit."

Vivian sat. "But before I make it, I want to be sure that you won't use it against me, pork barrel in something that has nothing to do with the wish."

"You just don't want to feel what I made you feel," Bell said. "I'm afraid I can't promise anything. I've made exceptions, but I'm hardly going to make one for you. You know that." His reply wasn't unkind, just matter-of-fact. "I think you'd benefit from a little empathy, but you've had more than your usual share since that day, haven't you, my dear?"

Vivian clenched her teeth.

"The longer you sit with your emotions and recognize them in others, the more you'll get used to them. You got used to living without them. You'll get used to living with them again."

"Fuck my feelings. I'm not here about that."

"But you are. If you're looking to atone, it's all about your feelings. You're just not used to guilt."

"Is that what this is?"

"Not quite. But it's as close as you're presently capable of. You see the benefit of atonement because you're not happy being the villain to the few cast members here that you've come to value. You see all these connections you've made as weaknesses, but if you're seeking their better impressions, perhaps you're beginning to understand that such connections are not always weakness."

"How sweet. About that wish…"

Bell smiled. "You have no idea what that word does for me."

"I don't want to give you the satisfaction if it's just going to bite me in the ass. You know what I want to wish for, so why don't you just tell me whether you're going to use it to hurt me like the last one or not?"

"Because you don't deserve to know." Bell intertwined his fingers and rested his hands on the velvet tablecloth. "Once you've made your wish, it's in my hands. That's the risk you take."

"Fuck." Vivian leaned against the table, pressing her knuckles against her forehead. She had two wishes left, and one was probably going to have to get her out of Arcanium before Bell wanted her out. She essentially had one wish left to work with. And this was what she was going to do with it?

Vivian couldn't help but think that this might be the *only* thing he would let her use it on, other than agreeing to feel what he'd made her feel that night. And she'd never choose that on her own.

"It's not going to get any easier to put your life in my hands. Vulnerability doesn't come naturally to you." Bell reached across the table and stroked her hair before taking one of her hands in his. "But you are always vulnerable to me. Not wishing doesn't change that."

Vivian slipped her hand away and sat back. She made fists but kept them in her lap.

"I wish I knew how to cook as well as the odd chef."

Bell closed his eyes and smiled through a soft laugh. "What a relief that you chose the least difficult path for the first time since you arrived."

"I want to throw a dinner party."

* * * *

404

"You're not welcome here. I thought we made that clear."

Vivian sat on the low dining table in the middle of the harem tent. Dom had taken a seat on Lily's cot. Moral support, Dom had called it. Really, Vivian just wanted a witness. She knew better than to underestimate a tent full of women, even if they weren't as hungry anymore.

Alicia looked down at her with hands on her hips. Shane stood behind Alicia at the entrance. She'd agreed to bring Alicia in first before any of the other Skellies arrived back at the tent, because Alicia would be hardest to convince.

"I'm not staying," Vivian said. "I'm trying to make amends. Kind of my own twelve-step program."

"You're not forgiven."

"I'm not asking for your forgiveness. I'm asking for your help."

"No."

"You didn't even hear what it is yet," Shane said.

"You're not the most objective person when it comes to Vivian, Shane," Alicia said.

"Neither are you," Shane retorted.

Dom looked down as they crossed their long legs in front of them and grinned.

"Look... I made a wish, and as a result, Bell told me I now have the ability to cook for the Skeletons in a way that satisfies. You'll barely have to grovel," Vivian said.

"Oh, wonderful. Bell gives you yet another thing to lord over the rest of us." Alicia crossed her arms, appearing even less impressed. But Vivian recognized the subtle frown. Even subtle expressions were clearer on skeletal faces, and Vivian had been party to this particular emotion during her tour of Alicia's head. All

Alicia needed was a pair of green contacts and she'd be the very picture of envy.

"I'm not going to lord it over anyone. Hell, I'm the reason you're not starving all the time now, because I apparently broke the dramatic irony machine around here."

"You break everything," Alicia said.

"I nearly poisoned everyone in Arcanium, but Bell still gave me a kitchen to throw a dinner party. I want the Skeletons to help me."

Alicia's arms loosened, sliding down her abdomen, and Shane let the tent flap fall.

"That's why the Ringmaster whipped you. That's why it was so many times." Alicia slowly approached the dining table. "I knew there was something off about you. God, you're a fucking serial killer."

"First of all, I'm not a serial killer. I would have been a mass murderer. Completely different." Vivian uncrossed her legs and stood up on the dining table.

"Are you crazy?" Alicia climbed up onto the table, taking Vivian's extra height from her.

"I'm a psycho bitch. We've all established that." Vivian stepped forward to meet her, less than a hand's breadth from her face.

"If you think I'm going to help you —"

"Bell made me drink the poison I tried to give everyone else. He made me drink it all before the Ringmaster whipped me."

Alicia scoffed, but her eyebrows twitched inward. "Am I supposed to feel sorry for you?"

"That's not what's important," Vivian said. "I want to make amends to the circus for what I tried to do. Hence, dinner party. No poison involved. Well, maybe a little, but just the usual kind."

"The usual kind?"

"Alcohol, naturally. And if I can swing it, fugu."

"Why should I trust you? Why should I do any of this for you?"

"You won't be doing it for me. It's just part of my plan. You might even enjoy yourself, not least because you'll be able to eat everything I serve."

"I wouldn't eat your food if it would save your life."

Vivian shrugged. "That's your choice."

"She's not going to do anything with Bell keeping his eye even closer on her," Shane said from the door, although she seemed more subdued than she'd come in. "And if she's such a psycho bitch, why did she save me?"

"You weren't in danger," Alicia snapped. "You'd been holding back on feeding your other mouths. That's on you."

"And she figured out how I can have sex."

That got Alicia's attention. Salacious details were good for that.

"How?" Alicia asked.

Shane shifted uncomfortably, cheeks flushing. "Doesn't matter. The point is that as long as Bell's watching, there's no reason not to trust her. At least hear what she has in mind. It actually sounds...fun."

Alicia turned back to Vivian, looking her up and down. "You fuck her into agreeing with this the way you fucked Dom to protect you?"

"Hey! Screw you, too, sister," Dom said, standing. "We didn't start until after that, thank you."

"I'd think you'd be more worried about protecting Dom from me." Vivian stepped still closer, almost close enough to kiss. Alicia had to step back. "Besides, I barely touched Shane. I just introduced her to someone who could. I'm trying."

"Here's the thing about amends, psycho bitch. Sometimes they still don't get you what you want." Alicia stepped down from the table. "I appreciate what you did to help Shane, and I appreciate she won't be moaning in her sleep anymore, but you're still not welcome."

"You ever heard of *nyotaimori*?" Vivian said.

* * * *

"I can't believe I agreed to do this," Alicia muttered. But she laid down on the dining table in the harem tent.

Two more tables had been provided for Lily and Nasreen to take their places on either side of their main dining table. The golems had also brought Shane's box into the tent and set it up on the higher table at the far end of the configuration. Half of it had been filled with semi-frozen ground meat, with more kept in the ice box they'd put in the bathroom. An iced container of sausages had been set up next to it.

Shane sat naked on the wax paper that presently covered the raw meat to keep her from eating too early. She'd wrapped her arms around her knees, shoulders tense and back a beautiful curve. The proximity of meat had made her mouths antsy. But she'd agreed to do it, and do it without her bandage dress — only because the other girls were naked as well.

"Why naked?" Nasreen had asked.

"Because we don't have to worry about health violations," Vivian had replied. "Come on. You all get naked in front of each other for Lennon. What's the big deal?"

"Psycho bitch," Alicia had muttered.

Vivian beckoned the golems to bring their chilled delicacies to each of the women. Vivian had a short amount of time to put everything out and keep it cold enough before body temperature changed everything. A cooler temperature in the harem tent helped, but the girls' stress would counteract some of that.

The golems understood most of her directives and their intentions, but they lacked their own sense of aesthetic. She could show them how to make a rose out of icing or modeling chocolate and they'd copy her, but they couldn't make their own variants. So she couldn't trust them to put out the food with anything approaching artistry.

Just a few days ago, Vivian would have drunk orange juice out of a carton to avoid putting it in a cup. Now she was decorating naked women with food, and it looked really good. And even though she'd done nothing to earn the knowledge she used to do it—nothing but risk her neck making a wish to a jinni—Vivian was ridiculously proud of what it looked like when she was done.

Life was weird sometimes.

"All right. Whatever you do, don't move," Vivian said as she put the floral finishing touches on the women.

"Really? So I can't do this?" Alicia tucked in all her fingers but the middle ones on both hands.

"Do you fuck yourself with those fingers? You look amazing." It wasn't a compliment. Vivian didn't do compliments. It was just true. It turned out that skeletal bodies were really good canvases to work with—all those raised edges acted like natural plates and bowls. "Shane, are you ready?"

Shane lay back on the wax paper and slowly spread her legs to drape over the sides of the box. A golem stood nearby, ready to pull the wax paper out from under her. She nodded. Her nipples were hard and flushed again, and she bit her lip as she shifted over the paper, her cunt mouth visible for everyone to see.

"This is really strange, Vivian."

Vivian rounded the room to stand next to the box, which, in addition to the bucket of raw sausages, had been surrounded by metal trays over ice that displayed crudos and tartare for the demons with a taste for flesh and humans craving clean, raw and savory. They could also feed them to Shane if they wanted. Her monster mouths weren't picky, but her human mouth might enjoy them, too. Chopsticks had been provided at all tables.

"It's harmless," Vivian said. She even heard the gentleness in her own voice and was almost unsure she was the one speaking. "Just have a good time. There's only more if you want more."

"Arcanium used to do things like this," Alicia said.

"Eating food off people?" Shane asked as she settled into the cushion of meat.

"No. Sex parties."

"This isn't a sex party," Vivian said. "It's a dinner party. You're mostly here as something pleasing to serve the food. It's up to you whether you want to be eaten."

Nasreen giggled.

"As long as you don't move," Vivian added.

"I notice you're not naked and covered in food," Alicia said.

Vivian knocked on the table as she passed it. "I've already done that. Now hush. Plates don't speak unless giving permission."

"You're going to sing, aren't you?" Alicia said.

Vivian stopped at the door. "Just to put people in a better mood to eat something I've prepared—if they've come at all. I assume word of what I did got around?"

Alicia didn't say anything, which meant yes. Vivian had assumed Alicia wouldn't be able to keep it to herself.

"You can sing Pink's *Sober* the next time we play," Vivian said. "Delilah and Dom sing all the time, and not because I live with them. It's because they asked. You ever thought about asking, Alicia?"

"I thought you said minimal groveling." The words sounded thick, as though pushed through an obstruction.

"Tears salt the food, but they'll smear your mascara. Asking isn't groveling. There was a whole stretch where I wasn't singing, and did you step forward once? Now, this is just a dinner party to reassure people I'm not going to try to poison them again. I'm singing to remind them why they still want me around. If they want to drink tequila out of my navel, I probably won't say no."

Lily snorted.

Vivian pulled up the tent flap and tied it off.

Bell was first in line with Dom and Delilah, who had to duck to enter the tent. A vote of confidence, Vivian guessed, because once Bell entered, the other members of the cast outside the tent gradually made their way in.

It wasn't the whole population of Arcanium, but it was enough for a party, and it filled the tent, with her guests in a double circle around the tables.

Vivian couldn't see the odd chef. *Fuck*. If he didn't come, this whole dinner was ruined. It wasn't for the rest of Arcanium, not really. It was an apology, but the apology was intended as the icing on the cake she'd intended to serve him.

She fought not to tell everyone in the tent to just leave. Looking at the Skeletons convinced her to hold her tongue. She'd worked so hard on arranging each of them, it would be a shame to waste the effort.

Vivian climbed onto the platform she'd had the golems set up for her. There were recordings on an mp3 player, speakers and a microphone — bare bones, like a cheap dive performance, but it was an intimate venue, and she wouldn't be screaming tonight. She arranged herself on the edge of the platform, her legs dangling over the side. She certainly wasn't going to stand in those killer heels the whole time.

"Good evening, everyone. I'm better at singing than at speaking, but I wanted to welcome you to my little dinner party. I…"

Vivian lowered the microphone to her lap and swallowed.

Every last particle of her body screamed that she didn't have to admit to anything, that she hadn't actually done anything, and even if she had, she'd paid for her supposed crimes and then some. They whined that she was wired differently and fuck anyone who didn't understand that, that they were lucky to have her voice and she didn't have to apologize to anyone.

Those thoughts were the thoughts of someone afraid. She was so scared that her hands were shaking.

But she brought the microphone to her mouth again. "I did something bad. Most of you know that by now."

The odd chef ducked into the tent. He wasn't wearing his chef's coat, which was strange in and of itself, since he always seemed to wear it, even when the circus wasn't open. He'd chosen a black sweater instead. She'd seen his closet. He hadn't owned a black sweater.

She'd wanted him there, but it made things harder. She swallowed again then forced herself not to look at him as she continued. "I'm not a good person. I don't think that can change. But I wanted to offer this experience to you as a way to show that I'm not dangerous — and that I'm trying, for my own sake and for yours."

No one said anything. It wasn't as though she'd expected applause, so she soldiered on. "What we have here are four tables to enjoy at your leisure. On the main table, we have sushi, sashimi and nigiri on Alicia, with soy sauce, creamy sriracha and ginger available on the side. Next to her, we have the fruit and dessert trays on Nasreen and Lily, with melted dark, white and espresso chocolate for dipping or drizzling. And up here on the meat tray, we have Shane, who is open to being fed as offered, or you may enjoy your own array of raw meats and charcuterie. The staff have wine and spirits to your taste, and I will provide light entertainment — or as light as I can provide. Now, a few ground rules…"

Vivian pushed herself off the platform so that she could stand and pace a bit while she spoke. "The food is presented and sometimes prepared on women with whom you are accustomed to working. They agreed to the arrangement of their own free will. But food is to be eaten or served using the chopsticks on hand, especially with Shane, whose mouths might be initially overeager. Given that Lady Sasha and Lord Mikhail are here tonight" — Vivian nodded to them, though their expressions remained neutral. Most of the cast, except the Patchwork Pirate, gave them a wide berth, even in the tight space — "the impulse to do more may strike you. You are allowed to ask. I must insist that, until their bodies are completely uncovered, they stay still. Keep that in mind before you ask. Remember, though, that this is a dinner party. You're here to eat, and we're here to serve."

"You tried to kill us," May said, the hair usually covering her face tied back to reveal her demonic face.

Vivian tightened her grip on the microphone. "Yes."

Those murmurs brought her right back to the big top ring, and her hands trembled even more.

"No one is forced to be here, and you're free to leave at any time. Anyone is free to leave. But I hope you won't. Because the food is good, the presentation is better and I think you'll have a good time. Tip your plates, please. *Salud.*"

She climbed back up onto the platform and stared down at the people in the tent, who still hadn't moved.

Her gaze inevitably rested upon Jonas, his expression as blank as ever. He still wasn't looking at her. Instead, he looked over the tables, the only movement in the room as he stepped between and around the other cast members to take in the sight of Lily, Alicia and Nasreen artfully covered by slices of sushi rolls, nigiri and fresh patterns of sashimi framed with seaweed salad and crab meat, slices of banana, mango and strawberry interspersed with sliced pistachio and almond, circles of rum-soaked vanilla sponge, dollops of whipped cream and chocolate accents that would stay soft with the Skeletons' body heat.

There were small glass bowls of honey next to the warming fondue pots of chocolate.

As he rounded Shane in her glass box, she licked her lips and lifted herself up by her legs over the edge and her grip on the glass. The golem next to her pulled the wax paper out with a deafening rustle in the otherwise silent tent. But when Shane sank back over the meat and her mouths began to consume, she whimpered, and that sound, too, filled the large room.

"You agreed to this?" the odd chef said quietly, but with everyone else not saying a word, they could all hear. "She asked you to do this, and you agreed?"

"Yes," Shane whispered. "We all did."

Jonas considered Shane for a few moments. Then he picked up a pair of chopsticks, lifted a thin slice of raw beef, laid it lightly in peppered olive oil then brought it not to the gashes on Shane's body but to her own human mouth.

"Really, Jonas?" Vivian said into her microphone. "You're making Shane your food tester?"

"There's no poison here" the odd chef said. "There's a light bit of tetrodotoxin in the fugu on Alicia's body, but it is expertly prepared, and it should cause only a light tingling on the lips and tongue. There is nothing to fear here, and I shall taste everything in due course. Shane, on the other hand, like the rest of the Skeletons, is hungry."

He lowered the meat into Shane's mouth. Shane caught it with her tongue first then groaned through the first bite. The meat would be tender, with the acidity of the olive oil, the spicy pepper and smooth beef fat to enhance the flavor. As Shane swallowed, the level of the meat in the box started to lower. Vivian didn't think she'd eat it all this time — or at least not as quickly. The mouths had been well fed during the last couple of days.

With Shane not dropping dead of cyanide poisoning, everyone else started to mill in toward the tables, kneeling on the extra cushions that the golems had provided.

Bell was the next to take a pair of chopsticks. He selected salmon nigiri, dipped it in the soy sauce and placed it in his mouth. Like Shane, he closed his eyes and groaned a little. He'd been responsible for procuring quality ingredients for her, but cut, proportion and preparation mattered, too. Everything from wasabi to the garnish to the temperature of the vinegar rice, fish and the Skeletons' skin affected the flavor.

The odd chef didn't sit with the rest. He stepped back to the walls of the harem tent to watch the rest of the cast eat with avidity he normally reserved for watching the Skeletons consume his feasts.

Ciarán didn't immediately partake—given his size, Vivian guessed he wanted to give other people a chance to eat before indulging in his own appetite—but Moss tortured Lily mercilessly as he slid mango and strawberries across her ribs. Apparently, Lily was ticklish.

Jonas put a hand on Moss' shoulder. Moss immediately stopped, grinning with teeth that didn't look meant for fruit as Lily struggled to control herself again, and the odd chef returned to the edges. It occurred to Vivian that he'd stepped in for her, to keep the experience the one that Vivian had intended.

Vivian turned on the music to avoid thinking about the tightness in her chest.

There was the odd tease after that, but otherwise, the cast settled into enjoying the meal, making the kinds of sounds that were difficult to distinguish between sexual or gastronomical satisfaction. The sex demons probably muddied the issue, especially for Shane, who'd collected piles of sexual dissatisfaction since arriving in Arcanium.

Despite the young woman's shyness, she seemed unable to keep herself from wordlessly pleading for whatever the cast around her gave, both to her own mouth and the mouths on her body. None of them had yet discovered what the sausages were for, though, and the odd chef hadn't decided to show them.

The music was synth only. Nasreen had recorded it for her that morning before Vivian had gone back to her new kitchen to continue preparations. Vivian wasn't going to do much in the way of screaming in a small tent, so she kept most of the edge out of her voice, using the clearer side on softer songs. They weren't exactly uplifting or even appetizing, but Vivian had chosen pieces that everyone loved to hear from her, like *House of the Rising Sun*, *My Immortal* — seriously, she couldn't seem to escape that song — and *People are Strange*. But she also pulled out *Familiar Taste of Poison*, despite the twist it brought to her stomach when the music started.

Most of the cast stopped eating while she sang it, watching her with solemn expressions that she feared masked animosity or accusation, but after she finished, they just continued eating — more subdued at first, but with greater gusto through the next songs, Muse's *Endlessly* and Marilyn Manson's *Tourniquet*.

Many of them got up to move to another part of the tables at various points, exclaiming to the people next to them at a particularly good bite or combination of flavors.

Things started shifting around the time the sex demons ended up around Nasreen and started feeding the Patchwork Pirate, which was also when Vivian started her own version of *Sally's Song*. Nasreen felt the effects of the sex demons' proximity as well as their rising interest that seemed to fill the cold tent with slowly increasing heat. Vivian worried for her ice, but it didn't seem to be melting any faster. The chocolate, however, was struggling.

Lady Sasha slid fruit through the chocolate on Nasreen's skin that marked her like henna and served it to Neve. The succubus didn't have to touch Nasreen directly for chocolate to start dripping down her sides.

With the incubus' hand tangled through her asymmetrical hair, Neve leaned over Nasreen and whispered something in her ear. Nasreen nodded, her upturned hands tightening into loose fists as Neve lowered her mouth over Nasreen's chocolate-enhanced breast. Vivian raised her eyebrows. She hadn't gotten any of that sort of vibe from Nasreen the way she had from Shane.

But it seemed like a good time to transition to the other side of her set. She'd had Nasreen do a stripped-down version of Halestorm's *Dirty Work*, Kamelot's *Static* and Puscifer's *Rev 22:20*.

"Don't forget to feed your plates," Vivian said before the synth shifted into the first sensuous introduction — just as Neve brought a chocolate-dipped mango to where Nasreen's thighs were pressed together, startling a cry from her.

Lennon was the first to figure out what the sausages were for and the first after Jonas to know what the monster mouth between her legs felt like, which meant he'd now tasted every Skeleton except Vivian. When he made Shane come — to the great pleasure of Ciarán and Moss as they fed themselves from the meat offerings — he glanced over at Vivian as she sang through a darker version of *Music of the Night*. She grimaced at him, which just made him laugh. She'd duet with him if he wanted, but she'd fuck Ciarán's massive cock before she joined Lennon's harem.

Only two abstained from the more sexual sensuality the feast provided. The odd chef remained an observer, although he had stepped forward a few times to try the things she'd made — the fugu, vanilla sponge paired with the pistachios and a slice of chocolate-covered strawberry, the oro, unagi and salmon nigiri and steak tartare. He sampled rather than settled down, moved from one end of the tent to the other almost without her noticing, using her blind spots to shift from view.

And Bell sat back on his heels to observe from the middle of the action, his loose linen trousers hiding nothing of his arousal. Yet he also did nothing to the woman in front of him, nor did he ply anyone else around him, though he seemed to focus on Neve more than anyone else.

Vivian closed out her set with a soft cover of Delain's *I Want You*. That song drew Bell's attention from the cast around him back to her, but it turned the odd chef away. He was the first to leave, like a food critic who had been less impressed than the restaurant's patrons. Vivian couldn't help but feel dismissed.

"Thank you, everyone, and good night," she murmured into the microphone before setting it down and stepping around the slowly developing sensual feast, all of her food presentation in disarray and her platters engaged in their own evening meals — of both sorts.

Vivian pushed out of the harem tent and closed her eyes to breathe the fresh air. It was warmer outside than in the chilled tent, spring well underway.

"You served everyone else, and the other Skeletons are being fed. But you haven't eaten."

Vivian spun around. The odd chef stood off to the side of the harem tent.

"I tried everything I made," Vivian said. "I can do that now."

"You're still hungry, and you have the stamina of a human in the kitchen. I'm sure you're tired."

He didn't insist, didn't come any closer, just waited.

"I thought you'd do more for Shane tonight," Vivian said.

"Did you think that because she needs to be fed and I can feed her that you'd created a love match?"

"That was the point, yes."

"Then you missed the point, Vivian."

"And what's the point?" she asked.

"I want to satisfy, and she wants me to satisfy her, but that is far from the need she will eventually have to satisfy — that, I'm afraid I cannot offer her. But you are in need right now, and I can give you what you need. Please, after what you did tonight, allow me to feed you."

She'd been taste-testing all day but always little bites, and she hadn't had her evening meal. Her stomach finally let her know how hungry she was, especially after being surrounded by the scents of her feast all evening while she hadn't had so much as a drop of wine.

She started toward the food court. The odd chef joined her, albeit from enough of a distance that they might not have been walking together at all.

Chapter Fifteen

He made her a simple Mediterranean plate, with halved olives, feta, pita and hummus. The pita was premade and warmed up with olive oil in a cast-iron pan, but he made the hummus fresh in front of her while she accepted a glass of pinot grigio.

She noticed different things about food that she'd never noticed before, her expanded palate and knowledge catching how everything was supposed to pair and recognizing the deceptive simplicity of his choices and skill. It was odd for her to consider anything other than calorie count or how she would have to pay her body back for consuming it. She noticed the care he put into both preparation and presentation, even for a light appetizer-like meal like this, and how that care was a sort of consideration—the culinary version of foreplay, even if he had no intention of engaging in the same literal foreplay as the rest of the cast.

Only in the silence of the kitchen, as she satisfied her more basic hunger, did she realize she *was* tired, that all the thought she'd put into the menu and prep had used a lot more creative energy than she was used to expending.

"Thank you," she said when she'd finished. For the taste alone, she meant it. She was too tired for it to mean something else.

"You're welcome." He rinsed each of the plates with his usual fastidiousness and put them in one of the dishwashers.

"You didn't have to invite me back."

Jonas closed the dishwasher and straightened, but he didn't turn around. "I didn't want to leave you hungry."

"I can feed myself now. And I don't burn water anymore."

"As fulfilling as it is to serve, it can be more satisfying to be served. You provided my meal tonight. I provided yours. It was an even exchange."

"I'll go, then."

"Vivian." Jonas washed his hands then dried them off on a clean dishtowel. He turned around and met her eyes as he removed his thick glasses, baring the one part of him that was irrepressibly demonic. "I know what he did to you."

Vivian stood, wary. "You're going to have to be more specific."

"I know what Bell did to you, before the Ringmaster. He told me you drank of the poison you'd intended for everyone else. So you know the taste of it now."

"Death's a little dry."

"Vivian…"

"I'm allowed to be flippant. If Bell hadn't killed me, the Ringmaster would have, and if they hadn't, you would have — if this wasn't Arcanium and Bell wasn't magic. You wanted to kill me, but that wasn't all you wanted, was it? More than wanting me dead, you wanted me alive to wish I were dead."

"You've wished yourself dead before. Do you remember or is the memory too distant? It still flavors your honey, child. It is one of the many reasons I crave it." He rested the dishcloth next to his glasses. "I want to show you something."

He cupped his hand over her elbow, and while her first reaction was repulsion, she allowed herself to be propelled past the blowfish aquarium to the mushroom garden.

"I'm not eating those again. I'm not even touching them," Vivian said.

"We're not here for the mushrooms."

The odd chef reached to the side of one of the shelves and pushed a hidden button that made the mushroom garden swing back into a dark room on the other side. Jonas led her inside then shut the mushroom garden door behind him. She could still see through the back wall of the garden to the kitchen, though she hadn't been able to see anything from the kitchen.

The room was unlike anything she'd seen in Arcanium. There had been industrial structures from wherever Bell had brought in the kitchens and the harem tent bathroom, but this wasn't industrial. This room was clearly part of a house. In the center of it was a monstrous grotesquerie of a dining room table, elaborately carved in a warm, dark wood that nonetheless looked cold, like a demon's altar. Surrounded by equally giant, Gothic chairs, it stretched the entire length of the room. The walls broke the illusion of age with built-in shelves backlit with almost psychedelic colors so that everything could be seen and inventoried, even in the dark.

"This is my home. All the doors are locked, and I'm the only one with the key, but I wanted my dining room always accessible. There's been no need for it in centuries, other than storage. I keep it for nostalgia, I suppose, even if I foreswore everything it meant. It's my room of poisons."

"And you're showing this to me because...?" She whirled on him, suspicious and angry because of it. "Seriously, you were so pissed at me for trying to poison everyone with the mushrooms you had on hand, and now you've shown me how to get into a room filled with more? What the hell are you playing at?"

"Have a look around, Vivian."

She narrowed her eyes, but when he didn't give her anything, not another word or hint of an expression, Vivian looked to the shelves. Some of them were too high for her to read the labels on the bottles, jars and boxes, but she got the gist. He had a whole collection of pre-twentieth jars of laudanum, medicinal bottles of arsenic, tins of mercury, old cocaine. He maintained other small gardens with UV lights – poppies, aconite, lily of the valley, rhododendron, foxglove, hemlock, nightshade. He kept extracts of cyanide, ricin and yew berries, among others. On one set of shelves, he stored nothing but modern drug paraphernalia and everything from medical-grade and black tar heroin to meth. One shelf was devoted to high-alcohol-content spirits, including a collection of absinthe bottles that would give the entire cast of Arcanium alcohol poisoning.

Then there was a set of shelves holding what looked like essential oil bottles with old-fashioned glass dropper lids. The ones at eye-level read with labels like *Jealousy, Lust, Melancholia, Paranoia, Perversion…*

"You keep trying to bring out the demon," Jonas said. "This home was made for one."

"And despite foreswearing your demon side, you didn't let this go." Vivian didn't move from the essence shelves, as though the red light behind them called to her. She wasn't hungry anymore, and the bottles were sealed tightly, so they didn't release any discernable scent, but her mouth watered at the sight of each handwritten label.

"Do you know what I was, this demon you reawaken?"

Vivian jumped when he slid his hands over her shoulders with far more familiarity than she expected from him talking about his demonic side, and with far more heat in his palms than she was used to, even through her jacket.

"When I left this behind, I chose a more Dionysian path, one of indulgence, decadence and experience — things that leave one full, comfortable and satiated in their wake, things that lead to deep sleep and hazy meditation. Those were things I was capable of before, but the demon, by his nature, twists these pleasures until they cannot satisfy. Gluttony encourages indulgence beyond satisfaction, decadence and experience that lead to cravings, sickness, addiction, each hollower than the last. Until I was assigned to the Skeletons, I did not interact with the human cast of Arcanium at all, preferring to satisfy them from afar without temptation. But the Skeletons taught me the satisfaction of the personal touch, each meal a gift that I package and present to them. You, however, are the reason I might have wished that Bell had let me keep my distance."

At the first beads of sweat on her neck, Jonas breathed her in through her hair and pulled her jacket down her arms. She didn't resist, but in addition to the scent of her heat, he had to also be aware of how tense she had become, with his large hands back on his shoulders, this time nearly bare, with nothing but the straps of a loose tank top to cover them.

"You tempt the demon with every emptiness inside you, every sickness, every addiction. I tried so to satisfy you, Vivian, but you are insatiable. And this kind of emptiness comes from years of someone else carving his way inside you to make himself a home. I may not know the specifics, honey child, but I know enough. It is why you run to me. I tried to satisfy you as a human, with all the things that bring me joy, but you kept pursuing the demon instead. One might say you chase the dragon."

He reached over her shoulder to retrieve two essences from the top shelf then put one in each of her hands.

Ecstasy. Despair.

"A toxic combination with which you are dreadfully intimate. And it is the combination you keep seeking from me. It is not my choice to offer it, but I crave it from you as much as you crave it from me. You find something much healthier from the people with whom you spend your time now — dysfunctional anywhere else, but it works here in Arcanium. And I have my kitchen, my Skeletons to serve. All we would have to do is avoid each other like the poisons that we are."

Ecstasy. Despair.

She turned around in his arms. Fuck, he *was* turned on. She couldn't tell if this was new or she was just in a better position to feel it.

She twisted open the stopper to *Despair*. The scent was of a musty, used bed, of cheap beer, of old sweat on an unclean man, of her shampoo, of the walls in the first apartment she'd taken Angelica to after stealing her away from their home. God only knew why she kept seeking its taste, but she could hardly deny it now. She wasn't sure how to apply it — topically or orally — until the odd chef guided it to her mouth and showed her how to squeeze two drops onto her tongue.

"No more," he murmured, taking the bottle. "Essential oils are toxic, and these are no exception, albeit in a different way."

She gave herself two drops of *Ecstasy* more quickly, so she could swallow both at the same time.

"Poison doesn't poison you, right?" Vivian backed away, the oils working fast and making her head spin. Her shoulder blades hit the shelves. Hundreds of bottles clinked in warning.

"Not in the same way."

"And you want these things from me." The labels blurred as the essences took effect. Her breath came faster, and she tasted the salt of mucus at the back of her mouth, the taste that followed tears.

"Yes." His voice lowered to its impossible place, quivering through her as though his desire was her body's frequency.

She opened *Despair* again, squeezed the dropper. More than two droplets hit her skin with a hiss as though it burned. She followed it with drops of *Ecstasy*. As soon as she put the bottles back on the shelf behind her, he darted forward, grabbed her upper arm hard enough to bruise and her hair tightly enough to lift her up so that he could crush her against the shelves and lick the essences from her skin with a toe-curling groan.

"You and your honey skin, child. How your lifelong despair has fermented to blend so perfectly with the fresh. Do you have any conception of what you have reawakened in me? Bell never asked for it. Locke could not convince it to the surface. But you pushed me against a wall and conjured me without effort? You should know better than to conjure a demon you cannot control," he whispered in her ear before kissing her neck just below, catching the flesh in his teeth and tasting her with an intensity that was almost pain.

Against her own will, it seemed, she wrapped her arms around him and moaned, almost a sob, into his shoulder, hooking her legs over his hips to bring herself flush against him. This... This was what she'd been trying to reach in Dom's bed. The sex with Dom was fine, good, better than what she'd had before Arcanium. But it wasn't this. Dom could scratch lines down her back, but they couldn't claw this far down, this deep inside — this brutal, beautiful soul-scraping — and it wasn't what she needed from Dom anyway. In Dom and Delilah's trailer, she'd found her port in the storm. But this was the storm she'd been chasing.

He made his way across her jaw to take her mouth, consuming her all the way, consuming her as she took him in. She tasted the same essence of despair and ecstasy on his tongue, but it tasted different coming from him, his chemistry drastically changing the flavor. From him, it brought her back to his bed — the smell of their mingling sweat, the taste of honey and cum, her arousal on his lips, the bed creaking, the sterile scent of his kitchen. What he tasted on her tongue had him thrusting against her right there against the shelves, making the bottles rattle in their places like windchimes.

She nearly came just from his kiss and his body using hers. But he pulled away from her mouth, gasping, and eased back. The darkness of his eyes didn't reflect the red light from behind her, so dark they had become as they peered into her.

She stroked his face, framed it with her hands then dug her nails into his scalp. He hissed, baring his teeth, but he whirled them around, and with impossible strength, leaped onto the table into a crouch. He lay her upon the wood like a sacrifice, but he continued to hold her hair, keeping her locked in place as he looked down upon her from his hands and knees.

"Why do you seek this despair, Vivian? Why, when it has flavored you for so long, when you built all your walls to avoid it, when you've run from it to the point of desiring the death of yourself and all those around you? Why seek it from me?"

She reached for the front of his trousers. "It never came with ecstasy before."

He tightened his fist in her hair, pulling at her scalp, and she arched up, arousal shooting up and down her spine, sparkling in her head and in her cunt at the same time. She hated being controlled, hated being used, hated this kind of arousal coming easily to her at the hands of a man, had never wanted anyone like him in her life before Arcanium, yet she ripped at his pants, pulled them open then tugged at his goddamn sweater.

He had to let go of her for her to pull it over his head, and as he removed the clothes from his lower half, she quickly removed her shirt and her leather pants. But he grabbed her wrists before she could take off her bra and panties.

"What about you, demon? Why do you seek despair in me?" She felt small, her wrists breakable in his grip, her voice weak and small in the massive room.

He slammed her wrists onto the smooth wood on either side of her head, startling her into a cry.

"To me," he whispered over her parted lips, "ecstasy and despair taste the same."

Jonas caught her legs on either side of his hips, thrusting against her so hard that her knees nearly reached her shoulders. He kissed away from her mouth, down to her breast. Without him to muffle her, her moans were far too loud in a room where her voice was far too soft, but she cried out again when he bit at her bra between her breasts, catching skin with teeth that didn't used to be sharp. He tore the bra away, the cups falling to the side. When he lifted his head again, the teeth that had been white, healthy, perfect and human were no longer human. They snaggled like nothing Vivian had seen before, with sharp edges that had no rhythm or reason, uneven razor blades in his gums.

"Why despair at all, Vivian?" Claws he'd hidden from everyone, as sharp as broken fingernails, tore her panties away, leaving scratches on her hips. "I could have given you endless satisfaction, ecstasy of the gods, all on its own. But you would not allow yourself to be satisfied, your heart so cold it could have already been dead. Only this ecstasy and despair, together, made you alive under me. Alive to die again and again."

"I don't know." Vivian sat up just long enough to grab the back of his neck and draw his heavy body over her own. "I don't care. Just cover me, fill me with both.

I know how much you want to. Fill the emptiness, fuck me into hell and make me scream for more. Cover me. Cover your despair, demon, and come into your ecstasy. Just, God, take me."

He seemed to become bigger over her, and his cock seemed larger than the last time, though when she opened her eyes, he hadn't grown, and when she encircled the shaft, she reached the same places. She drew him to her pussy and didn't bother with any kind of preparation. The poisons he'd given her had done their task.

He didn't go slow, didn't go sweet. He cradled her head in his hands as though he would crush her skull and pushed into her body, his grunts and groans low like a boar digging into the carcass of a kill. He didn't get bigger, but something about his appearance shifted, something so subtle that she couldn't put her finger on it except that he didn't look human anymore. It wasn't something as obvious as his eyes, his teeth or his claws. He still felt flesh and blood, had the same body, the same face. Yet the pure blackness of his eyes seemed to extend well beyond them, under his very skin, his whole body over and inside of her becoming darkness wrapped in humanlike flesh.

He fucked her until it hurt, fucked her until she cried, but when he tasted her tears, she kissed his neck, bit his shoulder, screamed into his flesh as she came. She tore at his back as she tightened around him and brought him deeper.

"Not yet," he growled. He yanked her away from him, leaving her abruptly empty in her aftermath, and shoved her down the table. Her skin burned where it skidded against the polished wood. He crawled with preternatural speed over her and flipped her onto her stomach to shove his cock into her again.

"Is this what you wanted?" He ground into her with every thrust, as though to show how completely and deeply he possessed her. "Is this what you needed? What you craved?"

She reached underneath herself with both hands, her cheek pressed to the table. She pinched her nipple with one hand, rubbed her clit until it hurt with the other. She hated it, didn't want him to stop, wanted to come again with this hatred like heartburn in her chest.

Vivian sobbed into the wood, her saliva joining with tears as she came again, and this time the odd chef followed her, shoving into her so hard that his thighs clapped against her flanks. He filled her hot and hard as she shook, pushing down against her climax but not enough to push him out.

He yanked her upright, wrapping an arm around her abdomen. As he rocked his hips, his cum squeezed out of her, trickling down her thighs like honey. He licked up her face from the corner of her mouth to her temples, where most of the salt from her tears had settled.

"Close your eyes." He slipped himself from her, smearing her ass with the mixture of his cum and her juices, a humiliation that had her panting as she obeyed.

He withdrew from her completely, which left her kneeling alone on the cold wooden table. She felt him, though, creaking the wood behind her then in front. His hot breath scorched her lips when he knelt in front of her.

"Now, open."

The table was filled from end to end with all manner of foods, from American pies to savory pies, casseroles and roasts, cakes and cookies, bowls of the richest, ripest fruits, goblets of wine, platters of cheese, tarts, pasties, pastas, flatbreads and loafs, stuffed peppers, spring rolls, curries. It was a long table, and the odd chef had covered it to the edge with a thought. The only place he had spared was where they were kneeling.

He smiled, a bigger smile than she was used to from him. It made the skin around his eyes crinkle in a surprisingly endearing way, even as a demon. "Like goblin fruit, nothing you eat here will satisfy anything but me, but it *will* make you crave more, at least until I grant you mercy. And it is not in the nature of a demon to grant such mercy easily." He passed his fingers over her lips, smearing saliva over her cheek and chin. "So please me, child. Please me with your appetite, and I will at least give you something to satisfy you in your despair."

"You can't be serious." Vivian looked around at the feast of Christmas Present he'd set for her, the scents sudden, strong and assaulting. Her mouth watered, but she knew what it was to eat and not be filled, had lost herself inside trash cans and filthy dumpsters doing exactly that, and the memories were new and fresh enough that she could almost smell and taste the filth of trash over the food right in front of her.

Jonas took a goblet of red wine and drank half of it down all at once. This wasn't a gentle sip for tasting subtlety, like a good chef would. He swallowed hard and fast, drinking like drowning. Then he abruptly splattered her with the rest.

She cried out, but as the wine dripped down her front, he gathered her in and licked up her body. Then he released her again without warning. She fell back, one elbow in pudding, the other in a bowl of plums, flipping half the fruit off the table.

"Do you have any idea what I want to consume from your body?" He followed her, stalked her down the table as she crawled backward from his hunting gaze. China and crystal hit the ground on either side, shattering, and food and drink splattered upon the wood and in other dishes. The odd chef continued in single-minded pursuit.

"If you aren't hungry, there's something I can inject you with that will stir your appetite, although I'm afraid it will also make you quite voracious in other ways...and thirsty. You'll wish you'd never seen water by the end of it."

Her foot caught in a bowl of mashed potatoes and gravy. The odd chef laughed as he snagged her ankle and sucked the remnants from her toes then made her twitch and jerk as he licked the bottom of her feet clean as well.

"Shall I find the needles?" he murmured into the arch of her foot.

"*Jesus Christo*, fine." Vivian grabbed a buttermilk biscuit from a pile and took a bite. The biscuit was like eating a bread cloud, the butter soaked through the golden top. After one bite, she groaned as loudly as she had when she'd come. She pushed the rest into her mouth, unable to chew and swallow fast enough.

"Yes. Show me how greedy your little mouth is, how greedy your cunt. Make yourself as filthy as you are. You're such a mess, aren't you?" He took a fistful of spaghetti and let it fall over her breasts and belly, an oddly erotic sensation like thin fingers over her skin. Then he took a handful of the marinara to pour over her, steaming the flesh around it. "I don't want you pretty, Vivian. I don't want you controlled. You're mine now, love, and I want you to glut yourself on what I have to offer — revel, wallow, waste, break, destroy."

He slurped up the spaghetti, every last bit, and sucked the marinara from her skin. There was nothing polite about it, nothing refined, just pure, unfettered hunger. Then he took a handful of the pudding and smashed it against her pussy. It oozed into her and over her, cold on her folds and her clit. She couldn't stop long enough to be disgusted, because she'd reached for a bowl of jasmine rice, covered it in goat curry and gathered it into her mouth with her hands. It wasn't as though the odd chef had provided utensils among the grand feast, and even if he had, she couldn't wait long enough to be dainty.

Her elbows slipped on the table and her head fell onto a roast with potatoes and carrots as Jonas ate the pudding from between her legs, swirling his tongue around her clit and digging into every crevice for more, finally sinking his tongue deep inside of her to reach the rest. She whined, pushing back from the onslaught of his own greedy mouth over her flesh as though she, too, would be swallowed down. But he followed her, knocking more food off the table in their wake, grabbing fistfuls and smearing them all over her skin until she didn't know what she was covered in anymore, except that her body sang with each texture everywhere he feasted from her.

She stopped her own eating to clutch at the back of his head as he ate something else he'd poured over her pussy — some kind of gravy, she thought, but it didn't matter. It was hot, like candle wax, but his mouth was hotter, and she shoved new things off the table as she screamed at the tray ceilings.

"Yes, scream, scream all you want, Vivian. No one will hear you. No one can feed on you here but me."

He brought powdered-sugar-covered ginger cake to her face, shoving it into her mouth almost too fast for her to keep up. She turned over on her side just to eat from his hand, licking and sucking the powdered sugar from his fingers. He crawled over her, smoothing his cock with ice cream. The cold did nothing to diminish him.

With his fingers in her mouth, he led her to his cock, which she took in with just as much gusto. She dragged her teeth along his shaft up to the ridge of the head to gather the melting cream. His shout was laced with a growl like an animal, and he shoved himself to the back of her throat, making her gag. She sucked him down like a snake, swallowing until she reached the base. He wound his fingers through her dirty hair to hold her there, groaning without restraint as he fucked her throat.

Her eyes rolled back as she struggled to breathe, but eating him was more important, and she kept swallowing until he came again, until what filled her stomach was something substantial, the only thing that could satisfy on a whole table of food as meaningless as saltwater to the parched. She moaned as though starving, pushing him as deep as he could go, until she briefly lost consciousness. Not for long, because when she came to, she could breathe, but his cock was still wet against her face.

Vivian fell back against the table, something squishing underneath her head. She panted, each exhale a sigh as she gradually came back into herself. It didn't take away the tastes in her mouth or the textures on her body, but at least she could catch her breath.

Fingers stroked over her forehead. She opened her eyes. The blankness of his expression seemed to alternate between tender and mocking, nuanced though the difference was.

"Is that all you've got?" he asked.

She knocked away his hand then climbed up and hit him across the head with a chalice. White wine went flying across the room. Though he fell to the side, all he did was grin his jagged grin as she climbed over him and threw food at his face, whatever she could find. But he caught most of it with his mouth and swallowed it whole, working his throat like she'd worked hers over his cock.

Finally, she dipped three fingers in honey and forced them into his mouth.

He swallowed them down, too, almost to the back of his throat, the suction a delicious, impossible pressure over her fingers. His moan shuddered through her with vibrations just as intense. She ground over his still-hard cock, rigid against his abdomen. A minor adjustment, and he was inside her again, drinking the honey from her skin at the same time he raised his hips to grind into her.

She grabbed another chalice but this time to down the whole glass of cabernet, triggering the goblin fruit spell all over again. She pulled her fingers from his mouth to taste them herself instead. As she rode him harder and harder, she tipped her head back and swallowed whatever she could reach — a dripping bunch of grapes so ready to burst in her mouth that they nearly fell off their stems, three bowls of panna cotta with strawberries and balsamic vinegar, the rest of the ginger cake.

But the odd chef drew her down again, guided her mouth to his chest, to his neck, to his face, where she'd thrown food at him, and she feasted from the salty plate of his skin until she tasted the honey in his mouth and lost herself in a kiss where she couldn't tell who was tasting whom. She rode him as though her pussy was eating him, kissed him as though she could swallow his tongue, smeared all the food covering them between their bodies as they fucked. He drew patterns in it over her back with his huge hands.

This time they came together, their mingling groans that of both feasting and fucking, raw, artless, animal, primitive, but they didn't part on either end.

Not until the odd chef reached between them to gather his cum dripping down her thighs to bring to their mouths. At its taste over her tongue, the spell broke again, and he kissed her into cold, unwelcomed sanity, moved his cock in her until her hips stilled.

"I have endless oblivion," Jonas muttered into her lips. "We could revel like this for months without seeing the sun before you cried out for mercy rather than more."

When she opened her eyes, the feast had disappeared, as had the mess on their skin — as though it never had been. There was just them and the mess that their bodies themselves had made. There wasn't even the taste of honey — at least not to her.

"I haven't cried out for mercy yet. Please, don't stop."

"Vivian." He sat up, bringing their hips flush together. "It never stops. Don't you understand? Your pain never stops. The pit of it is bottomless. That's what you brought in here. It's nothing that I did. Besides, Arcanium would never let me take you for months, tempting though it is." He stroked through her hair—

no longer plastered into thick strings on her back and shoulders. Then he brought her down to kiss her again, threatening to draw blood from her lips and tongue with his wicked teeth. But when he pulled away again, the demon had receded in both the obvious and subtler ways, except for his eyes.

"There will be other nights. This room doesn't even begin to tap into the poisons I would share with you. I have forever here for you at my table, if that is what you desire." He lifted her to slip out, but he enveloped her again, his arms tight and large and warm as she cooled and fought against the emptiness he left behind.

Vivian shivered in spite of his heat, clenched her teeth against the swell of emotions that rose and expanded in vain to fill that empty space he'd left raw. "Don't let me go," she said through chattering teeth. "I feel like I'm falling. Don't let me go."

Jonas slid them off the table, continuing to hold her to him. "The essences will wear off soon. You're safe here."

He carried her from the poison room into the bright, clean kitchen then drew back the sheets on his bed and slipped both of them between. When she guided his mouth to hers again, he didn't resist, and though he was gentler here, the intensity hadn't faded, nor had his arousal. He sank into her, took her hard enough to know where he'd already bruised her, but slowly. And he kissed her through more tears, each one less stinging than the last, until she came again, shuddering, the explosions in her head like bursting light bulbs instead of bursting ink wells.

"I like your honey with many flavors, love," he murmured, pausing to feel her clench around him.

"I'm not done with you yet, demon." She caught her breath again, smoothing her hands down to his ass.

"Oh, believe me. I'm nowhere near done with you." Jonas jerked his hips, gathering her legs to angle up her hips. "You've been running to me all your life, ran all the way to Arcanium for fate to bring you to me and I'm not going to let you go. There's no undoing what has been done, no putting back to sleep what you have awakened. But if I must be your poison, let me also be the antidote. Give yourself to me to break, and I will give you rest in my arms. You can stop running, Vivian, because with me, there's nowhere to hide."

This wasn't like agreeing to let Dom take her into their trailer. This wasn't like the Skeletons agreeing to the dinner party or Shane agreeing to follow her into the odd chef's kitchen with trust Vivian hadn't earned.

This was like making a wish, and she damn well knew it.

"Yes."

He came with her name on his lips, as though the honey he tasted became a vow and his hands on her wrists became shackles.

"Mine," he whispered as he drew her back into his warmth, wrapping himself around her more tightly than Dom in their dreams. "They never have to know, love, and you can have the rest of them all you want. You'll always come back to me, with your broken honeycomb and beestings. *Mine.*"

She closed her eyes, shivering out the last of the poison, and dreamed of serving his table.

Want to see more from this author? Here's a taster for you to enjoy!

Sanctuary: Winter Howl
Aurelia T. Evans

Excerpt

Renee took the last sip from her Samuel Adams and set the finished bottle down next to the first one. She smiled and nodded at Marie, who had come over to take the empty bottles and leave the receipt. There were no words between them. Usually Marie would chat to her customers, but she'd learned when she'd moved to Antoine five years ago that Renee Chambers would not look at her, half of the time wouldn't talk and the other half of the time would stumble through some painful attempt at conversation. Renee had got better as she'd come to know Marie, but it was still more comfortable for both of them when Renee didn't try to talk and Marie didn't try to make her.

Renee left the cash tip on the table, clenched the leash and slid out of the booth. Her legs stiffened when she saw Josh Beall and Marcus Levinson a few booths down. She had not seen them come in, and although she had heard their laughter, she hadn't recognised it as theirs. She would have to walk by them to leave. The warm body against her leg reassured her, nudged her in the right direction. She took one step, then two. Her knees loosened and let her walk. She instinctively — and fruitlessly — tried to hide in her long, light blue coat.

"...saw her at the supply store getting her checklist squared away," she heard Josh say.

"What's it been, two months since she last came down here?" Marcus asked.

"Three months. Won't come back down till spring. You can practically set your seasons by her." He belched, then coughed, pounding his chest a bit.

"What does she do up there all alone, anyway?" Marcus asked.

"Roswell says she gets a lot of mail," Josh said. "He says she has help, but I don't believe it. She wouldn't let anyone up there. I bet she does it all herself. Completely crazy."

Renee closed her eyes and breathed in. She was not so egotistical as to believe that everyone in Antoine talked about her, but it was just her luck that she had to walk by these two rubes when they were. Neither was too far into his mug for slurred speech, but they were far enough that they couldn't gauge their volume.

"Maybe she does porn," Marcus suggested. "You know, video stuff."

Josh snorted. "Frigid bitch like her? Don't think so." He leant forward conspiratorially. "Hey, what if we went up — ?"

"Hey, Renee," Marcus said, even more loudly then they had already been speaking. Josh turned around, his scruffy but reasonably attractive face lighting up with a sly grin when he saw her huddled against the booth table behind them.

"Speak of the scared little devil," he said, raising his glass. "Want a drink? You look a little tense."

Renee's eyes darted from Josh to Marcus to Marie to the door. At another nudge to her leg, and she stepped towards the door.

"Yeah, come on, sweetie," Marcus said, misinterpreting her direction. "We'll make it worth your while."

How? Renee thought. *By drooling on me and trying to feel me up with all those smooth moves you've cultivated over the last ten years?* She didn't say anything, of course, just kept inching along until she finally started past the table.

She lurched forward when Marcus delivered a hearty smack to her ass. It didn't hurt, but Renee could feel her face start to burn and her chest tighten. At least she could move her legs faster now that she was past them.

"Hey, now, none of that in here," Marie called from behind the bar. "Have a good day, Renee. Don't be such a stranger."

"You always run away," Josh shouted after her.

"I wonder why," Renee muttered, her tongue looser now that she was out of the bar and no one was looking at her. "Come on, Britt, one more stop before we go home."

"Hey, Mommy, can I pet the dog?"

Renee winced at the high frequency of the voice and hoped that the mother would know the appropriate way to answer her child. No such luck.

"Hello, miss. Can my daughter pet your dog?"

Antoine was not exactly a highly populated town, but it had a fair tourist trade, particularly downtown Main Street, which was described in most tourist guidebooks as colourful, cheerful, folksy, and unique. Renee did not know about unique or folksy, but many tourists liked to come by for the ambience. And like most townies, the Antoine population had both respect for tourist dollars and frustration with the tourists themselves.

Especially when tourists did not know a service dog when they saw one.

"I'm sorry, ma'am," Renee said, emphatically not looking at the woman. That sometimes helped, and the warm feeling of Britt against her leg reassured her. "She's working."

"Oh, I'm sorry... Hey, wait, you're not blind." The overly polite apology turned into a similarly grating voice of parental annoyance. "If you didn't want Lisa to pet her, you could've just said. There's no need to lie."

"I'm not lying," Renee said. In fact, she was a terrible liar, but that was not the issue at hand. "They do more than help blind people. Please... I need to..."

"Well, that's just rude, having a dog around when you're not really blind and then not letting a little girl pet it," the mother said indignantly.

"I'm sorry. She's working." The words came out short and clipped and curt, but Renee was not really that angry. Her throat was just tightening, and she could feel her shoulders curling in.

"Bitch," the woman muttered under her breath as she grabbed her daughter's free hand—the girl's other hand had been playing with Britt's tail. The little girl was lucky that Britt was an extremely well-behaved dog. The woman led her daughter across the street.

"Good girl," Renee whispered, rubbing Britt's ear gently. "Ready to go?"

She barely had to tug the leash in the direction of the grocery store. Britt had a deep bond with Renee, had been with her most of her life and been her service dog for about five years. She could feel where Renee wanted to go.

Renee admired Britt's beauty beneath the deep green service vest. So many people confused her for a Siberian husky, and Renee understood the mistake. They were both northern sled dogs, but malamutes were bigger, with thicker fur. Britt was a little larger than average, and the darkest parts of her fur—set off by the usual white accents—were almost black. Malamutes were not traditionally service dogs. But Renee had loved Britt since the first time she'd met her, and the feeling had been mutual. There was friendship and respect between them, a connection that she had never managed to make with any of the people at school. It was really no wonder she spent all her time around dogs—she understood them and got along with them so much better than she did with most people.

With Britt in front of her, Renee felt secure in her steps. The sides of her coat hood blocked out her periphery, like blinders on a horse, and she felt a little more confident where she put her feet. Besides, with a large dog like Britt with her—a dog that was occasionally confused for a wolf—she felt more protected. Like a celebrity with a bodyguard, thankfully without the paparazzi.

They made it to the grocery store in about a ten-minute walk. That was what she liked about Main Street. Almost everything was within walking distance, so all she had to do was drive into Antoine, walk around a bit, then drive back home when she was finished, rather than drive from one place to another, and another, and another. Renee was able to stretch her legs after the long drive into town, and certainly Britt needed the exercise as well.

Renee did not need to go to the grocery store often, and she did not necessarily need to go now, which just went to show how much better she had become in public places. But she wanted to get a few treats to tide herself over before all her orders were shipped in. That was actually how she did most of her shopping — online through bulk providers. She had the space, the money and the resources, and most of the things shipped in *needed* to be shipped in bulk. Besides, it was such a long drive between Antoine and where she lived.

There had been a time right after her father had died when she could not even walk into a grocery store without panicking, a time when she could not walk off her property without feeling everything coming in to crush her, as if the entire world had a force field of inhospitality. That was what each successive building had felt like once she stepped out into the world — like a heavy, unpleasant curtain surrounded each of them, and it would take all her effort to pass through. And sometimes she couldn't.

With Britt, though, she was able to walk into places much more easily about ninety per cent of the time.

A grocery store should have been easier, in theory. All those people should have made her feel less conspicuous — she should be able to do better in crowds where she was anonymous and no one really cared. She should do worse with one-to-one interactions. But quite irrationally, it was the other way around. While she was quite bad at one-to-one interactions outside her sanctuary, she was even worse in places that tended to attract more people. Marie's bar, The Benefit, was small and close, and although it tended to get more crowded by around four in the afternoon, Renee avoided it at that time. The grocery store, however, was another matter altogether. It was more than just a public place — it was a *frequented* public place, and that meant that the unwelcome energy surrounding it seemed to pulse against her.

Swallowing, Renee squinted at the people she could see inside. None of them were looking, none of them were judging. They were all going about their business. She was not the centre of the universe, she reminded herself sternly. The muscle of her heart felt as though it was forcing itself against the thin walls of her lungs, rattling her ribs.

Britt whined slightly as Renee retrieved a shopping cart. She could do this with Britt at her side. Then she could leave. If she could just get through this, she could go back home. That was good motivation to do what she needed to do. Her heart was still racing and her breathing was still a little shallow, but Britt stayed next to her, with her fur brushing Renee's jeans.

When she had finally finished, she pushed her cart to the self-checkout. Once she wheeled the cart out into the parking lot—relieved to be outside and breathing open air again—she saw a few dry flakes of snow fall on her coat sleeves. She guessed there was not going to be anything more than a flurry, but it would only be a sample of what was to come in future months.

Renee took the bags out of the cart and opened her duffel to pack them in. The bag was heavy on her shoulder when she started walking again, but aside from altering her gait, it did not bother her much.

The cold air felt great on her face, since she was beginning to sweat a little. She went around Main Street this time, behind the shops, among the employee parking and the dumpsters.

She rushed through the alleyway and finally reached the intersection between downtown Main Street and the beginning of Antoine proper. Her blue 2000 F150 was waiting at the end of the downtown parking lot. She was going to break into a jog to reach her truck that much faster, but two things held her back. One, Britt did not let her hurry. And two, Josh stepped out from behind the hood, where he had been leaning against the driver's side door.

"Hello, peaches," Josh said. "Plan to leave town for the rest of the winter and use the snow as an excuse?"

Renee hesitated at the edge of the last building, as if she had run into a glass window — but then she pushed through and circled around the truck, away from Josh. There was a chest in the covered bed of her truck that she usually put her groceries in. Her keys clinked as she pulled them out of her coat pocket and unlocked the back of the truck.

"Sit," she murmured to Britt. She needed both her hands to climb into the bed.

"Just going to ignore me?" Josh asked. "That'd be nothing new."

Renee opened the bed and lifted her duffel up into it, then crawled up to open the chest at the other end of the bed.

A low growl that made even the truck vibrate alerted Renee to the fact that something was wrong. She glanced back as Josh pushed himself up into the bed and started to crawl in after her. Renee had to hand it to him. He was crawling after a woman with a wolf-like dog growling at him, and although his face showed a trace of concern, he did not seem scared enough. He was either very persistent or just very stupid. Britt's brows twitched as she looked from Josh to Renee, waiting for Renee to decide what to do with the situation and whether she could handle it herself. But what Josh had not anticipated was that the truck was part of Renee's space, just like her land. And Josh had just entered her space.

"Don't you ever get lonely up there those dark winter nights?" Josh asked. "Don't you ever wish —?"

"I didn't go out with you in high school. What makes you think I'm considering it now?" Renee said.

Josh blinked.

"Time," he said, overcoming his surprise. "You're all alone, and it's been what? Seven years? Things change. *I've* changed."

"I'm not alone," Renee said.

"Oh, that's right," Josh said. "Your dogs. As though that's a substitute for good human companionship, especially in front of the fire with no lights on and sweet music playing... Unless they are a substitute, and I severely misjudged you."

Renee's face twisted in automatic disgust.

"Well, that's a relief."

"You haven't changed," Renee spat, unloading her groceries into the chest, then shoving his arm. "You haven't changed at all."

"And neither have you," Josh said. He grabbed her arm, and although it didn't hurt Renee, Britt's growl kicked up a notch. "Up there, nothing ever changes, and nothing ever happens. It's all safe and easy and alone, and don't you wish something would happen? Something new, exciting, different?"

Renee slid out of the bed and tugged Josh out. She felt a little shaky, but she knew Josh was mostly talk, no action, so she did not feel as threatened as she might have with Marcus or someone like that.

"Every day," Renee said. "You have no idea. But it's also not you I'm looking for. God, it's so not you."

Josh's jaw twitched as he clenched his teeth. She tried to pass by him, but he grabbed her arm again. His face was too close, and his gaze drifted down to her lips.

"You sure about that? You really sure about that? 'Cause it is awfully out of the way where you live, and if..."

It was Renee's turn to blink. Maybe she had underestimated him, with that glint in his brown eyes, the set of his jaw.

But she narrowed her eyes and murmured, her voice almost inaudible outside the truck, "You try and come on my land, and I promise it will go badly. And it won't be any fault of mine. I'm sorry."

She tugged herself away, and he let her go without much of a fuss. Renee looked around to see whether anyone had been watching their little altercation, because if they had, she would have been mortified. But where she was parked, the last building on Main blocked most of the view.

"So I guess this is the royal brush-off again," Josh said, leaning back against the truck as she fumbled with her keys. "Frigid bitch."

She unlocked the door and whistled to Britt, who came over and jumped into the driver's seat, then into the shotgun seat, settling down and keeping a sharp eye on Josh. Renee pulled herself up — it was a big truck for a small girl. Before she shut the door, she said, "Don't I know it."

Renee thought she heard Josh snort before she revved the engine and left him and Main Street behind. She breathed a sigh of relief and felt a muscle in her body unwind for every second she headed out of Antoine.

* * * *

In spite of the fact that Renee had always thought Josh looked down on her, she had been surprised when he'd asked her to the winter dance, a gathering between the two Antoine high schools — East and West — Barrington High School and Lex High School. At first, she'd been convinced that it was a *Carrie*-like joke, but by the third time he'd asked, she had discovered that in spite of the shiftiness of his glance when he'd asked her, he'd been serious. And she'd had no idea why. Why he would want a girl who seemed afraid of her own shadow — *seemed*, not *was*. Why he would want a girl who rarely talked and generally avoided his crowd — or any crowd, for that matter. Why he would want a girl who never stopped to give him a second glance, other than to get out of his way.

The third time she'd tried to walk past him in an effort to ignore what she thought was mockery, Josh had touched her cheek to stop her. And it had worked, because she hadn't been used to other people touching her at all. The next thing she'd known, he'd been kissing her. His lips had been soft and a little sloppy, but it hadn't been as bad as she had thought kissing might be. In spite of her nerves singing to get away from him, there'd been a strange warmth running from her lips down her spine to pool low in her belly. It hadn't quite been arousal, as she had discovered later, but it had been interest, new and a little exciting. Her panic had only magnified the feeling, as it magnified everything.

In spite of herself, in spite of the nervousness that Renee had taken for granted most of her life as just a part of her, she'd felt herself lean closer. The kiss had been nothing special. But they'd only been sixteen, and it was her first. Her fingertips had brushed against his neck. She'd felt the warm velvet of his tongue on her lips, and that was when she'd jerked back. It hadn't been that she didn't like it, but she had reached her quota for closeness. Her nerves had reached a screaming pitch.

Renee had not given him an answer, and while her father had bought her a dress for the dance, she hadn't gone. She'd sat at home in her dark blue, silky dress with the thin straps, corset-tie back and sparkles, and watched *Prom Night* and *Ever After*, in that order. She'd regretted not going to the dance, but she had known she would not be able to handle it, no matter what her father had said about it. The next school day, Renee had learned that Josh had gone with Kristin Fontaine. And she'd been just fine with that, although the touch of his lips had haunted her for months as she'd hidden under her covers and tried to sleep. After a while, the memory had faded. She hadn't even missed it.

She still did not miss it. Josh might have been more interested in her than any of her other classmates had been, but that did not mean she was interested back. It did not mean that Josh was anything good for her — he was quite innocently misogynistic, intentionally anti-intellectual, although Renee remembered he had been good at math. A lowest common denominator. Her father had told her to never settle, and she intended to keep to that advice. Not to mention that she was not nearly as lonely as Josh thought she was.

Home of Erotic Romance

Sign up for our newsletter and find out about all our romance book releases, eBook sales and promotions, sneak peeks and FREE romance books!

About the Author

Aurelia T. Evans is an up-and-coming erotica author with a penchant for horror and the supernatural.

She's the twisted mind behind the werewolf/shifter Sanctuary trilogy, demonic circus series Arcanium, and vampire serial Bloodbound. She's also had short stories featured in various erotic anthologies.

Aurelia presently lives in Dallas, Texas (although she doesn't ride horses or wear hats). She loves cats and enjoys baking as much as she dislikes cooking. She's a walker, not a runner, and she writes outside as often as possible.

Aurelia loves to hear from readers. You can find her contact information, website details and author profile page at https://www.totallybound.com